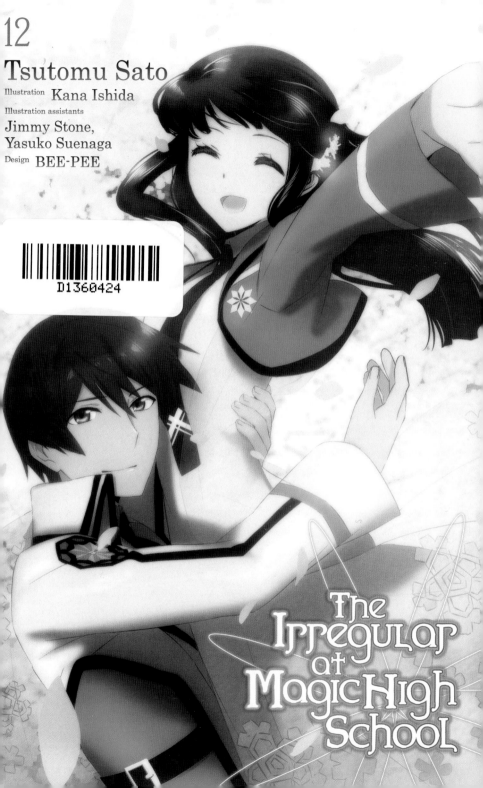

12

Tsutomu Sato

Illustration **Kana Ishida**

Illustration assistants
**Jimmy Stone,
Yasuko Suenaga**
Design **BEE-PEE**

The Irregular at Magic High School

Izumi Saegusa

A new student who
enrolled at Magic High
School this year. Mayumi
Saegusa's younger sister.
Kasumi's younger twin. Meek
and gentle personality.

Kasumi Saegusa

A new student who enrolled
at Magic High School this
year. Mayumi Saegusa's
younger sister. Izumi's older
twin. Energetic and lighthearted personality.

"I can't believe I'm
attending the same
school as someone like
Miyuki... I'm so moved."

"Step away from my big
sister, you womanizer!"

"I don't want a Weed like you telling me that!"

Takuma Shippou

The leader of this year's new students. Course 1. Eldest son of the Shippou, one of the Eighteen— families with excellent magicians.

Tatsuya Shiba

The older brother of the Shiba siblings. A student of the National Magic University Affiliated First High School. Part of Class 2-E. Now studying in the newly established magical engineering program. Sees right to the core of things. Serves as his sister Miyuki's Guardian.

"So you're unhappy that it's coming from me?"

Katsuto Juumonji

Former head of the club committee. Currently attends Magic University. Eldest son of the Juumonji, one of the Ten Master Clans. "A boulder-like person," according to Tatsuya.

"∘∘∘∘∘∘∘∘∘∘∘Hmph."

"It hasn't been a month since the graduation ceremony... but I hardly recognized you, Tatsuya."

Mayumi Saegusa

Former student council president. Currently a freshman at Magic University. Eldest daughter of the Saegusa, one of the Ten Master Clans. Said to be a once-in-a-decade genius in the field of long-range precision magic. Has a devilish personality.

"It suits you very well, Brother..."

"Indeed, Sister."

Miyuki Shiba

The younger sister of the Shiba siblings. Part of Class 2-A. An elite who entered Magic High School as the top student. A Bloom, referring to Course 1 students, whose specialty is cooling magic. Her lovable only flaw is a severe case of a brother complex.

Minami Sakurai

A new student who enrolled at Magic High School this year. Introduced as Tatsuya and Miyuki's cousin. A candidate for becoming Miyuki's Guardian.

The Irregular at Magic High School

DOUBLE SEVEN ARC

12

Tsutomu Sato

Illustration Kana Ishida

YEN ON

NEW YORK

THE IRREGULAR AT MAGIC HIGH SCHOOL
TSUTOMU SATO

Translation by Andrew Prowse
Cover art by Kana Ishida

MAHOUKA KOUKOU NO RETTOUSEI Vol. 12
©TSUTOMU SATO 2013
First published in Japan in 2013 by KADOKAWA CORPORATION, Tokyo.
English translation rights arranged with KADOKAWA CORPORATION, Tokyo, through Tuttle-Mori Agency, Inc., Tokyo.

English translation © 2019 by Yen Press, LLC

Yen On
150 West 30th Street, 19th Floor
New York, NY 10001

Visit us at yenpress.com
facebook.com/yenpress
twitter.com/yenpress
yenpress.tumblr.com
instagram.com/yenpress

First Yen On Edition: July 2019

Yen On is an imprint of Yen Press, LLC.
The Yen On name and logo are trademarks of Yen Press, LLC.

Library of Congress Cataloging-in-Publication Data
Names: Satou, Tsutomu. | Ishida, Kana, illustrator.
Title: The irregular at Magic High School / Tsutomu Satou ; Illustrations by Kana Ishida.
Other titles: Mahōka kōkō no rettosei. English
Description: First Yen On edition. | New York, NY : Yen On, 2016—
Identifiers: LCCN 2015042401 | ISBN 9780316348805 (v 1 : pbk.) | ISBN 9780316390293 (v. 2 : pbk.) |
    ISBN 9780316390309 (v. 3 : pbk.) | ISBN 9780316390316 (v. 4 : pbk.) |
    ISBN 9780316390323 (v. 5 : pbk.) | ISBN 9780316390330 (v. 6 : pbk.) |
    ISBN 9781975300074 (v. 7 : pbk.) | ISBN 9781975327125 (v. 8 : pbk.) |
    ISBN 9781975327149 (v. 9 : pbk.) | ISBN 9781975327163 (v. 10 : pbk.) |
    ISBN 9781975327187 (v. 11 : pbk.) | ISBN 9781975327200 (v. 12 : pbk.)
Subjects: CYAC: Brothers and sisters—Fiction. | Magic—Fiction. | High schools—Fiction. |
    Schools—Fiction. | Japan—Fiction. | Science fiction.
Classification: LCC PZ7.1.S265 Ir 2016 | DDC [Fic]—dc23
LC record available at http://lccn.loc.gov/2015042401

ISBNs: 978-1-9753-2720-0 (paperback)
        978-1-9753-2721-7 (ebook)

10 9 8 7 6 5 4 3 2 1

LSC-C

Printed in the United States of America

The Irregular at Magic High School

DOUBLE SEVEN ARC

An irregular older brother with a certain flaw.
An honor roll younger sister who is perfectly flawless.

When the two siblings enrolled in Magic High School,
a dramatic life unfolded—

Character

Tatsuya Shiba

Class 2-E. Now studying in the newly established magical engineering program. Sees right to the core of things. Serves as his sister Miyuki's Guardian.

Miyuki Shiba

Class 2-A. Tatsuya's younger sister; enrolled as the top student last year. Specializes in freezing magic. Dotes on her older brother.

Leonhard Saijou

Class 2-F. Tatsuya's friend. Course 2 student. Specializes in hardening magic. Has a bright personality.

Erika Chiba

Class 2-F. Tatsuya's friend. Course 2 student. A charming troublemaker.

Mizuki Shibata

Class 2-E. In Tatsuya's class again this year. Has pushion radiation sensitivity. Serious and a bit of an airhead.

Mikihiko Yoshida

Class 2-B. This year he became a Course 1 student. From a famous family that uses ancient magic. Has known Erika since they were children.

Honoka Mitsui

Class 2-A. Miyuki's classmate. Specializes in light-wave vibration magic. Impulsive when emotional.

Shizuku Kitayama

Class 2-A. Miyuki's classmate. Specializes in vibration and acceleration magic. Doesn't show emotional ups and downs very much.

Subaru Satomi

Class 2-D. Frequently mistaken for a pretty boy. Cheerful and easy to get along with.

Eimi Akechi

Class 2-B. A quarter-blood. Full name is Amelia Eimi Akechi Goldie.

Akaha Sakurakouji

Class 2-B. Friends with Subaru and Amy. Wears gothic Lolita clothes and loves theme parks.

Shun Morisaki

Class 2-A. Miyuki's classmate. Specializes in CAD quick-draw. Takes great pride in being a Course 1 student.

Hagane Tomitsuka

Class 2-E. A magic martial arts user with the nickname "Range Zero."

Mayumi Saegusa

An alum and former student council president. Currently attends Magic University. Has a devilish personality.

Azusa Nakajou

A senior and the student council president since Mayumi stepped down. Shy and has trouble expressing herself.

Suzune Ichihara

An alum and former student council treasurer. Calm, collected, and book smart. Mayumi's right hand.

Hanzou Gyoubu-Shoujou Hattori

A senior and former student council vice president. Head of the club committee since Katsuto stepped down.

Mari Watanabe

An alum and former chairwoman of the disciplinary committee. Mayumi's good friend. Somewhat belligerent in everything she does.

Katsuto Juumonji

An alum and former head of the club committee. Currently attends Magic University. "A boulder-like person," according to Tatsuya.

Midori Sawaki

A senior and member of the disciplinary committee. Has a complex about his girlish name.

Koutarou Tatsumi

An alum and former member of the disciplinary committee. Has a heroic personality.

Isao Sekimoto

An alum and former member of the disciplinary committee. Wasn't chosen for the Thesis Competition. Committed acts of spying.

Kei Isori

A senior and the student council treasurer. Top grades in his year in magical theory. Engaged to Kanon Chiyoda.

Takeaki Kirihara

A senior. Member of the *kenjutsu* club. Kanto Junior High Kenjutsu Tournament champion.

Kanon Chiyoda

A senior and the chairwoman of the disciplinary committee since Mari stepped down. Engaged to Kei Isori.

Sayaka Mibu

A senior. Member of the kendo club. Placed second in the nation at the Girls' Junior High Kendo Tournament.

Kasumi Saegusa

A new student who enrolled at Magic High School this year. Mayumi Saegusa's younger sister. Izumi's older twin. Energetic and lighthearted personality.

Takuma Shippou

The leader of this year's new students. Course 1. Eldest son of the Shippou, one of the Eighteen—families with excellent magicians.

Izumi Saegusa

A new student who enrolled at Magic High School this year. Mayumi Saegusa's younger sister. Kasumi's younger twin. Meek and gentle personality.

Kento Sumisu

Class 1-G. A Caucasian boy whose parents are naturalized Japanese citizens from the USNA.

Minami Sakurai

A new student who enrolled at Magic High School this year. Introduced as Tatsuya and Miyuki's cousin. A candidate for becoming Miyuki's Guardian.

Koharu Hirakawa

An alum. Engineer during the Nine School Competition. Withdrew from the Thesis Competition.

Chiaki Hirakawa

Class 2-E. Holds enmity toward Tatsuya.

Satomi Asuka

First High nurse. Gentle, calm, and warm. Smile popular among male students.

Kazuo Tsuzura

First High teacher. Main field is magic geometry. Manager of the Thesis Competition team.

Jennifer Smith

A Caucasian naturalized Japanese citizen. Instructor for Tatsuya's class and for magical engineering classes.

Haruka Ono

A general counselor of First High. Tends to get bullied but has another side to her.

Yakumo Kokonoe

A user of an ancient magic called *ninjutsu*. Tatsuya's martial arts master.

Masaki Ichijou

A junior at Third High. Participates in the Nine School Competition. Direct heir to the Ichijou family, one of the Ten Master Clans.

Shinkurou Kichijouji

A junior at Third High. Participates in the Nine School Competition. Also known as Cardinal George.

Gouki Ichijou

Masaki's father. Current head of the Ichijou, one of the Ten Master Clans.

Midori Ichijou

Masaki's mother. Warmhearted and good at cooking.

Akane Ichijou

Eldest daughter of the Ichijou. Masaki's younger sister. Enrolled in an elite private middle school near her family this year. Likes Shinkurou.

Ruri Ichijou

Second daughter of the Ichijou. Masaki's younger sister. Stable and does things her own way.

Retsu Kudou

Renowned as the strongest magician in the world. Given the honorary title of Sage.

Toshikazu Chiba

Erika Chiba's oldest brother. Has a career in the Ministry of Police. A playboy at first glance.

Harunobu Kazama

Commanding officer of the 101st Brigade of the Independent Magic Battalion. Ranked major.

Naotsugu Chiba

Erika Chiba's second-oldest brother. Possesses full mastery of the Chiba (thousand blades) style of *kenjutsu*. Nicknamed "Kirin Child of the Chiba."

Shigeru Sanada

Executive officer of the 101st Brigade of the Independent Magic Battalion. Ranked captain.

Anna Rosen Katori

Erika's mother. Half-Japanese and half-German; was the mistress of Erika's father, the current leader of the Chiba.

Muraji Yanagi

Executive officer of the 101st Brigade of the Independent Magic Battalion. Ranked captain.

Kousuke Yamanaka

Executive officer of the 101st Brigade of the Independent Magic Battalion. Physician ranked major. First-rate healing magician.

Inagaki

A police sergeant with the Ministry of Police. Toshikazu Chiba's subordinate.

Kyouko Fujibayashi

Female officer serving as Kazama's aide. Ranked second lieutenant.

Rin

A girl Morisaki saved. Her full name is Meiling Sun. The new leader of the Hong Kong–based international crime syndicate No-Head Dragon.

Xiangshan Chen

Leader of the Great Asian Alliance Army's Special Covert Forces. Has a heartless personality.

Gongjin Zhou

A handsome young man who brought Lu and Chen to Japan. A mysterious figure who hangs out in Chinatown.

Ganghu Lu

The ace magician of the Great Asian Alliance Army's Special Covert Forces. Also known as the Man-Eating Tiger.

Miya Shiba

Tatsuya and Miyuki's actual mother. Deceased. The only magician skilled in mental construction interference magic.

Honami Sakurai

Miya's Guardian. Deceased. Part of the first generation of the Sakura series, engineered magicians with magical capacity strengthened through genetic modification.

Sayuri Shiba

Tatsuya and Miyuki's stepmother. Hates them both.

Ushio Kitayama

Shizuku's father. A big shot in the business world. His business name is Ushio Kitagata.

Benio Kitayama

Shizuku's mother. Once famous as an A-rank magician known for her oscillation magic.

Wataru Kitayama

Shizuku's younger brother. A sixth grader. Adores his older sister. Aiming to be a magical engineer one day.

Kouichi Saegusa

Mayumi's father and the current leader of the Saegusa. An elite-class magician.

Maya Yotsuba

Tatsuya and Miyuki's aunt. Miya's younger twin sister. The current head of the Yotsuba.

Hayama

An elderly butler employed by Maya.

Mitsugu Kuroba

Miya Shiba and Maya Yotsuba's cousin. Father of Ayako and Fumiya.

Ayako Kuroba

Tatsuya and Miyuki's second cousin. Has a younger twin brother named Fumiya.

Fumiya Kuroba

A candidate for next head of the Yotsuba. Tatsuya and Miyuki's second cousin. Has an older twin sister named Ayako.

Maki Sawamura

An actress who has been nominated for best leading actress in a distinguished movie awards competition. Acknowledged not only for her beauty but also for her acting skills.

Ushiyama

Manager of Four Leaves Technology's CAD R & D Section 3. A person in whom Tatsuya places his trust.

Angelina Kudou Shields

Commander of the USNA's magician unit, the Stars. Rank is major. Nickname is Lina. Also one of the Thirteen Apostles, strategic magicians.

Virginia Balance

First deputy commissioner of the USNA Joint Chiefs of Staff Internal Investigation Office within the Information Bureau. Ranked colonel. Came to Japan in order to support Lina.

Silvia Mercury First

A planet-class magician in the USNA's magician unit, the Stars. Rank is warrant officer. Her nickname is Silvie, and Mercury First is her code name. During their mission in Japan, she serves as Major Sirius's aide.

Benjamin Canopus

Number two in the USNA's magician unit, the Stars. Rank is major. Takes command when Major Sirius is absent.

Mikaela Hongou

An agent sent to Japan by the USNA (although her real job is magic scientist for the Department of Defense). Nicknamed Mia.

Claire

Hunter Q—a female soldier in the magician unit Stardust (for those who couldn't be Stars). The code name Q refers to the seventeenth member of the pursuit unit.

Alfred Fomalhaut

A first-degree star magician in the USNA's magician unit, the Stars. Rank is first lieutenant. Nicknamed Freddy. Currently listed as AWOL.

Rachel

Hunter R—a female soldier in the magician unit Stardust (for those who couldn't be Stars). The code name R refers to the eighteenth member of the pursuit unit.

Charles Sullivan

A satellite-class magician in the USNA's magician unit, the Stars. Called by the code name Deimos Second. Currently listed as AWOL.

Raymond S. Clark

A first-year student at the high school in Berkeley, USNA, where Shizuku studies abroad. A Caucasian boy who wastes no time making advances on Shizuku.

Pixie

A home-helper robot belonging to Magic High School. Official name 3H (Humanoid Home Helper: a human-shaped chore-assisting robot) type P-94.

Glossary

Course 1 student emblem

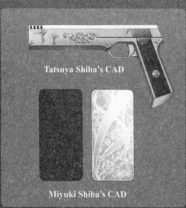

Tatsuya Shiba's CAD

Miyuki Shiba's CAD

Magic High School

Nickname for high schools affiliated with the National Magic University. There are nine schools throughout the nation. Of them, First High through Third High each adopt a system of Course 1 and Course 2 students to split up its two hundred incoming freshmen.

Blooms, Weeds

Slang terms used at First High to display the gap between Course 1 and Course 2 students. Course 1 student uniforms feature an eight-petaled emblem embroidered on the left breast, but Course 2 student uniforms do not.

CAD (Casting Assistant Device)

A device that simplifies magic casting. Magical programming is recorded within. There are many types and forms, some specialized and others multipurpose.

Four Leaves Technology (FLT)

A domestic CAD manufacturer. Originally more famous for magical-product engineering than for developing finished products, the development of the Silver model has made them much more widely known as a maker of CADs.

Taurus Silver

A genius engineer said to have advanced specialized CAD software by a decade in just a single year.

Eidos (individual information bodies)

Originally a term from Greek philosophy. In modern magic, *eidos* refers to the information bodies that accompany events. They form a so-called record of those events existing in the world, and can be considered the footprints of an object's state of being in the universe, be that active or passive. The definition of *magic* in its modern form is that of a technology that alters events by altering the information bodies composing them.

Idea (information body dimension)

Originally a term from Greek philosophy; pronounced "ee-dee-ah." In modern magic, *Idea* refers to the *platform* upon which information bodies are recorded—a spell, object, or energy's *dimension*. Magic is primarily a technology that outputs a magic program (a spell sequence) to affect the Idea (the dimension), which then rewrites the eidos (the individual bodies) recorded there.

Activation Sequence

The blueprints of magic, and the programming that constructs it. Activation sequences are stored in a compressed format in CADs. The magician sends a psionic wave into the CAD, which then expands the data and uses it to convert the activation sequence into a signal. This signal returns to the magician with the unpacked magic program.

Psions (thought particles)

Massless particles belonging to the dimension of spirit phenomena. These information particles record awareness and thought results. Eidos are considered the theoretical basis for modern magic, while activation sequences and magic programs are the technology forming its practical basis. All of these are bodies of information made up of psions.

Pushions (spirit particles)

Massless particles belonging to the dimension of spirit phenomena. Their existence has been confirmed, but their true form and function have yet to be elucidated. In general, magicians are only able to sense energized pushions. The technical term for them is *psycheons*.

Magician

An abbreviation of *magic technician*. *Magic technician* is the term for those with the skills to use magic at a practical level.

Magic program

An information body used to temporarily alter information attached to events. Constructed from psions possessed by the magician. Sometimes shortened to *magigram*.

Magic-calculation region

A mental region that constructs magic programs. The essential core of the talent of magic. Exists within the magician's unconscious regions, and though he or she can normally consciously use the magic-calculation region, they cannot perceive the processing happening within. The magic-calculation region may be called a black box, even for the magician performing the task.

Magic program output process

❶ Transmit an activation sequence to a CAD. This is called "reading in an activation sequence."
❷ Add variables to the activation sequence and send them to the magic-calculation region.
❸ Construct a magic program from the activation sequence and its variables.
❹ Send the constructed magic program along the "route"—between the lowest part of the conscious mind and highest part of the unconscious mind—then send it out the "gate" between conscious and unconscious, to output it onto the Idea.
❺ The magic program outputted onto the Idea interferes with the eidos at designated coordinates and overwrites them.

With a single-type, single-process spell, this five-stage process can be completed in under half a second. This is the bar for practical-level use with magicians.

Magic evaluation standards

The speed with which one constructs psionic information bodies is one's magical throughput, or processing speed. The scale and scope of the information bodies one can construct is one's magical capacity. The strength with which one can overwrite eidos with magic programs is one's influence. These three together are referred to as a person's magical power.

Cardinal Code hypothesis

A school of thought claiming that within the four families and eight types of magic, there exist foundational "plus" and "minus" magic programs that number sixteen in total, and that by combin-ing these sixteen, one can construct every possible typed spell.

Typed magic

Any magic belonging to the four families and eight types.

Exotyped magic

A term for spells that control mental phenomena rather than physical ones. Encompasses many fields, from divine magic and spirit magic—which employs spiritual presences—to mind reading, astral form separation, and consciousness control.

Ten Master Clans

The most powerful magician organization in Japan. The ten families are chosen every four years from among twenty-eight: Ichijou, Ichinokura, Isshiki, Futatsugi, Nikaidou, Nihei, Mitsuya, Mikazuki, Yotsuba, Itsuwa, Gotou, Itsumi, Mutsuzuka, Rokkaku, Rokugou, Roppongi, Saegusa, Shippou, Tanabata, Nanase, Yatsushiro, Hassaku, Hachiman, Kudou, Kuki, Kuzumi, Juumonji, and Tooyama.

Numbers

Just like the Ten Master Clans contain a number from one to ten in their surname, well-known families in the Hundred Families use numbers eleven or greater, such as Chiyoda (thousand), Isori (fifty), and Chiba (thousand). The value isn't an indicator of strength, but the fact that it is present in the surname is one measure to broadly judge the capacity of a magic family by their bloodline.

Non-numbers

Also called Extra Numbers, or simply Extras. Magician families who have been stripped of their number. Once, when magicians were weapons and experimental samples, this was a stigma between the success cases, who were given numbers, and the failure cases, who didn't display good enough results.

Various Spells

• Cocytus

Outer magic that freezes the mind. A frozen mind cannot order the flesh to die, so anyone subject to this magic enters a state of mental stasis, causing their body to stop. Partial crystallization of the flesh is sometimes observed because of the interaction between mind and body.

• Rumbling

An old spell that vibrates the ground as a medium for a spirit, an independent information body.

• Program Dispersion

A spell that dismantles a magic program, the main component of a spell, into a group of psionic particles with no meaningful structure. Since magic programs affect the information bodies associated with events, it is necessary for the information structure to be exposed, leaving no way to prevent interference against the magic program itself.

• Program Demolition

A typeless spell that rams a mass of compressed psionic particles directly into an object without going through the Idea, causing it to explode and blow away the psion information bodies recorded in magic, such as activation sequences and magic programs. It may be called magic, but because it is a psionic bullet without any structure as a magic program for altering events, it isn't affected by Information Boost or Area Interference. The pressure of the bullet itself will also repel any Cast Jamming effects. Because it has zero physical effect, no obstacle can block it.

• Mine Origin

A magic that imparts strong vibrations to anything with a connotation of "ground"—such as dirt, crag, sand, or concrete—regardless of material.

• Fissure

A spell that uses spirits, independent information bodies, as a medium to push a line into the ground, creating the appearance of a fissure opening in the earth.

• Dry Blizzard

A spell that gathers carbon dioxide from the air, creates dry-ice particles, then converts the extra heat energy from the freezing process to kinetic energy to launch the dry-ice particles at a high speed.

• Slithering Thunders

In addition to condensing the water vapor from Dry Blizzard's dry-ice evaporation and creating a highly conductive mist with the evaporated carbon dioxide in it, this spell creates static electricity with vibration-type magic and emission-type magic. A combination spell, it also fires an electric attack at an enemy using the carbon gas-filled mist and water droplets as a conductor.

• Niflheim

A vibration- and deceleration-type area-of-effect spell. It chills a large volume of air, then moves it to freeze a wide range. In blunt terms, it creates a super-large refrigerator. The white mist that appears upon activation is the particles of frozen ice and dry ice, but at higher levels, a mist of frozen liquid nitrogen occurs.

• Burst

A dispersion-type spell that vaporizes the liquid inside a target object. When used on a creature, the spell will vaporize bodily fluids and cause the body to rupture. When used on a machine powered by internal combustion, the spell vaporizes the fuel and makes it explode. Fuel cells see the same result, and even if no burnable fuel is on board, there is no machine that does not contain some liquid, such as battery fluid, hydraulic fluid, coolant, or lubricant; once Burst activates, virtually any machine will be destroyed.

• Disheveled Hair

An old spell that, instead of specifying a direction and changing the wind's direction to that, uses air current control to bring about the vague result of "tangling" it, causing currents along the ground that entangle an opponent's feet in the grass. Only usable on plains with grass of a certain height.

Magic Swords

Aside from fighting techniques that use magic itself as a weapon, another method of magical combat involves techniques for using magic to strengthen and control weapons. The majority of these spells combine magic with projectile weapons such as guns and bows, but the art of the sword, known as *kenjutsu*, has developed in Japan as well as a way to link magic with sword techniques. This has led to magic technicians formulating personal-use magic techniques known as magic swords, which can be said to be both modern magic and old magic.

1. High-Frequency Blade

A spell that locally liquefies a solid body and cleaves it by causing a blade to vibrate at a high speed, then propagate the vibration that exceeds the molecular cohesive force of matter it comes in contact with. Used as a set with a spell to prevent the blade from breaking.

2. Pressure Cut

A spell that generates left-right perpendicular repulsive force relative to the angle of a slashing blade edge, causing the blade to force apart any object it touches and thereby cleave it. The size of the repulsive field is less than a millimeter, but it has the strength to interfere with light, so when seen from the front, the blade edge becomes a black line.

3. Douji-Giri (Simultaneous Cut)

An old-magic spell passed down as a secret sword art of the Genji. It is a magic sword technique wherein the user remotely manipulates two blades through a third in their hands in order to have the swords surround an opponent and slash simultaneously. *Douji* is the Japanese pronunciation for both "simultaneous" and "child," so this ambiguity was used to keep the inherited nature of the technique a secret.

4. Zantetsu (Iron Cleaver)

A secret sword art of the Chiba clan. Rather than defining a katana as a hulk of steel and iron, this movement spell defines it as a single concept, then the spell moves the katana along a slashing path set by the magic program. The result is that the katana is defined as a mono-molecular blade, never breaking, bending, or chipping as it slices through any objects in its path.

5. Jinrai Zantetsu (Lightning Iron Cleaver)

An expanded version of Zantetsu that makes use of the Ikazuchi-Maru, a personal-armament device. By defining the katana and its wielder as one collective concept, the spell executes the entire series of actions, from enemy contact to slash, incredibly quickly and with faultless precision.

6. Mountain Tsunami

A secret sword art of the Chiba clan that makes use of the Orochi-Maru, a giant personal weapon six feet long. The user minimizes their own inertia and that of their katana while approaching an enemy at a high speed and, at the moment of impact, adds the neutralized inertia to the blade's inertia and slams the target with it. The longer the approach run, the greater the false inertial mass, reaching a maximum of ten tons.

7. *Usuba Kagerou* (Antlion)

A spell that uses hardening magic to anchor a five-nanometer-thick sheet of woven carbon nanotube to a perfect surface and make it a blade. The blade that *Usuba Kagerou* creates is sharper than any sword or razor, but the spell contains no functions to support moving the blade, demanding technical sword skill and ability from the user.

Strategic Magicians: The Thirteen Apostles

Because modern magic was born into a highly technological world, only a few nations were able to develop strong magic for military purposes. As a result, only a handful were able to develop "strategic magic," which rivaled weapons of mass destruction. However, these nations shared the magic they developed with their allies, and certain magicians of allied nations with high aptitudes for strategic magic came to be known as strategic magicians. As of April 2095, there are thirteen magicians publicly recognized as strategic magicians by their nations. They are called the Thirteen Apostles and are seen as important factors in the world's military balance. The Thirteen Apostles' nations, names, and their strategic-spell names are listed below.

USNA

Angie Sirius: Heavy Metal Burst
Elliott Miller: Leviathan
Laurent Barthes: Leviathan
* The only one belonging to the Stars is Angie Sirius. Elliott Miller is stationed at Alaska Base, and Laurent Barthes outside the country at Gibraltar Base, and for the most part, they don't move.

New Soviet Union

Igor Andreivich Bezobrazov: Tuman Bomba
Leonid Kondratenko: Zemlja Armija
* As Kondratenko is of advanced age, he generally stays at the Black Sea Base.

Great Asian Alliance

Yunde Liu: Pilita (Thunderclap Tower)
* Yunde Liu died in the October 31, 2095, battle against Japan.

Indo-Persian Federation

Barat Chandra Khan: Agni Downburst

Japan

Mio Itsuwa: Abyss

Brazil

Miguel Diez: Synchroliner Fusion
* This magic program was named by the USNA.

England

William MacLeod: Ozone Circle

Germany

Karla Schmidt: Ozone Circle
* Ozone Circle is based on a spell co-developed by nations in the EU before its split as a means to fix the hole in the ozone layer. The magic program was perfected by England and then publicized to the old EU through a convention.

Turkey

Ali Sahin: Bahamut
* This magic program was developed in cooperation with the USNA and Japan, then provided to Turkey by Japan.

Thailand

Somchai Bunnag: Agni Downburst
* This magic program was provided by Indo-Persia.

The International Situation
State of the World in 2096

West EU and East
EU are allied
states, but nations
are independent

New Soviet Union

Japan, Mongolia, and
Kazakhstan are in an alliance

USNA
(United States of
North America)

Indo-Persian
Federation

Great Asian
Alliance

Japan

Arab
Alliance

Taiwan is an
independent nation

African
Continent
(southwestern
portions are
mostly lawless)

Southeast Asian Alliance
(includes Taiwan, the
Philippines, and New Guinea)

Brazil

Other nations have
broken into regional
local governments

World War III, also called the Twenty Years' Global War Outbreak, was directly triggered by global cooling, and it fundamentally redrew the world map.

The USA annexed Canada and the countries from Mexico to Panama to form the United States of North America, or the USNA.

Russia reabsorbed Ukraine and Belarus to form the New Soviet Union.

China conquered northern Burma, northern Vietnam, northern Laos, and the Korean Peninsula to form the Great Asian Alliance, or GAA.

India and Iran absorbed several central Asian countries (Turkmenistan, Uzbekistan, Tajikistan, and Afghanistan) and South Asian countries (Pakistan, Nepal, Bhutan, Bangladesh, and Sri Lanka) to form the Indo-Persian Federation.

The other Asian and Arab countries formed regional military alliances to resist the three superpowers: the New Soviet Union, GAA, and the Indo-Persian Federation.

Australia chose national isolation.

The EU failed to unify and split into an eastern and a western section bordered by Germany and France. These east-west groupings also failed to form unions and now are actually weaker than they were before unification.

Africa saw half its nations destroyed altogether, with the surviving ones barely managing to retain urban control.

South America, excluding Brazil, fell into small, isolated states administered on a local government level.

The Irregular at
Magic High School

Ninety-seven years earlier, the starting point of modern magic, abnormal abilities were first observed in what was then the United States of America. It had been about eighty since mankind had shifted from the development of magical abilities toward the development of magicians and human alteration.

In this short time—even shorter, in fact, clocking in at only about fifty years past—mankind had created bloodlines that could stably supply magicians with powerful-enough abilities to warrant the term *magician elites*. If one thought about it carefully, this was a shocking development. A new race called *magicians* had been successfully manufactured in a mere half century.

Of course, behind it all was a fierce research race between the developed nations of the world, all pouring in enough scientific technology and financial resources to make such advances possible. The drying up of energy reserves, settling like a dark shadow in the minds of the people—at least for those who resided in the most advanced countries—was a curse upon the future that had been hanging over their heads since the latter half of the previous century. Ever since magical research began in earnest, many had hoped that magic would be a technology to solve the imminent energy crisis. This—combined with the Earth's rapid cooling, which had begun to manifest around the 2030s, and the food shortages that had come along with it—was what triggered World War III, which accelerated magician development enormously, and it also kept respect for magicians' fundamental human rights strictly secondary.

Even prior to the twenty-year-long war, human selective breeding and human crossing experiments had been conducted partially in the open throughout the world, with everyone vying to be the first to develop a race of people called magicians. The fact that magic ability was genetic had been discovered back when magic was still considered a supernatural power. It was both natural and necessary that magic development would eventually become the development of superior bloodlines.

During those human selective breeding trials, the most advanced countries had very skillfully trodden upon human dignity.

The development of artificial wombs had been the first thing those nations achieved.

Less accomplished countries wickedly engaged in the forced mating of those with magical ability—in other words, nationally endorsed rape—but richer nations more *efficiently* advanced magician development through the replication of unfertilized eggs and nonsurgical sperm retrieval methods such as ejaculation stimulants. Genetic engineering was actually an unpopular method—instead, magician development in these countries involved the birth of—or perhaps it would be more accurate to call it the manufacturing of—large numbers of test tube babies that hadn't been genetically modified.

Fortunately—though it was controversial to say so—the children born from these replicated eggs, for whatever reason, died early deaths. Not many of them had the chance to worry about their own descent. According to available statistics reported in Japan, their average life span was seven years. But it wasn't a high rate of newborn deaths that was the biggest reason for the average being so low; the life spans of these children were really just short. The ones who lived the longest only ever reached seventeen years of age at most. None of them had rapidly aged, either—they died of natural causes while still young. The engineered children born from original eggs were universally without this flaw of a short life span, so experts believed it was an issue with reproductive cell replication technology.

However, it was possible to measure latent magic capacity at the age of three. Because of the children's sacrifices, scientists discovered the proper combination of egg and sperm. The impact on the second and third generations was something they could address with genome map simulations. Now all these nations had to do was arrange formal marriage meetings to induce people to voluntarily marry.

And from that process came the families called modern magic elites.

Representative among them were Japan's Ten Master Clans.

Japan had been able to create these distinguished magician families more cleanly than anywhere else in the world because of a cultural background that made these types of marital relationships easier.

And thus, inhumane technological development was ultimately influenced by cultural factors, something that would be called ironic by some, and a stubborn last stand of people's "humanity" by others.

But in the end, it would be up to historians to pass judgment on the practice.

[0]

The village was in a narrow basin surrounded by mountains in old Yamanashi Prefecture, close to the border with old Nagano Prefecture. It had no name, and because of that, it wasn't on any maps. The term *village* didn't denote any sort of modern administrative distinction, but it wasn't a natural enclave that had been settled in premodern times, either. But in the end, there was, in fact, a settlement there, and people lived in it.

Aside from its lack of a name, the village was normal. One might even say it had everything it needed besides a name. It had a town office, a police station, a fire station, electricity, and running water. Its roads were paved like any other village's, and it even had a school—only one, a combined school.

Snow had been falling from the thick, heavy February clouds, and the village was currently covered with white. Outside, it was gravely silent, the villagers all cooped up in their houses.

It was hard to spot anyone. In fact, other than one group of ten people heading down the street, nobody was on the roads. The lone exception was headed for the school, which had its back to the skirts of the mountains that stood on the village fringes.

Snow covered the walkers like camo, including the uniformly

designed knapsacks hanging from their backs and the assault rifles dangling from their shoulders.

A girl in a sailor school uniform was watching the dangerous group approach from a second-story classroom. She rose from her seat and moved to the window, continuing to watch them.

She was the only one in the classroom. Actually, she was the only person in the school building at all.

But today wasn't a weekend or a holiday, nor was it part of a long school vacation. Perhaps the other students had learned of the armed group's approach and evacuated. That, however, meant the girl didn't have a reason to be there. Everyone had evacuated—not only the students, but the faculty, too. Under any normal circumstance, the odds that a middle school girl would stay behind were low.

The armed band came to the school gate as she watched on, then shrugged their weapons from their shoulders. Keeping the small firearms at waist height, they scattered left and right along the inside of the school walls. Three to the right and three to the left. Four remained in front, of whom two advanced with guns at the ready. The other two behind them lowered their knapsacks and took something out.

Meanwhile, the girl removed a long and slender device from her skirt pocket. It highly resembled something people a century ago had called a *cell phone*—an information terminal mainly for voice communication—and it had a straight shape with a keypad, which would have earned it the old classification of *feature phone*. She pressed the power button above the keypad to awaken the small device from sleep mode, then let psions flow into it.

The device in her hands was an information terminal–shaped CAD. And the girl was a magician.

The two people visible in the rear of the forward group aimed at the school building rifles that appeared to have rockets attached.

As they did, her fingers danced over her CAD, and her spell activated.

* * *

What the two people at the rear of the group in front of the school had taken out of their knapsacks was a pair of rifle grenades. Short and stocky, the projectiles were meant to inflict death via shrapnel rather than penetrative power.

After exiting the muzzles, the grenades traveled in a lazy arc through the air toward the classroom the girl was in. The combination of this particular type of grenade and rifle had an effective firing range of two hundred meters, so with the distance from the school gate to the building being at most one-fifth of that, she was easily within acceptable range.

However, the grenades never reached her classroom.

They made it to within ten meters of the window she stood behind, then exploded. The flames licked along a transparent wall, and the blast rebounded toward the armed group. The metal shards that had been encased in the grenades rained down upon the squatters. The pieces had lost most of their momentum by then, so it didn't wound any of them, but it was enough to whet their hostility and caution.

The two in front dropped their bags and affixed grenades to their muzzles as well, while the men who had fired the first shots also loaded their next.

They knew magic had caused that phenomenon. The windowpane was free of cracks even after the grenades exploded, because the barrier that had been erected in midair possessed properties that repelled at least heat, sound, and matter. However, if the magical barrier took an attack that exceeded its tolerance, it would become ineffective. The men knew that, too.

Four grenades were fired in a single volley. There was no sign that the attackers had made any particular signals, but their coordination was perfect. If one shot couldn't get through the barrier, then maybe, they thought, four exploding all at once would oversaturate it with heat and force and thus disable it. Even if they failed to disable the spell, the rebounded fragments and shock waves wouldn't hurt them. They'd just seen proof of that.

Once again, their grenades exploded in midair. Four grenades' worth of flames licked across an invisible wall, just as they had the first time. This time, though, the grenades exploded in a different position.

The barrier wasn't ten meters from the school building—but five meters away from *them*. Precisely speaking, it had been reconstructed five meters from them the moment they pulled their triggers. The blast bounced back at extremely close range, and the hail of shrapnel peppered them. They had goggles, but the rest of their faces were exposed below the helmet. Without any time to react, the shards tore at their faces. By the time the blast slammed them into the ground, all four had already lost consciousness.

After verifying that the four who had fallen were no longer moving, the girl turned around and left the window. Right when she reached the center of the classroom, the door in the back clattered open. Her fingers danced over the keypad, a boon from her training that had been ingrained until it was reflex. The spell activated a moment before an attacker stepped inside. The one who tried to enter ran into a transparent wall, lost his balance, and then stumbled to the floor.

Within less than a second, the classroom's front door opened. But the result was the same: They couldn't enter. As the man who had rammed into it with his shoulder stood helplessly stuck to the invisible wall like a mime, the frosted glass separating the classroom from the hallway cracked with a loud noise.

However, the glass fragments didn't fall into the classroom, instead raining down on the three outside who had broken the glass. The barriers she'd created hadn't only blocked the doors—she'd covered the entire area separating this room from the hallway.

As the girl sighed in relief at preventing the miscreants from entering, she realized something. She'd spotted a ten-person armed group. Four of them had remained at the front entrance, and the other six had split into two groups of three. She'd disabled the four in front with their own weapons, and she'd stopped three others in the hallway with her spell just now. So where were the remaining three?

The glass behind her exploded. Three men came crashing inward, hanging from the roof by ropes. They'd kicked off the walls above and used themselves as pendulum weights to breach the building.

The girl turned around as she threw herself to the floor in a twist that flipped her skirt wide open, but she knew this wasn't the time to worry about that—because as she fell, she saw her adversaries out of the corner of her eye, readying their rifles as they jumped inside.

A moment later, the sound of gunfire followed by the appearance of bullet holes in the blackboard and some of the lockers proved her judgment correct.

The barrier she'd erected in the hallway vanished. Her attention had been stolen by the new intruders, and she'd stopped updating her magic program. First, the unwilling mime rolled inside. Another man came in from the rear door, and a third jumped through the hallway window into the classroom. She was about to be surrounded by an armed group of six.

A normal middle school girl would have cowered in helpless fear. At most, she'd sit up and hide her fear behind her arms, turning a brave glare on the intruders. But this girl didn't fall under the category of "normal middle school girl."

She stood up, then raced for the rear door. One of the attackers was there, readying his gun, but she acted as though he didn't exist. She barreled straight toward the muzzle, and even her opponent seemed taken aback. By the time he reacted, the distance between them had closed to two meters.

She was too close for him to properly use his rifle. Up against a middle schooler, the chances of him losing in physical combat were close to nil. In the end, however, he decided to attack with his rifle anyway.

The other five made decisions more quickly. When the man at the rear door finally brought his rifle up, the other five already had their fingers on the triggers.

Five gunshots thundered, and one followed them.

A moment later, six screams went up.

Muffled cries of anguish escaped the men's mouths. She might have been a magician, but all that gunfire was clearly overkill for a single girl—and yet everything had bounced off the anti-object reflection barrier she'd created and hit her attackers instead.

The guns they were holding were high-powered assault rifles meant for fighting magicians. They fired armor-piercing rounds containing improved propellant to break through magical barriers. When such high-powered bullets were sent straight back at them, even their ballistic armor, with high-density carbon plates sewn into it, was no help at all. The impact of the bullets knocked them down, leaving half-conscious bloodied men and a girl looking down at them slightly flustered. She wasn't sure what to do now.

Then an old man's voice came to her over a speaker.

"The drill is over. Relief party, please begin treating the adversary team. Minami, please return to the estate. The mistress wishes to speak with you directly."

The last sentence caused her to straighten. Her voice laced with nervousness, she answered, "Yes, sir"—even though she knew he wasn't listening anymore.

At first glance, this village was a completely ordinary mountain settlement. One-story, flat-roofed buildings of reinforced concrete without windows were scattered about the village like flat boxes, but these structures were the aboveground portions of air-raid shelters built en masse all across Japan during the time of the third nonnuclear world war. It wasn't strange that they existed this deep in the mountains—at least not on the surface.

But below the surface, this was more than an ordinary mountain village: It was one massive test site.

In fact, it had been the most secretive and infamous one: the deadly fourth magician factory, known officially as Magic Development Institute Four. This village was where it used to be, and was now the headquarters of the Yotsuba of the Ten Master Clans, who conducted magician improvement and screening here.

And the largest mansion in the area held the Yotsuba family residence. Several houses stood on the vast property, but the biggest of them was the main building, where the Yotsuba's current leader, Maya Yotsuba, lived.

At the moment, in one of its rooms, a lone girl faced Maya with a tense, drawn-back face.

Her name was Minami Sakurai. A fifteen-year-old girl on the cusp of middle school graduation and of the second generation of the Sakura series of engineered magicians. She had impressive magic power, having been born of engineered parents who had been bestowed with great power artificially, through genetic manipulation.

Neither of those parents still remained in this world, though. Now that death had parted Minami from them, she worked as a live-in maid at the Yotsuba residence and received education to be a future Guardian.

The Sakura series' main trait was the generation of anti-object, heatproof barriers. It couldn't match the Juumonji's Phalanx in application and variety, but when it came to a single barrier, Minami, at fifteen, was already exhibiting talent on the Juumonji family's level.

"You did very well, my sweet Minami. More than enough for a passing grade."

"Thank you very much. Your words are too much for someone as inexperienced as I."

In contrast to Maya, who addressed her amiably, Minami's tone was nervous and rigid. One couldn't blame her for that, either: The woman sitting in front of Minami wasn't only her employer, but a person who reigned at the pinnacle of Japan's magicians. She was the leader of a particularly powerful family even among the Ten Master Clans, and was known as the strongest magician of her generation, referred to with awe as the Demon of the East.

"Oh, you needn't be so modest about it. Isn't that right, Hayama?"

Hayama, who had been waiting behind Maya without speaking or moving a muscle, answered the question solemnly. "Allowing entrance through the window was a negative, but you disabled all ten in the end, so in my humble opinion you have earned passing marks."

Minami's eyes widened in a display of surprise. The evaluation hadn't been too severe—this was the first time, to Minami's knowledge, that the butler overseeing all the residence's servants, who hardly ever praised his own family, had said the words *passing marks* in that order. The fact that he'd directed them at her only doubled her astonishment.

"By the way, Minami?"

"Yes, Mistress?"

She couldn't let her shock linger, though. She understood without having to think about it that the Yotsuba's leader wouldn't have called an apprentice like her just to praise her for the results of an exercise.

"You'll be graduating middle school soon. What will you do about high school?"

"…I haven't decided yet, ma'am."

"Ah, I see you're worried about it."

She wasn't worried—her future school prospects weren't up to her to decide. The Yotsuba *owned* her. If she said she wanted to go to high school and Maya or Hayama said there was no need, that was it. "I haven't decided yet" was synonymous with "I haven't received instructions yet." Minami herself wasn't worrying about it at all.

"Then I'd like you to go to Tokyo."

For Minami, this order was 30 percent understandable and 70 percent surprising. They'd let her know a year before that she'd eventually become Miyuki's caretaker. But she'd thought it would be much further down the road, once they'd welcomed Miyuki to the main house. The young mistress's house in Tokyo was certainly larger than normal, but it was still only a private residence. It would be a slight bit unnatural for Miyuki to have a live-in housekeeper, and Minami thought that housekeeper being a child who'd just graduated middle school would only invite more suspicion.

The questions she had were immediately answered by her mistress.

"I want you to enroll at First High."

A question rose in Minami's mind—*By First High, does she mean the National Magic University's First Affiliated High School?*—but it stopped there. The order was to go to Tokyo and enroll at First High, so there couldn't be any other interpretation.

Because applications were online now, she didn't have to worry about meeting a deadline. The problem was that First High was one of the most difficult schools to get into. She grew considerably anxious—would she be able to pass the entrance exam when she hadn't done any real studying for it?

"You won't need to worry about the entrance exam."

Minami honestly thought that meant Maya would do something shady to pull some strings for her.

"I'll write the necessary knowledge directly into your brain in the three weeks before the test date."

But it had been naive of her to think that way. Maya was right—they had a device in this village that applied the principles of brainwashing devices to forcibly record necessary information into a person's mind. It was a terrible mental drain, however. Once exams were over, she might have to stay in bed for a week.

"Do your best, all right? I'll allow you a little break once the test is done. And you can have off from your maid duties as well, starting tomorrow."

As though she'd picked up on Minami's unease, Maya pronounced gently and heartlessly that there was no getting out of this.

"And Minami?"

"Yes, Mistress?"

Maya's face, which had seemed amused until now, suddenly grew serious. Minami's own expression drew back along with it.

"I want you to go to Miyuki. Starting this spring, she will be your mistress."

"Of course, Mistress."

That had been her original mission, the one they'd informed her of in advance. With a certain determination even amid her nervousness, Minami accepted Maya Yotsuba's order.

[1]

Thursday, April 5, 2096. One day before the National Magic University's First Affiliated High School's new year opening ceremony, and three days before the entrance ceremony.

At the Shiba siblings' house, Tatsuya was standing in front of a long body mirror with a distressed expression on his face.

Next to him was his younger sister Miyuki, wearing a flowering smile. In fact, it felt like the cherry blossoms would go back to being buds in embarrassment if they had to compete with such an endearing expression. That was the magic that her smiles possessed. She was so beautiful that their new roommate, Minami Sakurai—sent there by their aunt Maya Yotsuba as a housekeeper, bodyguard apprentice, and boarder—who would become their junior at First High three days from now, seemed to simply fade into the background despite standing right next to her.

Expectation glistened in Miyuki's broad smile as she watched her brother in front of the full-length mirror. The jacket portion of Tatsuya's new school uniform, which had arrived the day before, hung on the hanger right next to the mirror.

"Brother, please hurry and let me see what you look like in your new uniform. Or are you trying to keep your sister in suspense...?"

If he left Miyuki alone, she'd probably start overheating any second now. He decided he'd have to put aside his own gloom for the sake of his sister's mental health. He'd already put on his uniform's slacks and the official vest. Now he just had to throw on the blazer. Resigned, he grabbed its collar.

Minami tried to move in front of him to help him get his arms through the sleeves, but Miyuki moved at the same time, cutting her off. Without seeming particularly offended, Minami withdrew to her previous spot.

Tatsuya took the blazer from his sister's outstretched hand and turned. After he put his arms through the sleeves, Miyuki pulled the long blazer up from his back to his shoulders, then smoothed out the wrinkles.

When Tatsuya turned back to face the mirror, Miyuki, watching him, put a hand to her cheek in rapture and let out a passionate sigh.

Its design and coloring were the same as the regular First High boys' uniform. But there were three spots that differed slightly.

Tatsuya's new uniform blazer: Its left breast and shoulder were decorated with an eight-toothed gear design. It was the same size as the eight-petaled flower emblem on Course 1 uniforms and had a similar design; the new emblem was embroidered onto his left breast pocket and the tops of both sleeves.

"It suits you very well, Brother..."

Tatsuya still had many reservations about the new uniform, but its design immediately cleared the resentment that was pent up in Miyuki whenever she looked at him in his uniform with the blazer's breast pocket unadorned.

This gear emblem was a symbol of the magical engineering curriculum, newly created starting this year. The school had decided it wouldn't be good for its reputation to continue treating Tatsuya, who had built up a repertoire of outstanding achievements over the past year that couldn't be ignored, as a "substitute." As a result, it had put together a new curriculum for magical engineering, abbreviated M.E.

Of course, the school couldn't change its whole organization just for Tatsuya. Whatever the actual events leading to it were, it would be absurd for a newly created course to contain only one student.

Instead, it had made a fundamental update to the First High curriculum.

New students would be split into one hundred Course 1 students and one hundred Course 2 students; there was nothing different there.

What had changed was the process of moving from freshman to junior. New juniors now had the option to choose between the general magic curriculum and the magical engineering curriculum. Those who opted for general magic would receive lectures separately, as before, with four classes of Course 1 students and three of Course 2 students. Meanwhile, those who went for the magical engineering courses and passed the exam in March would be placed in a new class and given a curriculum that put emphasis on technological concepts relating to magic engineering.

Because it was establishing a new prototype school system, First High had also received an influx of teachers dispatched from the university. At first it would only be for one class, but in the future, if the new system saw good results, the school planned to separate the general magic and magical engineering students at enrollment and recruit new students.

And as a side effect of the M.E. courses' establishment, however many Course 1 students moved to magical engineering, an equal number would be allowed to transfer to Course 1. The school selected the Course 2 students with the highest grades in practical fields; of Tatsuya's friends, Mikihiko would be moving to Course 1 this year.

And yet, however they glossed over things on the surface, it was clear to those who were in the know that the magical engineering curriculum had been established for Tatsuya.

So you couldn't exactly blame Miyuki for celebrating her brother's long-awaited triumph.

Several forced poses later, Miyuki seemed satisfied and finally permitted Tatsuya to change. He felt a little like she was using him as a dress-up doll, but he convinced himself it made sense because she was still a girl. (The fashion show for Minami, the new student, had been three days before.)

"Brother, Minami, why don't we have some tea?" said Miyuki to her housemates, her good mood lingering, before disappearing into the kitchen almost at a skip. Minami watched her go and lowered her eyes sadly, which was already a sight Tatsuya was accustomed to. She was young—practically a child, in fact—but a spirit of professionalism had been instilled in her. As far as he could tell, she approached her maid work with pride (though that, too, was a fairly impolite impression). For her, someone else preparing tea probably challenged her reason for existing. Still, it didn't seem like Miyuki had any wish to yield when it came to the importance of taking care of him. The first five days after Minami's arrival had seen the girls making fairly bitter deals with smiles on their faces. Had Tatsuya's heart been of weaker constitution, he might have complained that his stomach hurt and left. Thankfully (?), though, he was built like steel, mentally and physically.

At the end of their quiet warfare with their identities at stake, Miyuki and Minami had come to a vague compromise.

First, Miyuki would leave cleaning and laundry to Minami.

Second, Miyuki would leave tea and cleaning up after meals to Minami.

Third, Miyuki would see to meal preparation when Tatsuya was present. When he wasn't, Minami would make the food.

Fourth, Miyuki would see to tea preparation when Tatsuya was present. When he wasn't, Minami would prepare it.

Fifth, Miyuki would help with Tatsuya's dress. Minami would help with Miyuki's.

The reason this arrangement was vague was that either of them, if she saw an opportunity, would attempt to outwit the other. As far as Tatsuya could tell, though, their relationship for the moment was peaceful and friendly.

Tatsuya and Minami's relationship was, on the surface, also friendly. Of course, he figured—as though it didn't concern him—that if a boy going on seventeen and a girl who was currently fifteen *were* to grow completely comfortable around each other in just two weeks, that might actually be a bigger problem.

Still, the fact was that Tatsuya felt like keeping something between them—specifically distance. Her slightly down-slanted eyes, her wavy dark-brown hair, her slender yet thick eyebrows, and the way dimples appeared in either cheek when she smiled all reminded him too much of Honami.

Honami Sakurai: the woman who had been their late mother's Guardian. Someone who had passed away four years ago protecting Tatsuya in Okinawa.

Minami and Honami had had the same "mother." They had been "created" from the same batch of unfertilized eggs and undergone the same genetic modification, and then those eggs had been fertilized by sperm gathered from the same "father." A human genetically engineered to have a strengthened magic faculties—an engineered magician. They were "sisters," not twins but extremely close to being so. It only made sense that Minami, genetically a niece, would have such similar features to Honami.

Tatsuya knew all the logic, of course. But understanding it didn't solve the problem or grant him comfort. The reason the "thing between them" (or something like it) had emerged in Tatsuya wasn't her appearance itself, but the memories of the dead her appearance triggered.

To the Shiba siblings, Honami Sakurai had been like family. She'd been like an older sister, easy to get along with. When Miyuki thought about her, she grew full of both mourning and fondness. But Tatsuya felt more bitter regret than anything else. Even the memories of her taking the siblings to her heart were like bitter gourds that only amplified his regret. It wasn't that the gourds were inedible—it was that his face would scowl without his meaning it to.

————He hadn't been strong enough.————

That was, in a few words, a summary of the regrets Tatsuya had when it came to Honami.

She'd died of emaciation, but if Tatsuya hadn't tried to intercept the GAA fleet invading Okinawa, she wouldn't have had to die *there*, at least. The truth was that Honami had whittled down her life until it was a cinder via continuous application of large-scale magic to protect Tatsuya.

Tatsuya, however, didn't regret the decision itself. He didn't consider the choice to intercept to be wrong. He hadn't thought deeply about his actions at the time—they'd been the result of swelling emotions. But if he hadn't wiped out the GAA ships then and there, it was highly likely the situation would have gotten even worse. He wasn't the only one to believe that, either. The tactical simulations done at the Academy of Defense's lab had produced the same results.

His regret was having needed Honami's strength at all.

These days, Tatsuya didn't need much time to prepare Material Burst. Now that he'd learned to fire Dismantle as a stationary area-of-effect spell, he wouldn't need Honami to help him shoot down the enemy warships' artillery shells.

At the time, he hadn't had enough strength.

And now, when he saw Minami, it reminded him of how powerless he'd been back then.

"Brother?"

"Right, I'm coming."

Tatsuya had been trapped by pensiveness for no more than three seconds. Miyuki hadn't given him the prompting because time had passed, but because she had noticed the slight change in his mood.

In response, Tatsuya began to move.

Minami, who had been waiting for him, followed behind.

The siblings had essentially been living on their own, and just having an extra housemate meant they had to buy more of certain things and replacements for others. Their dining table was one of them. The new table, one size larger than its predecessor, had a surface made of heat-resistant, high-strength glass, its emphasis heavily on its design element. Still, it was quite a bit sturdier than plywood, so unless someone used a big two-handed hammer, it wasn't going to break. Considering its resistance to moisture, stains, and grease, it was actually highly practical as well—which, of course, meant it was on the expensive side. When Tatsuya sat down at it, Miyuki sat down across from him, and Minami next to her.

Miyuki, for some reason, was still wearing her apron. Minami wore an apron by default, and having two girls in aprons sitting across from him was an odd situation, now that Tatsuya thought about it.

Of course, they may have both been wearing aprons, but their fashion sense was significantly different.

Minami wore a simple, long-sleeved, long-length, high-necked dress. Her apron, too, was made of thick fabric that covered almost the entire front of her body—a design that stressed practicality above all else. It wasn't the style of "real" maids from nineteenth-century Europe, but it clearly had that in mind.

In contrast, Miyuki was wearing a bold off-the-shoulder minidress, despite it still being early spring. Her apron was the type that hung by slender braids as well—how many different aprons did she even have?—and it even revealed her clavicle. Her skirt ended over ten centimeters above the knee, and she was barefoot below it as though it were natural. He could see a fair bit of her thighs through the highly transparent glass table, brought together as they were in a ladylike manner.

Could his sister have been trying to seduce him—or was she just teasing him?

That has to be it. If I let it get to me, I lose, he decided, glad that he wouldn't need to worry about it even if it was true. He decided he should thank his mother and aunt for that—though Miyuki was likely of the opposite opinion.

Neither of the siblings breathed a word about any of that, though, and they each aimed for their own coffee cup and cookies.

"The entrance ceremony is in just three days. I'm sure you're excited, aren't you, Minami?"

Nothing like it had happened when they'd lived on their own, but Miyuki had recently gained a tendency to swing the conversation to Minami whenever Tatsuya fell short of her expectations.

"Yes, Big Sister Miyuki. I am excited."

Meanwhile Minami, whether she hadn't caught on to Miyuki's intent or did but couldn't do anything about it in her position, gave a much more sincere reply to her offhanded question.

"Miyuki and I have to go to school a little early that day. Is that okay with you, Minami?"

"That's fine, Big Brother Tatsuya. I will humbly accompany you both."

Incidentally, her "big sister/big brother" references were something Tatsuya had suggested and Miyuki had subsequently ordered.

Because of how cabinets—the modern-day public transportation system—worked, they'd never be riding with complete strangers. Nor could they meet up with others part of the way through the trip. If people were riding the same cabinet, they had to live in the same house, live extremely near each other, or at least meet up at the station first.

On the other hand, because of her additional role as bodyguard, Minami didn't have the option of going to school via a different cabinet from Miyuki. Still, it would be unnatural for a complete stranger to commute in the same cabinet every day—it would invite suspicion they didn't need.

The excuse they'd be using was that Minami was the siblings' cousin on their mother's side. The Yotsuba family had instructed them to tell people something to that effect as well, and besides, the siblings' family register was utterly red with lies already. Adding in a cousin not related by blood was trivial at this point.

The problem had been in how Minami had initially referred to them as "Lady Miyuki" and "Lord Tatsuya."

These days, save for a few exceptions, no high school girls used the term *Lady* or *Lord* for students one year their senior. Those exceptions were girls of high birth, servants in the employ of high families, and girls somehow otherwise belonging to high families. Magicians only used it for people from the Ten Master Clans or families of equal import. *Big Brother* and *Big Sister* were exaggerated, too, but they were more common forms of address than *Lord* or *Lady*.

Tatsuya and Miyuki really just wanted her to call them by their first names, but Minami rejected that out of hand. She'd expressed reluctance at the family relation tags, too, but she knew concealing their identities was of great import, and so they'd compromised on *Big Sister Miyuki* and *Big Brother Tatsuya*.

The siblings, who had been living on their own, were for the moment getting along well with their unexpected new housemate.

Their teatime topic, naturally, shifted to the entrance ceremony three days hence.

"This year's representative is a boy... First time in four years, is it?"

"Five years, Brother. The president before Saegusa was a girl as well."

The siblings' conversation had turned to this year's new student representative—in other words, the top-seated incoming freshman. It had been a long time since First High had seen a boy as the representative.

"Since Saegusa's little sisters are enrolling this year, I thought it would be a girl again."

"Yes...and if Minami had really tried on the exam, she probably would have been the representative."

"No, that would be out of the question..."

Minami, expression stiff, shook her head a little at Miyuki's slight tease. The fact was that she had been concealing the true extent of her magic power on the main family's orders so that she wouldn't stand out too much. Tatsuya agreed that if she'd taken the test for real, she probably could have taken the top seat, but it seemed Minami wasn't of a mind to let a conversation like this pass without saying something.

Before an awkward air could begin to drift, Tatsuya decided to get back to the topic. "His name is Takuma Shippou, right? *The* Shippou?"

Miyuki hadn't exactly wanted to trouble Minami, either. She followed her brother's intentions right away. "Yes—eldest son of the Shippou, of the Eighteen."

The family tree of influential magicians in Tatsuya's mind and the information Miyuki recalled from the student profiles in her memory came to matching conclusions:

"So we have the Saegusa and Shippou as classmates. Either it's an incredible coincidence, or some very deep-rooted fate... I hope it doesn't cause any trouble," muttered Tatsuya, frowning just a little.

"Wouldn't it be good camouflage for us if they did stir up a little bit of trouble?"

"Well, yes, but..."

Miyuki meant that if the eldest son of the Shippou and the Saegusa twins were to get into an altercation, the school's attention would be on them, meaning there would be nobody—or at least fewer people—left to poke into the relationship between the siblings and Minami.

Her comment was logical, but he started to get a headache when he considered who would have to settle the commotion.

"Oh, and about the party tonight..."

As Minami was about to get up and clear the table now that their cups and saucers were empty, Tatsuya gestured for her to stop and suddenly changed the topic.

"I still think Minami should attend as well."

Tatsuya and Miyuki had been invited to a party at the Kitayama residence (meaning Shizuku's house) that night. The plan wasn't for Minami to mind the house in their absence, but for her to come with them to the mansion and wait for them in the servants' waiting room, but Tatsuya thought that they should change it.

"If you order me to, I will obey."

Minami's response was the reasonable one for a servant. But her expression was especially impassive now, implying that she didn't really want to do it. Her features weren't very expressive, but she certainly wasn't emotionless. Compared to girls like Mayumi or Erika, who would deliberately construct overblown expressions, Minami had emotions that were easy to read—though of course, this was only due to Tatsuya's own insightfulness.

Tatsuya wasn't into forcing people to do things. He took no pleasure in ordering people to do things they disliked. Her answer that she'd obey if ordered was something he was reluctant to exploit, and it actually made him want to say, *You know what, never mind*, but he hadn't made his previous comment on a whim.

"I see. I know it might be difficult, but please do come with us."

He considered it necessary that she reinforce the lie that she was their maternal cousin, so a somewhat unhappy answer in response wasn't enough for him to withdraw the idea.

"Let's pick you out a dress right away. I'll help you, since we don't have very much time." Miyuki clapped her hands, her mood changing to a cheerful one, perhaps in consideration of her brother's unshown feelings on the matter.

It was certainly not—he was sure—because she wanted to see Minami getting incredibly flustered.

[2]

Though it may have been nothing more than a party in name, this event was being held by the business behemoth Ushio Kitagata, who was Shizuku's father. The venue was naturally very well attended.

Despite that, it didn't give the impression of being crowded. There were certainly a lot of people gathered, but—

"This place really is big…"

—the Kitayama mansion it was hosted in was so large it made even Tatsuya give a genuine sigh.

But his impression found no match in those with him. Miyuki simply gave an insincere smile and nodded. Beside her, Minami looked slightly confused, as though she were about to tilt her head. It seemed there was a gap in perception among the three of them stemming from their upbringings—Tatsuya, who oftentimes mingled with "commoners" in the military or laboratories; Miyuki, raised as the next leader (or a candidate) of the Yotsuba; and Minami, who despite being a servant had grown up in the Yotsuba main house since a young age.

The pretext for today's party was the homecoming of Shizuku, who had finished her short-term study abroad program in the USNA. The party doubled as a grade-advancement celebration. It had been two weeks since she'd returned to Japan, and as for why the party was only happening now, it was because she'd been swamped with having to make the rounds and say hello to people of all sorts.

Shizuku was an honor student at the National Magic University's First Affiliated High School, a talented magician-in-training in her own right. But she had another face: She was also the daughter of a major business leader. Socially, she actually had to prioritize her standing as a company president's daughter. In an extreme sense, she possessed a position as a future magician, but with it came added responsibility as the president's daughter toward her family, employees, stockholders, and clients.

That was why her family (?) party had been pushed to the eve of the new semester.

The Kitayama family comprised five people: father, mother, grandmother, Shizuku, and her little brother. But her father had a younger brother and five sisters—for someone of a wealthy class, a family of that size wasn't too unusual—and because he'd married late in life, almost all of Shizuku's cousins were older than she. Over half of them were married and had brought their families with them, while the unmarried came with fiancés and fiancées and those they'd be engaged to in the coming days. That was why the family party had ballooned into such a crowd...and thus the story Tatsuya was currently hearing from Shizuku's mother:

"Ushio comes from a family of businessmen who have prospered since the last century. I know there are many things he can't afford to neglect, but..."

Tatsuya nodded along politely with what she was saying, but inwardly he sighed for the tenth time. He didn't know what her aim was or what she liked about him so much, but as soon as he'd said hello to Shizuku, Benio Kitayama—maiden name Naruse, an A-rank magician who had once been famous for her oscillation-type magic—had accosted him and locked him in as her conversation partner. Miyuki and Minami had already fled to where Shizuku and Honoka were.

"That doesn't mean I feel right about brazenly bringing total strangers to a private family party. When it comes to business, even my little Ushio is soft on family."

Still, thought Tatsuya, *Shizuku's mother seems to have a very sharp tongue.*

Of course, even though she was a company president's wife, the business wouldn't have survived if she let her sharp tongue run loose *all* the time (though acting that way in the world of riskier business was another story). She probably chose carefully the time, place, and person—but why on earth had she chosen him, someone she'd essentially just met? No matter how much he thought about it, he couldn't come up with an answer.

This wasn't the first time Tatsuya had come across Benio. He'd said hello to her the day Shizuku invited him and Miyuki over to tell them all the information she'd learned in America. But it really had been just a hello. He had no recollection of her ever choosing him to have such a candid conversation with.

"My little Ushio," huh...? Is it okay for her to call him that, considering these people's status in society? remarked Tatsuya to himself as he tried to escape reality, fed up already with Benio's complaining.

Tatsuya knew the ages of Shizuku's parents. Her father went without saying, but it hadn't been hard for him to gather personal data on her mother, either, because she had been quite famous in her day. (Still, in an era where personal information was very strictly protected, no normal person would have been able to do it.) Despite the way she referred to her husband, she wasn't as old as he. Ushio dressed younger than his age, and Benio's features were appropriate for hers, so at a glance, they didn't seem to be very far apart. But supposedly, Ushio was actually nine years older.

Must be well loved.

Even in his thoughts, he hesitated to use words like *pampered* about his friend's parents.

* * *

As though she was satisfied she'd gotten that string of discontent out of her system, Benio's glare mellowed out. In exchange, of course, she began to look at him as though sizing him up. Sizing up not the total stranger a relative might have brought, but Tatsuya.

He kept a calm expression, but when it came to feeling uncomfortable, Tatsuya was the same as anyone else. He wanted to go back to Miyuki and the others as soon as possible, but Benio didn't seem about to allow that.

"By the way…"

Before Tatsuya could politely remove himself from the conversation, Benio began again. Despite his desire to be polite with his classmate's mother, he considered this a most regrettable failure—well, it wasn't all that serious, but that was how uncomfortable it made him.

For Benio, though, things were getting to the important part now. If Tatsuya had tried to make his escape, she would have found a way to keep him there.

"Would you happen to be the object of little Honoka's unrequited affections?"

An ambush—but Tatsuya immediately understood what was behind it. Only in hindsight, though. This verbal attack was one he should have predicted.

"Whatever 'object' I am aside, yes, something like that."

Still, he resisted in no small manner simply nodding and saying yes to the "object" part. Maybe it was a trivial hang-up, but it was a small bit of self-assertion that Tatsuya couldn't yield on.

"You're not getting flustered. You seem dependable."

But apparently that oddity only gave him extra points in Benio's mind. Or maybe she scored him high because he hadn't tried to lie about it. The smile she was giving him suddenly turned from a formal, courteous one to a friendly one.

"But why didn't you say yes?"

Still, she might be "friendly" in the sense of a person being friendly toward a pet.

"She may not be as beautiful as your younger sister, but she is cute, isn't she?"

That being said, this was closer to someone watching a small animal running for its life in a hamster wheel in enjoyment. Tatsuya had skillfully withstood her opening move, but he could see in her eyes anticipation that he would start spinning his wheels.

"I do think she's cute. Not just in looks, but in personality, too."

Tatsuya's attitude was haphazard, but a large part of it was for appearance's sake. Behind his gaze, which made it hard to know where he was looking, he was very attentively observing Benio for even the slightest change in expression that might clue him in to why she was asking him about this.

"Oh, well...then I understand even less. Her face, body, and personality are all A-plus, but you still turned down her confession."

Tatsuya didn't remember saying anything about Honoka's body, but he rationalized it by assuming Benio probably meant it figuratively. He considered what to say to ignore it, but he didn't need to.

Because Benio dropped the bomb on him first:

"And she would be a great help. She would serve you faithfully."

If that wasn't a bombshell remark, he didn't know what was. Her words were far too inappropriately serious to be teasing her daughter's classmate. As a comment from one magician to another, it was indiscreet and imprudent.

A *normal* magic high school student wouldn't have known what Benio was talking about. And if someone *had* understood it and possessed the natural emotions of a sixteen- or seventeen-year-old boy, they wouldn't have been able to hide discomfort.

But Tatsuya simply looked back at Benio impassively.

Her smile didn't falter—she really was the wife of a major businessman.

"...Ah. So you know, and yet you can still act like that."

But evidently, she couldn't stop her voice from stiffening somewhat.

"I don't intend to feign ignorance." Tatsuya's voice certainly couldn't be called amiable, either. Whatever Benio's reasoning was, she should never have delivered that comment. He refused to think he should be cordial with her just because she was his new friend's mother.

"I see… You know how valuable it would be to use an Element's power, and your position is to neither accept her nor push her away."

Honoka's bloodline—the Elements. She was a descendant of prototype magicians, developed in an attempt to recreate traditional magics, from before the modern magic system of four families and eight types was established. For those in high positions of authority, her blood had much value. Tatsuya knew that, and that was what Benio was commenting on.

The insincere smile fell away from her face. Her stiff voice turned into a hard, cold one. "A calculated move, perhaps?"

Benio didn't say who or what, but Tatsuya properly understood what the implications were—and that criticism and slander were part of them.

"I have no intent to take advantage of my classmate…"

Still, Tatsuya didn't back down, nor did he let the aspersion irritate him into arguing with her.

"But you were in her company during the vampire extermination, weren't you?"

Annoyance crept into Benio's voice—maybe she thought he was trying to play dumb.

"I didn't have any reason to leave her out, either." Tatsuya was keenly aware of how Benio was changing. He would overlook goodwill, but he'd never miss hostility. That was how he was put together. And he was trained not to let any hostility or malice, no matter how strong, disturb him.

Seeing that the blood wasn't rushing to his head no matter how much she tried to rattle him, she changed the topic. "…Honoka is like a sister to Shizuku. Both Ushio and I treat her the same as a daughter. And Shizuku has taken a liking to you, too. The trust she places in you goes beyond regular friendship."

Tatsuya returned her gaze, his eyes asking what exactly she was getting at. Any diffidence he'd maintained for her as Shizuku's mother had vanished at this point.

"So I took it upon myself to investigate you, Tatsuya Shiba." Benio directed a challenging gaze at him.

"That isn't very pleasant, but I can understand why." Tatsuya met it with an undaunted stare of his own.

"Who *are* you? Even Kitayama's… Even the cartel's information network couldn't get any personal data on you."

"I think you must be mistaken. If I had no personal data, I wouldn't have been able to enroll in high school."

Tatsuya's answer made sense, but Benio could only see it as splitting hairs.

"You'd do well not to underestimate adults. There is a bare minimum of personal data on you out there. It has an appropriate amount of extra information, and an appropriate amount of negative assessment in it. It's not overly clean. I'd never asked her anything about you, so I didn't have any particular doubts."

"Is there something suspicious in it?"

Tatsuya's tone in response was inorganic, like a machine's. His attitude made it seem that he'd seen through her, seen that she wasn't speaking of any real information or evidence.

"No, there's nothing suspicious in it. That's why it's strange."

As Shizuku's mother glared hard at him, Tatsuya looked back without saying anything. His honest-to-goodness feeling was that there was nothing he *could* say to that. At most, he mused privately (and partly to escape reality), that Shizuku's mother had a much more fiery temperament than he'd thought.

"Just from what she's told me, you have the abilities of a prodigy—no, a sheer genius. Now that I'm talking face-to-face with you, I'm growing more and more certain that you're not a normal person. There is no way your personal data could be that normal."

Even if Benio's comments were true, they were no more than guesses. And guesses were something he didn't acknowledge as necessary to submissively admit to.

"P.D. is just that—data. It's not the person himself."

Personal data was a mask, a persona, that allowed for distinction between yourself and others. Even if that persona was completely different from one's true face, as long as the fact that it was completely different stayed secret, one's persona could remain on one's face.

"...Are you trying to tell me it's only natural it would give me the wrong impression?"

"In terms of who I am, if you're asking my name or personal history, it's exactly how it is in my P.D. If you're asking about the impression I give, it's as you can see. There's not much else I can tell you."

In a way, this was how Tatsuya actually felt. Who was he? Someone who wielded large-scale destruction outclassing the most powerful nuclear weapons of the age, someone who could possibly destroy the world—*what* was he? Those were the unanswerable questions that oftentimes came to mind.

But Benio didn't take it like that.

"Are you playing dumb with me...?!"

She was keeping her voice down, but her tone had grown very rough.

Those of elite status, save for certain exceptions, tended to keenly pick up on the shifting of emotions those of equal rank or above showed. The sight of the party's hostess and a guest arguing was beginning to draw attention from those present.

"Benio, please settle down."

It was a family party, but not everyone here was completely *family*. There wasn't any way being seen like this would be good for her. Her husband's breaking in to cool things off was the right move.

It seemed Benio hadn't realized how excited she'd gotten. When Ushio reproved her, she caught herself before responding, surprised.

"Shiba, I apologize for my wife's rudeness."

"Not at all—I'm the one who said several forward things. The words of an inexperienced youth, as I'm sure you know, so I hope you will forgive me."

As Ushio bowed to him, Tatsuya politely returned the apology. It was quite an arrogant thing to say, though—a masterfully scathing backhanded stab.

Fortunately, Ushio didn't seem to mind Tatsuya's acting as if it had nothing to do with him. Without creating any more tension, like a tide going out, the other attendees began averting their stares from Tatsuya and Benio.

"If it's all right with you, I'd like to excuse myself from your presence for a while," said Tatsuya to Ushio rather than Benio, probably thinking it was a good chance.

"Ah, yes. I'm sure my daughter wants to talk to you."

Ushio probably figured his wife would need some time to cool down, too. Tatsuya bowed and headed for Shizuku and the others as Ushio put a hand on Benio's back and led her to a seat near the wall.

"I'm sorry, Tatsuya."

As soon as Tatsuya got close enough that she wouldn't have to raise her voice, Shizuku apologized and bowed before he could open his mouth. When she looked up toward him, he could see a little bit of shame in her usually expressionless face, as if she didn't know where to put herself. Her mother had picked a fight (in Shizuku's view) with a classmate she'd invited to her party—anyone, not just Shizuku, would definitely have been pretty embarrassed.

"No, I can understand where your mother is coming from. I'd probably worry too if a strange man were close with my daughter. I don't mind, so you shouldn't, either."

"...Okay. Sorry."

Shizuku refrained from objecting to one thing or another, not because she was quick to change gears (though that aspect wasn't wholly absent), but because her reticent nature had worked against her. She wanted to apologize about so much more, but she could only manage a couple of words. That overlapped with her embarrassment, and she gave an awkward look.

Tatsuya realized just in time that his right hand was reaching out to pat her on the head. Her being blameless but caring too much and getting down about it reminded him of how Miyuki looked sometimes, making him reflexively use his head-pat response.

He kept his bitter grin at his own carelessness to himself, then smiled a little and shook his head as if to say that the matter was over with.

Shizuku, Honoka, Minami, and Miyuki: a ring of four girls in gorgeous dresses—and one boy in a plain suit and tie among them. Normally this would be the time to start feeling uncomfortable, but Tatsuya didn't have those nerves. Honoka began talking to Minami out of consideration, with Shizuku pressing the brakes at times so that she didn't go too far, while Minami gave restrained answers to questions with support from Miyuki. Tatsuya was relegated to watching their conversation proceed as a listener, when suddenly a voice addressed him from behind.

"Umm, you're Tatsuya Shiba, right?"

Tatsuya turned, but the boy seemed to think he hadn't heard what he'd said, and when he repeated the question, Tatsuya told him yes.

Tatsuya didn't need to ask the name of the small boy, who was probably still in elementary school.

"Wataru."

His name came off Shizuku's lips.

"Sorry, Sis. Am I getting in the way?"

The boy's identity had been revealed from his own mouth.

"No, but introduce yourself properly."

Shizuku, a girl of few words, sounded quite curt, but her eyes were gentle as she looked at her much younger brother.

Wataru knew what he was doing, too, so after doing his best to fix his face to look serious—it was quite heartwarming to see him almost stand on his tiptoes—he gave a proper bow as his sister had told him to.

"I'm Wataru Kitayama. Pleased to meet you. I'll be in sixth grade this year."

Wataru introduced himself, turning fully toward Tatsuya. He was already in a relationship that could be called friendly with Honoka, so it could be called only natural that he wouldn't look in her direction for a greeting. However, he didn't turn to look Miyuki's way—evidently so that he wouldn't get (too) excited. As Miyuki was returning the introduction once Tatsuya was done, the boy looked away slightly, clenched his teeth, and put his strength into his whole body, so there was little doubt.

It was clear he didn't hate her and that he wasn't trying to ignore her, so Miyuki only found Wataru's attitude charming. However, Minami didn't seem able to prevent her own displeasure at the lack of manners shown toward her mistress.

"It is an honor to meet you, Master Wataru. I am Minami Sakurai, Big Brother Tatsuya and Big Sister Miyuki's cousin. Pleased to make your acquaintance."

Minami's behavior was excusably courteous, but in it one could glimpse the emptiness of a businessman's smile. It wasn't quite offensive politeness, but it certainly still felt like empty politeness.

The one who moved to dispel the uncomfortable air about to drift in was Honoka.

"Wataru, didn't you have something you wanted to ask Tatsuya?"

Still, it wasn't a forced change of topic. Wataru had indeed been acting as if he wanted to ask Tatsuya something earlier.

"Oh, right."

Wataru's attention immediately focused on Honoka, which seemed less like a reaction to the mood and more just an expression of his age.

"Shiba…"

There were two Shibas here, but nobody misunderstood which one Wataru had addressed, nor was there anyone who would purposely interrupt what he was saying—Minami included.

"There's something I'd like to ask you," Wataru continued, managing not to choke on his words, his nervousness apparent.

"Sure, if it's something I can answer," replied Tatsuya in a familiar tone.

"Umm, well, can you still become a magical engineer even if you can't use magic?"

The question itself was nothing strange, but coming from the son and heir of the Kitayama family, it sounded odd. In fact, Shizuku and Honoka both gave surprised looks.

"I'd say no. Magical engineers are technical experts with magic faculties. A technician who can't use magic wouldn't be called a magical engineer."

But Tatsuya didn't even pause, much less struggle to answer.

"Oh…"

Wataru's shoulders drooped. But it was still too soon for him to feel down.

"Of course, magical engineers aren't the only technical experts in engineering fields related to magic."

"Huh?"

As Wataru looked up at him hopefully, Tatsuya gazed down with a calm smile. Wataru's eyes sparkled with anticipation as he waited for the next words.

"You can still study magical engineering without being able to use magic."

Tatsuya didn't affect a pompous, self-important air. He might have been a bad person, but that didn't mean he was callous—at least, not if you asked him, anyway.

"It's difficult to tune CADs if you don't have a magical sense, but you can create them even without magic. The same goes for other products with magical technology in them. If you study hard, you should be able to learn what you need to and acquire the skills to help your sister out."

"I—that wasn't what I was…"

However much he denied it, the embarrassment on his face made his true intentions clear.

And the look he was giving Tatsuya also switched from caution and fear toward a strange adult (from an elementary school kid's point of view, high schoolers were adults) to respect mixed with aspiration.

The adults, unfortunately, were unable to adopt the same innocent attitude as the children.

As she watched the siblings, both now attached to Tatsuya, from afar, Benio began to feel like heaving an excessive sigh.

"What could be the matter, Benio?"

Even when Ushio, sounding worried, addressed her, Benio's expression was too fixed in its sigh-stifling state for her to reply. All she did was glance at her husband after he'd said it, then return her gaze quickly to the children having a pleasant chat.

"What on earth rubs you the wrong way about Tatsuya Shiba?"

Ushio Kitayama was a loving husband, but he wasn't henpecked. Actually, certain parts of him might be better described as submissive, but their relationship was not one where he couldn't air what he wanted to say.

"…Ushio dear, you seem to like him quite a bit," she said, finally looking at her husband directly.

"I think the kid has a lot of promise. Above all, he's talented."

Ushio's answer was straightforward—or, put more negatively, utterly frank.

Benio felt a reflexive burst of emotion, but she didn't lash out at him in hysterics. "…He's *too* talented."

But her tone of voice revealed that she was straining to clamp down on those emotions, betraying her mental state as a far cry from cool and composed.

"And he knows about too much, and he understands too much. Even the direct descendants of the Ten Master Clans don't feel this heavily guarded to me."

Finally, a sigh escaped her lips. The doubts she cradled would have gone unspoken otherwise.

"For magicians, being *too* talented isn't a fortunate thing. It could even be something that puts you farther away from fortune. Thankfully, Shizuku is *only* talented. But if she's close to a magician who is *too* talented, she could be wrapped up in the misfortune that too much power can draw."

Ushio couldn't laugh off his wife's words as indicating overthinking. Instead, he put a hand on her shoulder. "If you're right and Tatsuya Shiba does draw misfortune—he wouldn't bear the blame, right? I wouldn't appreciate you avoiding him because of an uncertain future he has no responsibility for. If his strength does invite misfortune and it seems like Shizuku will get wrapped up on it, it falls to us to get rid of the misfortune. They don't call me a tycoon for nothing. You can be sure I'll protect my family at the very least."

Benio nodded to her husband's firm affirmation, finally not arguing.

But it still didn't seem she was truly convinced.

It wasn't clear whether it was because of powers too great, but Tatsuya certainly had a tendency—or perhaps character—to summon trouble. Even now, a sort of trouble was sneaking up on him as he had a pleasant conversation with Shizuku's younger brother.

"Shizuku, I haven't seen you in so long."

A young man who looked to be in his midtwenties came up and began casually speaking to Shizuku. He came off as frivolous, but he had good looks. He didn't seem tawdry, at least. Shizuku simply returned a bow to him, so Tatsuya didn't know his name, but from the familiar mood, he must have been one of Shizuku's older cousins.

But Shizuku and Wataru both seemed confused when they saw the young woman standing at his side. She looked about the same age as the man. She had very good looks, but her dress and accessories were conscious of the occasion, so nothing about her appearance offered any outlandishness. The questioning expressions on Shizuku's and Wataru's faces indicated that the beauty was not any family member the two of them knew.

"Oh! I'm actually getting married this year. To her," explained the young man a little hurriedly as Shizuku and Wataru looked at him.

"You're engaged? Congratulations," said Shizuku, offering conventional regards for the situation.

"Yeah. Actually, we haven't gotten the engagement ring yet." The young man scratched his head, slightly embarrassed.

As Tatsuya looked on, reflecting that he seemed quite like a normal boy for someone who was a Kitayama extended family member, the beauty making a display of herself beside him noticed his gaze and offered him a friendly smile.

This time it was Tatsuya's turn to look confused. Miyuki immediately picked up on the change, looking to him, eyes asking what was the matter. She looked over to where Tatsuya was gazing.

When she realized what was going on, she probably would have bristled up to her eyebrows, but before she could, the woman began to speak—not to Tatsuya, but to the most important person of the day, Shizuku.

"It's nice to meet you, Shizuku. I'm Maki Sawamura. I'm quite pleased to make your acquaintance."

To Tatsuya, the short self-introduction felt like it wasn't due to a reserved personality unused to preening, but rather to a belief that everyone would know who she was without her having to explain.

As if to confirm his deduction, Honoka, who introduced herself after Shizuku and Wataru, asked her a question, her voice a little giddy.

"Umm, Miss Sawamura—are you the famous actress Maki Sawamura? The one who was nominated for Best Actress in a Lead Role in the Pan-Pacific Cinema Awards for *A Midsummer's Ice Drift*?"

"Oh, you watched that old thing?" replied Maki Sawamura, still smiling elegantly—though a little bit of pride was mixed in.

"I thought so! I saw it in the theater. You were wonderful!"

"Heh-heh. Thank you very much."

Tatsuya didn't watch many movies, but he knew the title *A Midsummer's Ice Drift*. He remembered the movie as having been quite the topic the previous summer. Judging by Honoka's attitude, it must have been an interesting film. At least interesting enough to make her go to the theater instead of watching the VOD (video on demand), which was mainstream these days.

The conversation had included that she'd been nominated for an international film award, so she must be a famous actress. Once he knew that much, his interest in her faded. He never had any interest in the entertainment world anyway, and there would be a lot of negatives, given his position, if he were to become acquainted with a celebrity who got so much media attention. He knew it was rude to Honoka, who was quite excited, but he wondered if she'd go away to some other guests soon.

Unfortunately for him, though, the situation moved in a direction he'd rather it hadn't.

"I apologize if I'm wrong, but…" She trailed off as though about to ask a question—of Tatsuya and Miyuki, who were standing off a bit behind the group. "Would you happen to be Miyuki and Tatsuya Shiba?"

The siblings were both experienced enough not to let any dismay show, but they *were* both caught off guard, though to different degrees.

He took a step forward to block Miyuki from moving up and introducing herself, then stood directly in front of Maki. "We are. You'll have to excuse me—have we met before?"

Maki's answer didn't clash with Tatsuya's memory. "No, this is the first we've met."

Then why? asked Tatsuya wordlessly, only to have Maki reveal her hand quite easily:

"He showed me the Nine School Competition broadcast. Since Shizuku was in it." *He* obviously referred to her fiancé, who had been standing next to her the whole time. "It struck me how picture-perfect the two of you are."

Maki lowered her voice so that Shizuku, who was talking to Maki's fiancé, wouldn't hear. Tatsuya decided it was so Shizuku wouldn't wrongly take her praising Miyuki as an implicit smirching of Shizuku. She brought her face closer to theirs as she quieted herself, though, so maybe she had a different intent. Tatsuya had no obligation to respond to whatever it was.

"Do you think so? My sister aside, I wouldn't think I'd be very picturesque."

He spoke to her casually in consideration of where they were and whom he was talking to. His attitude was even more aloof than it had been with Shizuku's parents.

Miyuki was staying silent under a mask of propriety for the same reasons as her brother. They both instinctively sensed something shady about Maki.

"You're very modest. I'm not the only one who thinks you two each possess beauty. My friends all thought the same way."

After that, Maki listed the names of several actors and movie directors, but unfortunately, Tatsuya didn't know who a single one of them was.

"Oh, I know! Do you have plans this weekend? If you can make it, I'd like to invite you to our salon."

Maki invited Tatsuya with an alluring smile. As she affected a pure air with an innocent expression, sex appeal began to worm its way onto her face as though trying to catch him in a net. It was a move that was fully appropriate for such a young and famous actress.

In all honesty, Tatsuya felt interested. At a glance, the celebrity had nothing to do with magic. What did she want from him? He couldn't help but wonder. He didn't believe for a second the nonsense about his appearance having attracted her. The light in Maki Sawamura's eyes was more thoughtful than that.

"I appreciate the offer, but I'll have to decline."

His answer, though, was refusal. His tone was polite, but the will he imparted to his voice left no room for misunderstanding or misinterpretation.

"Oh, I see."

For an instant, something akin to anger rippled through Maki's eyes, but an instant later, not even its shadow remained—a testament to her skills.

"In that case, Miss Miyuki...would you be interested in coming alone?"

This time, she directed a smooth smile at his sister. Her previous smile had intimated womanhood, while this one prevented any excessive femininity. She knew what smile to use when. Maybe her acting skills were the real deal.

"My brother has already declined, so I could never intrude on you by myself."

Miyuki's response was an immediate refusal, too.

It left Maki with no foothold whatsoever. She looked taken aback. While she was trying to recover her pace, Tatsuya and Miyuki each made a bow, his curt and hers elegant, and walked away toward the food table.

Minami, who had been watching them privately so as not to rouse attention, followed them. She glanced back quickly. Maki had been watching Tatsuya leave with a harsh look, but now she hastily turned away.

As though he'd misunderstood the look she was giving off, her (self-professed) fiancé, who had been talking to Shizuku, returned to her side. Maki welcomed him back with a comfortable smile in which not a trace of ire or unrest remained.

[3]

An electric car, made to look like a classic—in this case, one of the supercars popular domestically from the late 1970s to the 1980s—stopped in front of a high-rise apartment complex standing in the heart of the city.

Maki opened the gull-wing door and stepped out of the car, which was so low it almost touched the ground, and onto the pavement. She stood up in a motion dashing enough for a movie star, then went around the hood to the driver's seat—though the man in it was just sitting there, since it was a self-driving car—and peered in, saying, "This is fine. Thanks for driving me back."

Her "lover" (Shizuku's cousin) gave her a look that said he wasn't satisfied. But Maki crouched a little, touched her lips to his cheek, and smiled. The young man started the car again without further complaint.

She waved a little at the classic car replica as it drove off, but as soon as it made a turn at an intersection and went out of sight, her smile disappeared, replaced with a chilly glare. She sighed, driving her "lover," whom she'd manipulated with a simple, calculated smile, from her mind, and headed for the elevator lobby in the apartment building.

Excluding special super-high skyscrapers like Yokohama Bay Hills Tower, few buildings in Japan at the end of the twenty-first century exceeded one hundred meters in height, and among these, residential apartments were especially rare. This was because it was better from a federal land usage efficiency standpoint to build many high-rise apartments all in one area rather than to have a single super-skyscraper standing on its own.

Maki's apartment was in a high-class mansion area where eighty-meter-high, twenty-story apartment buildings stood at regular intervals. Hers was on the end of the twentieth floor. A combination of mirrors and optical fibers gave sufficient natural illumination to the lower floors as well, but tenants tended to like higher floors anyway.

Therefore, the top floor was also the most expensive. Having a room on the uppermost floor of a high-class apartment building in the heart of the city would have been difficult for someone so young, even with her career, without a patron. This would be true no matter how famous an actress she was—that is, if she really was just a normal actress.

"Thank you for minding the place," she said to two female bodyguards who had moved into the hallway upon learning of their employer's return. They weren't attendants, though those had survived as a tradition in the entertainment world. They weren't apprentices doubling as errand runners dispatched by the production company she belonged to, either—they were bodyguards her father had picked out.

Maki's father was the president of a holding company that owned several media corporations, including television stations. The Sawamura family might not have as much capital as the Kitayama family, but they were still members of the wealthy upper class.

After getting back, she went straight to take a shower. In a lounging dress and a gown, casual attire she never wore outside her own house—or *those* types of photo shoots—she sank down onto the sofa. Manipulating the menu on the side of the armrest, she had the HAR, or Home Automation Robot, ready a bottle of wine and a glass. She took the already-uncorked bottle and poured red wine into the glass.

Rather than putting it to her lips, she brought it close to her face and savored the fragrance. It wasn't that she wanted the alcohol. This was a kind of ritual that Maki performed to relax her strained nerves after coming back from a job. That being the case, it might be more accurate to say she was reveling in the mood rather than savoring the fragrance.

Still, she wouldn't leave the wine completely undrunk. When the halfway-filled glass had decreased to half that, a bodyguard opened the living room door and entered.

"Madam, Master Shippou is here to see you."

"Takuma? ...Oh yes. It's almost time. He's a little early, but I don't mind. Show him in."

Despite her clothing being something most would hesitate to wear in front of others, Maki's face held no hesitation as she ordered the bodyguard to let the visitor into the living room.

"Right away, madam."

Even after the bodyguard turned her back, Maki didn't bother hastily putting on makeup.

She was an actor. Even if she had none on, even if she was seminude, she could play the part of the Maki she wanted others to see. Her simple dress and gown would be sufficient armaments to see the inexperienced boy in.

After the bodyguard showed the young man in, said young man wasted no time going to the seat across from Maki and sitting down, as though thoroughly acquainted with the place.

He was about five foot eight, but like most boys his age, he was rather skinny. He looked fine, but there was some boyish charm still left in his face. However, he also gave off a somewhat impudent impression—it probably came from the strong light of self-assertion in his eyes.

"Good evening, Maki."

For his part, he had a tendency to be overly conscious about coming off like an adult in both his tone of voice and his behavior.

"Welcome, Takuma. You're right on time."

Maki decided to casually go along with Takuma's overreaching himself. Still, their relationship was not one where the act would lighten his mood any at this point. They'd known each other for close to a year now.

"Want something to drink?"

"No, thanks. Alcohol clouds my judgment."

Takuma shook his head at the offer. Maki hadn't intended to give him alcohol, but she didn't mention that.

"Anyway, could you tell me what you called me over for?"

"Sure. Let's get right to it."

Takuma's attitude was too impetuous for Maki's tastes, but the boy was almost a decade younger than she, so she didn't try to make an appeal with her figure. Takuma wasn't a younger boyfriend, nor was he *involved* with her.

"I contacted Shizuku Kitayama. But for now, all she knows are my face and name."

"...Doesn't care much for celebrities, I guess," said Takuma, not hiding his disappointment.

Maki gave him a smile, the relaxed one of an actress—no, of a star. "Well, her friend, Honoka Mitsui, seemed to have quite an interest in me."

"Really?" Takuma's attitude switched gears—a calculated move—and he leaned in toward the woman. "Honoka Mitsui is near the top of the new junior class. If we can ally ourselves with her, she'd definitely help."

"Most likely. And if her good friend Honoka Mitsui joins your faction, I think the probability of getting Shizuku Kitayama into it will rise."

Maki and Takuma were confederates. They both wanted magician allies for their own reasons—pieces on the board to use. Part of their plan was to create a faction using First High students wishing to become professional magicians in the future.

"I would have thought it'd be better to get other new students like you on our side at first…"

"Our goal is to achieve a new order in our respective worlds," broke in Takuma, "not to create a faction itself. There's no point playing king of the hill at school. We should prioritize getting people with a lot of influence on our side, like the Kitayama family. That's why you contacted that dull man with ties to the Kitayama in the first place, right?" He settled an overbearing gaze on Maki. "We'll target that Honoka Mitsui first. I can expect your assistance, I assume?"

Maki parried his eagerness, or rather childishness, with a smile. "Yes, that's the plan…but you should probably be courteous with her, since she will be your upperclassman, Takuma. You might accidentally find yourself not paying attention and slip up."

Takuma's eyes immediately began to wander awkwardly. In response, Maki wet her lips with her wine and changed to a slightly somber expression. It was an act, of course, but:

"Maki, did something bad happen?"

Takuma frowned when he saw it. His question was exactly what Maki had been going for.

"Something bad… I suppose."

Obviously, she kept that under her hat. The idea was to make it seem like the look had accidentally come onto her face, and that she'd only answered because he'd asked.

"Like you heard before, Miyuki Shiba and her older brother were at the party as well."

Takuma showed no signs of catching on. Either he had no ability to spot acting or he literally had zero interest in what Maki actually thought; his attention was focused on what she had to say.

"It seems like it'll be rough to rope them in."

"Did something happen?"

"No, I just talked to them…but they seemed to have a special relationship with the prior student council president."

At this stage, Maki was already lying. She hadn't had time to find out anything like that before Tatsuya and Miyuki gave her the cold shoulder. But Takuma had no way of knowing that.

"The prior student council president... Saegusa!"

His ability to think calmly and see through lies was firmly capped by his emotions, which centered around a hostility riled by Maki's words and by the name Takuma himself had said.

"This is just a guess, but I think the Saegusa family already has their hands on the Shiba siblings. If they are allied with each other, things would get sticky for us. The sister especially has many supporters at school."

The flames of enmity burning in his eyes, Takuma answered her in a strong voice—or at least one trying to be strong. "That's how it goes—the more allies you have, the more enemies. If they're Saegusa pawns, sooner or later we'll have to clash. And I'll be ready for it!"

"The sister is the student council vice president, so you might want to give up on making the student council a foothold."

Maki looked up at her guest, who had shot to his feet in agitation, as if he were the most dependable person in the world. A light of expectation glimmered in her eyes.

"According to what I heard, the sister dotes very heavily on her brother, and her brother is pretty much hated. You might be able to use that to make a strategy," she advised Takuma, with encouragement in her voice—or at least trying to get it there.

[4]

Tokyo, Osaka, and Nagoya were Japan's three biggest cities even now at the end of the twenty-first century. For a time, Osaka had suffered from severe land subsidence, but with a radical decrease in physical distribution costs (centered around the removal of airport usage fees and a quick conversion of ports to a twenty-four-hour system), it recovered its status as a commercial city.

But tonight, it was not Osaka where an incident was about to happen, but Nagoya.

The time was almost 11:00 PM. The place was a promenade in Atsuta Park, in the vicinity of Horikawa.

"I must say, having a secret meeting at this hour in such a deserted place is like asking for people to be suspicious of you."

Speaking softly and ignoring that she was also present at this hour and in this place—the thick brush beside the promenade—was a girl of fifteen or sixteen with long hair in soft waves, wearing a conspicuous outfit that made it seem she was coming back from a rock concert that had sold itself on extreme visuals.

"Gee, the way my big sister is dressed is already one step from *actually* being suspicious, what with the time and location, so I don't want to hear that from you."

The voice that responded was low for a girl's, but high for a boy's.

One might not have been able to tell just from hearing it which the speaker was, but they were wearing a black, mini-length jumper dress and leggings in the same color, indicating the speaker was female.

Beneath the jumper dress, incidentally, was a black long-sleeved turtleneck, so the only skin being exposed was that of her face and hands, but the chest was visibly sticking out slightly. Additionally, her hair was done in a straight, short bob, ending about where her jawline was. Externally, she seemed like she was definitely a girl. She called the first girl her "big sister" despite appearing to be the same age, so she was either a slightly younger sister or a twin.

"You just don't get it, do you, Yami?"

The younger girl, called Yami, scrunched up her face for a moment, but didn't complain.

"If I'm wearing this, then I can walk around this late *because* people will just think I'm some random delinquent."

The claim held a certain kind of persuasion, so Yami's words caught in her throat. Still, the job they'd been given tonight promised some real action, and for that, a fundamental rule was to wear clothing that was easy to move in. The sort of clothes that would catch on every little thing, like what her sister was wearing now, were supposed to be unsuitable. And yet even though Yami had chosen her outfit with a mind for ease of movement—though certain circumstances dictated she still wear a dress—her sister had said she "just didn't get it." Yami wasn't satisfied with that.

She wanted to argue, and she didn't care how. She tried to find the words, but her futile thought processes were cut off by a message coming in from the receiver hooked onto one ear.

"It looks like our targets are here," said Yami.

"I confirmed as well. I didn't expect them to come by boat, though—and by houseboat at that. It sticks out like a sore thumb... Hiding must not be what they're going for."

The thick bandage covering her sister's left eye was apparently an HMD, or head-mounted display, and she frequently rubbed the bandage surface while closing and opening her right eye. She didn't seem to be totally comfortable using it. *You didn't have to use it, you know,* thought Yami, instead giving voice to something more constructive (at least, so she thought).

"I don't think hiding is the idea. Even if there are witnesses, claiming to be providing information to journalists would do the trick."

"Journalists, huh…?" said her sister dubiously.

Yami shrugged her shoulders purposefully, though not so hard that it came off as exaggerated. "But we'll leave your distrust of the media for another time, Yoru."

"Yami…you've gotten really cheeky, you know that?"

Her indication that their pointless chatter was over seemed not to have been for nothing. Without sparing any thought for her older sister's remark, Yami directed her gaze to the excursion boat about to come ashore. It was a houseboat, and one couldn't see inside the rooms. The boat connected to a small pier that also served as a gondola platform, and two large men got off.

Greeting the two men was a middle-aged man of middling height and middling girth. At first, he appeared seedy-looking, but he didn't fool the girls. He wore a suit one size too big in order to hide it, but he was significantly physically trained for combat. And the scent of smoke was drifting from him.

"Is that the journalist? Looks more like a mercenary, if you ask me."

"Apparently he actually has mercenary experience, too. Didn't you get the data before?"

Yoru looked away smoothly as her younger sister gave her a *Didn't you see?* look. She'd gotten confirmation on the journalist earlier. The man seemed to think he was hidden, and he didn't show any signs that he knew the girls were sneaking a peek. The visual data had made his profile clear.

"It says he's a journalist with strong dissenter leanings."

"Hmm. A paragon of journalism, then."

"Yes, you can tell me all about your prejudices later."

"Prejudices... Yami, you really *are* cheeky."

"Let's just go. The boat comes first. If you don't mind..."

The indifferent evasion put a very unhappy look on her sister's face, but though she was young, she was no amateur. She wouldn't neglect her duty for personal feelings.

"Yeah, yeah."

Yoru answered casually, but her face was all business. She removed the leather accessory covering her left forearm. A multipurpose CAD shaped like a bracelet appeared from underneath it. She pressed a function button slightly removed from its keypad and initiated an activation sequence.

"Time to *blow them away!*"

Yoru went around behind her younger sister. She had a clear view of the houseboat from the gaps between the trees.

Suddenly, Yami's body disappeared.

A moment later, she was standing on the houseboat's bow.

Pseudo-teleportation—that was the name of the spell Yoru had used. The spell canceled the momentum an object (such as a human body) possessed, created a cocoon in the air around it, then a slightly larger vacuum tube to move the cocoon through. It was made up of four processes: weighting, containment, convergence, and movement. It wasn't a very complex spell. The flaw was that during creation of the vacuum tube, it created an air current as the air got pushed away from it, meaning an observer would sense where the object was moving to. If one had the skill to chain the spell and *fly*, one could use movement speed to dazzle the opponent, but that was seen as fundamentally unsuited for offense and more of an escape technique.

The pseudo-teleportation Yoru triggered, however, didn't even make ripples on the water's surface; she held even the air currents that emerged upon the vacuum tube's creation under her control. It was

proof that this seemingly flighty girl had an incredibly high level of magic skill.

Yami, sent straight into the midst of their prey thanks to her sister's power, lightly kicked off the deck and dived inside.

Five men were in there. Like the mercenary-turned-journalist, they were all bulky, but unlike him, they didn't give off an air of unruliness. In fact, they had an awfully single-minded and genuine light in their eyes.

"Who are you?!"

The voice asking her identity was somehow awkward. It seemed he'd been about to shout in his native tongue, then corrected himself and spoken Japanese. Still, there were North Americans, Europeans, and South Americans of Japanese descent as well, and there were even more East Asians you couldn't physically tell apart from a Japanese person. Yami figured looking into their identities could wait until after she captured them.

Under the illumination, one could see that Yami was indeed pretty. Large, almond-shaped eyes in well-balanced positions, well-shaped scarlet lips, and a perfectly straight, modest nose. A girl like that had suddenly jumped into a cabin full of men late at night. It was no wonder the men were at a loss. But Yami didn't have any obligation to watch them until they figured themselves out.

She stuck out her right hand. That was when the men first noticed that she was wearing a matte black knuckle-duster on it.

The act was intended to confuse the men even more. Knuckle-dusters were weapons for increasing the impact of a user's punch. If she couldn't reach them, it was pointless. Maybe it was some kind of roleplay, thought four of the men.

<"Hey, what's wrong?!">

All of a sudden, one of their number fell on his face, and his fellows finally realized something was happening that warranted a little more than jokes. One of them knelt by him and shook him. He probably didn't realize he'd been speaking English. The other three didn't have room to be conscious of that, either.

Before the kneeling man could confirm that the fallen man had lost consciousness, he felt like a blunt object had just slammed into him. He gave a yelp and fell down. Yami's right hand was pointed at the two victims.

"A magician?!"

At this point, they at last conceived that there might be a connection between their comrades collapsing and Yami's right hand. She pointed it, and one of them fell. There was enough distance between them that her hand couldn't reach, and there were no traces of anything that had flown out of her hand. The only possibility left that they could think of was a magic-based attack.

The man who'd asked the question probably hadn't expected an answer—he'd just yelled out of reflex.

Yami's right hand stuck out toward that man, and he crumpled to the floor along with the previous three.

"Damn monster!"

With a hateful yell, two guns came up at Yami. She could have absorbed a scream of that level with the soundproof field she'd set up ahead of time, but she wasn't confident it could block out the crack of gunshots. No suppressors graced the guns they'd pulled out, either—maybe they really didn't have any intention to conceal themselves.

But Yami didn't have any reason to wait for them to shoot.

She used her thumb to press a button on the end of the knuckle-duster. The main part of the CAD was the stick she held in her hand; the part covering her fist was mere decoration. The CAD, specialized for a single spell, expanded an activation sequence that would manifest her personal magic.

A spell that delivered pain directly to a person's senses. Feeling as though their abdomens had been smashed by a pile driver, the men immediately blacked out.

After taking little time to suppress the inside of the boat, Yami easily disabled the three men on the pier as well. As Yami was using a radio she'd taken from the pouch at her waist to request support personnel, Yoru walked up to her, the frills of her tri-layered skirt fluttering. She'd removed the bandage on her left eye; maybe it had gotten to be an annoyance. With her whole face visible now, the older sister had very girlish features, and while Yami was pretty as well, Yoru was the one whose voice easily matched her gender.

"Yami, did you learn who they are?"

"I got a match using physiognomic recognition right away. The guys on the boat were members of a humanist group active in the USNA. Maybe if we bring them back and investigate them, we can find out who's backing them."

"And the journalist?"

"There was a call record on his terminal with an opposition party member famous for hating magicians. They didn't try very hard, huh?"

"They didn't... It feels anticlimactic."

"Yeah. I don't think you had to come out here with your little brother to begin with," complained Yami, with a fair bit of serious-ness, as Yoru gave a deflated frown.

"Hey, Yami!" she scolded. "*Sister*, remember?"

Of course, Yami hadn't been complaining about the job itself. He groaned. "Come on, Sis."

"No girl would ever call herself someone's brother. You have to do what anyone else would do so you don't draw attention."

The phrase *That's funny, coming from you* was standing by in Yami's throat, but Yoru did have a point. He swallowed the retort back into his stomach.

However, Yami's emotional conflict became meaningless when the black-suited personnel shuffled in toward them.

"We've prepared your transportation, young one."

One of the people, who didn't seem like a stiff no matter how you looked at him, addressed Yami as *young one*.

"You idiot! Not *young one*—young *lady*! Would you ruin all the effort the young one put into hiding his shame and cross-dressing like this?!" said another man, knocking the first over. He seemed to be their leader. "I'm terribly sorry, young one—er, young *lady*."

"You…"

"Yes?"

"You're ruining this even worse!" said the trembling girl, who was actually a cross-dressing boy, in a cleverly hushed but still angry voice. "And I'm not cross-dressing. I'm *in disguise!*"

"Y-yes, and a wonderful disguise it is. I assure you, none of us would even begin to think that you were actually Master Fumiya."

"Stop blurting it out!"

"Yami, calm down."

Yami, also known as Fumiya Kuroba, was having more and more trouble keeping his voice low, so Yoru, also known as Ayako Kuroba, saw fit to scold him. Incidentally, *Yami* was a reversal of the last two syllables of Fumiya's name, and *Yoru* came from the character for "night" that was in the name *Ayako*.

"And the rest of you aren't being cautious enough either. I wonder how our great leader would see fit to scold you if she saw you like this."

The black-suits paled, and Fumiya's head cooled in seconds. Fear of their "great leader" had been instilled in them quite heavily.

"There is no reason to stay long. Let's withdraw."

"Yes ma'am."

The black-suits, their movements showing proof of good leadership, packed up the journalist and the foreigners, picked them up, and began to jog away.

Fumiya, left behind but still in the guise of Yami, bowed his head awkwardly. "Sorry, Sis."

"I suppose you can't help it, considering how you must feel right now."

"…I'm glad to hear you say that," he replied, shoulders drooping.

"It's only for a little longer. Once you start hitting puberty for real, you won't be able to cross-dress anymore. When that happens, we'll just have to go put in the brain work to think of a different disguise."

"Yeah…right…"

Fumiya nodded to try to encourage himself, choosing not to think about the fact that he still showed no signs of losing effectiveness at cross-dressing despite almost being in high school.

Gongjin Zhou, young owner of what was known to the public as a popular Chinese restaurant, had several other faces.

The relatively well-known one was that of a broker of defectors: He sent those stranded in Japan after fleeing GAA oppression to other nations. He didn't just help with defections—he supplied funds for them to engage in anti-GAA activities wherever they ended up.

Almost as if to strike a balance, he also had a spy-like role with the GAA. More specifically, perhaps, he was a local assistant to spies. He'd been the one to guide the GAA Army's saboteur team during the Yokohama Incident the previous October.

He'd also played a neutral role during the vampire incident that had occurred at the beginning of this year by arranging the parasites' illegal entrance into Japan.

His shadowy actions seemed unprincipled at first glance, bringing boons and banes to both opposing powers—Japan and the GAA—but he had a reason for them, of course. His own belief that governments should be weaker obviously influenced him, but above that, he was in the service of a certain person conducting operations to weaken anti-magician state power.

Chinatown, at midnight. In a room in the basement of his shop, one that nobody but him ever entered, Gongjin Zhou now knelt. The person hanging over his head was a life-sized doll sitting in a chair, the doll itself adorned with Chinese clothing excessively embroidered in silver and gold. It was a spell tool: The internal organs had been taken out of a corpse, anti-rotting measures had been applied, and the brain had been repurposed into a sorcery booster. A cable stretched from the case of a giant communication device behind the puppet that was as big as a commercial refrigerator and was connected to the back of the puppet's skull.

"Grand Minister."

At the young man's call, the spell tool corpse-puppet opened its eyelids. Wisps of light flickered on inside its empty eye sockets, the eyeballs having been removed.

"Gongjin. How did things turn out?"

A hair-raising voice emanated from the puppet. Its lungs were unmoving, yet it could produce a voice—because of ancient *jiangshi* magic from the mainland. By applying technology also used in CADs to convert psionic signals into electrical ones, it had made the corpse into a device whose communications couldn't be intercepted.

"The humanists I summoned from America have, unfortunately, all been apprehended, along with the journalist."

"Then our plan to mold them into honest witnesses has failed."

Behind the fear-inducing voice, the words and tone the corpse produced were modern and everyday. It was indirect proof that it was no spirit borrowing the corpse's mouth, but a living person.

"Master Hague," said Zhou, respectfully bowing. The corpse-doll had no eyesight, but the feeling would get across. Zhou's attitude, at least, was nothing slapdash. "Those men had a purely supporting role. Efforts to sabotage big media are proceeding apace."

"How far along are they?"

"Forty percent in visual media, and thirty in print media, I believe."

"Once the operation reaches fifty percent in visual media, set it up immediately. So that any politician who cares about votes will need to act."

"As you command."

As Zhou lowered his head deeply, the puppet almost seemed satisfied.

The wisps of flame in the empty eye sockets went out. When Zhou looked up, the puppet's eyelids were closed.

He rose, then exited the underground room, backing away so as not to turn his back to the puppet. He opened the door behind him, then closed it from the outside. The moment the puppet was out of sight, he breathed a relieved sigh.

Zhou was a user of the ancient Chinese magic of Dujia, but he hadn't dealt much with *jiangshi* techniques. No matter how many times he experienced a conversation with a cadaver, he never felt good afterward.

Still…perhaps it is a suitable vessel for a vengeful spirit of the Dahan, he thought, a disparaging monologue regarding the leader—but one that didn't taint his alluring face in the slightest.

[5]

April 6, 2096, the first day of the new school year. Tatsuya and Miyuki had gone to school, leaving Minami at home. The adverbial phrase *for the first time in a while* wasn't attached to that because they'd been back and forth from school frequently over spring break for preliminary student council meetings.

Today and tomorrow would be the last two days the siblings would be going to school by themselves. Miyuki, as though conscious of that, walked closer to Tatsuya than she usually did on the short road between the station and school. Seen from afar—or rather, unless seen from right up close, they were so near each other one might have thought their arms linked as they walked.

Among the admittedly small student population at Magic High School, the two were now firmly entrenched as celebrities. Almost no students were left who didn't know that they were siblings. More than a few people with common sense frowned at the immoral act of displaying themselves like lovers when they were blood relations, but nobody was stalwart enough (or rather, boorish enough) to speak up and criticize them. Still, there was certainly no lack of appalled eyes directed at them.

Of course, Miyuki wasn't one to let things like that—gazes simply watching from a distance—get to her. Anyone who couldn't say something to her face was, to her, nothing but rabble. In fact, she'd already garnered enough attention that the amount of time she spent *not* being looked at was shorter. For her, there was no point in worrying about every single person's stare. There would be no end to it.

Tatsuya, on the other hand, couldn't afford to ignore other people watching like his sister could. After all, he was Miyuki's bodyguard; he would protect her from any and all harmful intent. It was both the duty he'd been assigned and a right he couldn't surrender. He couldn't overlook any malice directed at his sister.

That wasn't actually very difficult, in the end, since the inconsequential malicious stares were always directed at Tatsuya himself, not at Miyuki.

It was hard for anyone to look at Miyuki in a negative way. For example, one might *harbor* envy toward her, but one would never *direct* it at her. Her appearance and talents were both so dazzling that the very thought of directing envy at her made people feel humbled. Diffident—and then they would hate themselves for their diffidence, and be caught in the swamp. One needed very firm, strong willpower to direct any negativity at Miyuki Shiba.

So it was certainly not a coincidence when Tatsuya noticed it happening.

A gaze on her, not with the vivid hostility that came with rigid determination, but one still not at all well disposed. This stare that was being directed at Miyuki was a rare sort, and it was even less ordinary considering it came from a member of the opposite sex—a boy.

Tatsuya remembered the boy's appearance from somewhere. They'd never met face-to-face, but Tatsuya had looked over his history, which had included a stereoscopic image. He was one year younger, the representative of this year's freshmen.

...I think that's the eldest son of the Shippou.

He almost scowled unconsciously, but he concentrated and stopped his expression from changing. He hadn't wanted to put the boy on his guard with an overreaction, but Takuma, perhaps realizing

Tatsuya had glanced at him, looked away and disappeared into a small street between two stores.

"Brother?" asked Miyuki doubtfully.

A moment later, she keenly picked up on a fragment of her brother's awareness turning away from her. She could ignore stares from the rabble, but not when one of those took Tatsuya's.

Tatsuya shook his head and said, "It's nothing," then, glancing over his shoulder, raised a hand when a certain redhead hailed them with "Good morning!" from behind.

Following Erika, they met up with Leo, Honoka, Shizuku, Mizuki, and Mikihiko. It wasn't unusual for them to be together when leaving school, but it had been some time since they were all together on their way there. Shizuku especially—they hadn't walked to school with her since the end of last year, before she went to study abroad.

This meant the gang was back together at last, but though their members were the same as before, certain ones had a different uniform design from those they'd been wearing until last month—in other words, as freshmen.

On Tatsuya's breast was an emblem of an eight-toothed gear.

The same design was embroidered on Mizuki's blazer.

And on Mikihiko's left breast was First High's school symbol—an eight-petaled flower.

"Mikihiko, how does it feel to be wearing a Course 1 uniform?" asked Tatsuya, smirking in a mean kind of congratulations.

"Quit teasing me, Tatsuya," he answered, giving a pained grin but not appearing altogether uncomfortable. They'd learned Mikihiko would be transferring into Course 1 the previous month, but this was the first time they were seeing each other's new uniforms.

"What about you—how does your brand-new blazer fit?"

"I guess it's new, but it's really just a billboard at this point."

Mikihiko's words had implicitly mentioned the newly established magical engineering curriculum. Tatsuya's words in response had indicated that it was still only a name, and that independent classes had yet to start. Still, independent classes along with everything else would be getting off the mark today. Nevertheless, the school hadn't revealed the teaching staff until today, the day classes began. He couldn't deny feeling like the school hadn't prepared well enough. His line that only a signboard had changed had been a joke, too, but it wasn't without basis.

"Well, that sure is sobering."

But his calm, or rather uncaring, attitude seemed to have belied his friends' expectations. They knew he wasn't the kind of person to jump for joy at the class split, but they'd probably envisioned him being at least a little excited.

"Seriously. When Mizuki over here is smiling away, too."

After Leo, Erika grumbled about it. Her bored sidelong glare was on Tatsuya, but the arrow of her gaze was going through him to pierce the one on the other side.

"I...I am not!" protested Mizuki defensively. She thought she'd been showing consideration toward their friends who were still Course 2 students (meaning Erika and Leo). But her face was, at Erika's mention of her, colored with an expression of happiness she couldn't quite hide.

"You don't need to force it," said Erika with a mean grin—from which, as far as anyone could see, it was doubtless that Mizuki never needed to be so careful with her friends.

The magical engineering classroom was next to the central staircase on the main building's third story. The class's letter was E. In other words, Tatsuya and Mizuki were directly above the classroom they'd been in the previous month.

Meanwhile, Erika and Leo were both in Class F. When they learned that after exchanging info on their homerooms, which they'd been notified of via intraschool wireless, the two of them made a show of looking incredibly unhappy. Was it how they truly felt, or just them trying to hide embarrassment...? Only they knew, and Tatsuya, at least, didn't really care that much. Mizuki and Honoka seemed to find it very interesting, though.

When Tatsuya entered the classroom, half of the seats were filled. They were arranged five by five, same as last year, and the alphabetically ordered seating arrangement was the same as when they'd been freshmen, too. Still, was there a special reason they weren't separated by gender, instead alphabetically ordered by Japanese pronunciation starting at the front of the room and going across, or was it just caprice?

Cutting off his meaningless line of questioning within a single second, Tatsuya headed to his seat. He was at the column nearest the hallway, second seat from the front. Next to him was Mizuki, same as last year. Considering their last names were Shiba and Shibata, this was neither confusing nor a surprise.

"Mizuki, you're sitting next to Tatsuya this year again, huh? Maybe I should have put in to switch classes, too."

That complaint, the tone of which made it sound like it wasn't necessarily a joke, came from Erika, who was leaning on her elbows on the rail of the hallway window, which was wide open.

"Why bother? We're right next door," continued Leo, squirming himself between the window frame and Erika to peek in, a hint of disappointment underneath his words.

"True. Being in separate classes isn't any trouble."

One year ago, the scene would definitely have turned into a stream of inflammatory responses, but Leo wasn't trying to pick a fight, and Erika wasn't trying to buy into it. The change was a little bit funny to Tatsuya, but without showing even a slight hint of it, he agreed with what Leo had said—or at least, what he'd said on the surface.

"Yeah, it's not like we're not allowed to go into other classrooms," Tatsuya noted.

"We're just having class in a different room, that's all," Mizuki cut in.

Mizuki immediately chimed in agreement with Tatsuya, which was presumably because she thought he was trying to keep Erika in check. Still, even though Erika seemed like the free-spirited, adventurous type, she'd almost never escaped the classroom. Tatsuya had gotten out during class time far more times than she had.

"That's true."

Erika probably didn't feel like she was being criticized, so she easily agreed with what Mizuki said.

"Anyway..." said Erika, switching gears and looking around the classroom. "There's a bunch of people here I don't recognize."

Erika, who was *outwardly* a sociable person, knew the names and faces of most of the other hundred Course 2 students in their year. That meant any she didn't recognize must have formerly been in Course 1.

"Yeah, now that you mention it...it's a little unexpected."

The students in the classroom steadily increased as the beginning of classes grew nearer; now two-thirds of the seats were full. Leo was, unlike Erika, *actually* sociable, and as he looked around at the faces again, he agreed with her, his voice filled with surprise.

The two of them—and Mizuki as well, for whom Erika's words didn't quite make sense—had predicted most of those wishing to transfer after the magical engineering program's establishment would be kids from Course 2. They hadn't thought any prideful Course 1 students would decide to sit at desks right next to Course 2 ones.

For Tatsuya, the Course 1 students transferring wasn't surprising or anything, but he could perfectly understand why Erika and the others would think that, so he didn't put in any comment.

"By the way," said Erika, switching topics, "she's really got an eye out for you, Tatsuya."

Tatsuya gave a light shrug of his shoulders, an affirmation. He hadn't needed her to point it out—he'd already noticed the hateful eyes on him, staring him down.

He knew whom they belonged to, as well. If he hadn't known why she was looking at him like that, it might have bothered him, but he knew both that he was disliked and the reason for it. Tatsuya generally tended to let sleeping dogs lie, as long as all they were doing was looking, but it seemed to be something Erika couldn't do. Her unhappy voice spoke up:

"After putting all those people through all that trouble, she still doesn't understand that she's just venting for no reason?"

"She might know, but I'm sure it's not easy for her to let go of."

"Not easy... It's been almost half a year."

"Just half a year," answered Tatsuya, looking behind him at an angle and glancing at the source of the stare.

Chiaki Hirakawa, glaring spitefully at him, hastily looked away. A moment later, as though angered by her own display of weakness, she turned back, an even more dangerous stare trained on Tatsuya.

Her attitude rubbed Erika the wrong way even worse than before. In contrast to Sayaka, who'd been tricked into cooperating with a terrorist group but had shown pure-hearted repentance after the incident, Chiaki had willingly become a pawn for people she knew were foreign spies in order to have her misguided revenge, and even now didn't even try to apologize to Tatsuya for it.

Erika didn't have any patience for that. She wouldn't poke her own nose into it because she wasn't very bullheaded, but she truly felt that if it came to a fight, she'd accept a challenge in Tatsuya's place—or even start one herself. And right now, Erika felt Chiaki's brassiness was, in fact, picking a fight.

A severe light came into Erika's eyes. Rather than narrowing them, she pulled them open even wider. Erika's looks were already somewhat feline, but now she took on a more ferocious beauty akin to a tiger's or a panther's. Tatsuya was personally interested in appreciating the look for a few more moments, but if this situation continued, he was sure to get dragged into the middle of more trouble. The viewing fee seemed a little too high to him.

"Erika, you don't need to meddle."

She gave him a wholly unsatisfied look. A look with enough punch that, had he been a man of weaker constitution, he might have flown down to his hands and knees to apologize. But unfortunately, Tatsuya was not so commendable (?).

"The embers are falling on me, and I'll swat them away. But only if she has the grit to light the flame."

Tatsuya gave a cold-blooded grin. After she realized from his expression that he had no intent whatsoever to get familiar with the girl, Erika's own expression softened—into a slight smile to hide embarrassment, possibly indicating she regretted overstepping herself.

Then, with perfect timing, another voice interrupted them and altered the mood.

"Hey, do you have a minute?"

The voice came from directly behind Tatsuya, so he turned around in his seat. A male student who had just entered the classroom sat there, looking at him with an amicable smile on his face.

"This is the first time we've been able to actually introduce ourselves, isn't it? I'm Hagane Tomitsuka. Nice to meet you, Shiba."

"You're right—I know your name, but for all intents and purposes we've just met, I suppose. I'm Tatsuya Shiba. Nice to meet you, Tomitsuka."

Tatsuya answered in his usual tone of voice as he returned the handshake. To tell the truth, he felt like shaking hands with a classmate after self-introductions was an overblown act, but he didn't let a wink of that show. Nor did he give any indication of his surprise that Hagane Tomitsuka was here in the first place.

But Tatsuya's friends couldn't keep a poker face like he could. Mizuki, for example, had been staring hard at Tomitsuka, who had plunked himself into the seat directly behind Tatsuya. She appeared to snap back to her senses suddenly, and her face reddened. She was probably embarrassed that she'd been so rude. With a bashful smile, she spoke up.

"It's nice to meet you, Tomitsuka. I'm Mizuki Shibata."

"Yes, it's nice to meet you, too."

Tomitsuka gave an affable smile, dissolving the tension from Mizuki's face. The exchange was pretty normal, in a way, from a high schooler's standpoint, and after seeing it, the other two seemed to break out of their petrifaction.

"I'm surprised... Tomitsuka's fifth in our grade, but he chose the engineering program."

Still, Erika's voice—directed to no one and everyone—was filled with surprise.

Tatsuya couldn't blame her. Like she said, Hagane Tomitsuka was a top-ranking student in their grade, one who had scored fifth highest across all subjects during final exams. (The order for final exam grades was Miyuki in first, Honoka in second, a male student named Yousuke Igarashi in third, and Eimi Akechi in fourth. Shizuku had been studying abroad at the time.) His grades were more than good enough for a Course 1 student, so one wouldn't have thought he'd need to transfer into the magical engineering program—had one been an objective observer.

"Chiba, right? You probably know this since you're one of the Hundred, too, but my family's forte is this, not combat or rescue, and I...have some issues with my practical skills."

Though the remark hadn't been directed at him, Tomitsuka still turned to Erika with a slightly wry grin and responded. And then Erika (and Leo, too) remembered the rumors surrounding Tomitsuka's nickname.

Range Zero. The nickname was both a term of respect for his unrivaled strength at point-blank range and a reference to his inability to use long-range magic. It wasn't actually that he couldn't use it at all, but the undeniable truth was that he wasn't very good at aiming long-range spells, and Tomitsuka was undeniably aware of the flaw.

Erika let her eyes wander, unable to find the words to reply with. Tatsuya threw her a life raft. "Well, everyone has strengths and weaknesses."

It wasn't completely clear whether his "life raft" was supposed to be comforting or dismissive, but Leo interjected quietly and seriously with "Can't argue with someone like Tatsuya saying that."

Tomitsuka's wry grin shifted into something more bitter.

"Tomitsuka! Found you!"

A moment later, a voice, cheerful enough to blast away all their intricately intertwined emotions, burst into the classroom of Class 2-E.

"Akechi?!"

Tomitsuka turned around in a fluster as Eimi Akechi, also known as Amy, came stampeding toward him from the entrance in the back of the room. She was a personal acquaintance of Tatsuya's as well, since she'd been a competitor in last summer's Nines. She stopped next to Tomitsuka's desk almost with an audible skid, and one hand shot up while a full smile came over her face. Tatsuya had no idea whose style she was emulating by putting on this display.

"Morning, Tomitsuka!"

Her greeting was energetic, the sort a heart or even a music note might have followed. Unlike Erika, who had an equally bright personality but convoluted ideas lurking beneath the surface, Eimi had a personality that was cheerful all the way down. A valuable type of person—when you watched her, she'd make you feel stupid for fretting constantly over this or that. Now was no exception—her arrival had blown away the awkwardness about to settle in the air.

"Ah, yeah. Good morning, Akechi."

Tomitsuka drew back at her fervor, perhaps out of courtesy. Actually, judging by his expression, it didn't feel like Eimi was drawn to Tomitsuka so much as she was *overpowering* him.

"Morning to you, too, Shiba."

"Morning, Amy. That's right—you were in Tomitsuka's class last year, weren't you?"

"Yep! You sure do know a lot," said Eimi, her eyes widening.

"Well, I know some things," said Tatsuya, giving her a somewhat exhausted grin. "Amy, this is Mizuki Shibata. Over here is Erika Chiba, and also Leonhard Saijou. All three of them were my classmates last year."

He figured Mizuki and the others wouldn't have had any contact in the past, and this estimation of his wasn't wrong.

After he gave a simple (sloppy?) introduction, Eimi immediately replied with one of her own. "Nice to meetcha. I'm Eimi Akechi, but you can call me Amy."

"Okay—Amy, right?" Erika was the first to respond, perhaps expectedly. "You can just call me Erika."

"Feel free to call me Leo."

"It's nice to meet you, Akechi."

After Leo's self-introduction (or self-introductory supplement), Mizuki bowed to her.

For some reason, when she did, Eimi puffed out a cheek unhappily. "Amy."

"Huh?"

"I just said to call me Amy, didn't I?"

Mizuki blinked in confusion, unable to comprehend why Eimi was mad at her. From an objective standpoint, Eimi's insistence bordered on unfair, but cases where energy won out over logic could be observed quite frequently in this world. Erika and Leo aside—they were mildly appalled, since they didn't know what kind of girl she was—even Tatsuya, who had a degree of familiarity with her, didn't show any signs that he would intervene for whatever reason. Tomitsuka, the other person who would have known what Eimi was like, looked like he was too busy being flustered to put a word in anytime soon.

"Umm… It's nice to meet you, Amy. And you may call me Mizuki as well."

Mizuki, though bewildered, was the first to break in the end.

"Yep! Nice to meet you, Mizuki."

When she did, Eimi immediately gave an innocent smile. It wasn't a normal "sweet" smile so much as it was a naive and unsophisticated one, and it packed enough punch to single-handedly dissolve the slight discomfort Mizuki had felt at her selfish objection.

Eimi nodded, satisfied, then whirled back around to face Tomitsuka. "Then next it's your turn, Tomitsuka."

"I'm sorry?" It was all so sudden that Tomitsuka basically didn't understand why she was suddenly talking to him or what it was his turn to do.

"Amy." Eimi said her own nickname once again.

He still didn't know what she was asking of him. He looked left and right at a loss, then noticed Tatsuya making a face like he was trying not to laugh.

He used his eyes to beg for help. Tatsuya crafted an unnaturally serious expression, then answered his distress call:

"She doesn't like you calling her *Akechi*, does she?"

Tatsuya's deduction seemed to have hit the mark. Eimi nodded in agreement.

"I think she wants you to call her by her nickname, too."

Eimi's being visibly frustrated at Mizuki had been a hint. Still, Tatsuya had seen this development coming, which was why he hadn't said anything.

Meanwhile, Tomitsuka's face was so drawn back, it looked like he would start sweating at any moment. "I, uh, well, you call me *Tomitsuka*, too, so..."

"I do? Do you want me to call you Hagane?" She bowed slightly and put her hands together in a gesture of apology, her eyes saying, *Come on, you should have said something sooner,* as she peered into Tomitsuka's face. Meanwhile, his panic was clear to everyone present. As his face stiffened even further and he leaned back, Tatsuya and the others watched him with warm gazes.

"Uh, no, that's not exactly what I meant by—ack!"

The direly distressed Tomitsuka, trying desperately not to meet Eimi's gaze as she watched him in apparent amusement, spotted the eyes on him from two seats over, stood up, and spoke in a tone of contrived politeness.

"Akechi, we can leave this conversation for another time."

Deftly evading Eimi, who was taking up half his vision by leaning forward at him, Tomitsuka walked over to the seat of the female student who was watching him.

"Hirakawa, right? I didn't know you were in this class, too."

His voice could just barely be made out from where Tatsuya and the others were sitting. Chiaki's words, though, were muttered and reserved, completely inaudible.

"Amy, shouldn't you go after him?" asked Erika, keeping her tone low as Eimi made an unhappy face at being left behind so suddenly. "I really don't think you should back down now..."

Were those the whisperings of a devil luring a heart to corruption, or of a divine envoy directing her to a path of hardship? —It was nothing so theatrical, of course, just some words from an imp spurring on a classmate, but it took effect instantly. Eimi nodded, her expression pumped up, then rapidly walked toward Tomitsuka.

"...You're a scary woman, you know that?" muttered Leo, his tone serious.

"Isn't this more constructive, though?" answered Erika with a grin.

"You're not wrong," noted Tatsuya. "Things could get pretty interesting."

Mizuki looked at Tatsuya—who, as his words had implied, was watching Tomitsuka, Eimi, and Chiaki with a gaze that didn't hide any of his interest—in mild astonishment mixed with a bit of exasperation.

The bell rang, putting aside for the moment the coming-of-age drama wherein Tomitsuka was the main character (or possibly the prey). Eimi skipped happily out of 2-E, and Erika and Leo headed for the 2-F classroom as well.

There wouldn't be any student body–wide opening ceremonies for the first day. The school's stance was that students should take it upon themselves to make sure they saw any messages the school gave. For this class, the program was for their practical skills instructor to show up now (same as in classes A through D). Enough students to form a majority here in Class 2-E felt that the school was being full of itself by not announcing the teacher's name until the day of, but Tatsuya belonged to the minority who didn't think that way.

They'd probably only decided on someone with very little time to spare—and his deduction was completely on the mark. Magicians with teaching talents were in such short supply that First, Second, and Third High, which all had a lot of staff to begin with, still had to cut off half their students from them.

The labor shortage was always in his mind, so he predicted that Class 2-E's practical skills instructor might be an eccentric, maybe someone generally thought of as on the edge of teaching fitness. Very old, for example, or conversely extremely young. They were only going to teach engineering-related skills, so the position didn't demand that much capacity as a magician, but Tatsuya's predictions also included the possibility that they'd be dispatched a scientist without any teaching certifications.

But thirty seconds after starting time, the instructor who stood in front of all the Class 2-E students was beyond anything Tatsuya had expected. The other students seemed surprised, too; a hushed murmur rippled through the classroom.

She was a woman he estimated to be in her forties.

That, of course, wasn't enough to strike them as unexpected. Just because there was a clear majority of male teachers at magic high schools didn't mean women were a rarity. The surprise was at her appearance.

Her hair color was silver, her eye color blue, her skin color white. She was tall, and her waist was high off the ground. Judging by her other physical characteristics as well, it was clear that the woman was a Caucasian born in a northern region.

"I'm Jennifer Smith."

Her name was very Anglophonic as well—actually, her last name was *the* last name of the English-speaking sphere.

"I was born in Boston, in the USNA, but I naturalized here eighteen years ago."

Those words dispelled most of the students' doubts. If so much time had passed since she'd naturalized, there wouldn't be any concerns on the confidentiality front. Normally, a stronger sense of love for one's country was demanded of naturalized citizens than of those born here. Unless you were more faithful to the country you naturalized in than to the one before, they'd never permit you to naturalize. That was what it meant to be an expatriate. This was particularly thoroughly enforced when it came to magic researchers with many opportunities to be involved with state secrets. It still begged the question of why she had rescinded her USNA citizenship and naturalized in Japan when the USNA was, in the modern world, the wealthiest and stood at the cutting edge of magical technology, but that was a relatively uninteresting topic for Tatsuya.

"Until last year, I was a lecturer at the Magic University, but this year I'm here to instruct magical engineering classes as well as this class. I look forward to teaching you all."

Her position is the same as Mr. Tsuzura's, thought Tatsuya. Tsuzura in particular had a background—he too was free-spirited, and that had been his downfall. He wondered if Ms. Smith had a similar background…although he also admitted that assuming she was another problem child was terribly rude.

First period was allotted for course registration, they'd very abruptly started their usual curriculum in second period, and now it was lunch break.

Tatsuya had come to the student council room.

Starting today, he was the vice president. A "secret agreement" between Azusa and Kanon had made him switch from the disciplinary committee to the student council, the execution of which was performed regardless of Tatsuya's own wants. He didn't resist, since he didn't have any attachment to the disciplinary committee, but he didn't dislike the idea of being in the student council overall. However, even if he had taken a stance of refusal, a certain someone would probably have convinced him to do it anyway—not Azusa, but Miyuki. Perhaps he hadn't resisted in the first place because he knew all that going into it.

Whatever the background, this was how 2096 First High's new system had safely set sail. There were new members in the disciplinary committee, too. Mikihiko was one, chosen as Tatsuya's successor by the student council in their one allotted recommendation slot. Shizuku had been chosen as the club committee's allotted replacement recommendation; that committee had lost their other replacement at the end of the previous year. In the student council room today, the first day of the new year, were Azusa, Isori, Tatsuya, Miyuki, Honoka, Shizuku, and Mikihiko. They were having a good celebratory luncheon together for the new committee members.

Even the student council room's meeting table was somewhat cramped with eight people. To alleviate that—or maybe just using that as an excuse—Kanon was clinging right to Isori. Everyone watched the passionate—though a little awkward on Isori's part—behavior differently, with Azusa and Mikihiko embarrassed, Tatsuya and Shizuku maintaining poker faces, Honoka looking rather envious, and Miyuki with a warm smile as they all continued to enjoy their peaceful lunchtime. Incidentally, Honoka would have liked to reuse Kanon's reasoning that the table was cramped to cling to Tatsuya herself, but when even Miyuki held herself back—or rather, in her seat—she couldn't make any moves either.

Coffee cups and teacups were passed out according to specific tastes. Serving them was 3H type P-94, Pixie. The female-modeled housekeeping robot had originally been on loan from the robotics research club, but due to several circumstances—*first and foremost Pixie's own wishes*—starting today, she would now be put to use by Tatsuya in the student council room.

At first their lunchtime conversation was about the unusual instructor for the newly established magical engineering program. But as their break reached its halfway point, everyone's interest shifted to the entrance ceremony just around the corner.

"Is there rehearsal after school again today?" asked Mikihiko politely, knowing their upperclassmen were present, despite the fact that he wasn't involved with the ceremony's preparations.

"It is more of a preliminary meeting than a rehearsal," answered Miyuki in the default polite tone she used with male students. "There are only two rehearsals for the address—one during spring break and one right before the ceremony. Even then, they'll only be practicing the program. They won't actually be reading any scripts."

"Was it the same last year?" asked Shizuku.

"Yes," answered Miyuki. She had been the one to read the address a year before.

"Wait, really? It definitely didn't seem like it," said Kanon, with surprising energy. The reason, though, came from her own mouth right after: "It was pretty awf—er, difficult when it was us, so I thought they decided to have more rehearsals next time."

"Well, it *was* awful…"

Kanon had corrected herself just before her slip of the tongue, but it seemed she had been too late. Azusa, who had been the new student representative the year before the last, cowered, her face incredibly disappointed.

"Y-you were just nervous, Nakajou," said Isori hastily, trying to fix his fiancée's mistake. "It wasn't anything strange."

Meanwhile, Tatsuya set up a defensive perimeter before Miyuki could get strangely awkward at Isori's follow-up, saying, "Of course, that doesn't mean Miyuki was strange for not getting stage fright, either."

"Oh, you joke, Brother. I can assure you, I was quite nervous."

With incredibly natural timing, Miyuki placed her hand overtop Tatsuya's, where it sat on his thigh. She brought her upper body closer, peering into his face. He grinned drily at the slightly miffed look she was giving him, gently patting her hair and gently pushing her head back to its original position. Miyuki made a soft "ah" sound and directed a bashful smile toward him. Shizuku elbowed Honoka—whose face was frozen in an expression of surprise—in the side as Kanon gave a weary look, putting herself aside (while still snuggled up next to Isori).

Mikihiko cleared his throat purposefully, returning the chaotic mood to normal. His face had the traces of considerable effort on it. Tatsuya spoke to him, acting as though nothing had happened. "Miyuki and I actually haven't ever met this year's freshman representative," he remarked.

"The school leads all the preparations for the incoming students, after all," said Isori, shifting into explanation mode; he knew more about it than Tatsuya did. "They respect student autonomy, but official events with a lot of guests are probably a different story. The student council does most things related to students who are already enrolled, though."

"Because...the incoming freshmen still aren't students at this school?"

"Nah, Mikihiko, I think you're reading too much into it."

Mikihiko probably hadn't meant much—he was just trying to keep the conversation going—but Tatsuya came back with an unreserved retort. Isori looked somehow envious of how easily they got along with each other, but maybe it was an illusion.

"I don't know the real reason. It's only what we figure is happening," said Isori, smiling it away. He didn't give a single hint as to his feelings on the matter before changing the topic. "Nakajou, you've met him, right?"

Kanon immediately perked up. "She's met Shippou?"

With eyes brimming with curiosity bearing down upon her, Azusa looked down in thought. "Yes, well… He seemed very...*motivated*."

She clearly didn't want to offer a negative evaluation of her new classmate.

"Ambitious, you mean," said Kanon, rephrasing it bluntly. Considering Azusa's vaguely pained smile in response, it seemed she had the same opinion.

The living room after dinner. Leaving the dishes to Minami per their work-distribution agreement, Miyuki brought coffee to Tatsuya. She put her own cup on the side table, then sat down next to him.

"Considering he's the Shippou's eldest son, I can understand why he's ambitious," began Tatsuya as if to soothe her.

"Brother, why are you suddenly thinking about Shippou?"

She placed both hands together on her lap, her pose a polite and ladylike one as she tilted her head in confusion. Her formal expression, of course, wasn't enough to deceive Tatsuya.

"But that doesn't mean we have to make concessions for him. If you don't fight with him, you don't need to be any more friendly with him."

"I would never fight with someone," said Miyuki, grumpily turning her cheek. She only assumed such an attitude openly because they were both aware of what had happened; Miyuki and the Shippou's eldest son's first meeting hadn't been a friendly one by any stretch of the imagination.

Miyuki hadn't tried to pick a fight with him, of course. At first she had tried to welcome him warmly as an underclassman and the incoming student representative. But...

"Allow me to introduce Takuma Shippou. He'll be the new student representative this year."

The student council room after school. Its members had already assembled—Isori, Miyuki, Honoka, and Tatsuya—and after an introduction by Azusa, Takuma Shippou gave a bow. The attitude was passably ordinary for a new student, but...

"I'm Tatsuya Shiba, vice president. Nice to meet you, Shippou."

...that impression changed when Tatsuya introduced himself after Isori.

"I'm Takuma *Shippou*. It's a pleasure to meet you."

His last name came out unnaturally stressed, but his choice of words was still tolerable. His attitude, though, couldn't be called very polite. Takuma wasn't looking at Tatsuya's face—he was looking at his left breast pocket.

"...Shippou?" asked Azusa quietly.

Takuma appeared to come to his senses. He gave an uncomfortable and insincere grin. "I'm sorry. I just didn't recognize the gear emblem Shiba happens to be wearing."

After hearing his excuse, Azusa said, "Oh, I get it," and nodded. "That's the emblem for the magical engineering program that was just established this year."

"I see," said Takuma casually, seeming disinterested—either truly or by design.

Tatsuya didn't consider it unpleasant. The Shippou family's trump card, Million Edge, was exceptional among modern magic in that it didn't use a CAD. Tatsuya had heard rumors among engineers that, possibly because of that, the family tended to malign magical engineering technology.

But he didn't mind it so much—everyone had their own way of thinking. Something might be valuable to you, but you couldn't force others to share that sense of value.

However, it was something Miyuki couldn't personally overlook. In her eyes, it was a pompous attitude, absolute insolence. He believed without basis that he was of higher position, and therefore looked down on others without reason. He wore the same colors as his Course 1 classmates who had disparaged her brother for being a Weed. That was how Miyuki took it.

Takuma turned to face the next person, meaning to continue his greetings. He didn't intend to cause a stir in a place like this, and besides, he didn't feel he'd done anything rude to begin with. Without any particular preparation, he looked toward the next student council member, Miyuki.

A moment later he winced, doubtless a humiliating act for him. But none could blame him, for upon that face...

...the queen of snow and ice had descended.

Her presence was not so simple that she could be called "Blizzard Princess" or anything of the sort. The prim, aloof facial expression was a common one for her, but it had driven a former student council member to ready himself for a death match. It was still a far cry from that time, which had been during the student council elections last year, but she still gave off such pressure that Takuma's losing his cool upon seeing it for the first time was nothing for him to be ashamed of.

But Takuma himself didn't think that way. Frustration rose to his face, unable to be kept down. He quickly constructed a courteous smile in its place, but it didn't go so well from an objective standpoint.

"I am Miyuki Shiba, also vice president."

Those were the only words she gave in self-introduction, fitting for her cold look.

"...I'm Takuma Shippou. It's nice to meet you."

His voice trembled slightly, not from fear but from anger. He was mad at himself for letting Miyuki overpower him. He still had the restraint not to transfer his anger to someone else, but he'd always been a boy subject to violent changes of mood. He gritted his teeth to hold himself back. Gritted them so strongly that no expression he could put on his face could hide it.

Miyuki and Takuma's attitudes couldn't be called absolutely peaceful. Steadily the level of unrest in the air increased, and Azusa began to fidget. If this were the previous year's student council, someone like Suzune would have patched things up, but Isori, who was in her position this year, looked like he didn't know what to do. Miyuki's response had been childish for someone who was Takuma's senior, but he was hard-pressed to call Takuma's behavior suitably polite for someone who was a new student. The sense of imbalance bound him.

Out of all the members here right now, the only one who stood a chance to pacify Miyuki and thus resolve the situation was Tatsuya—but all he did was observe Takuma's expression without speaking.

...After that, thanks to Honoka doing her best to introduce herself as cheerfully as possible, the prickly mood dulled somewhat. The strained air, however, remained in the student council room for the duration of

the meeting. This wasn't any sort of proper rehearsal; they were just reviewing and confirming the previously determined program, so they finished in a short time.

If the mood had continued for much longer, though, it might have given concern for the success of the entrance ceremony itself—and considering the tradition whereby the new student representative was invited to the student council, things were already at the level where people worried about negative effects on the government body this year.

"Well, I didn't think it would suddenly turn into a stare-down. The eldest son of the Shippou seems to like fighting."

Miyuki didn't believe the attitude she'd adopted had been wrong. But however *legitimate* the reason—that she'd *felt* scornful eyes had been looking at her beloved brother—the fact was that she'd made the mood worse in an official setting. She'd been prepared for a *few* harsh words coming her way, but her brother seemed to be dodging the issue and not criticizing her. Her tone as she replied to him was a hesitant one.

"I do not believe his attitude toward you was simply of the insolent sort, Brother. It felt as though it had a much clearer vector, that there was underlying hostile intent."

Now that she thought back on it calmly, Takuma's attitude had seemed a little different from her classmates' right after she'd started school the previous year. It wasn't that Takuma was scorning Tatsuya as unimportant and beneath him, but that Takuma had to make himself *believe* he was, in order to be at a mental advantage against an enemy...

Miyuki suddenly changed her mind: *That* was the sort of lack of composure she'd glimpsed from him.

"Yeah. He was being cautious of us."

Tatsuya knew that Takuma had actually been directing his hostility more toward Miyuki than toward him. The person staring at them while they were coming to school this morning—Takuma Shippou—had been glaring at his sister, not him. Tatsuya felt like the hostility toward him was just an add-on to that.

On the other hand, Miyuki didn't consider for a split second that she was the main target and her brother was just a supplement. She noticed Tatsuya said "of us," but she believed that her brother was the main target, and she only an accessory.

"I do not know why, but I believe we should give it serious thought. We don't know when something like last year will happen again."

Miyuki was referring to the incident caused by an international terrorist organization named Blanche that had happened right after they'd enrolled the previous year. It had become an emergency wherein terrorists had invaded First High, and the siblings had only become deeply involved with it after Sayaka asked Tatsuya for help. At first, he'd assumed she was trying to recruit new members for a school club or something.

He had to wonder if, had he thought about it more seriously at the time, the later developments would have been different. In the end, it hadn't been a big deal (at least not for the siblings). But Tatsuya responding to Takuma's challenging behavior with an attitude of *Just don't get in a fight with him* overlapped with what had happened with Sayaka, so she couldn't resist warning him about that.

"Last year? Oh yeah. I don't think it'll come to that. He *is* still one of the Twenty-Eight."

"The Twenty-Eight" referred to the Ten Master Clans and the Eighteen Support Clans together, and was not an expression that saw much use. However, within the Ten Master Clans and the Eighteen Support Clans—which added up to twenty-eight families—it was used as a term to refer to all of them as having come from one place: magician development laboratories.

"Now I don't exactly know what Takuma Shippou is like, but," said Tatsuya almost to himself, still holding his coffee cup, "because of how opposed they are to the Saegusa, people say the Shippou have a particularly strong attachment even among the Eighteen to the idea of being one of the Ten Master Clans."

Miyuki knew about the feud between the Saegusa and the Shippou, but the rest, about having a position in the Ten Master Clans, must have been new to her. A curious expression came to her face.

"Boys our age already want other people to acknowledge how strong we are. We strive for the recognition."

"Oh, even you, Brother?" his sister teased.

"Well, yeah. I want that as much as the next guy," answered Tatsuya, giving a dry grin. "That sort of desire seems exceptionally strong in Shippou. He probably wants to show that he has the strength to be in the Ten Master Clans. I think that's why he gets aggressive with people who seem like they're going to get in his way."

"But we haven't gotten in Shippou's way."

"For someone who wants everyone to recognize them for how great they are, anyone who's already lauded is an obstacle," he explained, the pained grin still on his face.

Miyuki nodded deeply. "I see. In other words, Shippou is envious of your fame."

She seemed to have herself completely convinced. Tatsuya almost spat out his coffee. "No, I don't think it's *me* he's envious of—or rather, sees as a rival. It's probably you, Miyuki."

"What, me?"

Her eyes insisted that nobody could ever leave her brother aside for her.

Tatsuya shook his head several times. "He's this year's freshman rep, and you were last year's. That by itself is enough reason for him to view you as a rival. Add that to how well you did in the Nines, and I'm pretty sure he only sees me as an enemy accessory to you."

"But that's...! You are not an accessory of mine, or anything of the sort!"

"Look, you don't need to get so worked up... I'm trying to put myself in his shoes. This is all just a theory."

"I refuse to accept such an appalling theory."

"That doesn't exactly mean it's going away..."

With a switch suddenly flipped within Miyuki, Tatsuya kind of had his hands full.

"I'm the one who is your—no, even *if* I give a big concession, you're my dear partner."

The part she was a little embarrassed to say sounded like "I belong to you," but Tatsuya made the decision not to worry about it. Even the way she rephrased it seemed pretty bold and embarrassing to him, but he let that slide off as well.

"The other possibility I can think of is that he's hostile because he knows we're related to the Ten Master Clans."

This remark, spoken offhandedly, was weighty enough to drag the floating, excited Miyuki back down to earth.

"That we're related to the Yotsuba? I think that's overthinking it, don't you?"

"Maybe. I doubt he or his family has the power to break through the Yotsuba's information control…but something tells me the prejudice in his eyes was strong enough for it."

Tatsuya wasn't recalling the eyes he'd used to glare at Miyuki in the student council room, but rather the ones on her on their way to school. That was a Takuma Shippou she didn't know, which was why his thoughts didn't quite make sense to her right now.

Still, she took her brother's concerns to heart. "I see… He is one of the Twenty-Eight. We should probably take caution."

…He was right in that Takuma's animosity was related to the Ten Master Clans, but completely incorrect about their being related to the Yotsuba. Takuma suspected a connection to the Saegusa, but neither Tatsuya nor Miyuki came to that conclusion. They were friends with Mayumi, but they never forgot about the awkward relationship between the Yotsuba and the Saegusa, so they never considered that others might see them as part of the Saegusa's team.

[6]

Time: April 8, morning. Place: National Magic University's First Affiliated High School. Event: entrance ceremony.

Tatsuya, Miyuki, and Minami arrived at First High two hours before the ceremony, this time without being ambushed by any ill-mannered staring. The reason they came so early went without saying—to prepare for the ceremony. The three of them went straight to the lecture prep room, where their final meeting would be held. Minami was worried about being an outsider, but Tatsuya, experienced in coming to school with his sister and having time on his hands, forced her to come anyway.

Isori and Honoka were already in the prep room.

"Good morning, Tatsuya!" Honoka chimed. "And you, too, Miyuki!"

"Good morning, Shiba," added Isori. "You're right on time."

While Miyuki exchanged morning salutations with Honoka, Isori chatted with Tatsuya.

"Good morning. You're early, Isori," the latter greeted him.

"Well, it's who I am. I can't calm down unless I arrive early," answered Isori with a smile. He looked over at Minami, who was waiting behind Miyuki. "By the way, who is she? A new student, right?"

"That's right. Minami?"

"Yes, Big Brother Tatsuya?"

At Tatsuya's call, Minami trotted over. Isori made a somewhat surprised face at the response. "Big Brother? Shiba, I didn't know you had another sister."

In a way, his question was exactly what Tatsuya had expected. "No, she's our cousin," he replied, giving the lie they'd prepared in advance. "Minami, this is Isori."

"It's nice to meet you, Isori. I'm Minami Sakurai." Minami kept in mind Tatsuya's instructions not to be overly polite.

Isori didn't seem to think anything was off, either. "Nice to meet you, Sakurai."

"The pleasure is all mine."

It was as Minami was giving another bow to Isori that Azusa, Kanon, and the new student representative, Takuma Shippou, entered. (Kanon, incidentally, had just gone through a seating check.)

"Good morning... Am I the last one here?" asked Azusa, her face looking a little shaky.

"Good morning, President. You're right on time," replied Miyuki with a smile. She was actually about three minutes late, but Miyuki's smile had enough sternness to imply she wouldn't accept either apologies *or* excuses.

As Azusa swallowed down her planned apology, Takuma stepped out from behind her and spoke. "Good morning, Isori, Shiba."

"Good morning, Shippou," said Isori in return, bowing.

Takuma turned to face Miyuki and Honoka. "Shiba, Mitsui, good morning. I look forward to working with you today."

Was he nervous? Tatsuya wondered. His attitude was actually commendable today, unlike two days ago.

"Good morning, Shippou. Please do your best today."

It would take more kindness than that, however, to move Miyuki. Her smile was lovely, and her tone gentle. Her face was the perfect picture of a gentlewoman's—but that was an impenetrable mask for social occasions. Takuma had only changed his attitude; he hadn't apologized for his rudeness the other day. As long as he didn't apologize *to her brother*, she had no intent to compromise.

Her smile was aloof, but nobody could complain about it, and so Azusa and Isori both floated expressions of distress. They couldn't chide Miyuki, because there was nothing to chide. But that didn't mean they could ignore the awkward mood beginning to drift about. Azusa, not knowing what to do, looked to Tatsuya for help.

"It looks like we're all here, so let's start by going over the program." Tatsuya's response to her was to push the conversation forward like nothing had happened.

Kanon immediately laid down covering fire. "Yeah, no point wasting time." She probably also figured they needed to divert the conversation's momentum.

"Let's start with our positions thirty minutes before opening. Miyuki will be guiding visitors in, and Honoka will be in the broadcasting room..."

This was technically Azusa's job, but Tatsuya ignored that and began their prerehearsal meeting. The unnatural fact that Minami was here was eventually forgotten without anyone pointing it out.

Their preceremony rehearsal ended without issue, the air palpably tense and strained as the real thing drew closer. Azusa, for example, breathed a sigh of relief as it ended, seeming to relax completely—or rather, collapse—even though the ceremony was in thirty minutes. It seemed to Tatsuya that she was being a little *too* loose about it, but it wasn't his job to point that out. Besides, he revised his thinking, it was better than her getting too high-strung and ending up useless during the ceremony. He decided to get on with his own job.

"I'll go guide in the new students."

"I will see you soon, Brother."

"Oh yes—thank you."

After being seen off by Miyuki and Azusa at the side of the stage, as well as by Minami, who bowed without a word, Tatsuya left the lecture hall.

His preceremony role was to guide new students who didn't know where to go. He'd run into Mayumi before the entrance ceremony the previous year because she'd had the same job. When he'd heard of that at the end of March, during their debates about this year's job assignments, Tatsuya had felt like it wasn't something the student council president should have to do before an important event like an entrance ceremony. Now, though, he'd changed his mind. Maybe it had been an excuse for her to distract herself from her nerves.

He hadn't personally been that anxious. He did, however, still feel something of a sense of release. This was probably just who he was—he felt more comfortable outside where he could feel the wind than indoors setting up for a stiff, formal ceremony. Perhaps Mayumi was similar in that respect.

And perhaps that was exactly why he ran almost headlong into Mayumi as soon as he exited into the front school grounds.

"Oh, Tatsuya?"

"Saegusa? Good morning."

"I would say it's been a while…but it really hasn't. Are you showing the new students where to go?

"Yes, more or less."

"So you joined the student council after all."

There were non-council members doing the guidance work as well. The disciplinary committee was keeping an eye on the venue, too, partly for security's sake, and they even had provisional members patrolling. Mayumi shouldn't have been able to conclude from his answer alone that he was in the student council, but he made no objection as she giggled in amusement. After all, he had, in fact, joined the student council, and something else was bothering him more.

It didn't need to be stated at this point, but Mayumi had graduated First High the previous month. She wasn't wearing a school uniform, which of course made sense. A single outfit swap, however, shouldn't have been able to make her look *this* much like an adult.

This wasn't the first time he'd seen her in something other than a uniform. The summer dress she'd shown them on the way to and from the Nines the previous summer had been quite captivating. But at the time, despite her exposed skin, she hadn't seemed like a different person.

But now, garbed in a women's suit, she came off as so mature she seemed like a completely different person from last month. She wore a short jacket over a blouse with frills decorating the chest, along with a tight skirt that ended below the knees, none of which even gave a much different impression from First High's girls' uniform. Was it her cardinal-red high heels? Her makeup, which was light but still added color? The amber barrette holding her hair instead of a big ribbon? Most likely all of them combined and enhanced one another to produce the result—and more importantly, Mayumi herself had taken her first step toward adulthood.

"It hasn't been a month since the graduation ceremony...but I hardly recognized you, Tatsuya."

It was unavoidable, then, that when she suggested something similar about *him*, he'd be taken aback. "Really?" he managed.

Mayumi gave him a warm smile. "Yes. Your uniform—it's the magical engineering curriculum one, right? Completely different from last year."

"Only the uniform is different, though." Tatsuya wasn't trying to hide embarrassment—he was telling the truth. That was what he seriously believed.

"No, no. You probably can't tell, but your face is totally different from when you had the Course 2 uniform on at the beginning of last spring. You look like you feel...*freer* than last year," Mayumi pointed out.

It wasn't that Tatsuya *didn't* argue—it was that he *couldn't*.

A fact he hadn't noticed. A truth he hadn't been aware of.

He'd thought he hadn't been taking anything seriously, and yet he'd still allow the sense of inferiority another person might feel imprison him.

"I surrender. I suppose it's always hardest to understand oneself."

Tatsuya raised the white flag gracefully. His declaration of defeat wasn't only lip service, either. He genuinely decided to take the wisdom of his predecessors—that even if you think you understand yourself, you actually don't—to heart as a warning from now on. But when he saw Mayumi puff out her chest proudly a moment later, the seed of rebelliousness began to sprout.

"I should say the same for you. You've changed quite a bit yourself."

"What? Really?"

"Yes. You can tell you're a college student. You look very mature."

"D-do you think so? Our entrance ceremony was only just the other day."

She responded in the negative to his thoughts, but her slackened expression and fidgeting behavior made it clear that she didn't find it altogether disheartening. (Incidentally, Magic University's entrance ceremony had been on April 6.)

"Yes. The sober barrette and the adult high heels suit you very well. You're almost like a different person."

"Ee-hee-hee, you think so? …Wait." As Mayumi let her facade crumble, evidently not trying to hide herself anymore, her face suddenly stiffened as though in epiphany. "Tatsuya…what did you mean by that…?"

No, it was not *as though* in epiphany—she had, in fact, caught on.

"I'm not sure I follow."

"You said I matured, like a different person."

She'd caught on to the fact that Tatsuya had been teasing her.

"Do you mean to say I used to look childish…?"

"You're thinking about it too hard." Tatsuya, though, wasn't endearing enough in personality to so easily admit to his own wicked deeds (?). As Mayumi glared up at him, he constructed the perfect expression of seriousness and honesty, answering her in a voice to match. "I have never once thought that you have a baby face or that you have the build of a child."

"Baby face… Build of a child…"

For some reason, Mayumi seemed to be in shock. From an objective standpoint, she was simply short—she didn't, in fact, have a baby face or childlike body. If Tatsuya had to judge, her face was more cute than pretty, but that didn't mean it was childish, and her balanced proportions actually made her look mature next to others her age.

But it seemed the fact that she was too short—and it wasn't like she was *extremely* short or anything—was a secret complex of hers. Tatsuya had given a clear denial, but nevertheless, she'd interpreted his words in a bad way.

"Are you feeling all right?" he queried, not sounding overly worried.

"Yes, I'm fine," she answered firmly, half of which was a front, once again staring at him with upturned eyes. "Then what did you mean by 'a different person'?"

"I didn't really mean anything in particular. It's a common expression."

With the young woman persistently questioning him, Tatsuya wondered to himself if he'd messed up. He hadn't broached the topic intending for it to drag on for this long. He wasn't about to blow her off, but he couldn't spend all his time occupied with her, either. And now that he thought about it, why had Mayumi come to her alma mater?

"Really? That's not how it seems to me," she grumbled, stepping in without hesitation. Her upturned stare turned into a point-blank glare. She probably didn't realize it, but she was close enough to invite misunderstandings from outside parties.

"No, I'm serious… By the way, what brings you here today?"

He saw Mayumi's expression of startlement at about the same time that he heard an angry, shrill voice shouting "Hey!"

"Step away from my big sister, you womanizer!"

At first, Tatsuya didn't know those words had been directed at him. There was no reason anyone would be calling him a philanderer. But then he saw a girl, petite enough to fit the high-pitched voice, dashing straight for him along the cherry tree–lined path and realized she'd misinterpreted this situation—the positional one, in which

Tatsuya appeared to be hanging over Mayumi because of the height difference.

"Kasu?!"

Mayumi, for her part, understood by the term *big sister* and the voice's characteristics that the line had been directed at her. She looked back toward the girl running at them, quickly brought her face back to Tatsuya, then took a vehement step backward. She was obviously flustered. She must have figured out that they'd been misunderstood.

Tatsuya knew without having to look at the new student register that this girl Kasu was Mayumi's younger sister. And if Mayumi had been misunderstood by her younger sister to have been getting too cozy with a male underclassman, Tatsuya could understand her losing her composure. Her reaction did, however, feel a little too spirited.

His momentary doubts proved correct. Had her heels brought about the disaster? No—Mayumi would have had many chances to attend formal parties, so she couldn't have been unaccustomed to high-heeled shoes. Had she slipped, then, out of the sudden confusion?

Tatsuya thought about all this calmly as Mayumi's feet were about to fall out from under her. They were the thoughts of an outside observer. Had he simply seen it through to the end, he would have earned the title of "insensitive clod" and deserved it—but even *he* wasn't that inhuman.

Tatsuya quickly moved to support the staggering Mayumi by grabbing both her shoulders. He didn't do anything overly familiar like put his arms around her waist, of course, nor were there any unpardonable accidents like his touching her chest.

"Th-thanks…"

So when Mayumi thanked him, her face embarrassed, the only thing she would have been concerned about was the fact that she'd been about to trip over nothing.

Unfortunately, her sister didn't seem to think that way.

"I told you to get away from her!" she yelled.

A moment later, her sister Kasumi's body floated into the air. Her petite body *accelerated through the air*, not in a parabola but in a straight line, and her outstretched knee flew toward Tatsuya's face.

Tatsuya stopped her knee with one hand, not guarding with his forearm but catching it with his palm. By adding force like that of an uppercut, he dissolved the impact upward, and the momentum escaped into the ground.

Mayumi's eyes ballooned at the sight, but Kasumi was even more surprised than her sister. Blocking or smacking her away would have been one thing, but she was being raised just as a ballerina might lift a leg. Because her state of movement had been forcibly altered, her compound acceleration/movement spell lost its effects.

"Uwah-wah?!"

Her posture was unstable, one leg kneeling atop a palm without any magic-based assistance. Perhaps expectedly, she lost her balance. Her body began to tilt over.

Before Kasumi could continue to flip, Tatsuya pulled back one foot, opening his stance, and lowered his hand.

"Waah!"

With a cry that was decidedly not very cute, Kasumi fell, still in her leaning-forward posture. If she continued like this and made contact with the front schoolyard's soft-coat pavement, she might not hit her head, but she would probably scrape her knees and palms. One could say she'd be in a fairly miserable way as one about to attend her high school entrance ceremony. It would doubtless be a bitter first-day experience for a girl.

To stop the tragedy, Tatsuya could have caught her body in midair—but he didn't. The reason wasn't that he had no time to react. He'd been watching his new underclassman's descent with calculating eyes. The fact that she was Mayumi's younger sister didn't have very much weight in his decision making. What meant more was that she had, even incompletely, carried out an attack on him. Besides, if he caught the girl's body as it fell, he'd give the other girl an opening.

"Ah?!"

Tatsuya *saw* the reason Kasumi cried out dumbly and understood it.

A magic program was attached to her body, slowing her rate of descent. Without even damaging her eidos-skin—the layer of Information Boost protecting her. This sort of phenomenon normally only happened when the person applied a spell to herself—but it had emerged by way of a third party's magic.

At about the same time Kasumi made her soft, unharmed landing, Tatsuya took a big jump backward. After opening up three meters' worth of distance, he saw another girl, with exactly the same face and build as Kasumi but a different hairdo, running to the kneeling Kasumi's side.

"Kasumi, are you all right?!"

"Thanks, Izumi."

Standing side by side, it was obvious that they really *were* twins. Had anyone who didn't know their profiles seen them like this, they would have thought they were identical. And, of course, Tatsuya was aware that they actually were.

Kasumi and Izumi Saegusa. The sisters were known among the Numbers as the *Saegusa twins*, a simple nickname lacking any creativity or witticism.

But despite their identical features, they gave off noticeably different impressions. Kasumi, with her smooth hair and short haircut, appeared to be the energetic type, one who might lean toward physical education or martial arts over book studies—someone who was always ready for a fight.

On the other hand, Izumi, with straight, evenly cut hair that brushed her shoulders, was more the introvert, with a mild-mannered air of bookish grace about her. What she'd just said, both in tone of voice and expression, evidenced how alarmed she was, but she seemed to be somehow lacking apprehension—on the surface, at least. Still, Tatsuya felt as though *she* was the one to be careful around.

He was now on the receiving end of a pair of unmannerly gazes from people he'd never met before, but the feeling went both ways. In terms of how blunt their gazes were, Tatsuya's was practically reserved.

"Izumi, this guy's real strong for a philanderer."

"Wait, umm, Kasumi?"

But there was a clear difference in energy between them. They both watched him curiously, but Kasumi was the only one with enmity burning in her eyes.

"I think you'd better calm down..." said Izumi, soothing her.

"My gut's telling me that this guy's not ordinary."

But Kasumi wasn't listening. Still on one knee, glaring at Tatsuya, she pushed up her left sleeve to reveal a CAD.

"Izumi, let's do the thing," she said, about to let her fingers at the CAD's console.

Usage of magic without permission—a blatantly illegal act. And the second time, too. Even removing the fact that they were aimed at him from the equation, that wasn't something he could overlook. They might have been students about to go to their opening ceremony, but he didn't have the option of *not* subduing them.

He decided all this in an instant, but fortunately, before he could act, the illegal magic usage ended before it began.

"Give it a rest!"

Mayumi, who had been frozen in place, unable to keep up with the situation, had brought her fist down on Kasumi's head.

"..."

Judging from how Kasumi squatted holding her head, unable to talk, it must have hurt a considerable amount.

"...What did you do that for, Sis?"

"That's my line! Kasu, what on earth are you doing?!"

Mayumi looked down, hands on her hips, at her sister, as the girl looked up at her teary-eyed. Mayumi was seriously mad. Kasumi's excited mind cooled at her older sister's threatening countenance, and her face shifted from a warm color to a cool one.

"I told you many times that using magic without permission is a crime! And on the very day you start high school... How do you explain yourself?!" she said, rattling on in a voice that was half an octave higher than normal.

Tatsuya watched her, a little bit appalled. He'd seen her get upset before. But this was the first time he'd seen her *furious*. It was a guileless, straightforward attitude he couldn't have imagined from her normal approach—hiding her feelings behind a meaningful smile.

Meanwhile Kasumi, exposed to her naked wrath, tried to make herself small but didn't give up her resistance. Because she was family? Or was she used to this?

"B-but that guy was trying to do lewd things to you, Sis…"

And her counterattack was certainly effective—

"I… Le-lewd?!"

—in terms of dealing damage to her opponent, at least.

"We were doing nothing of the sort! What are you thinking?!"

Looking at the big picture, though, it was nothing more than fuel for the fire.

"You were the one who said you wanted to look around before the ceremony, and that you'd be all right since you're not a kid, Kasumi! You haven't been bothering other people this way, too, have you?!"

I see. So that's what's going on, thought Tatsuya. Mayumi had brought her sisters to the entrance ceremony in place of their busy parents.

"That would be outrageous, Big Sister."

The challenge to Mayumi's scolding in interrogative form came not from the trembling Kasumi but Izumi, standing close to her twin.

"Aside from Kasumi's misunderstanding just now, we have not done anything that would bother anybody else."

"Really…? Can I believe you, Izu?"

"You can, without a doubt."

Izumi's words, insisting on their innocence in a way that almost seemed *too* polite, seemed to let Mayumi regain some of her cool.

"All right," she said after seeing Izumi's eyes and nodding. "Tatsuya, I'm sorry!" She bowed deeply toward him. "My sister isn't behaving herself. Kasu, you apologize to him, too!"

Whether or not Kasumi truly understood how serious her older sister was, she didn't express displeased behavior as she had earlier.

She went next to Mayumi and bowed her head without complaint. "I'm terribly sorry," she said.

"I would like to offer my apologies as well. Please, forgive Kasumi's rudeness, Shiba."

Not only Kasumi, the perpetrator, but even Izumi followed suit.

With three beautiful girls—no, one beautiful *woman* and two beautiful girls—apologizing to him at once, Tatsuya felt uncomfortable. Miraculously, no one had witnessed the violent act earlier, but now he could feel a few curious stares. If they saw him as bullying the girls or something, the damage and aftereffects would be much worse than Kasumi's flying knee.

"Please, raise your heads, all of you. Nothing ultimately happened, so it doesn't bother me anymore."

Actually, *Please don't let it bother you anymore* was closer to how he really felt. He wanted to get out of here as quickly as possible to escape the gazes of the ever-increasing curious onlookers. But saying he didn't care anymore wasn't a lie, either.

Mayumi probably understood that, too. A relieved look came over her face, but it quickly faded to an apologetic, guilty one.

"Umm, look, Tatsuya?"

"What is it?" The air had turned odd, somehow. Tatsuya mentally prepared himself.

"I know… I know that normally you'd have to report this to the faculty office, but…" Mayumi, facing Tatsuya, shut her eyes and put her hands together. "Please! Could you make an exception just this once and overlook it?!"

"Oh, that?" murmured Tatsuya. "I never intended to make a big deal out of something so small."

In reality, if *she* had taken issue with things "so small," he had no idea how many times she would have lectured him or Miyuki. He didn't say it out loud, but his unadorned feelings were that the feeling was mutual.

"Thanks so much, Tatsuya!"

Which made him worry when she was so strongly thankful. And...

"No, I knew from the start she was going to stop right before hitting me."

There was also the flying knee being a bluff. If she'd *actually* attacked him, Tatsuya wouldn't have responded so amicably.

The compound acceleration/movement spell Kasumi had cast on herself had been made to quickly decelerate her thirty centimeters from Tatsuya's face, stopping her dead in midair ten centimeters away. No matter how well trained he was, it wasn't possible to use one hand to stop forty kilograms of body mass hurtling at him at fifty meters a second. He had known when she would start decelerating and when she'd stop, so he had literally given her a hand stopping herself and the spell right before that would have happened anyway.

"Right... I should have known, Tatsuya."

While Kasumi uttered, "But how...?" in bafflement next to her, Mayumi nodded, impressed. She was used to how abnormal Tatsuya could be.

"In any case, I need to show the new students in. The venue is open by now," said Tatsuya, forestalling Mayumi's next remark—which probably would have been an unnecessary one—before leaving without waiting for an answer.

"Pixie?"

After parting ways with the Saegusa sisters, he moved to a mostly deserted spot and brought his mouth to his voice communication unit.

"*Yes, Master?*"

The soft whisper in response came via active telepathy. It was from "Pixie," *inside* a 3H type P-94.

"Delete all psion sensor data from the lecture hall entrance to the front yard area, starting now and going back ten minutes."

"*Of course, Master.*"

Mayumi seemed to have accidentally forgotten, but Tatsuya

couldn't cover up Kasumi's unlawful magic usage just by keeping quiet. Sensors that surveilled magic usage were set up all over the campus, and except during special intervals like club recruitment week, all improper magic usage would be recorded by these devices.

"Deletion completed."

Tatsuya hadn't, of course, withdrawn Pixie from the student council to make her run errands. Perhaps because she had originally been a housekeeping robot and she wanted to do it, he was letting her, but his intentions lay elsewhere—to hack the school's surveillance system.

Up until March, when Mayumi had still attended the school, he could have asked her to do most of these things. She had codes to get into the school's surveillance system beyond the level normally permitted to student council presidents. There was obviously no way she'd obtained that ability via any *proper* means. Thus, it naturally hadn't passed down to the next student president.

Tatsuya, in many ways a shady customer himself, needed to figure out his own way of getting into the surveillance system now that Mayumi was gone. And that had led him to the way Pixie was put together.

Right now, Pixie's main body, a parasite, was operating in direct control of the Humanoid Home Helper's electronic brain. In other words, "Pixie" had the potential to control electronic systems directly, without needing any sort of interface. Tatsuya had assumed this would be the case.

And so Tatsuya had taught Pixie as many hacking techniques as he could cram into their spring break. Originally the techniques had been taught to him by Fujibayashi, the Electron Sorceress. His efforts had borne fruit, and though it was limited to First High's internal systems, Pixie now had the skills to freely infiltrate the systems keeping an eye out for magic and overwrite their data.

Although he called his job new student guidance, it wasn't very hard to figure out where the entrance ceremony venue—the assembly hall—was, and nobody would ever get lost if they had a device equipped with an LPS, or local positioning system. Cases like Erika last year, when she hadn't had her terminal and hadn't known where to go, were an exception. Tatsuya's job, as well as the others', wasn't to give new students directions but to give a heads-up to the ones who seemed like they were going to be late.

"Excuse me, where might the assembly hall be?"

So Tatsuya hadn't expected to run into someone who had *actually* gotten lost.

The place: the tree-lined path between the library and small gymnasium number two—the opposite side of campus from the ceremony location. There, Tatsuya had spotted an incoming male freshman who looked very much like he didn't know what to do. After Tatsuya called out to him, that had been the response.

This new student is quite conspicuous, though, thought Tatsuya. Among his own classmates were several sporting different colors from most Japanese people, with red hair or blue eyes or dark skin. But there were none so dazzlingly colored as the short student standing in front of him.

His hair was platinum, his eyes were silver, and his skin was white. The colors weren't the only thing that set him apart—his features were devoid of any Japanese characteristics as well. A manifestation of strong northern Caucasian genes? Come to think of it, Tatsuya noted, he resembled his instructor, Mrs. Smith.

"I'll show you. You can come with me."

Despite what was on his mind, his answer came without delay. The new student gave a relieved expression and bowed deeply. "Thank you very much. Umm, my name is Kento Sumisu."

"Sumisu—Smith…?" repeated Tatsuya in spite of himself. He seemed to have the same family name as the person Tatsuya considered the boy similar to. But Smith was the most common last name in the English-speaking sphere. A coincidence, he decided.

"Oh—yes, written with the characters for *corner* and *defense*. My parents naturalized here from the States before I was born. When they did, they put those kanji to the name Smith... I know, it must sound like a strange name."

Apparently, though, this Kento boy seemed to have taken the reaction for a different kind of confusion. His voice tapered off at the end. Maybe he had experience being teased for his last name in elementary or middle school.

"No, I don't think it's strange at all."

Middle school was one thing, but elementary school kids might display such innocent, unthinking cruelty. Tatsuya, though, had no ties to that sort of foolishness. What he'd been thinking was that if both the boy's parents were naturalized Japanese citizens, it made sense he didn't have any Japanese physical characteristics.

"By the way," said Tatsuya, something more important on his mind. "Doesn't your information terminal have an LPS function, Sumisu?"

When Tatsuya had spotted Kento, the boy had been looking at his information terminal screen like he was about to cry. If the device had an LPS function, he wouldn't have lost his way.

"Oh—you can just call me Kento. As for LPS, well...it does have one, I guess, but..." he said, removing a rather large information terminal from his pocket. The boy only came up to Tatsuya's chest. Considering ethnic characteristics, he was quite short. He would even be classified as short among Japanese boys his age. Perhaps deciding that his holding it made it too hard to see, Kento raised his information terminal above his head and pointed it at Tatsuya.

The terminal was a fairly old model. That was all Tatsuya knew about it, but it was actually more than twenty years old. And it wasn't from a domestic manufacturer, either, but was a model made in the USNA that had been popular there.

"All I had was one of the virtual terminals, so I borrowed the one my dad used a long time ago for today... But the LPS is a different standard, so..."

Ah, thought Tatsuya. LPS was a public infrastructure, and it had retained backward compatibility ever since its first version update, but that only went for domestic terminals. Japan and the USNA processed data slightly differently. Plus, the USNA's LPS was no more than a supplemental system for GPS, not a standalone feature like Japan's.

"Here, let me borrow it for a moment."

Tatsuya reflexively took the terminal from Kento and checked its processing power and free space. It was an old model, but it had been tuned up in several ways. Maybe Kento's father was an electronics engineer. Deciding it was fit for the task, Tatsuya connected his own terminal to Kento's and sent it a location information app.

"I've installed a GPS-based map of the school. It isn't as precise as an LPS app would be, but you should be able to see where to go, at least." Finished with the installation, he returned the terminal to Kento.

"Thank you so much!" Kento, despite the simple act, looked at Tatsuya awfully impressed.

"Of course, you should buy a new terminal. This is just a quick fix."

Tatsuya gave that obvious advice because even he, behind his poker face, was taken aback. He quickly became aware of the reason for Kento's overreaction.

"U-umm, if you don't mind me asking, you're Tatsuya Shiba, right?!"

"Yes, I am… You've heard of me?"

"Yes! I got to see you during the Nine School Competition last year!"

Tatsuya wasn't surprised by Kento's answer. There was nothing strange about a student enrolling at Magic High School, despite being a Course 2 student, having watched the Nine School Competition. Monolith Code was the center-stage event, even though he'd only been in the rookie one. Kento probably could have coincidentally remembered his face.

That's what Tatsuya thought, anyway—

"Brilliant tactics! Genius tuning! I picked First High because you're here, Shiba!"

—But it turned out that he was half-incorrect. Kento didn't know of Tatsuya as an athlete, but as an engineer.

"I planned to go to Fourth High until I saw last year's competition. I'm not great at practical skills, you see. But when I saw your super technique, I decided I had to go to the same school!"

Tatsuya listened to Kento's excited words with detachment.

"As you can see, I'm only in Course 2 right now, but I'll do my best to get into the engineering program next year, just like you!"

"...I see. Well, good luck. With your enthusiasm, I'm sure you'll be fine."

"Thank you!"

His intentions were rather different, but he seemed like a male version of Honoka. As Kento gazed at him eagerly like a puppy, Tatsuya found himself somewhat at a loss.

After leaving Mayumi at the entrance to the assembly hall, Kasumi and Izumi chose seats near the front row. Kasumi sat down immediately, and as Izumi was politely taking her own seat, Kasumi eagerly brought her face close in.

"Izumi, do you know that philanderer?"

There were still almost twenty minutes until the entrance ceremony began. Many other new students were there, too, sitting in groups and talking among themselves. Izumi, who had braced herself at hearing a conspiratorial whisper, gave her sister a deflated look once she understood her aim.

"Yes… Kasumi, do you mean you actually *don't* know who he is?" The more she realized Kasumi had been asking seriously, the more appalled her expression became.

"...Is he famous?"

"Yes, in a way." Izumi gave a light sigh, then turned in her seat to face her little sister. "His name is Tatsuya Shiba. He was a Course

2 student last year, but he transferred into the magical engineering curriculum this year."

"Huh... If he went from Course 2 to magical engineering, he must be pretty smart."

Kasumi's reaction was somewhat impassive; she didn't sound impressed, though she was also not making fun of him. Izumi looked at her as if to say, *What am I going to do with you?*

"What?"

"Well, he is certainly an intelligent individual... I'm simply not sure such a commonplace word is enough to describe him."

Izumi assumed a feigned posture of confusion, with a hand to her cheek. Kasumi huffed at the attitude, but she knew that if she got angry, it would just give Izumi the advantage. The twins had always been together, ever since they were born. Their tendencies and countermeasures for all sorts of different situations were pitch-perfect. Kasumi kept her mouth shut, waiting for Izumi to continue.

"Last year, he was an engineer participating in the Nine School Competition—not only as a freshman, but as a Course 2 student. The athletes he was in charge of took first through third place in the rookie women's Speed Shooting and Ice Pillars Break, first and second place in the rookie Mirage Bat tournament, and first place in the regular one."

"No way! You mean all the athletes he was assigned to only lost to each other? Like, they were practically undefeated?"

"Yes."

"You've got to be joking..."

"It's not a lie, and it's not a joke. His achievements were staggering—for all intents and purposes, every athlete he was assigned to went undefeated."

While Izumi answered her question, Kasumi stared hard at her twin's face, watching for even the slightest hint of a lie. But when she realized Izumi's answer was serious, her eyes—already wide—widened even more.

"He worked as Big Sister's support in Cloudball, too—you really didn't notice that, Kasumi?" followed up Izumi, her face not even appalled at this point, but rather pitying.

"I had no idea…"

"It seems it was a sudden assignment, but Big Sister showed no signs of any inconvenience."

Kasumi was crushed; she didn't know what to say. The twins had watched Mayumi's matches together during last summer's competition. She was in shock that only Izumi, and not she, had noticed the presence of an annoying bug clinging to their older sister.

"Still, I don't quite like him," said Izumi to herself as Kasumi sat there dazed. "Big Sister appears to be quite lax around our upperclassman Shiba… This may be an unexpected ambush."

That was as much as she said aloud. After her disquieting soliloquy, she sank deeper into her own thoughts, with Kasumi still unable to recover from the shock.

The entrance ceremony finished up as planned, without any accidents or incidents. Takuma's address in particular ended without issue. It was a safe speech, without all eyes in the venue glued to the dais like last year, or students both old *and* new watching over the address giver in suspense like the year before that.

After that was the traditional student council invitation. There was an unwritten rule that discussing the student council with the new student representative/head of the class waited until the entrance ceremony ended, the reason being that that person wasn't a student until it did. It felt too formal in a way, but nothing had ever gone wrong in the past. Even if there was a disturbance like last year, there had never been a failed invitation. However…

"I'm very sorry, but I must refuse."

That was Takuma's answer to Azusa's invitation to join the student council.

"...May I ask why?" pried Isori. He was the only other one who had come with Azusa to make the invitation, and he spoke in her place, as Azusa was now petrified at the unexpected no.

"I'd like to focus on improving myself," replied Takuma, returning Isori's gaze. "My goal is to grow into a magician as strong as the Ten Master Clans. For my extracurricular activities, I would prefer to work hard in a club instead of learning organizational management in the student council."

His answer came smoothly—he'd probably prepared it in advance. Which in turn meant that his resolve was firm. Isori decided that convincing him would be an uphill battle.

"I see..."

But it wasn't Isori whose voice drifted into the depressed air, but Azusa. She'd broken free of her paralysis surprisingly quickly, hanging her head without energy as though she would heave a sigh. Had it been such a shock to her? Isori, at least, thought so as he watched from next to her.

"Then there's nothing we can do. We can't force you to join." Her next words in response to Takuma, though, came unexpectedly easily. "We're sorry to hear it, but if this is a decision you're sure about, then please do your best in whatever club you end up joining."

Her attitude was a surprise to Takuma, too—she seemed too ready to give up. But if he hung around here any longer, they might start to think he actually kind of wanted to be a member. Or, since they'd expected they'd be able to keep him, they could take it as rude. That was what Takuma thought.

"I'm sorry. Please excuse me."

Hurried by the thought that he was thinking too much about this, Takuma walked quickly away from Azusa.

At about the time the pair of seniors were fighting to invite Takuma in (and losing), a trio of juniors—Tatsuya, Miyuki, and Honoka—were busy with work of their own.

Honoka was on cleanup detail for the entrance ceremony. Her eyes were almost spinning with checking guest attendance, organizing the congratulatory messages, and exchanging photographic data with a company representative.

Tatsuya was directing and supervising the juniors who had been roped into helping with the ceremony. His having been in Course 2 the year before was one thing, but nobody voiced any complaint at taking instructions from him with his eight-toothed gear emblem on. He was currently in the middle of collecting smaller items such as armbands and headsets from his classmates as they finished their assistance.

And as for Miyuki...

"If there was anything disappointing about this year's ceremony, it's that we didn't get to hear a speech from Shiba."

"Some things simply cannot happen, Mr. Kouzuke. The only students who take the platform during the ceremony are the student council president and the incoming freshman representative."

"Ha-ha-ha. You're right, come to think of it."

...She was being earnest in keeping a friendly smile, surrounded by adults who were making much ado about nothing.

The man called Mr. Kouzuke was a politician by trade. A Diet member belonging to the party currently in power whose constituency was in Tokyo, the young up-and-comer was said by many to be a shoo-in for a ministerial position should that party win in the next election. He was also known as one of the Diet members friendlier toward magicians, and he'd worked as an extramural inspector for Magic University in the past. With anti-magician demonstrations steadily rising in intensity, neither the Magic University nor First High could afford to alienate someone like him.

And Miyuki understood that. That was why she'd been smiling along with his pointless conversation for some time now. It honestly wasn't something a sixteen-year-old girl should have to be concerned about, but she was tolerating it well.

For his part, Mr. Kouzuke's eyes were flickering with shadows of lust. They weren't strong enough to link to any direct action, and it was closer to an instinctual yearning toward a young and beautiful girl of a man who was starting to realize his own physical decline, but even if it was a mental thing (though not a platonic one), it was doubtless uncomfortable for a girl to be on the receiving end of such leering. Still, Miyuki endured it, pretending not to notice the rude gaze.

His long-windedness was starting to become a bother to the faculty as well. With a Diet member of high status among the rest of the guests remaining at the venue, the faculty found it difficult to leave as well.

In fact, Mr. Kouzuke hadn't even rambled for so long until this year. Nevertheless, it didn't mean he'd suddenly become fond of empty loquaciousness. He'd been reserved last year and the year before that with Mayumi.

Reserved not toward Mayumi personally, but to the Ten Master Clans' Saegusa name.

Mr. Kouzuke didn't act friendly with magicians out of goodwill or interest. He certainly didn't hate them, but as a *politician*, he used defending magicians as a way to use their power for his own political activities later. Kouzuke and magicians had a utilitarian relationship; thus, he'd shown restraint with someone from the Ten Master Clans, since they occupied a representative position among magicians.

Had Miyuki made her connection to the Yotsuba clear, Kouzuke probably would have given a forced smile and left that place right away. The Yotsuba name had even more impact than the Saegusa. The Saegusa might have had more political value, but the Yotsuba went above and beyond when it came to striking fear into those with influence.

However, the only last name Miyuki was permitted to use was Shiba, not Yotsuba. And though she was reaching the limits of her endurance at this point, she didn't want to rely on the Yotsuba's power for something so trivial. After all, they weren't allies she could unconditionally rely on.

What saved her from the quandary and irritation she couldn't do anything about wasn't a Yotsuba, but a Saegusa.

"Hello, Mr. Kouzuke."

Kouzuke turned toward the voice suddenly calling his name, and as soon as he saw the maturely smiling Mayumi in her grown-up suit, his face drew back.

"Thank you for attending again this year. I know how *busy* you must be."

"This day is a cause for celebration for all the talented young men and women with this country's future on their shoulders. I should be thanking you—I consider it an honor to be invited year after year."

With Mayumi addressing him in a polite tone of voice, one that wasn't *too* stiff or formal, Kouzuke very quickly seemed like he wanted to leave. He wouldn't be a ministerial hopeful if he couldn't read signs like Mayumi placing unnatural emphasis on *busy*. Politicians could be insensitive—but they couldn't be fools.

"By the way, what brings you here, Mayumi? Accompanying your younger sisters?" asked Kouzuke, glancing over at Kasumi and Izumi, who were standing behind Mayumi. He'd derailed the conversation in a way that seemed natural, and in doing so begun his escape preparations.

"Yes. Both my parents were coldhearted enough to insist they simply couldn't make it today."

"Ha-ha-ha." Kouzuke's insincere, friendly smile pulled back a little. "Well, they're very busy people as well."

"Kasu, Izu, say hello."

Either satisfied her joke had gone over well or not willing to pursue the topic any further, Mayumi turned back to her sisters.

"It is nice to see you again after so long, Mr. Kouzuke."

"I'm terribly sorry—it really has been a very long time."

Once they'd been addressed, the pair waiting obediently in the wings greeted him, Kasumi briskly and Izumi politely.

Their by-the-book greetings were a good opportunity for Kouzuke. "No, no. I'm sure you've been busy with your exam studies, so you don't need to worry. I hope everything goes well for you in high school."

"Thank you, Mr. Kouzuke."

"We will apply ourselves even more."

Kasumi and Izumi gave another deep bow, and an air of completion settled over them. Kouzuke didn't let the chance escape.

"I have high hopes for both of you. Now then, Mayumi, if you'll excuse me."

With a simple goodbye, Kouzuke quickly left the place.

And Mayumi didn't press the attack from behind.

"Miyuki, are you okay?"

"Yes, and thank you, Saegusa."

As Mayumi addressed her with a genial smile, Miyuki answered with a modest one of her own. The ears and eyes of the faculty were still about them. Giving too clear an indication of her agreement might lead them to think Mr. Kouzuke had caused her distress.

Still, though, Miyuki wasn't seriously cautious about the school's staff tattling on her. She was only acting in such a way that she would never be taken advantage of, out of habit, without particularly noticing it. As long as it didn't involve Tatsuya, her feline skin was impenetrable as a stab-proof sheet woven with poly-paraphenylene terephthalamide (Kevlar).

You needed a very discerning eye to see through her mask, harder than steel, to her face. It wasn't possible for one female high school student she'd just met, at least. Even if that student *was* a direct descendant of one of the Ten Master Clans and used to seeing foxes and tanuki regularly. For most people, Miyuki's suppressed display of emotion surely would have looked ladylike and graceful, the epitome of the neat and trim *Yamato-nadeshiko* woman.

"Izu?"

At least, that was how she appeared to Izumi. Izumi was entranced, her eyes and attention stolen.

"Izumi? Hey, Izumi!"

"Yes?" she replied, the elbow from Kasumi next to her finally cluing her in to the fact that Mayumi was talking to her.

"Aren't you forgetting something? Be polite and say hello to Miyuki."

Her older sister's words permeated Izumi's consciousness, and she hastily turned her eyes in front of her. They settled on Miyuki, looking a little troubled but still smiling gently at her.

She's like a goddess...

Izumi, of course, had never met an actual *goddess* before. Miyuki's appearance was so detached from reality in Izumi's eyes, however, that the word naturally sprang forth into her mind. Her sister Mayumi was an unabashed *beauty,* and she even thought Kasumi was cute in her own right, an opinion that others might have taken as narcissistic. But she knew this was the first time she'd ever seen a woman as beautiful as the upperclassman floating an ephemeral smile right in front of her. Miyuki was the ideal image of what Izumi wanted to be.

"I'm Izumi Saegusa. Excuse me, but may I call you Miyuki?"

"Yes, I don't mind."

Izumi's eyes clouded as though a sudden heat had entered them, and her voice was a little off. The shift was enough for Mayumi and Kasumi to be anxious about why she'd suddenly gotten like that, but Miyuki nodded, her kind smile still on her face.

"Miyuki, I had the pleasure of watching you during the Nines. You were simply wonderful."

"Thank you."

Miyuki accepted Izumi's passionate gaze with the smoothness of upperclassmen.

"But now that I've met you in person, I have to say you look many times more beautiful than when I saw you from the stands."

"I-is that so?"

However, as a lunacy that went above and beyond mere idol worship began to creep into her feverish eyes, even Miyuki was taken aback.

"I can't believe I'm attending the same school as someone like Miyuki... I'm so moved."

"Izu, what on earth has gotten into you?"

The sight of Izumi's emotions running amok when she was normally so hard to read behind her calm smile was enough to thoroughly confuse Mayumi. Kasumi, who knew her twin sister actually had an impassioned streak, simply watched in exasperation, though.

"Miyuki…will you do me the honor of being my big sister?"

"Big sister?!"

"Wait a minute, Izu! Calm down! You have an older sister right here!"

Miyuki and Mayumi's voices broke into a higher pitch at the same time. Izumi, the very one who had created this rare sight, just kept on staring at Miyuki. Next to her, Kasumi had her cheek turned, not wanting anything to do with it.

"I don't believe it will be possible for you to become Big Sister Miyuki's younger sister, Saegusa."

It was Minami, who had been listening in on the four for a short while now from a slight distance, who tossed a stone into the chaotic stalemate.

"Minami?" Miyuki, who hadn't noticed Minami standing there, said her name, meaning to indicate she was wondering, *How long have you been there?*

But Minami left answering that question for later. "It is possible to become Big Brother Tatsuya's younger sister, however. Should Saegusa's older sister be wed to Big Brother Tatsuya, you would become his younger sister-in-law."

Once Minami finished her supplementary explanation to Izumi, she whirled around to face the other way.

"In this case," cut in a very male voice, "wouldn't Saegusa, sister-in-law to Big Brother Tatsuya, who is Big Sister Miyuki's younger sister, qualify as her sister?"

"Brother?!"

It had been, as Miyuki proclaimed, Tatsuya who asked that question of Minami.

"I will not approve of this!"

But Tatsuya couldn't respond to Minami's question or Miyuki's outcry. Before he could open his mouth, Kasumi voiced her own objection at what Minami had said:

"I want everyone to know that I'm against my sister being Shiba's wife!"

Kasumi, who had been keeping to the sidelines, suddenly broke in between Tatsuya and Mayumi, facing him as if to shield her sister. Her previous meek attitude was nowhere to be found, and now she was fully giving off an aura that said, *Don't come close to my sister.*

"Kasumi, we were only speaking hypothetically..."

Perhaps it was a division of labor only available to twins. Kasumi and Izumi seemed to have things set up so that when one of them was beside herself, the other would make up for it. Izumi, who had been looking up at Miyuki passionately until just a moment ago, suddenly cooled and began to soothe Kasumi.

Mayumi rubbed her temples as she watched them. It wasn't just a pose she was assuming—she looked like she actually had a headache.

"Tatsuya?" she said, downcast, hand to her forehead.

Tatsuya tried to move close enough to Mayumi to have a normal conversation with her, but Kasumi stood in his way again, a threat in her eyes.

But a moment later...

"Yowch!" Crying out like a cat whose tail had been stepped on, Kasumi grabbed her head and squatted down.

"And Miyuki?"

Behind her, Mayumi had swung her fist down, her eyes still on the floor. A truly miserable-sounding voice came from her lips.

"I'm, um, really sorry for my stupid sisters..."

Her face, looking down as it was, was completely red around the eyes. It must have seriously been embarrassing for her. Tatsuya supposed he could understand—if his sister had gone out of control so many times in a row, he probably would have been ashamed to stick around, too.

"I don't mind it. Right, Miyuki?" said Tatsuya, trying to draw Miyuki out.

"Not at all. Please, don't worry about it." Miyuki shook her head brightly. Izumi's scandalous conduct aside, Kasumi had very much been treating Tatsuya like a harmful insect—but for some reason, Miyuki was in a good mood. Mayumi felt suspicious and uneasy at her attitude, but she didn't have the emotional wherewithal to pursue the topic.

"I'll make it up to you, I promise. And you two—we're going home."

"Ow! That hurts, Sis!"

"Big Sister, you're hurting me! Why must I be punished, too?"

Grabbing her twin sisters' collars in either hand, Mayumi escaped the area.

On a specific corner of the road to school leading from the school gates to First High Station was Einebrise, the café that Tatsuya and the others visited often. He'd come to the shop again today on the way back from the entrance ceremony, along with Miyuki, Minami, Honoka, Shizuku, and Mikihiko, all amusing themselves with light conversations with coffees in their hands.

After the Saegusa sisters left, Tatsuya's group had briefly met up with Azusa. She'd told them firmly, however, that they could go home for the day, so he had decided to leave school with Honoka's group, which was already there.

"By the way, how did inviting the new representative go?"

Shizuku's question came the moment there was a pause in the chatter. She didn't have any special intentions, but neither did she ask the question out of curiosity, whether innocent or snoopy. If anything, the remark had been dragged out from the sudden lull in the conversation.

"...Not well."

So when Honoka—even though it wasn't her fault—suddenly looked as though she were about to be crushed under the weight of dark clouds, Shizuku ended up regretting asking it.

"Huh? Did Shippou refuse to join the student council?"

Which was why this statement from Mikihiko, who actually did sometimes prioritize his curiosity, was such a skilled play, preventing an uneasy silence from settling over them.

"Apparently, he said he wanted to focus on club activities. If there's something else he wants to do, we can't do much about it."

Tatsuya's answer wasn't aimed at Mikihiko so much as it was telling Honoka not to worry about it.

"Right. We can't force him."

Mikihiko, either sensing Tatsuya's intent or through pure coincidence, backed him up, restoring the storm clouds over Honoka to a mere slightly cloudy sky.

"It would be more constructive to think about who to invite to the student council in his place," said Miyuki to Tatsuya, moving all six of their attentions completely away from the new boy.

"Yeah," nodded Tatsuya with a serious look. "If none of the new students join, things might be shaky later on."

Miyuki clapped her hands together lightly. "I know. Why don't we have Minami join?"

Minami had been listening to the older students talk in silence. Her face froze at the idea.

"Miyuki, I don't think Minami would like that much." But before Minami could open her mouth, Tatsuya turned down the proposal. "It's a tradition to invite the top student to the student council, so we should select alternate candidates by their test scores, too."

Minami looked relieved. Miyuki, even with her proposal rejected, didn't seem dissatisfied in the slightest. Instead, she was smiling brightly. She must not have seriously been considering Minami for the student council—she just wanted to tease her a little.

"Who was second?" asked Shizuku—who had taken Tatsuya's

statement at face value regardless of Miyuki's ideas—of Honoka, who as the student council secretary would know all the entrance exam grades.

"Umm, that would be Izumi Saegusa. Our senior's younger sister." Honoka remembered the exam results just fine without having to check her terminal.

"Third place was her other sister, Kasumi. The two of them and Shippou were first, second, and third by a really tight margin. Their grades were a lot higher than fourth place." Miyuki, too, knew the results, so she added to the explanation for Shizuku.

"Then it would not be odd for one of Saegusa's younger sisters to join the student council." Mikihiko seemed to still be using a polite tone of voice, even when talking to Miyuki.

"But if we go in order, it would be Izumi, right?"

Depending on how one viewed Mikihiko's attitude, his observation might have invited groundless suspicion or come off as amused, but Shizuku objected flatly, not sounding very interested at all.

Miyuki made a slightly distressed face at this. Maybe she'd realized from earlier that she wouldn't be very good at handling Izumi.

"It's up to the president, but ultimately it depends on whether she wants to."

Tatsuya must have understood why her expression had changed, but none present could quite figure out whether that line was meant to respect her feelings or not.

As Tatsuya was washing his hands in the bathroom, Mikihiko came in. That, by itself, wasn't particularly meaningful. Thinking the timing happened to be coincidental, Tatsuya moved to pass him by and exit.

"Tatsuya?"

But he was stopped by Mikihiko's low, conspiratorial tone.

"What? …Something you can't talk about out there?"

"Mm… I don't want too many other people to hear this."

"All right. I'll keep it quiet."

Mikihiko's face, which had been locked with hesitation and vacillation, softened a bit. "I'm glad you catch on so quickly."

"It'll be strange if we're holed up in here for too long, so you might want to keep it short."

Like Tatsuya said, staying too long here was, hygienically speaking, bound to garner disgraceful suspicion. With that made clear, Mikihiko somewhat hastily began to speak. "Tatsuya, did you know that the new president of Rosen's Japan branch was at the ceremony today?"

Rosen was, of course, the German magical engineering device manufacturer, Rosen Magicraft, one of the two leading manufacturers of CADs in the world, competing for the top position with Maximillian Devices. The president of its Japan branch was a VIP to Magic University, and consequently to magic high schools.

"I did. I had a chance to say hello briefly."

Tatsuya had obviously known the branch president had been invited, and had even seen him in the seats.

"Briefly? At last year's post-Nines party, I think the previous branch president was very eager about his scouting efforts."

"*Fortunately*, he didn't have that time today." Tatsuya's face puckered as Mikihiko dug up a particular set of irritating memories. But his expression went back to normal a moment later, before he prompted his friend, "Anyway, what about this new branch president?"

"Do you know his name?"

"Ernst Rosen. Apparently a member of the main Rosen family."

"Yeah. The industry papers are buzzing with news about them having their first big shot in a while."

Mikihiko's words caught there for a moment. But right after that, he cast away his hesitation and lowered his eyes in a way that might be considered a little desperate, and whispered the next words:

"And he happens to be Erika's mother's cousin."

Even Tatsuya couldn't keep up his poker face against *that* bombshell. "Erika's mother is related to the Rosens?" he asked, the shock clear in his eyes.

Mikihiko very slightly—but very certainly—nodded. "Erika's maternal grandfather apparently eloped with a Japanese woman."

"*Eloped?* That's pretty old-fashioned."

"I guess..." Mikihiko gave Tatsuya a little pained grin. It was rare for him to express surprise at something other than the main point, and it somehow made the grave air calm slightly. His face looking rather more relaxed, Mikihiko continued. "He ran away to Japan against his family's wishes, so they're currently estranged from the main Rosen family. Her grandmother's—maternal grandmother's—family didn't seem to think highly of their relationship, either, and I hear Erika's mother has had a pretty hard time of things."

"That's unfortunate, but what are you getting at?"

Even Tatsuya considered Erika's home situation infelicitous, but Mikihiko's goal probably wasn't to get him to sympathize with her. Tatsuya prompted him to get to the point quickly.

"...Ever since then, Japan hasn't had a very good opinion of the Rosen family. Sales-wise, their headquarters are in Japan, but no main family member has ever been placed at the branch."

"You know, you're right." Tatsuya tried to go back through Rosen Magicraft Japan branch executive names from the last decade. Mikihiko was right—there were no Rosens in that list.

"I might be thinking about this too hard, but...I don't think Ernst Rosen coming to Japan is unrelated to Erika."

Tatsuya thought he might be overthinking it, too. But more importantly, the question of why Mikihiko was talking to him about this tugged at him. "And what would you like me to do?"

"I didn't want you to do anything. I just wanted you to keep it in mind, that's all." When Tatsuya looked at him dubiously, Mikihiko grinned bitterly at himself. "No, that's not it... It's just a little hard for me to carry this alone, so maybe I wanted to get you involved with it," he muttered, sounding a little mad at himself. "I know, I'm terrible."

Tatsuya's frank impression of Mikihiko, despite what he had to say about himself, was completely free of dark criticism.

◇ ◇ ◇

Even after Tatsuya and the others had left, Azusa had remained by herself in the student council room until just before closing time. (Pixie was in sleep mode.) The council had a whole mountain of work to do for the new year after the entrance ceremony ended. It wasn't odd that she, the president, was staying this late. If anything, what was odd was the other members going home before her.

Then was Azusa doing the work of five people on her own? No, she wasn't doing that. For a while now, she'd only been idly staring at this month's schedule. Occasionally she would give a heavy sigh and shake her head to snap herself out of it. Those were the only times she faced her terminal with enthusiasm, and even then she quickly reverted to idly staring at her monitor again. The process had repeated several times already.

She was sighing again, having lost count of how many times she had, when change finally showed up. A beep and a display message informed her simultaneously of a visitor's arrival. She switched the screen to the camera and saw Hattori in it. Hastily, she pressed a button or two and unlocked the door.

"I'm coming in, Nakajou... Wait, it's only you?"

"Oh, um, yes. I wanted some time alone to think," said Azusa, politely standing up and offering him a seat.

And in another display of politeness, Hattori sat down in the chair she'd offered.

"You could have just used your ID to come in. You wouldn't have needed me to unlock the door," she said airily as she moved to put on tea.

Hattori gestured that she didn't need to. "I'm not part of the student council anymore. I need to keep things separate, you know."

"That's very like you." Azusa giggled and went back to her seat. It might have come as a bit of a surprise, but Hattori was one of the very few male students she could talk with normally and informally. "Anyway, what did you need?"

"It's about the freshman representative this year."

One of the good things about Hattori was definitely that he didn't start joking about *I just came to see you* or *What, I can't come if I don't need something?*

Still, she couldn't deny that he was a little too straightforward, and lacking delicacy besides. "You mean Shippou...?"

Seeing a forced smile come to Azusa's face, Hattori knew he'd messed up. Unfortunately, it was too late. The option to stop the conversation now didn't exist in Hattori's creed anyway. "Yeah... I heard he turned down the invitation."

Azusa was well aware of how inflexible and overly serious Hattori could be. She wasn't going to get mad at him or feel hurt about it at this point. "Yeah. He says he wants to make himself better through club participation."

"Seems like it. Anyway, I thought I should explain something to you in advance." Hattori went on without stopping, thinking it would be ruder to be too considerate.

"Huh? Explain what?"

"This year the club committee, like the student council, has decided to groom an officer candidate from the freshmen. Now that I've succeeded Juumonji, it's really hitting me how much we need to do that."

"People like Juumonji only come around once in a lifetime. But I think you're doing fine..."

Hattori gave a wry grin at Azusa's attempt at comfort. No helplessness or self-loathing could be seen in his expression. She was relieved—he didn't seem to be depressed about it.

"I'm trying to keep that in mind, too. That's why we need to start right away."

Finally, Azusa realized what Hattori had come to say. "You want to put Shippou up as that candidate, don't you?"

"Yeah. It might seem to you like I'm snatching him away from the student council, but..."

"He already turned us down, so I don't feel that way," said Azusa with a smile and a wave of her hand.

"Oh. That's good." Hattori lowered his head in gratitude.

"Really, you don't have to worry about it. I had a feeling Shippou would turn us down from the start anyway... Oh, right!" Azusa clapped her hands together particularly brightly. "Since you're here, would you mind giving me your opinion on something?"

"My opinion? On what?"

Without answering Hattori's question right away, Azusa called up the data on her own monitor onto the big wall display.

"Data on the new students?"

It was detailed information on the freshmen, including their grades by subject on the entrance exams.

"Shippou got away from us, but I still think we should get one of the new students into the student council."

"And you were worried about who to invite in his place?"

It was exactly what Tatsuya and the others had been discussing at Einebrise. It was clearly a waste for them to be worrying about the same thing in different places, but only if you looked at the two events with a bird's-eye view. This sort of redundancy happened all over the world all the time.

"Mm-hmm. I kind of feel like they're all really talented..." said Azusa, seeming at a loss.

"Do you need to think about it that much?" asked Hattori, cutting her musing down swiftly. "If the top student turned you down, go to the next one. The second highest this year—let's see, it's..."

But when the sorting changed to show names in grade order, Hattori suddenly trailed off with a grimace.

"I guess Saegusa's younger sister would work... Hattori, what's wrong? You don't look very good."

"No, it's nothing. I think that's the best option, too," answered Hattori, standing up, quickly bowing to say goodbye, and leaving the student council room.

"I wonder what was wrong..." murmured Azusa as she watched him go. The reason behind Hattori's grimace was still unclear to her.

April 10, 2096. It was lunch break on what was, for the freshmen, the third day of school.

Tatsuya sat facing Kasumi and Izumi in the student council room. He wasn't up against them alone—he was sitting in as a member of the student council.

For him, the situation induced déjà vu. He'd been called to this room the previous spring, also on the third day of school. He hadn't been the only one invited, of course, nor had he been the guest of honor. He'd merely been an extra for Miyuki. And then, by some mistake, he'd been stamped with the official title of disciplinary committee member.

Ever since then, his high school life had been forced to deviate massively from his plans. If he hadn't come to this room that day, maybe he would have been enjoying a *peaceful* high school experience. At least that was what he thought—though whether he could have gotten anyone else to agree with him was doubtful.

At the time, Mayumi had been the one to invite Tatsuya and Miyuki here. And now, it fell to Tatsuya to ask Mayumi's sisters to be on the student council. Maybe this was fate, thought Tatsuya, a little off track.

"Then which one of us do you suggest to be a student council member?"

Izumi's remark, touching on the main topic, pulled Tatsuya back to the scene. As always, Kasumi was glaring at him as though she intended to start barking. That was why he'd been fleeing from reality.

"To be able to do the same work as Miyuki... It's like a dream."

And with Izumi putting a hand to her cheek and giving an entranced sigh, Miyuki had on an impenetrably friendly smile. He couldn't tell what she was thinking or feeling. Kasumi had her enmity on full display, and Izumi her desires. Even Azusa, Isori, and Honoka seemed entirely absorbed in the twins' strange behavior. As a result, it fell to Tatsuya and Miyuki, the objects of that enmity and those desires, to negotiate with them.

"If you both want to, we're okay with you both coming."

Tatsuya felt like something was wrong with him being the negotiator when he was a target, but he couldn't let his sister bear the brunt of this assault alone, which was why he'd returned to the table to begin with.

"I have no intent to join the student council."

But his efforts succeeded only in drawing a brusque reaction from Kasumi. The strength of her rejection toward Tatsuya was expressed in her polite choice of words. Maybe her politeness was what she used in public, and the opposite had been an accidental glimpse at her true self when she'd been in a frenzy.

"Kasumi, you've been very rude to Shiba this whole time." Even Izumi found her sister's clear sharpness inexcusable, and warned Kasumi harshly. She didn't do it in a soft voice, possibly out of an attempt to create an alibi for herself with the others present.

Meanwhile, Azusa, Isori, and Honoka couldn't hide their surprise at how Miyuki wasn't saying anything. Her fraternal love for Tatsuya, which bordered on worship, normally rewarded malice toward him with a burning (freezer-burning?) wrath. And yet the way she looked at Kasumi made it seem like she found it *heartwarming*. That made the three of them feel more afraid than suspicious. It was the calm before the storm.

Of course, they were thinking about it too hard. Miyuki was sensitive to malice directed at Tatsuya, and she instinctively realized that Kasumi's attitude was not one of contempt but of jealousy and caution. She was empathetic to Kasumi's feelings, sensitive to the fact that it was her love for her sister driving her to hostile behavior with a man getting close to her. Kasumi, who had little chance of being friendly with her brother in the future, was an adorable underclassman Miyuki could manage with relief.

"Oh. That's a shame." In that sense, it *was* a shame for Miyuki that Kasumi had turned down the student council. "Will you join the student council then, Izumi?"

But without letting on about those feelings even a bit, and without giving so much as a hint of her true desire to respectfully avoid Izumi, Miyuki delivered her question brightly.

"Gladly!"

And her perfectly ladylike smile didn't even falter when Izumi gazed at her with ever-increasing feverishness.

After school and after spending some time in the library, Kasumi went by herself to the café. There was still about half an hour until she had to meet back up with Izumi, who had gone to the student council room right away. It was a somewhat long time to wait on her own. Izumi had told her it was okay if she went home if she got tired of waiting, and as she was idly wondering what she'd do...

"What's the matter? You don't seem to be well."

...a voice suddenly addressed her. She looked up and saw a young faculty member in a pantsuit.

"Ah, no, I don't feel sick or anything like that," answered Kasumi, implying she'd rather not be bothered right now. But the only thing that made it past her lips was a voice more unsteady than she'd intended, which surprised her.

The female staff member smiled as though she'd seen through to Kasumi's worries. She took a seat opposite her without asking permission. The one-sided behavior got on Kasumi's nerves a little, but considering the totally harmless way the woman was smiling, Kasumi quickly stopped caring about that.

"I'm a counselor here at First High. My name is Haruka Ono."

"I'm Kasumi Saegusa, a freshman."

Haruka had taken careful aim at the moment the annoyance left

Kasumi's expression to introduce herself, so Kasumi had returned the greeting without time to think.

"If I recall correctly, you are in Class 1-C, right?"

"I am, but..." Once the first move was made, Kasumi had fallen completely into step with Haruka.

"I'm not assigned to 1-C, but if you're worried about something, I can give you an ear."

"I'm not exactly *worried*, but..."

Without time to feel any psychological resistance, Kasumi honestly explained that she had more time than she knew what to do with since her sister had joined the student council.

"I see. That must feel rather complicated for you," said Haruka quietly after listening to her story with a serious look.

What about it is complicated? thought Kasumi, but Haruka continued before she could ask.

"Would you be interested in the disciplinary committee, Saegusa?"

For Kasumi, that proposal was abrupt and completely unexpected. She found herself unable to react immediately.

Haruka peered into Kasumi's eyes and smiled sweetly. "Do you know much about the disciplinary committee system at First High?"

This time, the question had a simple yes-or-no answer. "Yes...I've heard from my older sister." Even Kasumi, still not free of her surprise, could answer it.

"Good. That will make things quick."

Haruka didn't ask who her older sister was. The last name Saegusa was unusual and famous, so she probably didn't have to ask anyway—and besides, she'd known who Kasumi was before asking for an introduction.

"There's actually an extra faculty recommendation spot open," she explained. "A few things happened, so we decided to make up for the missing person by choosing one of the new students."

"And you want me? I don't want to sound rude, but is this really something I should be deciding right now without asking anyone else first?"

"If you accept the position, there wouldn't be anyone who would complain." Now that Kasumi had returned to normal and asked the obvious question, Haruka smiled a little to brush it away. "I think you would do just as well as Shiba did last year."

And when that line came out, delivered in a way that seemed on the *surface* to be casual, Kasumi's eyes, after not having been very interested, changed. "By Shiba, you mean the brother?"

"Yes." For an instant, the words *got her* practically appeared on Haruka's face, but Kasumi didn't notice. "Shiba was the student council's recommendation, and he was just as conspicuous as Watanabe, the chairwoman last year. Morisaki, the faculty's recommendation, had steady and safe results himself, but I can't deny that he paled a little in comparison to Shiba. And there was an issue last year with another of the faculty-recommended members. If that keeps happening, people will start to blame the faculty, so I would be obliged if you accepted."

Haruka might not have needed to talk about the second reason. As soon as Kasumi heard that Tatsuya had stood out the most, she found herself broiling with a blend of fighting spirit and competitiveness.

"I understand. If you'll allow me to join, I will." She was so enthusiastic that flames might have gone up behind her at any moment.

"…Thank you. I'll contact the committee chairwoman. She should contact you tomorrow."

Having known there was trouble around the time of the entrance ceremony, Haruka had used levers to manipulate Kasumi. But when the effects were so far beyond what she'd expected, she had to question what on earth had *really* happened.

[7]

There was the unexpected accident of the new student representative turning down an offer to join the student council, but without any other major upheavals, First High entered its club recruitment week. (The second-year members all pretended not to hear Azusa when she muttered, "It sure is peaceful this year...")

But every year, troubles large and small (though maybe not so many of the small ones) sprang up during club recruitment week; there was no way it was going to end peacefully this year. On its second day, Friday, April 13, Azusa's prayer that things would end without anything going wrong was dashed like an ephemeral dream.

That day, like the previous one, Tatsuya and Miyuki waited on standby in the club committee headquarters after school. This way, if any trouble happened during club recruitment activities, they could immediately go in and use force.

Last year it had been Mayumi and Hattori in this position, but with the student council's irregular dual-vice-president setup this year, their both being away from the student council room seemed like it would create a poorly balanced formation. Still, not a soul had any doubts about Miyuki's magic power, and Tatsuya's abilities had been proven by his real-world exploits (and in real combat) far beyond what he scored on practical testing. Whatever someone's true feelings on it were, nobody would oppose the siblings' moving over to the active team as a pair.

The executive group, which was the club committee's peacekeeping team, also waited in that room. Before Hattori assumed the chairman position, the executive group had been a system that dispatched people here from other clubs when the need arose, but now that he was in charge it had been changed to a permanent system and its scope expanded. Their lineup was stationed at headquarters and rotated regularly, with each group comprising two boys and two girls, so it boasted the largest active force in school, even beyond what the disciplinary committee had. One couldn't deny that Hattori was lacking in the charisma department compared to the previous chairman, Katsuto, but as an organizational manager, he was, at least for the moment, showing more skill than his predecessor.

The executive members packed into the HQ yesterday had all been students Tatsuya didn't have any connections with, including the second-years. At most, he knew their names and faces. Today, though, an upperclassman was present whom he was a little more than passingly familiar with.

"I still don't get it, though. I almost caused an incident that got me expelled last year, and now I'm on the side dealing out punishment?"

"You're saying that about *yourself*?"

"Kirihara, please, don't say anything you don't need to... What would we do if someone took that the wrong way?"

Tatsuya's reaction was one of mild shock at most, but Hattori's was quite overblown: He put his elbows on the desk, rubbed his temples, and heaved a sigh.

"It'll be fine. Nobody else is listening."

Right now, only Hattori, Kirihara, Tatsuya, and Miyuki were in the club committee HQ room. There were another four executive members assigned for today, but two of them had gone to check to make sure nobody was overusing their allotted time in the small gymnasiums, while the other two had been out patrolling from the start.

"Whoops, speak of the devil. Let's leave it at that."

But as soon as Kirihara said nobody else was around, a senior female executive member returned from a small gymnasium.

"The kendo club's demonstration should have just begun, right?" said Tatsuya, changing the topic as ordered, his eyes shifting from the back of the girl reporting on the gym's status to Hattori and over to the clock.

"Yeah. It looks like the *kenpo* club stuck to their time limit."

Kirihara said it that way because a lot of clubs went past the allotted times for their demonstrations.

"Are you not going? I feel as though you were spending more time practicing at kendo club than your own club in March."

"How do you even know that...?"

"I was a disciplinary committee member until last month. I went to watch practice from time to time."

"Wait, when...? I never even noticed." Kirihara turned a look of trepidation and caution on Tatsuya. But when he saw his transcendental expression, he immediately relaxed. He'd changed his mind—after so long, there was no point. "Yeah, I was *practicing* with the kendo club, but I never transferred into it. They've got a practice match the week after next," he said, naming a high school known nationally for being strong kendo performers. "I ended up on the roster."

"So that's why you were practicing with them."

"Basically. It was a good opportunity, so I didn't want to waste it."

Tatsuya and Kirihara had met almost in the worst of ways, but now they were friendly enough to make small talk like this. Miyuki watched over them silently, seeming happy.

But their quiet time was interrupted by the alarm on Hattori's desk going off.

The call sound had been set to an old-fashioned telephone ring;

Hattori picked up the receiver on the table. After a short discussion, he stood up and addressed Tatsuya and Miyuki.

"Shiba, other Shiba."

It was an annoying way of putting it, but he called them both that by default.

"Yes?" answered Miyuki in a calm tone. Tatsuya stood up without a word and waited for Hattori's next words.

"Trouble in the robot club's garage. Could you go break it up?" he asked, looking at Tatsuya. Which had no deep meaning behind it—he just found it easier to give orders to Tatsuya.

"Understood," answered Tatsuya, with Miyuki bowing to indicate her understanding before they both headed to the scene.

Freshman recruitment activities were limited to one week, and when that week ended, registration was restricted to the new students putting in applications of their own free will. The main reason for that was the wars between magisport-related clubs. But that certainly didn't mean that conflicts didn't arise during freshman recruitment between clubs that weren't sports related. In fact, in front of the garage the robotics research club used as a clubroom, a new student was now caught in the middle of a stare-down between the robot club and the motorcycle club.

The motorcycle club wasn't a club for riding around on motorcycles, but for building and customizing them. Originally, it had been part of the robot club. One could fairly say the two had parted ways over whether to use legs or wheels for movement. Their history led them to be on bad terms with each other daily. If one had to distinguish, the motorcycle club, which rented what used to be a former auto repair workshop close to the school, had a stronger sense of antagonism against the robot club, which used an on-campus garage.

The two clubs now had their eyes on a very conspicuous new

student with platinum-blond hair, silver eyes, and pale white skin. A short stature and charming facial features gave an impression of cuteness to everyone who saw the freshman. The *boy* had whetted the desires of junior and senior *girls* who wanted to make him their club mascot. Both of the students at the fronts of the battle formations happened to be senior women as well.

"Why don't you just give up already? Sumisu said he wanted to join the robot club."

The name of the freshman and the prize of their battle was Kento Sumisu. He was the one Tatsuya had come across who was lost before the entrance ceremony.

"Have you used those press machines so much you can't hear anymore? He didn't say anything remotely like that. We're the ones who talked to him first, so I would much appreciate you minding your own business."

"First? We're not in elementary school anymore. It looks like your outdated reciprocating engines have been shaking your brains around, too."

"Outdated?! Leave it to the forefront of the nerd community to be too infatuated with playing around with life-sized machine dolls to be reasonable."

A group of onlookers had formed, quite interested in what was, objectively speaking, a considerably ugly duel of disparagement between women. Still, the male students waiting behind the girls got riled up then, as though they'd spoken the key words.

"'Outdated'…?"

"Did she just call us nerds…?"

"Um, I'm…"

——And they disregarded the cause of all this: Kento.

The mood was on the brink of explosion. The first ones who rushed to the scene weren't part of the student council *or* the disciplinary committee—it was a pair of executive members of the club committee who had been patrolling on their own.

"Both of you, please calm down!"

The first one to intervene was Hagane Tomitsuka, junior executive member. Next to him was Takuma Shippou, an apprentice of the executive group.

Takuma, who had accepted an invitation to the club committee's executive group with an active attitude that *seemed*, at least, to be much like a freshman's, was on his first job as Tomitsuka's assistant, who was assigned to mediating disputes between clubs.

Kento, pushed by Takuma's momentum, left to the outer circle of the quarrel.

"Is that you, Kento?"

Just then, a moment later than Tomitsuka, Tatsuya and Miyuki arrived.

"Oh, Shiba!"

Kento turned around to face Tatsuya happily, despite the fact that Miyuki was standing next to him. This could be said to be an extremely unusual thing. Feeling somewhat uncomfortable at Miyuki's deeply interested stare, Tatsuya asked him, "What happened?"

At this point, Tatsuya still didn't know that the trouble in front of them had started because of Kento. He stood out, and Tatsuya had met him before; that was the only reason he'd spoken to him.

"Um, I'm, uh, really sorry!"

Even with the sudden apology, Tatsuya wasn't getting any grasp of the situation.

"I haven't decided what club to join yet, so I wanted to just go and look at some of them today, but then they told me they'd tell me more about it inside, and just as I was about to go in, all of a sudden, from behind…"

He must have been rattled. His diction was completely breaking down. As Tatsuya struggled to make heads or tails of his explanation, a new development occurred.

"I'm with the disciplinary committee!"

He turned to the other side of the conflict, to where the familiar voice had come from. Not from the robot club or the motorcycle club, each insisting loudly to the other that it was right, nor from Tomitsuka, who was raising his voice in the middle of them.

"Oh? Brother, it's Kasumi."

"Yeah…"

Tatsuya had been purposely trying not to look over there, but there wasn't much point. He didn't need Miyuki to tell him—he knew it was Kasumi who had introduced herself as a disciplinary committee member.

"Kento?" said Tatsuya, getting Kento's attention—the boy's eyes had gone wide as he turned around at Kasumi's fiery voice.

"Oh, yes, I'm sorry."

"You don't need to apologize."

Tatsuya smiled gently at Kento, who was almost pathetically tense right now. It was very much an amused smile, but Miyuki, watching from the side, found it to be nostalgic—though it didn't seem to work on the important one, Kento.

"Yes, I'm sorr—er!"

"…It's fine." Tatsuya continued before an awkward silence was upon them. "What you mean is, the motorcycle club misunderstood, and then the robot club got involved with them?"

"Umm, yes, I think…"

"I see… Well, they should be fine now."

The arguments they'd heard until now had changed to something different. A stormy debate had begun—one leaving both clubs aside. The air was uneasy, as though a magic shootout would begin at any moment. Both the robotics club and the motorcycle club members were holding their breaths, watching the source—Takuma and Kasumi confronting each other.

"Kento, you can go now. I'll talk to the clubs myself."

Feeling a psychological headache at his underclassmen for trying to start trouble when they were supposed to be stopping it, Tatsuya instructed Kento to leave.

"Okay… Thank you." Kento seemed to waver for a moment over whether it was okay to push the cleanup onto Tatsuya, but in the end, he bowed and followed the instructions.

"The club committee's executive group already responded to this. Disciplinary committee members should go somewhere else."

That remark from Takuma had been what started the debate.

For a moment, Kasumi flinched away from the overbearing objection. But when she saw his face and realized he was a freshman like her, she shot back angrily: "I thought arguments between students were the disciplinary committee's job to handle." With that, she made to stride past him.

"Hey, wait!"

Takuma reached out for Kasumi's arm as she was about to go past. But his hand never grabbed anything. Kasumi deftly sidestepped to avoid it. Takuma was taken aback by the unexpected miss, but when he saw Kasumi grinning at him arrogantly, the blood went to his head.

Of course, he wasn't simpleminded enough to let that lead to a violent act.

"Don't be stubborn," said Kasumi in a fed-up-sounding voice after swiftly moving around in front of him. "Could you *not* get in my way?"

"I told you we were handling this, Saegusa. Or do you need me to spell it out for you? *There's no place for you here.*"

"Huh… I see you know about me, Shippou." Kasumi leveled a meaningful look at Takuma. As he opened his mouth, she continued, swiftly cutting off his opportunity to speak. "I get that you want to treat me like a nuisance. But it's too bad for you—there's no rule saying a disciplinary committee member has to do what an executive member says."

The smile was thin on her face, but her eyes flashed with a defiant glint.

"Saegusa…are you picking a fight with me?"

Takuma, on the other hand, was red in the face, while his eyes alone held a colder light.

"No, not at all. I'd be willing to take *you* up on the offer, though."

"Really…? A Saegusa wants a fight with a Shippou, does she?"

Takuma casually pulled his left sleeve back, showing his bracelet-shaped CAD. The only students officially permitted to carry their CADs with them in school were student council members and disciplinary committee members—everyone else, club committee executives included, was forbidden. But during club recruitment week, the CAD-carrying restriction was lifted. The one Takuma had just flashed wasn't one whose place and method of use restricted him to competitive use—it was his own, one fit for combat.

"Yeah, and we'll beat the snot out of you no problem. You'll never think of picking a fight with the Saegusa again!"

Kasumi also pushed up her left sleeve. Wrapped a bit above her wrist was a top-of-the-line CAD of her own, which, though smaller than Takuma's and more stylish, didn't lose to it in specifications.

"Your other half isn't here—you want to do this alone?"

"What, did you want an excuse for when you lost two to one?"

Takuma and Kasumi weren't looking at anyone but each other at this point. They took no notice of the fact that the argument between the robot club and the motorcycle club that they'd tried to mediate had been suspended, nor that Kento had used the opportunity to leave in the meantime.

"Hold it right there!"

In the crowded area, filled by the robot club, the motorcycle club, and quite a few others in the peanut gallery, a male student stepped between them, having decided their clash was inevitable.

"Both of you, calm down!"

It was Tomitsuka, who had been watching in a daze, affected by the poisonous air coming off Takuma and Kasumi.

"Please don't get in the way of this."

"Just calm down, Shippou!"

"Tomitsuka, you're going to take *his* side?"

"No, I'm not! You need to calm down, too."

…Though the dangerous mood softened somewhat when Tomitsuka stepped in, the stare-down showed no signs of stopping. Thanks to that, the robot club and motorcycle club, left aside for the moment, ended up looking at each other, wondering where to lower their raised hands.

"Why don't we all go back now, everyone?"

And thus, when a voice addressed them from the side, it was as welcome—well, *convenient* anyway—as a voice from an angel.

"The student council will not make an issue of this incident. I'll talk to the disciplinary committee and executive group as well."

Tatsuya followed on Miyuki's heels, and his statement that they wouldn't make an issue of it sent the robot club back to its garage and the motorcycle club back to the tent it had been assigned for recruitment. Tatsuya and Miyuki returned to the club committee HQ as well, leaving only the peanut gallery and what its attention was on—Takuma, Kasumi, and Tomitsuka.

[8]

"…And it felt totally awful."

"I see… I'm surprised you remained calm."

It was that night, April 13, 2096. They'd been told there were guests today, so after the kids had finished dinner by themselves (though their eldest and next-eldest brothers hadn't gotten home yet), Kasumi visited her twin's room and had been griping about the after-school events ever since.

"Yeah, well. I guess it was a good thing, too, considering all the stuff I would have had to do after. But if you ask me, I wanted to knock his lights out."

Kasumi, who had been sitting on the carpet hugging a cushion, took that cushion as though it were a virtual Takuma and slammed it against the floor a few times.

"Anyway…from what you've told me, Shippou's attitude seemed to go beyond unfriendly."

"Oh, don't put a ribbon on it. He had a chip on his shoulder was what it was."

"All right, all right. Regarding his *belligerent* attitude, I find it hard to explain simply through the lens of a club committee exec being aggressive toward a disciplinary committee member."

"That's right! That's why I said he was trying to pick a fight with a

Saegusa as a Shippou," insisted Kasumi firmly, slamming the cushion again.

Izumi didn't deny it. "Leaving aside whether he did so *as a Shippou*, I also sense some personal hostility in him."

Her unexpected comment led to Kasumi blinking several times, her cushion still in its down-swung state. "You mean he has a personal grudge against us outside of the family one?"

"A grudge? Kasumi... Well, perhaps it is something along those lines." Izumi, showing confusion at Kasumi's hyperbole, nodded, then made a face like she was listening to something inside herself. "I hear the current head of the Shippou is the mild-mannered sort. Judging solely from rumors, I don't think he'll come at the Saegusa directly, but..."

At about the same time, the current head of the Saegusa, Kouichi Saegusa, was welcoming an expected guest.

"It's a pleasure to meet you. My name is Maki Sawamura."

"We've been waiting for you. I am Mayumi, eldest daughter of the family. Please—this way."

Mayumi was the one to receive her. This was no coincidence— Kouichi had ordered her to show the woman in. As she showed Maki to the visitors' dining hall, she had a hidden curiosity—or rather, a suspicion.

This woman is Maki Sawamura the actress, right? What could a celebrity want with the Ten Master Clans...?

Had a politician or businessperson visited, regardless of gender, Mayumi wouldn't have thought it was strange. Also, celebrities wanting magicians' assistance wasn't exactly commonplace, but it wasn't rare, either. The Ten Master Clans, however, were *too* powerful to be used for troubles in the entertainment world.

"Father, I've brought Ms. Sawamura."

She thought this was shady but didn't show it on her face. With the perfect attitude of a well-bred young woman welcoming a guest, she led Maki to the dining room in which her father waited.

After turning Mayumi back at the door and having the house-keeper who showed Maki to her seat leave as well, Kouichi, still seated, addressed her.

"Is this the second time we've met?"

Maki, also seated in a chair, smiled nicely. "I'm honored you remember that."

"You're very welcome. Please—before it gets cold."

Everything from appetizers to the main course had been laid out on the table. Dishes weren't being served separately because Kouichi thought of this as a secret meeting. Maki wasn't displeased with this, either.

"Thank you very much," responded Maki before taking her knife and fork in hand. Behind her word choices, carefully picked to be casual but still polite enough, her table manners were perfect.

When Kouichi saw that, it seemed to Maki that he smiled with satisfaction.

"Oh, I'm sorry," said Kouichi apologetically, though it wasn't clear how he'd interpreted the gaze—perhaps he'd misconstrued it. "I understand that wearing these glasses indoors is somewhat rude."

"No, I certainly understand the need for them."

Kouichi had been wrapped up in an international kidnapping incident targeting magicians when he was fourteen, and during a bat-tle he'd lost his right eye. Now that he was an adult and had stopped growing, he used a false one, but when he was in his teens he had been famous in magic circles as the Eyepatch Magician. Even now, he favored slightly tinted glasses that would help others feel more com-fortable with the fake eye. It was readily available information.

Once they finished the main dish while exchanging small talk, Maki straightened her posture. She'd wanted to bring up the topic in a more spontaneous manner, but Kouichi had never given her an opening during their meal.

"To tell the truth, there was something I wanted to let you know about, which was the reason for this visit today."

Just as Mayumi had finished changing into normal clothes and was taking a break, her door intercom went off.

"Big Sister, it's Izumi. May I intrude?"

"Sure. Come in."

Come in was the password. Their HAR's voice-recognition interface picked up her voice and released the lock on the door. Izumi and Kasumi both came in.

"I apologize, but there was something we wished your opinion on."

Mayumi was a little surprised by the business Izumi had come to her with. Since they'd asked for her *opinion*, this didn't have anything to do with their school studies or magical training.

"What is it?"

"Sis, do you know what kind of person the Shippou family head is?"

The first thing Mayumi thought was *Why would you want to know that?* but she quickly realized the answer.

"Kasu…"

Mayumi realized her own eyes had glossed over without having to see her sisters react.

"Wh-what?" Not only did Kasumi's voice crack—her eyes were wandering. Seeing that response, Mayumi realized her gut instinct was correct.

"You got into a fight with Shippou, didn't you?"

"How did you know?!"

Kasumi suddenly confessed (or did something like it) without trying to play dumb, when in reality, she had intended to try to lie her way out of it. Mayumi's tone had been so forceful that she'd accidentally answered honestly.

"What am I going to do with you...?"

"Please wait a moment, Big Sister," interrupted Izumi when Mayumi immediately assumed a pose like she was about to launch into a lecture. "It is true that Kasumi very nearly got into a personal bout with Shippou, but I would say that Shippou holds more of the blame for this incident than she does."

Mayumi looked at Izumi suspiciously. But Izumi's gaze was firm and steady. Mayumi heaved a sigh and her expression loosened. "All right. I believe you."

Upon hearing those words, Kasumi sighed in relief, and her tension dissolved. She glanced at Izumi, probably to signal her deepest gratitude.

"You wanted to know what kind of person the Shippou family head is, right?" Mayumi narrowed her eyes, clearly thinking about it a little. "Let's see... I haven't ever directly met him, but I think he's a dependable, careful person."

"Dependable and careful?" repeated Izumi, not getting it. *Dependable and careful* applied to so many people that it didn't even seem like a real description to her.

"Yes. He's dependable, careful, and you never know what he's really thinking. He puts together plans and makes deals, keeps risks to a minimum without getting greedy for results, and always gets to where he needs to be. That type of person."

Mayumi gave that answer fully aware of what her sister's question had meant. But it only gave her sisters more questions.

"But that seems like..."

"Yes. It would seem to be the opposite of the attitude Shippou had with you, Kasu."

"Then that means he's not scheming something for his family?"

"But whatever he *is* planning, he can only do so much as a high school student. No matter how high his magic power is, he must understand it will only take him so far."

"Maybe he has some kind of support from outside his family?"

"...Isn't that a bit of a stretch?" asked Mayumi, unable to stop herself from interjecting into her sisters' inferences as they escalated.

"...Ha-ha, I guess so."

"...Yes, we must be thinking too much about it."

That's what they said, and they smiled, but neither of them looked really convinced.

Kouichi didn't say a single word while Maki was talking. When she was finished, he took the wineglass on the table in his hand. After downing the remaining quarter-glass of ruby liquid, he set it back down, making a soft noise.

"So," he said, finally looking back at her, "you mean to say your father plans to go back on his word on his secret pact with the anti-magic advocates?"

Maki nodded, a clear yes to his slowly spoken question. "I believe that ideologically opposing magic is unrealistic, harmful propaganda. Taking such a stance will only lead to strangling oneself in the end, and I've been able to make my father understand that."

"Thank you. You seem like someone capable of rational judgment." Kouichi bowed slightly in thanks, his eyes encouraging her to continue.

"I believe magic's benefits should be treated as more valuable to society. My thoughts are that there is still room to see it put to good use in many fields—not only for military and police, but for other things, like the media and visual entertainment."

"The media aside—entertainment? That's quite a novel idea."

"Just to be sure you don't misunderstand me, I do not mean to treat magicians as display objects. I've no intent whatsoever to create a new form of magical street performance."

"Really?"

"Movie filming, more often than not, comes with danger. And there is never a time we don't worry about whether special effects or stunt artists will be able to accurately portray reality. It goes without saying for the film crew, but magic has limitless value for actors, actresses, and the support staff as well."

"...Go on," prompted Kouichi, his face one of keen interest.

"Many magicians face unfortunate treatment because they haven't reached a level where they can use magic in actual fighting—but I fully believe there are just as many places for them to display their power in the movie and news worlds."

"I see."

"I would like to ask you to allow me to scout magicians who are stuck without opportunities and give them a chance to use this precious talent of magic. In that vein, I've prepared compensation that I'm sure will meet with your approval."

Maki paused here and peered into Kouichi's face. She took a breath, *pretending* to muster her courage, then pressed her case further.

"To magicians, I'm an outsider. I haven't had the chance to become familiar with any, either. However, I would like to be good neighbors and close friends with them. That is what I'd very much like you to understand."

"Which is why you're disrupting anti-magic advocate plans?"

"It may be a drop in the ocean, but even so, I wanted to express my sincerity."

"And in exchange, you want me to approve of you scouting magicians?"

Kouichi preempted Maki's demand, but Maki didn't seem rattled. She'd planned for this level of insight from him. "I would never be shameless enough to demand you approve of it—simply giving your tacit approval would be enough."

For a short while, Kouichi looked at Maki's face, amused. "Ms. Sawamura, you seem to be someone talented not only as an actress, but as a negotiator as well."

Kouichi, of course, hadn't simply complimented her as his words would imply on the surface. Maki focused so that she wouldn't miss his true thoughts. However, there was no need to.

"You're too skilled at concealing your motives, though. A regrettable thing, I feel. Depending on the time and place, revealing your real motives can draw people to the negotiating table who otherwise wouldn't have listened."

Kouichi laid his own cards on the table easily.

"You never told a lie. But your goal in making game pieces out of magicians isn't just to produce television shows. You'd *also* like to gather them as a more direct form of strength. Am I wrong?"

Unrest shot through Maki's face. But it only lasted for the slightest of moments. Using her natural acting skills, she forced her emotions back down. "I fear I've underestimated you."

Even from where Kouichi sat, Maki seemed to be apologizing sincerely. That bonus point with him earned Maki victory.

"As long as you stay away from magicians with connections to the Saegusa, I will not interfere with you."

Maki's downcast eyes shot back up. "Really?"

Just like that, she relinquished control over her own emotions, but it didn't subtract any points with Kouichi.

"I promise it."

"Thank you so much."

Maki realized she'd won her gamble. She'd lost her deal with Kouichi Saegusa in terms of points—but she'd succeeded in removing the greatest threat to her realizing the new order of her dreams.

After sending Maki away, Kouichi returned to his quarters, and after locking the door tight, he headed for the telephone. He pressed the call button and waited ten seconds. The small display on his table came up. It was the face of the elder Kudou.

"Sensei, I apologize for calling so late."

Kouichi didn't call Retsu Kudou "Old Master" or "Your Excellency," but "Sensei," the Japanese word for *teacher*. It was an old habit from back when Kudou had taught him privately along with Miya and Maya Yotsuba.

"I don't mind. It must be important, hmm?"

"Yes. I have something incredibly important to discuss," said Kouichi, leaning over the desk a little. From the other side of the camera, it would have looked like he'd brought his face closer to speak privately. In fact, what Kouichi was about to start *was* a secret meeting—and a conspiracy.

"I just had a visit from a guest related to the mass media," he began, before explaining that USNA humanists (anti-magic advocates) were manipulating the mass media there and plotting negative campaigns against magicians. "From what I heard today, their machinations against the media have progressed very far."

"I know you—this isn't the first you learned of it. You've been doing an exhaustive investigation of these media manipulations, haven't you?" asked Kudou, not even smirking.

"You've seen through me," said Kouichi without compunction, confirming what Kudou had said.

Kudou, actually, was the one whose expression changed then. *"I suppose I'll ask you."* With tiredness creeping into his face, he asked, *"What is it you're planning?"*

"The Yotsuba are too strong. So strong that they could upset the balance of the Ten Master Clans in the near future—and even the nation itself. Do you not think so as well, Sensei?"

Kouichi's answer to Kudou's question appeared unrelated at first.

"You want to use the anti-magic movement to reduce the Yotsuba's power?"

But Kudou read between the lines perfectly. Put differently, that meant the Kudou elder nursed the same concern as Kouichi.

"There is a student at First High who is deeply involved with the

101ˢᵗ Brigade. There is a cozy relationship between the military and the high school in charge of the teenage boy. Don't you think the media and *humanitarian* politicians would find that subject to their liking?"

"Your daughters are going to First High, too, aren't they?"

"In this case, the students would be victims and nothing more."

"First High's principal is in a neutral position…and he's turned down joining your faction, yes?"

"That's right—but that's a trivial matter. What I see as important is the link between the 101ˢᵗ and the Yotsuba."

It was more than ten seconds before Kudou could respond to that. *"…So that's your aim."*

"Not all of it, but the rest is still firmly in the area of speculation. What do you think, Sensei? I believe that tolerating negative campaigns on a limited basis would also relieve some of the anti-magic movement's tides. Their target of attack is still in high school—if we play our cards right, we could even turn public opinion against the movement. I think this has numerous merits *for the Ten Master Clans.*"

"I'm in no position to authorize your plan. And I've never had that sort of authority to begin with."

"You may not have authority, but you have influence."

"…I will not oppose your plan."

"That is all I ask. Thank you very much."

Kouichi ended the call with satisfaction on his face. Kudou Retsu's expression on the screen just before it disappeared was one devoid of ambition, as befitted one his age.

[9]

Saturday night, April 14, 2096. A rare visitor had come to what was in name Tatsurou Shiba's residence, and what was in practicality Tatsuya and Miyuki's house.

"Is this where Tatsuya lives?"

Ayako smiled and nodded as her younger brother, standing in front of the gate, looked at her as if to ask why the house was so average-looking. "I can't say I don't understand why you'd feel compelled to ask that," she replied, "but this is the place."

In these siblings' minds, Tatsuya and Miyuki were very far away from the word *average*. It would be considerably fitting were they to live in an old mansion off the beaten path, or a secret laboratory surrounded by high walls. The siblings were of like mind: They *should* live in a place like that.

But Ayako had received the map data directly from Hayama. It couldn't be fake. Fumiya, still feeling unconvinced, rang the doorbell on one of the gate's pillars.

"Yes? Who might this be?"

What came back was a voice neither of them had ever heard before. The last time the Kuroba siblings had heard the Shiba siblings' voices had been January 3 of this year, when the Shibas had visited the main house to deliver New Year's greetings. Over three months had gone by, but they were certain they'd never mishear either Tatsuya's or Miyuki's voice.

"I'm Fumiya Kuroba. Would this be Tatsuya Shiba's residence?"

Still, Fumiya named himself without letting his voice get cut off unnaturally and informed the voice of what they'd come for. There was a little bit of time before the response came back—probably for someone to check to make sure Tatsuya was okay with it. They'd visited abruptly, without having given advance notice, but it seemed to Fumiya that the visit wouldn't be a failed one, as he breathed a sigh of relief.

"*Please come in.*"

The sound of a tiny motor undoing the lock on the gate went off. When it was done, Fumiya gave the gate, carved in an open-work foliage design, a push. Before he could set foot on the property, however, the front door of the house opened. The girl who appeared from within, wearing a black dress and a white apron, bowed deeply to them.

When Minami led them to the living room, Tatsuya was the only one waiting there for them.

"Fumiya, Ayako, it's been a while."

Tatsuya greeted them while seated, but Ayako didn't seem offended. She took a seat across from him—without waiting for him to offer it.

"Sis!"

Fumiya, standing alone politely, rebuked his older sister for her lack of manners, but it seemed to go in one ear and out the other.

Still, she wasn't ignoring *everything*. As soon as she sat down, she directed her gaze straight ahead, put her hands together on the lap of her skirt, and bowed courteously.

"Tatsuya, it has been a long time since we've seen you. Please, forgive us for not arranging an appointment in advance and for visiting you at such an improper time."

"That's nothing you need to worry about. You might be second cousins, but you're still relatives, and we're all in high school here. You don't have to feel the need to arrange visiting other high school–aged relatives in advance."

"I thank you for your magnanimity," said Ayako. "…Fumiya, what are you doing? Say hello to Tatsuya already."

That was a disdainful remark indeed, but Fumiya, who was a serious person in general, couldn't ignore any wrongdoings he might have committed.

"Fumiya, you can sit down. You have to loosen up, or we won't be able to talk," said Tatsuya with a smile to Fumiya, who was standing there feeling not entirely satisfied.

Prompted to sit, Fumiya seemed to manage to calm himself down, because he took a seat right next to Ayako like she'd told him to. "Tatsuya, hello again."

He lowered his head in a simple bow, but not because he felt like he needed to keep his distance with Tatsuya or because he was treating Tatsuya lightly. He was nervous in front of the second cousin he respected, whom he hadn't met in three months.

At that exact moment, Miyuki and Minami entered the living room at the same time. Miyuki was empty-handed, while Minami carried a tray with four cups of tea on it.

"Ayako, Fumiya, welcome."

Handling her mature, ankle-length flared skirt with grace, Miyuki took a seat next to her brother. She'd been wearing well-ventilated clothing before, as she always did in the privacy of their home, but she'd gone to change into an outfit she'd wear outside when the sudden guests had arrived.

"Sister Miyuki, pray forgive the intrusion."

Ayako, not wanting to be outdone, stood up first before bowing politely to her. Her classic-style dress, skirt spread out, moved in time with her fluttering, gorgeously. The sense of rivalry in his sister made Fumiya shake his head, his face implying he had a headache.

(Incidentally, his outfit was a normal male one today, and he wasn't wearing a wig, either.) Meanwhile, Tatsuya watched the two young women with warm eyes.

Once Ayako sat down again, Minami arranged the tea on the table.

"We're sorry for coming so late at night…but we have to go back to Hamamatsu tomorrow morning."

Now that Fumiya had given what appeared to be an introductory remark, the air in the room settled.

"It's not really *that* late at night."

In actuality, it was late in that they'd already finished dinner. But it wasn't so late that they felt bothered by the visit. Fumiya and Ayako were the closest in age to Tatsuya and Miyuki in their family, and among the few they knew who weren't enemies.

"Oh, I forgot to tell you. Congratulations on getting into Fourth High."

"I never had any doubts about either of you. Congratulations, Ayako, Fumiya."

After Tatsuya spoke, Miyuki smiled and offered her congratulations. It was long past the exam results—they were already a week past the entrance ceremony—but it had been three months since they'd spoken face-to-face.

"Thank you very much, Tatsuya, Sister Miyuki."

"We were actually considering going to First High, too."

Once Ayako offered her thanks, Fumiya followed up, his expression just a little too wry to be a wry grin. "Apparently it wouldn't be good for too many of us to be in one place."

"Did Aunt Maya say that?" Miyuki asked.

Ayako nodded. "The mistress did not give us those words so directly, but yes."

"Our father received instructions through Mr. Hayama, so we had to give up on that."

Her true feelings aside, Ayako's expression at least didn't make it seem like she was that hung up on the subject, but Fumiya looked like he really regretted it.

"If Aunt Maya forbade it, then that's that," said Tatsuya in a voice that sounded regretful *enough* to comfort him, then casually changed the topic. "So, what brings you to Tokyo today? I didn't think you were assigned to any jobs in the Kanto region, Fumiya."

When the word *jobs* came out of Tatsuya's mouth, Fumiya straightened up as though he'd just remembered. "Actually, there's something we needed to tell both of you," he said, glancing over at Minami, who was standing behind Miyuki and to the side.

"You don't need to worry about Minami," said Tatsuya, answering the unspoken question. "This is Minami Sakurai, Miyuki's Guardian."

Fumiya and Ayako both looked clearly surprised at the additional explanation.

"Wait, but doesn't Miyuki have—"

"Tatsuya, have you retired from being Sister Miyuki's Guardian?"

Tatsuya smiled and shook his head at Ayako's sudden leap in logic. "No, not at all. I'm sure Aunt Maya has all kinds of ideas."

"I see." Ayako leveled a meaningful stare at Minami, but Minami kept her eyes down, not showing any particular reaction. "Understood. It won't be a problem if she is here, then."

Before things got awkward, Fumiya brought the topic back on track. "Anyway," he said, "the media is currently being manipulated by anti-magic factions from outside the country."

Miyuki's eyes widened a little.

"Where are they from?" Tatsuya, in his turn, didn't look surprised at all. There was no change discernible from the outside, anyway.

"It's the USNA's humanist movement."

The humanist movement referred to partly religious demonstrations that discriminated against magicians, claiming that magic was an *unnatural* power for humans to have and that humans should live only with the *natural* powers granted by heaven, or God.

"These so-called humanists infiltrated the country some time ago—are these ones different?"

The humanist movement had spread its influence out from the East Coast of the North American continent, and there were too many sympathizers in Japan now for magicians to ignore it.

"No, I think it's mostly the same. I wonder if it means they've entered a new stage of their plans."

Tatsuya knew the "true form" of the humanist movement from a certain information source. He didn't report that here, but he wondered if the Yotsuba core had a grasp on the movement's mechanisms.

"Media campaigns to sway opinion against magicians, then?"

Of course, he couldn't ask something like that. It would be like confessing he'd been keeping information from them. He switched his focus to the problem being given to him.

"It's not only the media. Diet members from the opposition party are involved, too," said Fumiya, adding his words to Tatsuya's question. "First they criticize military magic use, claiming human rights issues for magicians. Then they create a fictional structure where magic learning institutions are hand in hand with the military, based on how forty percent of Magic University graduates belong to the military. Their third phase is to target First High, which sends the most of its graduates to Magic University, and appeal for 'liberation' of children the nation is trying to use for military purposes. That's what we have on their plans right now."

As soon as Fumiya finished his long explanation, he wet his throat with his tea. When he looked up again, Tatsuya was watching him with a proud gaze.

The Kuroba family was the branch of the Yotsuba clan that handled intelligence. Its methods for gathering information didn't stop at magical means—they ranged from wiretapping and hacking to investigations using traditional manpower. But no matter how much equipment or personnel you had, you had to master it in order to reveal the scenarios hidden at the bottom of individual events. That he'd not stopped at learning what was happening now but had even predicted their next move was proof that Fumiya *had* mastered the Kuroba family's organizational strength.

"Fumiya, I'm surprised you figured that much out. It's really something."

"Ah, no, I... Thank you, Tatsuya." Immediately, Fumiya, who had finished such a long-winded explanation without stopping at all, began to let his voice falter. Looking more closely, you would have seen that his face was reddening as well. Based solely on this, it might seem as though Fumiya's tastes lay outside the norm, but that would be a misunderstanding. He was purely happy, that was all.

"You really like Tatsuya a lot, don't you, Fumiya?"

But he still had the kind of air around him that made others want to tease him about it.

"Sis! They're going to get the wrong idea!"

"The *wrong* idea? I guess you don't like him after all."

"That wasn't how you meant it when you said *like*!"

"Hm? What did it sound like I meant?"

"Well..."

As Tatsuya, Miyuki, and Minami watched them argue, their thoughts all agreed on one thing: that they were close siblings. However, their expressions betrayed how different the rest was: Tatsuya grinned a little painfully, Miyuki watched as though it was a heartwarming scene, and Minami looked on coolly.

After a somewhat more detailed conversation on the propaganda war against First High, Fumiya and Ayako headed for a hotel in the heart of the city. They hadn't spoken of their source or how they'd gotten the intel, but they likely intended to keep those hidden. Tatsuya wasn't about to criticize it as standoffish. He'd wanted to tell them to stay over since it had gotten late, but in the end didn't, so it went both ways.

Besides, their methodology aside, he didn't have to ask about their information source—he knew. The topic of a conspiracy between

Kouichi Saegusa and Retsu Kudou had made its way into the details, after all.

Fumiya's intelligence abilities—Ayako's, actually—were doubtless incredible, and the Kuroba's organizational capacity was foremost in the Yotsuba clan. However, the Saegusa's head wasn't one to let his tail be grabbed so easily. Ayako might have managed had it been someone like Mayumi, but Kouichi Saegusa was too great an opponent for either of them right now. The information had probably come through an unknown intelligence-gathering method their aunt had.

Tatsuya thought about all this while lying on his bed, his hand resting under his head as a pillow.

It didn't feel very good to think he was being made to dance in the palm of Maya Yotsuba's hand, but he couldn't leave this alone, either. In the very near future, anywhere from weeks to a month from now, First High would come under direct attack by the media and politicians in the anti-magic movement's pockets, and he hadn't known about it. That definitely made it useful information. Feeling unsatisfied with the whole affair, he mentally searched for the right way to deal with it.

[10]

The National Magic University was where the Japan Ground Defense Force's old Nerima Base had once stood. It used the space left vacant after the Asaka Base was expanded and the Nerima Base absorbed into it—but that Nerima-Asaka merge had also been rushed because of the decision to establish a magic university in the first place.

This establishment process made the relationship between the university and the military a tight-knit one. A solid 40 percent of university alumni graduated into the military or related organizations, and though that number might seem rather biased, it wasn't unnatural considering the societal demand for magicians. Still, if one were to ask if the campus had the orderly—or one could say *rigid*—atmosphere of a military education facility, the answer would be no. The students could wear whatever clothing they wanted, for example, and even significantly gaudy or overly casual outfits would never be censured as long as they weren't utterly unsightly. And even if clothing was criticized, in most cases things ended at advice from another student. Several other factors also contributed to the university's feeling more free than magic high schools did.

Mayumi had taken all this in over the past half a month. Today, her ensemble consisted of a pastel-colored, bare-top A-line dress with a three-quarter-sleeve cardigan over it. It was a knit cardigan, with thick stitches and thin fabric, and while her skirt was long, about six inches was lace fabric through which her legs showed, covered in thin stockings. The outfit was far more revealing than high school uniforms, but nobody, neither students nor faculty, gave her any disapproving stares.

She'd just been headed to the cafeteria after being called there. The call had been from a male student, a freshman at Magic University like her. Nevertheless, she wasn't nervous or excited. The one who'd summoned her was someone she knew quite well.

When she set foot in the cafeteria, she felt dizzy for a moment. Not because there was anything physically wrong. The extremely heavy percentage of couples inside had mentally damaged her. She knew that the greater part of them weren't just fooling around but were in serious relationships, but that wasn't much comfort to the single Mayumi. She had as much desire for love as anyone else. When she saw couples who looked happy and intimate together, two thoughts skimmed across her mind: one that she was envious, and the other that she wanted them to go away. Of course, she was also similar to other people in that she'd never admit she felt like that nor try to come to terms with it.

Maybe the fact that her relationship with the person she was meeting here was about as far from a romance as it could get was amplifying that emotion. It wasn't actually *completely* different, but in a way, she and this person were *too* close, so she'd unconsciously been removing that possibility from her vision.

"Sorry for the wait, Juumonji."

As soon as Mayumi said something, the eyes in the vicinity moved toward her table. Nobody at the university would fail to know what *Juumonji* meant. But it seemed quite a few people hadn't known what he looked like—some of their faces said, *Oh, that's him?*

"No, I just got here five minutes ago."

Not only *I just got here*, but *five minutes ago*. Mayumi smiled a little—it was very like Katsuto to speak like that.

"Thanks for coming, Saegusa."

When Katsuto added that, the number of people glancing over increased. Even the students with the good sense not to look over at the name Juumonji couldn't resist reacting to the name Saegusa. Almost no students were unaware that Mayumi had enrolled at Magic University this year. Unless you lived under a rock, the news that she'd enrolled was something you couldn't ignore, regardless of gender—and it went without saying that the male students held a stronger interest.

For her part, Mayumi casually ignored the dozen or so stares on her and sat down across from Katsuto. "Don't worry about it. It's probably pretty important if you called me here, right?" She smiled a bit and peered into Katsuto's eyes. "And to a place with so many people."

Mayumi knew she was rumored by the public to be a marriage candidate for Katsuto. If you looked at their relationship on a surface level, that certainly wasn't a far-fetched flight of fancy—in fact, anyone well acquainted with magician matters would definitely believe it. And the idea existed between the Saegusa and Juumonji families, too. Right now, the Itsuwa family was taking a more zealous approach to Mayumi's marriage than the Juumonji were—the Itsuwa son and heir was currently twenty years old. However, it was for the Juumonji family to make the first move; the Saegusa family had made no concrete moves to try to marry Mayumi to Katsuto, but the rumors of her being a candidate were correct.

Mayumi had mischievously mentioned the crowded place to question whether they should be giving fodder to such societal gossip. She meant it as a joke, of course, but if asked she wouldn't be able to completely deny having it on her mind. Whatever she liked or disliked about Katsuto aside, if they *did* become candidates for marriage, even if that came second, it would get more difficult for her to think of him as a friend.

"I thought it would be better than meeting somewhere empty and it seeming suspicious."

So whenever he replied to her in what was at a glance a gentlemanly way but in actuality an obstinate way, his treatment made it seem like she was the only one worrying about their relationship and left her unsatisfied. Katsuto wore an average, casual suit and tie, looking entirely humorless, and just the fact that she could tell right away he didn't possess any romantic feelings made it worse. But she was able to think of such *peaceful* things only until she noticed the contents of the newspapers spread out at Katsuto's hands.

"...Not very agreeable, is it?" she muttered.

An array of electronic papers were set on the table, bearing titles like *The True State of Magicians in the Military*, *JGDF Drafting Young Men as Weapons*, *A Defense Force Dominated by Magicians*, and *Do Magic Officers Receive Favorable Treatment?* The tones of the articles were split into two extremes—criticism of Japan's defense forces for taking advantage of magicians at one end, and criticism for magicians being shown favoritism at the other. But they shared something: They were all critical pieces associating magicians with the military.

"Some of these pretend to speak for the rights of magicians, but what they really want is for society to expel magicians. Hypocritical articles—and I'd say they're worse than the rest. Don't you think so?"

Without responding to Mayumi's complaint, Katsuto took out his portable terminal-shaped CAD from its case on his belt and began to use it, his hand motions practiced.

Magic University didn't forbid the carrying of CADs indoors like high schools did, and magic usage itself was less restricted than elsewhere as well. Lab rooms and practice rooms only forbade especially dangerous magic, using a blacklist format, and even those unrelated to research or practice used a whitelist format to allow the usage of most spells. The soundproofing field Katsuto had just constructed was the result of one of the spells permitted inside school buildings.

"It's that important?"

Soundproofing fields were obviously used for secret conversations, but Mayumi and Katsuto didn't have a private life to not want others to hear about. Judging by the look on his face, it was clear this was not a matter that could be resolved by jokes or small talk.

"Anti-magician reporting has seen a sudden rise in the media since the start of this week," he said, displaying a filtered list of articles on his e-reader.

"I've been feeling it, too," said Mayumi seriously, gazing into Katsuto's face. "Umm, what?" His look was so serious you could call it severe, and she wanted to know why.

"Because the reason the media's tone is split like this is because they each have different sources."

"You mean there are two different factions backing the media?"

"As you know, the Juumonji don't make a specialty out of information gathering." Rather than directly answer her question, Katsuto intimated that what he was about to say was a result of what the Juumonji family had investigated. "I have no proof for what I'm about to say, but it's not completely without evidence. Will you hear me out without getting mad?"

"Sure. Let me hear it." Mayumi straightened up unconsciously, understanding that this wouldn't be a very pleasant conversation for her.

"Of the two writing tones, the ones encouraging the criticisms of the JDF are most likely the Saegusa."

"What...?!" What he'd just said, though, was over and above what she could tolerate.

"There may be other conspirators. But the Saegusa is, at least, playing a large role in it."

"There is *no* way that's right!" Mayumi pounded the table and stood up.

The people outside the soundproofing field couldn't hear her voice, but the spell didn't block light, so the sight of her shooting to her feet drew attention from the cafeteria. She withered in embarrassment at the dubious stares attacking her from all angles, then sat back down. But after she took her seat and looked up, her eyes were locked squarely on Katsuto.

"Our father may be a tactician, and he may take pleasure in shady dealings. Even I, his daughter, don't completely understand the way he thinks."

There was a flame in her eyes now, strong enough to repel the pressure of Katsuto's own expression.

"But no matter what the reason, he would never forget his duty to the Ten Master Clans. He'd never do anything that would bring disadvantage to Japan's magic world."

Katsuto caught the heat in her gaze and replied calmly. "Then Mr. Saegusa must have thought this would be a benefit for it." And with enough weight that his words echoed in the bottom of her stomach.

"Don't be absurd. All they're saying is," she said, pointing at one of the articles displayed on a tablet, "that it would be better if magicians didn't exist. Even an idiot could see their call for protecting magicians' human rights is a front. Do you really think it would fool my father? You may be a friend, Juumonji, but that's insulting, and I can't ignore it."

"I never thought to say anything that rude."

Katsuto's answer to her flaring up at him had none of the properties of an excuse. His attitude exuded confidence, and it cooled Mayumi's head a little. "Are you trying to say he's making them do this for some other goal, even though he knows their intent is to oust magicians?"

"I don't know what that might be. All I know is that it *appears* that Mr. Saegusa is manipulating the media in a way that would betray the Ten Master Clans."

Mayumi turned an even stronger glare on him.

His eyes didn't even flicker for a moment.

"...Fine. Do you have plans tonight?"

"No."

"Then would you mind coming to my house? I'll ask my father

directly whether he's doing what you're insinuating, and I want you there to witness it."

"All right. That would be a help to me, too."

The Ten Master Clans, representative of all Japan's magicians—but they weren't exactly a famed lineage going back hundreds of years. Still, normal university students didn't need to make engagements between their families in order to visit each other's houses, but the visit today was Katsuto and Mayumi together seeing the Saegusa family head, Kouichi Saegusa. As the proxy head of the Juumonji, Katsuto requested a meeting with Kouichi, and received instructions and permission to come at 8:00 PM.

Seven fifty-nine PM, Wednesday, April 18. A black-painted passenger vehicle stopped in the driveway apron at the Saegusa house's front door. The back door opened first, and out climbed a giant of a young man in a suit and tie. Objectively, he wasn't especially big—he only had a normally large physique. What made him seem giant was his overwhelming presence far beyond his youth. Katsuto Juumonji, proxy head of the Juumonji family, was an unmatched figure now that he'd graduated high school and escaped the category of secondary school student.

Welcoming him was Mayumi Saegusa, eldest daughter of the Saegusa family. In a formal dress in subdued colors, the skirt reaching down to her ankles, she bowed to Katsuto and led him inside. The time was eight o'clock on the dot.

Like that, Katsuto set foot on the Saegusa family property.

"Excellent investigative work."

Kouichi Saegusa, who had taken his meeting with Katsuto in the reception room, easily admitted he was the one instigating one side of the anti-magician media.

"Father, what do you mean?!" cried Mayumi, beside herself at her father for nodding unashamedly.

"Please calm down, Mayumi," Kouichi calmly admonished her. "What has you so excited?" He was honestly confused at his daughter's extreme reaction.

"How am I supposed to remain calm?! What you've done is a betrayal to the Ten Master Clans—no, to the entire world of magic in Japan!"

As his daughter rose from the sofa and glared at him, Kouichi remained seated to receive the glare. "It's not a betrayal. Mayumi, you misunderstand."

"Misunderstand wha—"

"Saegusa."

Mayumi tried to interrogate her father even more. But when Katsuto, who was sitting next to her, stopped her, she remembered she and her father weren't the only ones in attendance right now. Reluctantly, she closed her mouth and sat down.

"Mr. Saegusa," said Katsuto once he sensed that Mayumi had calmed down for now, turning his eyes toward Kouichi. "I do not understand what you have in mind. That's why I'd like to ask for an explanation."

Kouichi leaned forward somewhat and returned the gaze. "Is that a demand from the Juumonji family?"

"It is a *question* from the Juumonji family."

Kouichi pulled his upper body, which was leaned forward, back into his seat, then breathed a long, quiet sigh. "A question from one of the Clans to another is something I will answer honestly." Taking his cue from Katsuto, who hadn't shown even the slightest break in his calm yet, Kouichi straightened himself up. "First, I will say this so there are no misunderstandings. These campaigns you've mentioned were ones that foreign anti-magician groups have started. Not only have they simply given information to the media, they've been supporting them financially as well."

"They're financially backing the media?"

"They can give whatever reason they want—donations, advertisement—but even their own pride is up for grabs."

Kouichi answered Katsuto quietly, radiating confidence. Backroom dealings such as these were more Kouichi's field than Katsuto's. Katsuto understood that, too, which was why he didn't interject with any pointless questions. "Do you mean that your media interventions have been a measure to oppose that?"

"Katsuto, do you know the most effective way to oppose public opinion?" asked Kouichi, his tone of voice suddenly sounding like a lecturer's.

Katsuto didn't bother to respond. He knew Kouichi wasn't asking for the answer—he wanted to tell him.

"Public opinion is just that—opinions, judgments. Some suggest them, and others bear them. Opinions are the property of those who assert them, and those who assert them shoulder the responsibility for doing so."

Had Kouichi's tone changed consciously or unconsciously? The age gap between him and Katsuto—between a leader of one of the Ten Master Clans and a son of another of its leaders—based on the surface-level difference in positions, Kouichi's choice of words could actually be said to be *more* natural than a more blaming tone would have been.

"If you understand the *person* who asserts an opinion, it's easy to object to them as well. You ask them questions, smoke out the contradictions in their logic, and get them to admit their mistake. It's also possible for each person to point out the flaws in the other's opinion and come to a compromise."

That was why Katsuto didn't feel any resistance to Kouichi speaking as though he were above him.

"But it's difficult to object to *public* opinion. After all, there's no specific person to object to."

Even if Kouichi's conversation happened to be a boring one for Katsuto.

"It may be public, but it is a single opinion, so one person must have suggested it, and it must reflect someone's interests. But whoever suggested it hides in the shadows of the populace, of society, and doesn't come to the table to debate it. The media only conveys the voice of the *citizens*, activists only present the demands of the *public*, and politicians only follow the opinions of the *nation*. Even if it was clear who first suggested it and what they stood to gain or lose from their position, that person will act as the speaker of public opinion, and as the master of that opinion, does not shoulder the responsibility of bearing the brunt of the backlash."

But Katsuto couldn't help but wonder as to Kouichi's true motives for being so roundabout with him.

"Public opinion is partly based on whoever gets there first."

Perhaps the harsh viewpoint toward Kouichi showed on Katsuto's face—Kouichi exhaled and gave a slight grin, then returned his tone to polite and soft.

"Whatever public opinion gains supporters the fastest becomes justice, right then and there, and it turns into pressure against those who disagree. Even if the dissenters have the truth, even if the public opinion has childish fallacies, you can't fight it by pointing truth or fallacies out. After all, there is no one person to argue against, as it was never an argument in the first place."

"Are you trying to say the anti-magic demonstrators were faster, Father?"

Mayumi, who had been listening quietly, though with a dissatisfied look on her face, interrupted, her voice irritated.

"The seeds of anti-magic movements were scattered over a year ago. And they were scattered by those knowing we wouldn't be able to argue from our position."

Having deftly handled his daughter's tantrum before it exploded, Kouichi immediately moved his eyes back to Katsuto.

"It's not very effective to argue against public opinion. Then do you know what one *should* do to counter it, Katsuto?"

"You'd divide them."

Katsuto's answer came easily, without any thoughtfulness or arrogance. Even if it hadn't been he, this was one of the answers anyone educated to shoulder one of the Ten Master Clans would figure out naturally. It wasn't the only one, nor was it absolute. It was an answer that *might have been* correct.

"That's right." With both of them knowing it wasn't the *only* right answer, Kouichi resumed his loquaciousness. "If there is something one can agree with approximately in the leading public opinion, it won't turn into the target for a witch hunt. The differences are in the unimportant details, and those are what easily divide public opinion. Divided public opinions lose steam, and they're eventually forgotten. As long as someone doesn't keep offering that opinion."

"Wouldn't that controvert your definition of public opinion, Mr. Saegusa?" pointed out Katsuto.

Kouichi nodded, a satisfied smile on his face. "That's exactly right, Katsuto. As long as the person hides their identity, they cannot maintain a public opinion that has already lost its momentum. If they try and relight the flames of that opinion with their identity still hidden, the people will only see through it and repel it. The public is foolish in that it will fall for it once—but wise in that the same trick can't fool it again."

"Which is why you directed an anti-magician campaign with a different focus?"

"Think of it as letting out the steam, Katsuto. The have-nots will feel envy toward the haves—there's nothing we can do about that. The power called magic is no exception. One cannot suppress envy awakened, either by the whip or by the rose. The only thing to do is let them vent to a certain extent. It's faster to extinguish a flame by separating its kindling and making small fires before letting them combine into a firestorm."

Kouichi stopped talking at last. Mayumi was making a face like she wasn't convinced, but also couldn't argue.

"Better small flames than a large one. I see—that is one way of looking at it," muttered Katsuto, his words low and rumbling, before directing a penetrating stare at Kouichi. "But small fires can still take lives. If separating the kindling means the extinguishing can't keep up, those small fires won't stop at small fires—they could turn into an incident responsible for human lives."

"That idea is based on assumption."

"Respectfully, so is yours."

His gaze met Kouichi's, and after predicting that the older man wouldn't speak any further, Katsuto got up.

"Master Saegusa," he said, referring to Kouichi respectfully as someone of an equal position in the Clans Conference. "The Juumonji family hereby expresses its regrets regarding the Saegusa family's media manipulation and requests that it immediately cease its involvement in anti-magician campaigns."

"The Saegusa family hereby requests an objection in writing from the Juumonji family. I'd like to see the answer on an official objection missive."

Kouichi stood up as well, looking up casually at Katsuto for his answer.

"Understood. I shall pen one when I return home."

"I apologize for you having to take the trouble to come here today. Mayumi, Master Juumonji will be leaving now. Please show him to the door."

Katsuto bowed to Kouichi without a word, and Kouichi returned the bow in similar silence. Mayumi hastily moved in front of Katsuto as he turned on his heel and led him toward the front door.

When Mayumi returned from showing Katsuto out, her father was still in the reception room, lounging on the sofa. She scowled and marched over to him.

"What's wrong, Mayumi? Have a seat. You can talk to me."

Kouichi was the picture of luxury, his legs crossed comfortably. Without saying anything, Mayumi sat down across from him with a huff.

"I have an idea of what you'd like to say...but you can say it."

"I believe your idea is correct, Father, but I think Juumonji's opinion holds weight."

Kouichi smiled at his daughter's self-control—he could see the emotions raging within her powerful gaze, and yet she was moderating herself. He nodded. "I don't blame you for thinking that way. Both Katsuto and I were only speaking at a surface level earlier."

It sounded like he was bragging. Mayumi balled her hands into fists. "There's something else, isn't there?"

"You couldn't tell? It seemed like Katsuto realized it."

Mayumi shook her head a little, biting down in frustration and hiding her face from his sight.

"Like I thought, Katsuto is of a higher caliber than Hirofumi is."

Hirofumi was the Itsuwa family's eldest son. The Itsuwa desired an engagement between him and Mayumi; comparing him and Katsuto meant that her father had intentions along those lines as well, but fortunately, those words didn't make it to Mayumi's ears.

"Mayumi, Kudou-sensei is aware of this incident. He didn't oppose my idea."

In place of his quiet murmur, he instead dropped a bomb on his daughter's ears.

"The Old Master...?" As Kouichi wanted, Mayumi stumbled over her words, stricken with confusion, but she wasn't burying the hatchet just yet. "I don't understand how the Old Master thinks. What I do know is that it's wrong to interfere with the lives of magicians like oneself, in one's own country, for nothing."

His daughter's unexpected tenacity surprised Kouichi, but it didn't give him pause. "At most, it'll be a month. I don't plan to let this develop into a crazy situation like that, where it's interfering with people's lives."

"Even if it's just for a month, or even a week, your thoughtless slander *will* leave scars that will last a lifetime for some. Using a pen for evil can leave deeper wounds than swinging a sword... I don't think the phrase *the pen is mightier than the sword* only applies to forces of good."

The normal Mayumi would have withdrawn long ago. His daughter's attitude was uncharacteristically resolute—and suddenly Kouichi had a doubt.

"Mayumi, for whose sake, exactly, are you getting angry?"

"Hm...?"

This question, delivered on a sudden idea, dealt unexpected damage to Mayumi.

"Is it for Katsuto? Or is it for one of your underclassmen from First High?"

"No, that's not..."

Mayumi, who hadn't even cowered at the name of Retsu Kudou, cringed, now clearly rattled.

[11]

Public pressure against magicians was growing stronger as the days went by, but school was a sort of autonomous zone. It didn't have so much independence that it possessed extraterritorial rights, but it was definitely a society somewhat estranged from the rest of the world. First High's school grounds were no exception, maintaining peace and quiet for the time being. But Tatsuya was certain now that he'd heard what Fumiya had to say that this was nothing but the calm before the storm.

And sure enough, the news came through the phone lines to inform him that the storm had arrived on the evening of Thursday, April 19.

"Tatsuya, thank you very much for your warm welcome the other day despite our sudden visit."

"You're very welcome." All he'd done to warrant the term *warm welcome* was serve tea and snacks. Tatsuya realized Ayako was saying it to be diplomatic, but he didn't take her up on the back-and-forth of flattery and modesty. "What news do you have for me today?"

"Won't you ever engage in even a paltry bit of small talk, Tatsuya?"

"Maybe next time."

Ayako, wavering between two reactions—being mad or giving an amazed sigh—eventually chose to simply give up. "Well…that will do for today. This is something quite important, after all."

"I'm ready to listen."

Tatsuya's mind had been focused on this important matter since before she'd started talking. Ayako, facing down a stare strong enough to poke holes through her despite being on the other side of a screen, averted her eyes in mild embarrassment.

"A concrete schedule regarding the incident Fumiya informed you of the other day has been decided." But even an embarrassed Ayako could perform her duties properly. In this sense, she wasn't as lowbrow a girl as her appearance might suggest. "On April twenty-fifth, next Wednesday, a Diet member will be coming to observe First High."

"Is it Kanda from the Civil Rights party?"

"Yes—I'm surprised you knew."

"Well, isn't *that* surprising."

Kanda was a relatively young up-and-coming politician in the opposition party, known as a civil rights activist extremely critical of Japan's defense forces. He'd suddenly been appearing frequently in the media since the beginning of the week. And while the words and actions media outlets displayed seemed at a glance to make him an ally to magicians, it was a ploy—anyone even a little bit cautious would have understood he was actually attempting to remove magicians from the JDF.

"Indeed," said Ayako, letting out a giggle, perhaps feeling the sarcasm was warranted. "Mr. Kanda plans to barge into First High with his usual group of correspondents."

"Barge in and do what?"

"We don't know that much, unfortunately."

"Meaning they're not setting up for anything *too* big," nodded Tatsuya, convinced, not even pretending to think about Ayako's answer.

"How, exactly, did you mange to twist things into that interpretation…?"

The only people in the conversation were Tatsuya and Ayako. Miyuki wasn't beside Tatsuya, nor was Fumiya next to Ayako. Perhaps eased because nobody was watching the conversation, she made a blank, confused face, a juvenile expression suitable for her age.

"If they were planning something large scale, there's no way you wouldn't know about it, right?"

"...I'll take that as a compliment," replied Ayako, at a loss but managing to stay cool (or so she believed, at least).

"It *was* a compliment."

However, after receiving an even more serious-sounding follow-up attack, she was *actually* dumbstruck.

"Tatsuya...you're doing this on purpose, aren't you?"

"Doing what?"

"It's people like you who... No, never mind."

Ayako appeared ready to pursue the point, but presented with an ironclad poker face that perfectly hid Tatsuya's feelings, she swallowed what she had been about to say. The other reason was that she'd remembered a moment before doing so that it wasn't why she'd called him.

"As you've said, we don't believe this to be anything large scale. It will probably be one of his regular performances. But might not his entourage of journalists plan on padding it out many times over and make a song and dance of it?"

"I see. Yes, they might do that." For the first time tonight, he pretended to be deep in thought for his second cousin. But it only lasted a few seconds before he returned his gaze to Ayako, a slightly appreciative smile on his face. "Thanks for contacting me. This will be a big help."

"I very much look forward to observing your skills, Tatsuya."

Ayako returned an affected smile and, after bowing, ended the call.

On the next day, Friday, April 20, Tatsuya called Azusa and Isori to the student council room before the morning bell.

"Huh? But isn't that a major affair?!" After hearing a Diet member from the opposition party would be coming to observe, Azusa lurched to her feet, shoving out her chair, and wailed.

"...Do you really need to get that upset over it?" Kanon, stuck to Isori like usual, offered up.

"No, this is a bona fide incident, Kanon," Isori chided. "On a surface level, Mr. Kanda's opinions appear to be safeguarding magician rights. But his argument is to declare it evil that the military takes in magicians. His intent to block magicians' involvement in the military is hiding under the surface."

"Well, even *I* get that. But he's trying to target the military and the school, right? Not us." Kanon responded to Isori with a slightly miffed look; maybe she didn't like how Isori had taken Azusa and Tatsuya's side instead of hers.

"Even if it leads to us losing our freedom?" Isori asked.

Kanon looked startled. She still didn't quite get what Isori was concerned about.

"If people who want to stop the military from using magicians get into power, they would definitely prohibit magic high school students like us from choosing the Defense Academy route after graduation, and Magic University graduates from entering the armed forces. They'd probably try to restrict us from having any interest in national defense at all."

"You mean they're trying to censor the way we think?" asked Kanon, not buying it.

Isori lowered his eyelids a little and shook his head. He wasn't denying the question Kanon had voiced, but rather the one that had shown up on her face.

"Principled pacifism doesn't allow for analyzing military threats to one's country or for debating the necessity of defensive military preparedness. They try to completely wipe out any speech that seems to accept the presence of an armed force. They would even use violent methods to enforce it. They probably don't have any reason to hesitate to instate thought censorship. After all, they claim to champion magicians' human rights at the same time that they try and take away their freedom of employment."

It was an unexpectedly scathing criticism. Even Kanon, who thought she knew Isori best, was a little embarrassed. Tatsuya felt surprised, too—maybe that was natural. Did Isori have some kind of bad memories of this "principled pacifism"?

"...So we have to assume it *will* have to do with us, Kanon. And Shiba—how do you plan on dealing with it?" Perhaps sensing he'd gotten a little too excited, Isori gave an awkward, insincere smile and tried to change the topic. "I'm sure you called us because you have some ideas."

"Yes." Tatsuya turned around to glance at Miyuki. Having waited patiently behind him ever since Azusa and the rest had arrived, she now handed the e-blackboards in her hands to Azusa and Isori. Tatsuya went on the moment he saw them lower their gazes to the boards:

"They want to criticize magic high schools, saying they've turned into places for military education and that they force their students to enter the armed forces. In which case, all we need to do is show them that we see good results in magical education aside from classes aimed toward militaristic goals."

Tatsuya spoke the conclusion straight from the shoulder. Nobody vocally agreed, or argued, or even raised a question.

"Therefore, I'd like to have a somewhat showy demonstration when Mr. Kanda arrives at our school."

"...'Somewhat'?"

"...This is '*somewhat*'?"

Finally there was a reaction from Azusa and Isori. Indirect expressions of objection, given with appalled faces. But their voices couldn't quite express the appalled nuance like their faces; their tones seemed superficial.

"The preparations will be a lot of work, but the demonstration itself won't be much different from the electric discharge experiments or implosion experiments done on a daily basis. At least not on the surface."

"Maybe just at a glance, but..." Even as Azusa weakly protested, her face didn't change—she still seemed to be trying to endure Tatsuya's dry grin.

"They'll look similar on the outside, but this will mean something completely different...but I guess that's what will make it work so well. Still, Shiba—" Finally seeming to have pulled out of his shock, Isori nodded and spoke as though to himself before turning a troubled look on Tatsuya. "Can we really do this? A thermonuclear reactor with a resident gravity-controlling magic program is one of the Three Great Practical Problems of Weighting Magic."

Now that Isori asked about the core part of his plan, a slight hint of hesitation passed over Tatsuya's face.

"We can't make a real one yet."

However, that didn't reveal a lack of confidence as to the plan's practicality, but instead that he'd been wondering how he was going to answer this question.

"We can't even call it an *experimental* reactor, because it's not an actual reactor. But we can show it off in a more flashy and more easily understandable way than last year's Thesis Competition, when all we did was suggest that creating a nuclear fusion reactor was possible."

"...With a stellar reactor?" Azusa mumbled. She hadn't looked up from her e-blackboard throughout any of the conversation, and was still in that pose. "A *continuous* thermonuclear reactor with a *resident* gravity-controlling magic program. It seems like the opposite of the concept Suzune suggested of an intermittent type of nuclear reactor."

As Azusa gazed fixedly at the e-blackboard, she couldn't see either boy's face. "And the energy it can draw per unit of time is leagues more than her system... If we create your stellar reactor, Shiba, it would be possible to provide energy whether it's day or night, without receiving influence from meteorological conditions. Factories could operate electric power supply without fear, and we wouldn't have to fear a second global cooling. This demonstration is probably as good as you can get to appeal to the peaceful uses of magic."

Her mutterings, which seemed spoken to herself, broke off, and she turned her face to Tatsuya. "Was this your plan all along?"

"It's not exactly my own idea, but it is what I've been aiming for. The magic skill needed is still too high, so it's pretty far from being implemented, but if we get all the students in school together to help, we can create a working experimental reactor."

Tatsuya nodded more firmly to Azusa's question—as if to say a thermonuclear reactor with a resident gravity-controlling magic program was the very pinnacle he was striving to attain. A stellar reactor was nothing but a central piece to accomplish his real goal, but right now, he didn't intend to let them know about that.

"I see... All right."

Azusa, too, nodded in an uncharacteristically strong manner. Tatsuya hadn't told them everything, but he was sincere in his intent to realize this stellar reactor. And Azusa had nodded because she'd sensed his earnestness.

"Isori?" She turned to face Isori. "I think we should help Shiba with his plan. What do you think?"

"I'll help, too. A public experiment of a stellar reactor—I'd be more than willing to get involved, not only to deal with Mr. Kanda but as someone who wants to be a magical engineer."

Perhaps it was just the fact that Azusa had been the one to ask, but Isori, too, nodded vigorously.

During lunch break that day, Tatsuya visited Jennifer Smith in the faculty room. The rule was that if someone wanted to conduct an extracurricular experiment, they had to speak to their club adviser if it was for a club, or to their homeroom teacher if it was independent and outside club activities, and if they were a Course 2 student without a homeroom teacher, they needed to submit a request form to the main office and get the school's approval.

Jennifer suddenly frowned after seeing the list of magic to be used at the top of the application form.

"Gravity control, Coulomb repulsion control, a fourth-phase shift, a gamma-ray filter, a neutron barrier… Shiba, are you doing an experiment on a high-powered laser cannon, or…?"

"That was not my intent, ma'am."

Tatsuya answered his homeroom teacher's question with an artless, standard phrase. The situation didn't exactly call for an amusing response, but part of it was probably that he'd been too taken aback to choose anything other than a platitude that he wouldn't have to think about. He hadn't realized until Jennifer pointed it out that the combination of spells he'd placed on the list could also be used to create a laser weapon that used nuclear fusion explosions.

But Jennifer hadn't been listening to Tatsuya's answer, either, so maybe it went both ways. Her question was more of a monologue—her eyes were plastered to the form.

"This is quite the ambitious experiment…" She looked up from the e-paper with the form displayed on it and over to Tatsuya, who stood next to her. "But can you guarantee it's safe?"

"Mathematically, yes."

Tatsuya's answer may have seemed irresponsible, but Jennifer didn't rebuke him for it. One of the points of experiments was to see whether something that was possible in theory was also possible in the real world. Prohibiting an experiment because one didn't actually know whether it was safe would be, in a way, putting the cart before the horse. And she was a scientist, a person far removed from any such foolishness.

"In our school's presentation at last year's Thesis Competition, you used a proton-proton chain reaction to avoid neutron radiation exposure. You've opted to use a deuterium-deuterium reaction for this experiment—why is that?"

Of course, that didn't mean she hadn't considered the risks. Keeping risk to a mathematical minimum was something that automatically made its way into her considerations.

Needless to say, Tatsuya had thought about that, too. His answer came fluidly. "By its nature, a P-P chain reaction has conditions that are too strict to be used as an energy source. With Ichihara's experiment, we used a probability-controlling spell to induce the reaction, but given its usage as an energy reactor, one could say it's better to have as few spells injected into the system as possible. Besides, even with a P-P chain reaction, the danger of radiation exposure is small, but that doesn't mean neutrons won't emerge at all."

Jennifer folded her arms and thought his answer over. "...All right. But I can't give permission alone. I'll forward your form. We should have a decision by after school today."

"Thank you very much, ma'am. I'd also like you to treat this experiment as strictly confidential."

Tatsuya hadn't believed he'd get permission to use the radiation lab and the schoolyard immediately. After adding that final thing, he bowed to Jennifer and left.

"So did you get permission for the experiment?" Azusa asked.

They were in the student council room after school. In response to her, Tatsuya held out the application form on which was written the principal's electronic signature and message. "Conditionally, but yes, it was approved."

"What are the conditions?" Isori inquired, causing Azusa to look up from the e-paper displaying the form.

"It's an obvious thing," Tatsuya explained, "but a teacher has to oversee it. That's the condition."

"Makes sense. Which teacher will be with us?"

But at the same time Isori layered another question atop Tatsuya's response, the chime indicating a visitor rang.

"Mr. Tsuzura," Miyuki answered, checking the monitor. She turned back to Isori. "It looks like he took the trouble to come all the way here."

The one who quickly rose to her feet was Izumi. She didn't appear to be moving briskly in the slightest, but, suitably for a freshman, she headed for the door before one of her upperclassmen could respond and welcomed their guest in.

With Tsuzura's visit, the student council's activities temporarily ceased. Honoka and Izumi, who had been training in student council operations, had also stopped their work and were now at the conference table. Tsuzura took a seat where the student council president usually sat, and the student council room quickly changed into a meeting room for discussing their experiment. The one who had planned this experiment was Tatsuya, and its collaborators for the moment were limited to student council members, so it couldn't be said that meeting here in this room was without reason.

"I've looked over the experiment's procedure, and I think it's an interesting approach."

Wetting his throat with tea brought out by Pixie, Tsuzura made the first statement of the meeting.

"Shiba, how were you thinking of splitting up responsibilities?"

Splitting up responsibilities in this case referred to who would oversee what magic. The spells to be used were gravity control, Coulomb repulsion control, fourth-phase shift, a gamma-ray filter, and a neutron barrier.

"First, I was thinking of asking Mitsui to handle the gamma-ray filter."

"Me?!"

Suddenly named, Honoka raised a dumb-sounding voice. She hadn't heard about the details of the experiment at this phase, so one couldn't blame her.

"I can't think of anyone who is superior to you when it comes to magic for controlling the oscillation frequency of electromagnetic waves, Honoka. Will you do this for us?"

"I understand! I'll do my best!"

But in the end, Honoka, without asking anything important,

enthusiastically nodded at his request. Considering her feelings, this, too, was perhaps inevitable.

"The Coulomb repulsion I'll leave to Isori."

Perhaps having heard everything already, Isori nodded without a word.

"I have an idea as to a freshman who can handle the neutron barrier, so I was thinking of asking her."

At this line from Tatsuya, Izumi's expression twitched.

"A freshman? Will that be all right?"

Tsuzura probably couldn't help feeling uneasy as well. He cut in with a remark that seemed involuntary.

"Yes. She has a natural talent for anti-object barrier magic."

"Who would that be?"

"Her name is Minami Sakurai. She's my cousin."

"I see."

But upon hearing Tatsuya's explanation, Tsuzura returned his posture to his previous leaned-forward one with an eased expression. To Tatsuya, the change in his attitude seemed like it had come too easily. In all likelihood, Tsuzura's concerns hadn't been allayed because she was Tatsuya's cousin; he'd decided he could trust her because she was *Miyuki's* cousin. That was how Tatsuya interpreted it.

"I haven't decided whom to ask about the fourth-phase shift yet. And I'd like to leave the central factor, the gravity control, to my sister."

At the same time Tatsuya said that, Miyuki bowed slightly in her seat.

"I think those are all appropriate selections."

Tsuzura appeared convinced this time as well. He, of course, knew as well as anyone else that the student with the highest magic power in First High, leaving the seniors aside, was Miyuki.

"In which case, the first issue we'll need to resolve is who to ask for the fourth-phase shift spell." Saying that, Tsuzura looked over to Azusa. "Would Nakajou not work?"

In the end, the one who answered his proposal wasn't Azusa herself, but Tatsuya: "I'd like the president to keep watch over everything in balance."

"I see. Yes, that would be more appropriate."

As he withdrew his own proposal, Tsuzura's face became thoughtful again. At that point, Izumi raised her hand.

"Excuse me, but if it's all right, would we be able to undertake that particular job?"

This proposition should have been unexpected, but Tatsuya responded in a businesslike tone without letting his true feelings to the surface. "When you say *we*, do you mean both you and Kasumi?"

"Yes. We may lack strength alone, but together I'm sure we'll be able to help."

Hearing Izumi's words, of the other six in this place (Tsuzura, Azusa, Isori, Tatsuya, Miyuki, Honoka), four looked hesitant.

"...Mr. Tsuzura knowing about it aside, I hadn't thought even you, Shiba, would have been aware."

Of course, from Izumi's own perspective, it was natural for the others to be dubious about her proposal, and when it was accepted like it was natural, she couldn't help but brace herself. There was no way an upperclassman chosen as an engineer for the Nines and as a representative for the Thesis Competition wouldn't know the meaning of two people being assigned to one spell. No surprise being expressed despite that meant nothing other than that Izumi and Kasumi's skill was already known.

"Why don't we discuss that at another opportunity? Not that such an opportunity will come for sure, but..."

Tatsuya smoothly turned aside Izumi's searching gaze and projected a model diagram of the experiment onto the large screen on the wall.

"Mr. Tsuzura, Mitsui and Saegusa don't know the details of the experiment. I'd like to explain everything from the beginning for them, and also to make sure everyone knows."

Gaining Tsuzura's agreement, Tatsuya revealed the experiment's details once again to the student council members. The contents were such that Azusa, Isori, and Miyuki already knew them, but nobody in the room looked bored.

"...The stellar reactor system, from a technological standpoint, is still full of parts that aren't mature yet. But if the people here work together and function as a team, we can definitely succeed at this experiment, said to be one of the Three Great Problems. That is what I believe."

Thus wrapping things up in the end, Tatsuya got his stellar reactor off to a small start.

The practical preparation period for the stellar reactor experiment was four days long, from April 21 to April 24. Considering the time that had been needed to build the Thesis Competition's experiment equipment, the lack of time seemed hopeless. And they couldn't fully mobilize the entire student body this time, either.

Tatsuya and the others shouldn't have even known about Mr. Kanda's plans to come observe. On the face of things, this experiment needed to be something planned and executed without any connection to the opposition party member and media visiting the school. They didn't need to keep the stellar reactor experiment itself a secret, but because of the discreet nature of the reason behind it, the only people they could use for it were the student council members and those who volunteered to help.

But even from such a humble start, Tatsuya and Miyuki hadn't viewed the situation pessimistically—though they were the only ones. Like he'd told Isori, they wouldn't be creating an energy reactor as an actual structure this time; they would just show its mechanism. This experiment was fundamentally a demonstration of magic; they weren't attempting to assemble an experimental device that could actually operate, as they had been in the Thesis Competition.

Tatsuya had kept that difference firmly in mind. Miyuki, for her part, wouldn't ever take a pessimistic view of *anything* her brother was trying to do.

Preparations steadily advanced, and as their goal started to come into a more concrete, physical view, the urgency began to fade from the faces of the other members participating in the experiment. Even Kasumi, who was always making that irritated face like she was doing all this reluctantly, had applied herself to the experiment enough to rival Miyuki's own contributions. Even Chiaki Hirakawa, with a dubious attitude and always wondering how it had come to this, never stopped working. Even Tomitsuka, who had dragged Chiaki into it in an ill-informed act of benevolence—the anxiety was starting to disappear from all their faces, replaced by something like determination to see things through. Though there were outsiders mixed in—namely Kento Sumisu—the silvery-haired freshman did nothing but look at Tatsuya with a yearning gaze, appearing to exude joy from every pore just for being able to help.

And so it was that on Tuesday, April 24, the day before the real deal, one final rehearsal was held in the radiation laboratory after school. They injected a solution of 50 percent heavy water and 50 percent light water into a globular water tank, which was built with a transparent, high-durability, heat-resistant resin that could withstand great pressure.

Tsuzura had been the one to prepare all the heavy water. While it was possible to industrially produce it from normal seawater, it was still very difficult for a *mere* high school student to procure so much of it. They'd acquired it in such abundance because Tsuzura had put his own connections to full use.

"All right, let's get started. Miyuki?"

"Yes."

The first spell, to control gravity, activated.

"Kasumi, Izumi?"

"Fourth-phase shift is go."

The twin sisters spoke at the same time, executing their fourth-phase shift spell.

"Honoka, Minami?"

"The gamma-ray filter is in effect."

"Neutron barrier stabilized."

Rather than relying on their reports alone, Tatsuya checked each step of the experiment with his "eyes" as they went on.

"Miyuki?"

"Focus set."

Tatsuya called Miyuki's name one more time, and she reported that all preparations were now complete.

"Isori?"

"Starting the electromagnetic repulsion dampening."

And as the final safety valve was released, the members positioned in front of the measurement device began talking over one another as they checked the various statuses.

"Gravitational field stability level is okay." "Gamma rays within error tolerance." "Neutron rays within error tolerance." "…"

As he listened to the voices, Tatsuya watched calmly and closely the first step of his own dream.

The final rehearsal was over. Had it been a normal experiment, today would have seen its completion, as it had given them satisfactory results. However, this experiment was for a demonstration for the anti-magic activists—the real show would be tomorrow. The team members left the lab with hearts filled with anticipation.

Azusa and Isori had volunteered to clean up and close up, so the rest of the members moved to the student council room. School was about to close, but Tatsuya thought some sort of emergency call might have come. The other members were in a long line; Miyuki and Honoka were behind him, Izumi and Minami stood behind Miyuki, and Kasumi stood behind Izumi. Kasumi and Minami weren't part of the student council, but nobody was here to worry about that right now.

"Welcome back."

Shizuku was there to greet them. She wasn't a student council member, either, but like her superior (?), the disciplinary committee chairwoman, she was frequently in the room thanks to the stairs linking them directly. It was hard to imagine from her restrained appearance, but Shizuku actually had a pretty free-spirited personality. But her sense of responsibility was stronger than average, so if they ever asked her to mind the place, she'd do the job properly.

"Sorry for making you wait, Shizuku," Miyuki offered appreciatively. "Thank you."

"Nothing happened in particular." Shizuku shook her head, then turned to face her best friend. "Honoka, what's that?"

Honoka immediately grimaced and let out a short groan. As though that was enough to answer the question, Shizuku shook her head and sighed.

She stood up, then moved behind Honoka and grabbed her friend's shoulders. Honoka stood about a half head above Shizuku, but without caring about that, Shizuku turned Honoka's body in such a way that it faced Tatsuya directly. Then, after removing her hands for now, Shizuku gave a glance around, found Honoka's bag, and without asking took a small, neatly wrapped box out of it. After pressing the box into Honoka's hands, she went around behind her again and firmly pushed against her back.

Honoka, having stopped after a step and a half, looked up into Tatsuya's face from closer than before. She was positioned just a little too far away for it to seem like a romantic scene. Still, it wasn't easy for Honoka to do anything too bold with so many people watching, despite her tunnel-vision habit. What she was about to attempt was innocuous.

"Umm, Tatsuya!"

After speaking, Honoka shut her eyes tight and held out the small box in her hands.

"Today—today is your birthday, right?"

Tatsuya didn't have time to respond before Honoka continued. She spoke so quickly it seemed like she might not have even taken a breath, but it certainly wasn't difficult to understand her.

"It's not much, but I really tried hard to pick it out! Please—this is for you!"

A voice from Kasumi saying, "Are they like that?" reached Tatsuya's ears, but obviously Honoka hadn't heard it.

"Of course—gladly."

The moment Tatsuya's hands touched Honoka's present, he felt a gaze, a stabbing one. But by the time he took a quick sidelong glance behind him, the icy blade of a glare had vanished without a trace.

"Thank you."

"Y-you're welcome. Umm, please don't unwrap it until you're alone, if that's okay."

"Hm? Yeah, got it."

Tatsuya nodded, his face a little mystified. Honoka let out a big breath. She looked so exhausted she might collapse at any moment, but thankfully she just staggered a bit. Perhaps realizing from her expression full of accomplishment that she couldn't do any more than this, Shizuku walked up next to her.

"Tatsuya, are you free this Sunday?"

Shizuku starting conversations abruptly was par for the course. Tatsuya was completely used to it, but he couldn't avoid feeling a moment's bafflement.

"What time?"

Of course, it only lasted an instant. He carried on the conversation without any gaps.

"Evening. Around six."

"…That should be fine."

He had a conference at FLT R & D Section 3 regarding development on a fully thought-controlled CAD on Sunday, but he had more than enough time to make it back by six. The rest of the company was one thing, but Section 3 would never drag on longer than expected and keep him there.

"It's a little late, but I want to have a birthday party at my house for you. Is that okay?"

The *Is that okay?* had three meanings packed into it: *Would you be okay with joining us? Is my house okay to have it at?* and *Is it okay that I planned you a birthday party without telling you?*

"Of course. If you're willing to throw it, I'm willing to be there."

He knew without having to ask that her proposition was an expression of goodwill and not her trying to use his birthday as an excuse for something else. He nodded without pretending to think about it, and Shizuku gave him a small nod back. Her face looked impassive, but the corners of her lips had softened just the slightest bit.

"What about you two, Miyuki and Minami?"

She immediately addressed Miyuki and Minami—maybe an unnecessary hiding of embarrassment.

"Yes, that will be fine."

"I will gladly attend."

Away from Miyuki answering cheerfully, and Minami answering reservedly, Kasumi was sizing up Tatsuya. She hadn't thought he'd be the type most women would go for, but now her assessment was wavering.

[12]

On the way home from school, after everyone split up and the three of them climbed aboard a cabinet, Miyuki started to act strangely. On the surface her behavior wasn't that abnormal. A close friend might have wondered if she was brooding about something. But in Tatsuya's eyes, she looked awfully worried. The strangeness continued, deepening more and more as they alighted from the cabinet at their stop and drew nearer to the ticket gates.

"Mi—"

"Brother, may I ask you something?"

At the exact time Tatsuya had tried to say her name, she brought her downcast head up.

"…Sure. What is it?"

Instead of immediately answering his question, Miyuki came to a stop in a spot where they wouldn't get in the way of others passing through the gates.

"You see, well… Would you mind terribly coming with me for a bit of shopping?"

"No, not at all…"

But why? Tatsuya swallowed those words. Miyuki wasn't the type to go out and enjoy shopping as entertainment on a weeknight. If she absolutely needed to purchase something, she could order it online and it would arrive the very next day. Still, this didn't seem like a good time to ask her about it directly.

"Minami, I'm sorry to ask this, but would you go ahead by yourself and get dinner ready in advance?"

"Of course, Big Sister Miyuki. Big Brother Tatsuya, please excuse me."

Without appearing worried, Minami walked briskly toward the commuter boarding location. This, too, was an attitude that invited suspicion. Though maybe not as much as Tatsuya, Minami must have realized Miyuki was acting strangely, too. If she trusted Tatsuya to be her bodyguard, Minami's attitude made a kind of sense. But he couldn't wipe away the somehow unnatural impression she gave him.

After Minami left, Tatsuya brought Miyuki to the closest café. He'd figured that whatever the case was, he'd ask what was going on first.

When she entered the shop, Miyuki seemed somehow relieved. This, too, struck Tatsuya as suspicious. She'd told him she wanted to go shopping, but now that they'd sat down in a café, her expression implied that she'd accomplished her goal. Even Tatsuya didn't understand why.

When the waitress came to take their order, Tatsuya asked for hot coffee, while Miyuki thought for a moment and then ordered black tea, not a cup but an entire pot. She didn't seem like she planned on leaving here soon. He wondered if she really just wanted to talk to him alone.

"Miyuki?" said Tatsuya, growing ever more worried, unable to wait for their drinks to arrive.

"Yes, Brother?" she answered, the same girl as usual. She smiled, as though happy he'd said her name. Her leaden mood from earlier was gone as though it had never existed.

But that didn't mean he could leave this unsettled. He decided to be straight with her. "Are you worried about something?"

"What? Oh, no. I'm all right now."

Miyuki, too, seemed at least to be aware that she'd been acting oddly. Her shaking her head quickly, hastily, made her look like she was holding on to something.

The waitress then brought their drinks to them, suspending the conversation. Miyuki opened the pot's lid and checked the tea leaves inside, closed it again, waited for a little bit, and then filled her cup with the black tea. Her movements were unnecessarily careful—or, in different terms, very slow.

Miyuki bent her neck to take a sip of the tea, then added half a spoonful of sugar to her cup and stirred it without making a sound. Twice around, thrice, four times... Once the number had exceeded twenty, even Tatsuya couldn't keep quiet. His tone somewhat reserved, he asked, "I doubt this is what it is, but is me getting a present from Honoka bothering you?"

The spoon hit the cup and made a high-pitched clacking noise. "That would be absurd. No, it's certainly nothing like that!" she denied quickly and firmly, her cheeks flushing.

"Sorry. You're right. I didn't really think it was that, so forgive me," Tatsuya apologized with an awkward look.

"No... It's not that I don't like it, or that it made me angry. I just felt like she beat me to it again... Yes, so it wasn't a complete misunderstanding. So you have no need to bow your head to me like that."

Miyuki, this time the one confused, entreated Tatsuya to raise his head. Losing out to her vehemence, he did so, but the question remained in the back of his mind. Like he'd said, he hadn't seriously thought Miyuki wasn't herself because of jealousy. The reason for her suspicious actions was still unexplained. But Tatsuya decided going any further would just make things more awkward, so he gave up on pressing the issue. Seeing his expression of incomplete combustion, Miyuki tilted her head in mild worry. When their gazes met, each with a nondescript expression, they both began to laugh without knowing who started it.

* * *

After enjoying a little under an hour's worth of window-shopping, the two of them went back home. Tatsuya hadn't asked again what Miyuki had been worried about. That wasn't to say it wasn't still on his mind, but it seemed like she'd figured it out for herself, so he'd decided he didn't need to smoke it out.

What had Miyuki been worrying about? Once he'd gotten changed in his own room, been called over the in-house line, and opened the door to the dining room, he immediately learned the answer.

The sound of poppers greeted him. A shower of colorful paper strips blocked his vision and fell to his feet.

"Happy birthday, Brother!"

Miyuki had removed the outer piece of her uniform and its tie and was now only wearing the dress. The pure-white, sleeveless one-piece perfectly matched her slender silhouette. He was used to seeing her in her school uniform daily, but with the outer piece removed, it seemed to give quite a different impression. It was as though the dress had been specifically designed for her.

Minami, waiting behind Miyuki, was wearing the same high-necked dress and apron as always. And on the table was a colorful plethora of what must have taken her a long time to make.

"So you wanted to stall me to get this ready..."

Tatsuya looked at Miyuki through narrowed eyes. She shrank back and averted her eyes.

"Well...I'm happy for the effort. Thank you."

Basically, she'd wanted to surprise him. She certainly couldn't have pulled this off until this year, since it had only ever been the two of them. He did feel like the idea was a little childish, but he didn't fail to understand that she'd done it because she loved him.

"Please take a seat, Brother. I'll bring out the cake."

When Tatsuya gave a smile, Miyuki's face lit up like a light show. She began to work eagerly. With Minami standing off to the side and looking resigned, Miyuki brought over the cake, put candles in it, placed a fork and knife in front of Tatsuya, lit the candles, and instructed Minami to sit as well before finally turning out the lights and taking her own seat.

"Blow out the candles, Brother."

Tatsuya, who had been watching over her in silence as she bustled around in her work, responded to her by blowing out all seventeen candles in one puff.

Despite this unannounced birthday party being only a small group of three, it nevertheless ended in a lively way. Tatsuya had made noise, too, doing things like clapping along to the songs, drawn in by his sister, who was in high spirits the entire time, but right now he was relaxing alone in his room.

It had been a good change of pace, too, before the demonstration coming up tomorrow. His sister was too good for him, so she must have thought about that as well, he thought. And then, suddenly, he remembered that the present he'd received from Honoka was still sitting there untouched, ribbon and all.

He took the long, slender box out of his bag. It was very heavy relative to its size; expecting some kind of mechanical device, he untied the ribbon and neatly took off the wrapping paper. What came out was a box made of unvarnished wood with a high-grade feel. When he opened the lid, he found an antique clockwork pocket watch inside. Pocket watches no longer had much value as practical accessories, but in modern times mechanical devices like this were beloved as pieces of art.

"This has to have been expensive...," he whispered to himself suddenly before turning the box over to check the manufacturer's logo.

A subtle expression came over his face. The marking on it belonged to the corporate group Shizuku's father operated. In other words, this had originally come from Shizuku.

It was made so that you could put a picture on the inside of the case, but it was empty, as he'd expected. Shizuku probably would have at least put in a photograph of Honoka there, but the girl herself had probably argued against it. He let out a smile as the scene vividly played itself out before his eyes.

A soft knocking reached his ears as he smiled to himself.

"It's Miyuki. Brother, do you have a moment?"

Her voice was just barely audible from inside the room—as soft as a whisper. For whatever reason, she seemed to not want their other housemate to hear. In consideration for that, Tatsuya opened the door quietly.

His sister was standing there, dressed up gorgeously, with a light layer of makeup on. She wore a light-pink, lace-abundant dress—a *robe décolletée* that boldly exposed her back and neckline. Her long hair was done up in a complex manner, as if to show off her alluring, pale-skinned back, without a single spot or pimple on it. The skirt, which reached her ankles, was made of several layers of thin fabric of differing lengths, and her flawless leg lines were visible through it from about halfway down her thighs. Her form was charming enough that even Tatsuya, robbed of his impulses, felt a momentary shiver.

"Brother?"

"Right, sorry. Come in."

Unintentionally, Tatsuya had been lost in admiration. Having been standing in the doorway in a daze, he regained his senses at the sound of Miyuki's bewildered voice. He shifted to one side and let his sister in.

And she hadn't come empty-handed. His sister had some sort of bottle in her right hand, two stemmed glasses in her left, and a purse hanging from her left elbow.

In place of Miyuki, who had her hands full, Tatsuya gently shut the door. With a polite thank-you, Miyuki bent her knees slightly and set the bottle on Tatsuya's desk, then arranged the glasses.

"Is this the present Honoka gave you?" she asked, eyes stopping on the pocket watch he'd left on the desk.

"Yeah."

"It has a very elegant design."

"It does."

Miyuki probably had no ulterior motives, but Tatsuya felt a hint of awkwardness anyway and put the gift, along with the box, inside his desk drawer.

"Anyway, what's all this?" he asked as he unfolded the spare seat from its wall storage and offered it to Miyuki before sitting down in front of his desk, looking at the bottle and glasses.

Miyuki moved the backless caster stool next to Tatsuya, and repositioned herself so that their knees faced each other. Bashful, she smiled. "Brother, do you remember what happened last year on April twenty-fourth…?"

"Of course I remember."

Tatsuya was dubious at a completely unrelated question being the response to his own, but realizing she wouldn't answer his unless he answered hers first, he replied truthfully.

"I had no idea what was going on when you showed up all of a sudden in a *furisode*."

He'd been surprised by her dress this time, too—but he didn't say that yet.

"Yes, that happened, too, didn't it?" Miyuki said softly, as though to herself, looking away just slightly. She'd been very serious about it then, but now that some time had passed and she looked back on it, she didn't seem able to prevent herself from feeling shy about it.

"That aside… Last year, it was…just you and I, Brother."

"Yeah."

At this point, Tatsuya had a guess as to what Miyuki wanted to say. He gave a smile full of compassion, and she returned a clear one of her own.

"The year before last, we celebrated alone as well."

"I remember."

"This year we have Minami, so we celebrated together, but…"

She paused, looking down in embarrassment. "But I still wanted…

some time together alone. Would you do me the honor of allowing me to celebrate your birthday alone for a short while...?"

Tatsuya leaned forward in his seat and reached a hand out to Miyuki's face.

His hand touched her cheek.

Miyuki's shoulders jumped.

Her face came up as his hand gently stroked her in the same direction, and their gazes met.

Miyuki's eyes moistened, and her cheeks reddened.

Abruptly, she looked away.

As though trying to prevent her brother, still touching her cheek, from sensing the heightening heat through his hand.

"Shall we raise a toast, Brother?"

"Is this champagne?"

Tatsuya obediently lowered his hand—but his gaze was still filled with her.

"Yes, but that's all right. There is almost no alcohol in it."

"All right, I'll open it."

Tatsuya took the bottle from Miyuki's hands—her fingers were trembling, as though the cork was in tight. He easily removed it without popping it and returned the bottle to his sister.

"Thank you... Here."

She poured about half a glass of champagne and set it in front of Tatsuya. After pouring some for herself in the same way, she lifted her glass in her right hand.

Tatsuya took his glass in his left and brought it to hers.

There was a clear-sounding *clink*.

"Brother...happy birthday. I'm so grateful that you are here."

"Thanks. I'm grateful that I can be your brother."

They tilted their glasses at the same time.

Incidentally, the present Miyuki had brought for him was in her purse. Inside the box was a somewhat large, circular locket pendant, its metal wrought elaborately into a motif of the moon, the stars, and the sun. Inside it was a 3D photograph of Miyuki's head and shoulders, taken with her in the dress she wore now. She'd been frustrated earlier at Honoka's beating her to the punch, but it seemed she still held the lead in ways like this.

——And Tatsuya, without comprehending his sister's intent, subsequently wondered about this situation for over an hour.

[13]

Tuesday, April 24. On the day of Tatsuya's birthday celebrations with Miyuki, Takuma Shippou had just returned from a tête-à-tête with Maki Sawamura, his ally in aiming for a new order.

The time was already 11:00 PM. He'd eaten out so that he wouldn't bother those in the house (including the servants), and he'd given advance notice of it so that they wouldn't worry about him. Most of the live-in servants would already be asleep in their chambers, so he entered the house quietly through the back door so that he wouldn't wake them up.

"Takuma?"

But as soon as he'd removed his shoes, a man slightly older than he addressed him. He'd been waiting.

"The professor is waiting in the study."

"The professor" was the head of the Shippou, Takumi Shippou. This young man before him now was his father's aide, probably ordered to wait for the son's return. *What a pain*, he thought, but he couldn't ignore it. With an "All right" to the servant, he headed for the study.

Publicly, the Shippou family business was investment advising, and they specialized in the field of weather derivatives especially. More and more agricultural work was being done in factories, diminishing the role of weather derivatives in the food industry, but on the other hand, sunlight-based energy had finally achieved the status of most-used power supply in advanced nations, and daylight prediction had now been established as a major factor in corporate earnings programs. Another reason Takumi Shippou was called *professor* was that he was acknowledged as the leading expert in annual weather forecasting in Japan.

But right now, the Takumi Shippou whom Takuma was facing was the leader of one of the Eighteen Support Clans and a magician with magical faculties rivaling those of the members of the Ten Master Clans.

"Take a seat," came the voice as soon as he entered the study.

Takuma sat down on the lounge-suite sofa, positioned apart from the imposing desk his father used, which was part of the same set.

Takumi stood up from his desk and sat directly across from his son.

"Takuma, how is school going? Are you having fun?"

He called me at a time like this to make small talk? Takuma wondered. He understood this was a preface, but his irritation won out over logic.

"Dad, I keep telling you that high school isn't a place to have fun for me."

His father looked like he wanted to sigh. "You're so obstinate. You don't need to try and look big and tough about it."

"No, you're just too carefree about it!" Takuma's irritation erupted. "The next Ten Master Clans Selection Conference is in only a *year*. At this rate, those opportunistic Saegusa will snatch away our position among the Clans again, and the Shippou will *have* to put up with being subordinate to them!"

"The Selection Conference is to choose ten families from the Twenty-Eight." A feeling of vain effort seeped through Takumi's voice in spots. "I know you understand there's really no point in being obsessed with just the Saegusa, Takuma."

This wasn't the first time Takumi had told him this. In fact, excluding days where he didn't see his son at all, he realized he'd been telling him something similar every day for the last year.

"There *is* a point." And yet Takuma had never accepted what he had to say.

"The Saegusa are only one family out of the Twenty-Eight."

"They're different." His attitude was just as stubborn today.

"Takuma!"

"They're not the same. The Saegusa are different."

Takumi let a tired sigh drift into the air. "Who on earth planted this mistaken obsession in you?"

"It doesn't matter who! Anyway, the Saegusa betrayed the three and stole the results of the seven in order to gain their current position!"

"Takuma…the Saegusa's number changed from Three to Seven before the Ten Master Clans system was put into place. By the time the Old Master put forward the new system, they were already the *seven grasses* Saegusa, not the *three branches* Saegusa. And their abilities at the time outclassed everyone else in the Twenty-Eight."

"Outclassed? But their abilities are just from stealing research from Labs Three and Seven. They were Lab Three's best and final test subjects, but they broke out. The Shippou were involved in the colony control development ever since its basic, theoretical stages—but then the Saegusa came in right before it was complete, and even though they only contributed a little bit, they took advantage of it and acted like they owned the place. It's not just the Shippou family—it's the Mitsuya, the Mikazuki, the Tanabata, and the Nanase, too! The Saegusa are making fools out of all of us! How can you possibly be okay with that?!"

"Takuma, Saegusa's magicians were test subjects just like we were," asserted Takumi bitterly, causing his outraged son to be at a loss for words for once. "Created beings, just like us. But even though they had to put up with being guinea pigs, they chose their own path, unlike the other twenty-seven—no, twenty-six. That isn't something they should be criticized for. It's something they should be *praised* for."

"…Are you saying that betrayal and clever plots are praiseworthy acts?" managed Takuma in reply.

"Aren't you trying to outwit the current Ten Master Clans, too?"

"But that's…!"

But his argument came right back to him like a boomerang that had missed its target.

As his son fell silent in frustration, Takumi exhaled slightly. "Well, fine. No matter what I say, I know it's not going to convince you."

Takuma's denunciations and Takumi's persuasions hadn't just begun today. As already mentioned, this same sort of conversation between the father and son had repeated itself dozens of times in the past. But they couldn't resist arguing about it—a paradoxical indication that their father-son bond couldn't be severed.

"I called you for something else today."

"…In the middle of the night?" said Takuma, mustering the strength to roll his eyes.

"I needed to tell you today. Look, the next time you stay out this late, let me know your plans beforehand. I would have told you right when you got back from school."

But that, too, was a self-destructive act on Takuma's part. "…Sorry."

"You don't need to apologize to me, but go say sorry to your mother. She should still be up."

Crap, thought Takuma, his eyes wandering.

His father ignored him and got to the point. "Takuma, I want you to stay home from school tomorrow."

"Dad? What are you talking about?" His dubious look wasn't affected. He was actually suspicious now.

"Mr. Kanda, a Diet member from the opposition party, is visiting First High tomorrow to observe."

Takumi, predicting that his son would question this, revealed his reasoning without putting on airs.

"Kanda—the humanist, anti-magician activist?"

"Yes. Along with his entourage of reporters."

"Why?" asked Takuma, but he actually did have a guess. Considering Kanda's words and actions that had been stirring up the media recently, he had a good idea of what he wanted to do by coming to First High. Takuma's question had been for confirmation alone.

"He probably wants to put on a performance to make it look like he's protecting the human rights of young boys and girls being forced to do magic."

"Human rights?!"

Takuma might have known, but he couldn't help blurting out like that. The words *He should mind his own business* were written all over his face.

"I know what you want to say, but he *is* a Diet member. We shouldn't cause problems."

Takuma's face grew irritated again at this, but in a different way from last time. "I might not like him a whole lot, but I wouldn't pick a fight with him without thinking about the consequences. I'm more grown-up than that."

"Even if *he* were to pick a fight with *you*?"

"…Of course not. I'd never get riled up that easily."

Tatsumi relaxed and leaned more deeply into the back of the sofa. "Then fine. You're adamant about this, so you get to take responsibility."

"I know that! Are we done?"

Considering how he recoiled at every word meant to warn him, anyone, not just Takumi, would have doubted that Takuma really wouldn't get riled up.

"Takuma, Master Saegusa will deal with this matter. I don't want you getting involved when you don't need to."

But Takumi's words weren't caused by his unease at his son's attitude—they'd been specifically timed.

"Saegusa?!"

As usual, Takuma gave a violent rejection.

"Don't get involved. You're responsible for what you say."

But the promise had already been made.

"The Shippou family will not interfere in this matter. Understand, Takuma? This is final."

He had no way to go back on his previous statement at this point.

"...All right, fine!"

He had no other answer available to him.

For most First High students, the guest was unplanned for, and probably to almost everyone related to First High, he was unwelcome.

Ten men and women had intruded in three pretentious black-painted vehicles.

The group included Diet member Kanda and his secretary, his entourage of journalists, and his bodyguards.

It was the middle of fourth period, the first class of the afternoon, when they suddenly asked for a meeting with the principal. Without any appointment, of course. Normally the staff might have politely declined and asked him to leave, but with his Diet member badge on, he could force the issue anyway. This was no different from how it had been in the previous century.

Yaosaka, vice principal of First High, met Kanda with a bitter look as the Diet member ignored manners and demanded a meeting.

"Mr. Kanda, as I've already explained, Principal Momoyama is on a business trip to Kyoto today and is absent. Would you be able to come back again once the principal is in?"

"Ho. You would tell me, Kanda, to come back later as if I were some child?"

"I never implied anything of the sort."

"Then you'll do just fine, Vice Principal. I would like to observe some of the classes going on at your school."

"I cannot admit you on my own authority. I will still have to directly request this of the principal."

Kanda and Yaosaka were both in their early fifties. At just a glance, Kanda would appear younger, having special makeup professionals and stylists on hand for his television appearances. But when you got up close and really looked, you would see an age-appropriate fatigue in him as well. Of the two men, one argued vehemently from his high horse, and the other, sweat forming on his brow, endured it without arguing. It was a common sight in society, but this iteration seemed somehow comedic.

Also, Kanda had known from the start the principal was away. It would be more correct to say he'd made his intrusion for that precise reason.

First High's principal, Azuma Momoyama, was currently seventy-one years old. This was his eleventh year as the school's principal. Along with his fame for great contributions to higher education curricula for magicians, on the flip side, he was also criticized for leaving the discriminatory treatment of Course 2 alone, and even having provoked the emotional antagonism between the two courses. Of course, the only voices accusing him of such provocation were those of backbiters. Azuma Momoyama was an authority in not only magic education but higher education in general, and he had widespread contacts in both worlds. He was someone even Diet member Kanda wouldn't want to take on directly.

Kanda had aimed for when Momoyama would be absent, wanting to make his performance a success, and Yaosaka wanted to stop the media from gathering info using the principal's absence as a shield. Their quarrel continued, time drifting onward with Kanda's position of superiority never changing. If they ran out of time like this, the result would be just what Vice Principal Yaosaka was planning for. From Kanda's point of view, he would have won the battle, but lost the war. Just as he began to grow impatient and tried to force his way through, a bell whose sound was modeled after a carillon's began to blare through the principal's office.

At the same time the sudden bell rang, the wall-mounted display projecting a famous Impressionist landscape painting blacked out. Immediately, the screen switched over to a clear, real-time video feed.

"Principal?! Is the conference over?"

The one who appeared on the screen of the videophone that could forcibly be switched to a receiving state from the sender's end was Principal Momoyama, who was supposedly in a conference at the Magic Association.

"I had them make a little time," he answered shortly to the vice principal's question.

His eyes swiveled to Kanda. The way the cameras fitted at the four corners of the display calculated positional relationships created for the viewer the illusion that the person on the other end was physically present. Receiving Momoyama's gaze *directly*, Kanda shifted uncomfortably.

"And you, Mr. Kanda. What might you be here for?"

Momoyama, in the computer screen, wore his pure-white hair tied back into a knot, and the lower section of his face too was covered by a completely white beard and mustache. The area around his eyes that wasn't covered by the beard was buried in deep wrinkles, through which one couldn't pick out subtle facial expressions. Nevertheless, the piercing light coming from within his sunken eye cavities unmistakably displayed anger at the rude visitation.

Kanda's reply was a withdrawn one, a complete change from when he'd been talking to Yaosaka. "Oh, well. I do apologize for having intruded without clearing my plans with you first—"

"If you understand that, then might I ask you to come back another day?" interrupted Momoyama, keeping the end of his sentence steady as he made his demand: that Kanda go home and come back later.

As he was the one responsible for the entire school, the principal's request that Kanda come when he was present was certainly logical. Kanda almost accepted out of reflex, but when one of his journalist entourage whispered, "Mr. Kanda, Mr. Kanda!" to him in haste, he barely managed to hold out on the edge of the ring.

"I would heartily agree with what you're saying, but there's an idea on my mind as well."

"Is there?"

Momoyama urged him on with a harsh stare. Despite being separated by a screen, Kanda was clearly on the defensive, but his tongue continued its wily motions.

"As of late, there have been disquieting rumors circulating society regarding the curriculum at magic high schools. They wonder if the nine schools are brainwashing their students into becoming soldiers."

"That's absurd," spat Momoyama, displeasure plain to see.

He was First High's principal, and not in a position to speak for all nine schools, but the curriculum he'd formulated for magic high schools was being used at the other eight as well. He took great pride as an educator in the magician-fostering programs he'd created.

"Have you not seen the breakdown for advancement for students at our school, Mr. Kanda? Last year, for example, sixty percent of our graduates went on to Magic University. Less than ten percent advanced to the Academy of Defense."

Momoyama counterattacked by presenting clear-cut numbers. But Kanda gave a hint of a smile to the argument, as though he'd been waiting for it.

"But when you look at National Magic University's graduation paths from last year, forty-five percent now work in the armed forces or related organizations. If you tally up the students who went straight to the Academy of Defense out of high school, you can see that a majority of students who have studied at a magic high school are now working with the military."

Kanda's *got you* look barely even made Momoyama budge. *"And those were paths chosen by the students themselves. They're fully fledged adults by their final year of university. What effect would purposely trying to sway their decisions even have?"*

"Perhaps." For some reason, Kanda nodded deeply to Momoyama's reasoned argument. "I think you're right about that, Principal. And that is precisely why I arrived at the conclusion that I'd like to observe the classes—in order to wipe out the irresponsible impression people have that magic high schools are an agent organization of the JDF."

Between the lines, Kanda was implying that he'd then spread whatever image *he* wanted regarding magic high schools. Momoyama was a masterful man, and saw right through his thinly veiled intent.

"It isn't so easy. Classes where magic is practiced are delicate ones. If you were to suddenly barge in, you would throw the students into confusion."

"I would never be a nuisance."

At this point, Kanda's attitude had turned into a high-handed one. He'd regained his pace—or rather, was growing stubborn, unable to let himself lose to Momoyama in an argument.

"...If you insist, then I will allow it."

After *pretending* to think for a moment, Momoyama turned around and said *that*. As Yaosaka looked on, a look of surprise mixed with doubt on his face, Momoyama continued preemptively.

"However, you may only observe fifth period."

"I— No, that would be fine."

The condition was unexpected, and Kanda almost raised an objection out of reflex. But he'd just told the principal he wouldn't be a nuisance. He couldn't object now.

"Vice Principal, which classes have an experiment planned for fifth period?"

Pretending not to notice Kanda's mental conflict, Momoyama posed a question to Yaosaka.

The blend of surprise and doubt within Yaosaka changed to be only 10 percent doubt. He didn't need to ask—Momoyama was fully aware of all classes for all grade levels at all times.

"There are no classes planning an experiment in fifth period."

Nevertheless, in his position, he had to answer the question now, not make a suggestion of his own. He answered exactly what he'd been asked.

"However, while it isn't part of the regular curriculum, students from 2-E plan on conducting an extracurricular experiment, which they've put in for, in the schoolyard."

"There you have it, Mr. Kanda. I believe it would be a good idea to come back another day after all."

"But that's—at least allow me to observe the rest of fourth period!"

If he rearranged his schedule to come back at a later date, it would allow Momoyama time to shore up his defenses. The principal had friendly relations with even the top echelons of the Civil Rights party Kanda belonged to. He'd barged in as a surprise attack out of fear of Momoyama's influence, and if he had to regroup, he'd lose that advantage.

Standing his ground was a calculated move, but he'd already given his word.

"Mr. Kanda, microphones and cameras during practice would ruin the students' concentration. At worst, that could mean a student experiences a magic failure and suffers irreparable damage. I don't think you wish for that to happen, either."

Kanda was, after all, not knowledgeable when it came to magic. He had no grounds on which to reject Momoyama's words. His pretext was that he was for the students—he couldn't force his way in now that he'd been told it could bring the students' future to naught.

"…All right," he said, frustrated. "Could you let me at least observe this extracurricular experiment, then?"

"I suppose. Vice Principal, call Mrs. Smith and have her show Mr. Kanda where it is, please."

Without seeming especially proud of the victory, Principal Momoyama gave Vice Principal Yaosaka those instructions and hung up.

Fifth period began, and as they were led to the in-preparation radiation lab by Jennifer, one of Kanda's group of journalists spoke to him in a hushed tone.

"Doesn't this seem strange, sir?"

"What?"

What came back from Kanda was a clearly angered, irritated voice, but the journalist continued nevertheless. "The fact that there's no practice going on. It's almost like they knew we'd be coming."

"No…it was a coincidence. They couldn't have known about what we were doing. We never even reported it to the party, after all."

"I'm just saying all this has been a little off since the beginning. Usually just planning to do any magic-related reporting gets inter-ference about this or that, but for once nobody's come to us to say anything."

Kanda was about to argue that it only made sense, but instead he fell silent. Nobody from the Magic Association had interfered with this little performance because someone had pulled some strings in its upper echelons. They'd kept their name a secret, but Kanda had a decent guess as to who it had been. When he thought about it again, however, there was indeed something about it that didn't sit well with him.

Kanda was acting as an anti-magic activist, but that didn't mean he considered magicians inhuman creatures. He truly acknowledged the benefits of magic. He was simply preaching anti-magic sentiments as a political talking point *in front of the press*. To put it in more blunt terms, he was attacking magicians to please the masses. Whoever had manipulated things behind the scenes to prevent interference into today's news coverage (which was what they were calling this political propaganda) would have known that, so he'd figured they were giving tacit approval of his play to the crowds so as to not let a politician who *actually* loathed magicians rise to power.

But was that alone enough to excuse his anti-magic performance? Sure, the person he had in mind might have wanted to take advantage of his carefully calculated political plans. Still, there was no guarantee *all* the Ten Master Clans thought that way, and this person wasn't an absolute ruler among them anyway.

As he was mulling things over, leaving the journalists to their unease, the party arrived at the radiation laboratory.

After entering the radiation laboratory, Kanda's group just stood there, feeling unfriendly gazes on them. The students who had been preparing for the experiment had turned icy stares on them as though they'd known they were coming. But it only lasted for a short moment before they refocused on their work as if they had never noticed the politician and his troupe of journalists, leaving both Kanda and the reporters wondering whether those stares had been an illusion or not.

"Mrs. Smith, who is this?"

The only one who addressed them—the only one who displayed clear interest in them—was Tsuzura, the teacher overseeing the students' work.

"This is Mr. Kanda and his journalists. They've come to our school to observe."

"An esteemed Diet member is one thing, but why does he have all these journalists with him? They should have needed permission to do news coverage inside a school. I haven't heard a word of any such thing."

Hit by an unexpectedly strong stare from someone who appeared at first to be a gentle, scholarly man, Kanda very nearly winced.

"The principal gave them permission."

Thankfully, he didn't need to reply to Tsuzura. Jennifer answered his doubts instead.

"I thought the principal was on a business trip."

"He made time, apparently, and called here."

"I see."

Tsuzura seemed easily convinced by the scant explanation, and Kanda and his reporters found themselves taken aback. But convincing himself that this would make his job easier than if Tsuzura had been hostile toward them for no reason, Kanda turned to the teacher. "Please pardon the intrusion during class."

"Actually, this isn't my class."

But suddenly, his start was spoiled. He heard someone snort softly, but when he looked over, all the students were continuing their work with serious looks on their faces, so he couldn't tell who had laughed. Suppressing the unfocused anger with willpower, he tried talking to Tsuzura again.

"This is extracurricular, right? What is all this, exactly?"

"The students are conducting an independent experiment not in the curriculum."

Tsuzura's answer was one of feigned ignorance. (At least that was how Kanda felt.) The politician had to take a deep breath to keep his irritation inside.

"What kind of experiment are they trying to do?"

That question came from one of the journalists. Tsuzura directed a stinging gaze at the reporter, probably because the man hadn't introduced himself. But neither an answer to the journalist's question nor an inquiry as to the journalist's identity were carried out in this place.

"Mr. Tsuzura, we're finished getting ready. May we start the experimental device?"

Isori, the de facto leader of this experiment, addressed Tsuzura, and the conversation between the journalist and Tsuzura was cut short.

"…Yes, go ahead."

When Tsuzura gave permission after scanning the checklist Isori had sent him on his A4-sized information terminal, a support member of the robot club flipped a switch on the wall as though he'd been waiting for this moment.

Kanda managed to keep his face straight, but his journalists' eyes ballooned almost comically.

The radiation laboratory wall silently began to open.

It was just a passage to bring in large equipment, but the way part of the wall in a windowless laboratory opened up made the place seem somehow like a secret base.

Of course, the only ones who felt that way were the outsiders. The students, used to this gimmick, didn't wait for the wall to open all the way before they began to push in a spherical water container two meters across filled halfway with a mixture of heavy water and light water (the other half was filled with water vapor) and the stand it was on. To be fair, the stand's casters had motors on them, so they didn't have to use strength to move it so much as just guide its direction. The students filed into the courtyard, and Tsuzura followed after them.

"We should go as well," said Jennifer. Diet member Kanda and the journalists hastily followed after her.

"Come to think of it, why are they conducting an experiment that isn't part of a regular class during class time? Does this happen often?"

"No," answered Tsuzura indifferently to the question from a journalist who had caught up to him. Still, even he seemed to think that one word was too unkind, so he soon gave additional information. "We originally planned to do this experiment after school. But when the staff learned about it, a lot of them wanted the students they were in charge of to observe it as well, so we stopped all practice during this hour so that the students who wished to could freely come and watch. That's why we're doing the experiment in the schoolyard."

"A student proposed this experiment, right?" asked another journalist, mystified.

"Well, this experiment has a lot of academic significance and practical significance both."

"When you say practical, do you mean this will relate to weapons development that can bag entire enemy fleets at once like that secret weapon used for the Scorching Halloween?" asked one of the journalists with a snide grin.

Tsuzura turned a cold gaze on him. "This experiment is to challenge one of the Three Great Practical Problems of Weighting Magic," he replied, walking over to the students gathered around the spherical water tank.

When the journal gathered himself and tried to interrogate Jennifer this time, she spoke first instead. "They're starting."

Perhaps because of their occupational awareness as members of the media, their attention was drawn to the experimental device fixed near the center of the schoolyard, slightly closer to the building.

The experimental stellar reactor had a simple construction—a spherical water tank placed on a stand. The pump had already been removed in the radiation laboratory. Around the water tank's equator was fitted a metal ring fifteen centimeters wide, with four support pillars. The water outlet at its uppermost point was shut with a disk thirty centimeters across, and another disk was attached to the opposite pole.

A crowd of students watched the experimental device from the windows of the school building. Most classrooms weren't getting through classes normally, and because that had been anticipated, the faculty room had suspended all practice during this hour and switched to classroom learning via terminal.

The students who couldn't be satisfied just seeing things from the windows came out into the schoolyard. Class 2-E in particular was fully present at the scene, including the students who hadn't taken part in the experiment. Aside from them, the other members of last year's Class 1-E and the female representatives of last year's Nines were all in attendance. It wasn't only students, either—there was no shortage of teachers here.

"We're starting the experiment."

The announcement over the megaphone came from Tatsuya. The

students gathered in the schoolyard stopped their conversations and fell deathly silent. As students and teachers alike waited with bated breath, Tatsuya gave the signal to begin.

"Gravity control."

Miyuki activated the gravity-control spell. A gravitational field, defined only with direction and no range limitation, emerged within the water tank, and the mixed-water solution created a hollow cavern in the middle as it stuck all around the inside of the tank.

"Fourth-phase shift."

Kasumi and Izumi activated the phase-shift spell—a dispersion-type one. The spell would move the liquid into the fourth state of matter: plasma. Deuterium plasma, hydrogen plasma, and oxygen plasma emerged from the surface of the water facing the cavern Miyuki's gravity-control spell had created.

"Neutron barrier, gamma-ray filter."

Minami inserted a neutron barrier between the two spells, the gravity-control spell and the fourth-phase shift spell. The neutron barrier was, as its name implied, a spell for creating an energy field that repelled neutrons.

On top of that, Honoka inserted a gamma-ray filter between the neutron barrier and the fourth-phase shift energy field. The gamma-ray filter was a spell that scattered gamma rays, captured their heat energy, and converted it into visible light rays.

The gamma-ray filter and neutron barrier were both classified as emission-type spells. The definition of emission-type spells included any magic that interfered with the motion and mutual action of elementary particles and composite particles. Spells that manipulated gamma rays were categorized as emission type because they interfered with photons, but in a sense, this categorization was a retroactive one. These two spells had been developed to render fission weapons harmless, and their development had been advanced with high priority at the dawn of modern magic. And because of their properties, they were often researched as a pair. Research convenience had led to the gamma-ray filter and neutron barrier being placed in the same category.

"Gravity control."

Miyuki activated a second gravity-control spell.

In the center of the spherical water tank, a high-gravity area ten centimeters across appeared. In more precise terms, it reversed the gravity vector from the first gravity-control spell, which had been pointing outside the sphere, generating a field that pointed toward the center. The gravitational force between matter was also increased.

A metal ring fit around the sphere's equator. This ring was a linked chain of sixty targeting-assistance devices used for specialized CADs. This device converted the mass and distribution state of the matter in the center of the water tank into data that magical targeting could use. The data was fed through the cables inside the pillars supporting the tank to the large fixed-type CAD in front of the operator, who was Miyuki for this experiment.

With this fixed-type CAD, which had far higher calculation power than portable-type CADs, all sixty chunks of targeting data were unified and transmitted to the caster along with an activation sequence. Thanks to this targeting assistance data, Miyuki could build a gravity-control magic program corresponding to the mass within the target region, which was changing by the second, and execute it without too much of a struggle. This, of course, was only possible because of her magic power. However, without the know-how about the consecutive influence of gravity fields gathered from the flight magic, and the precision targeting assistance system combining the sixty data chunks, even Miyuki would have found it impossible to keep the high-gravity field this stable for a prolonged period. This targeting assistance system ring was the very core of the experimental stellar reactor.

"Coulomb repulsion control."

Isori's Coulomb repulsion control spell lowered the electromagnetic repulsion force in the high-gravity region to one-ten-thousandth.

The electromagnetic forces at play between protons were multiplied by 10^{360} the force of gravity acting on the heavy hydrogen nuclei. The electromagnetic force was reduced to one-ten-thousandth and the gravity increased one hundred times, but that wouldn't be enough to induce nuclear fusion by itself. However, the kinetic energy of the heat energy (plasma) required to trigger the nuclear fusion reaction was definitely now much lower. Enough to fulfill the conditions for the reaction through a plasmification-based pressure increase.

A pale light appeared, and a silent stir ran through the observing students. The light increased in brightness, continuing to shine for one minute, then two.

The water inside the spherical tank began to boil. This experimental device drew heat based on the same general principle as a magnetically sealed thermonuclear fusion reactor. It caused accelerator neurons to collide with a moderator, then converted the neutrons' kinetic energy into heat energy. Because of this mechanism, nuclear fusion reactors of this type caused a large amount of high-speed neutrons to collide with the wall surface of the heat-gathering device, meaning a weakening of the construction materials due to neutron radiation was unavoidable. This neutron radiation embrittlement was the main bottleneck in giving a reactor a practical level of durability. This experimental device, however, used water as a moderator for the neutrons and completely surrounded the reaction source in the sphere's hollow, created by that water, which resolved the problem of needing to deliver a moderator to the neutron rays through the container itself. The mechanism was useful as a check on erosion of the wall surface as well. And the creation of this hollow water sphere was made possible by gravity-control magic.

The digital thermometer fixed to the side of the spherical tank showed that the mixed-water solution boiling in the tank had exceeded three hundred degrees Celsius. The number meant the average pressure inside the sphere had reached about a hundred atmospheres. As long as the gravity-control spell was maintained, the container would never break—but aside from the reinforcing magical effects, the actual container's pressure-resistant capacity was nearing its limit.

"The experiment is over."

Three minutes after the experiment's start, Tatsuya announced its end. The Coulomb repulsion control spell and the second gravity-control spell ceased, and the light inside the experimental container disappeared.

"Release the gamma-ray filter."

After verifying that the nuclear fusion reaction had completely stopped, the gamma-ray filter protecting against the neutron capture–induced gamma-ray emission was released.

"Release the gravity control, but keep the neutron barrier up."

The watery walls covering the inside of the container fell to the bottom with Earth's gravity.

A mechanical arm operated by the robot club attached a duct to the top of the spherical vessel. It led to a gas composition analyzer. When they opened the valve, the gas inside the vessel rushed quickly into the analyzer because of the pressure difference.

"Gas composition is water vapor, hydrogen, heavy hydrogen, and helium. No readings of any mixtures containing tritium or radioactive matter!"

A simplified version of the measurement results was announced in a shrill voice by Kento, who had taken up position in front of the analyzer. It was only simplified in that the actual ratios hadn't been calculated; uncontainable excitement rippled through the ring of observers.

"Start injecting the water, please."

Following Tatsuya's instruction, a hose was attached to the duct, and the water injection to cool down the vessel's interior began. A thick haze developed in the spherical tank, but it disappeared soon after, and the tank was filled with clear water.

"Release the neutron barrier."

He directed a grateful look at Minami, whose shoulders relaxed in relief, then directed it toward Honoka, Kasumi, Izumi, and Miyuki in turn. Lastly, he and Isori exchanged looks and nods, and Tatsuya handed the microphone to Azusa, who had been busily scanning the multiple measurement devices behind him during the experiment.

Azusa shook her head vehemently, trying to push the microphone back into his hands. But she was unable to oppose the smiling Isori or the pressure from the silently watching Tatsuya, and when she took the microphone, she looked like she was about to cry.

After several deep breaths, Azusa brought the microphone to her mouth. Her face sharply stiffened with determination—though it also looked like an expression of desperation—before she announced to all the students who were present there:

"The continuous thermonuclear fusion experiment using a resident gravity-control spell as its central technology has achieved its expected objective. The stellar reactor experiment is a success."

In the schoolyard, and in the building, a cheer went up all at once. It was a crazed one, almost violent, almost sounding like a cry to celebrate the possibilities and future of magic.

Overwhelmed by the students' cheering, Mr. Kanda, frozen in place, and his entourage of journalists only snapped out of it once the spherical tank had been returned to the radiation laboratory and the students in the schoolyard had begun to go back to their classrooms.

"What on earth *was* that?" one of the journalists asked Tsuzura and Jennifer, who were talking to each other, in a fairly incredulous voice.

"An experiment for a thermonuclear fusion reactor with a resident gravity-controlling magic program."

But with the way he'd asked, that was the only answer he'd get. The reporter, irritated, tried to raise his voice angrily. Kanda, however, was trained in the world of politics, which was filled with black-hearted individuals, and didn't lose his temper so easily.

"What sort of thing is it? I thought the idea of a practical nuclear fusion reactor had been abandoned," he asked.

"Whether or not it has—"

"It certainly hasn't—"

Tsuzura and Jennifer answered simultaneously. The two whose voices had overlapped made eye contact, and after one of them yielded, Jennifer opened her mouth to speak again.

"It certainly hasn't been abandoned. Its priority was only lowered because sunlight-based energy systems were completed first. Research using such large experimental devices was stopped because it hit financial issues, but the research itself is still continuing even in nonmagic fields."

The quiet words "Oh, really" could be heard from Tsuzura's mouth, but both Kanda and Jennifer ignored him.

"Magic-based nuclear fusion research is one part of the overarching research. Nuclear fusion systems based on electromagnetic control magic were abandoned because of the complexity, meaning those based on the relatively simple gravity-control method have been the ones researched in the world of magicology."

"Nuclear fusion research—is it to try and create magic-based nuclear fusion explosions?"

"Like the kind used during the Scorching Halloween?"

With questions with malicious intent leveled at her from two reporters one after another, Jennifer scowled.

But she wasn't able to hurl a thorn-covered argument their way.

"Ha-ha-ha-ha-ha!"

Tsuzura's arrogant laughter took the poison out of Jennifer and embarrassed the journalists.

"Nuclear fusion explosions? Forgive my rudeness, but what exactly were you watching?"

The request for forgiveness seemed a pretty bold one considering his words. It didn't take much insight to realize the connotation there was, *Are you all blind?* This man named Tsuzura seemed to be possessed not only of scholarly insolence but of a mean personality as well.

"You don't need precise spells like this if all you want to do is cause a little explosion. And you couldn't use a technique like that to cause a huge one like the one you're all talking about, either. Besides, the only large-scale nuclear fusion explosion was a report of a success case from a strategic-class spell called Synchroliner Fusion from Miguel Diez of the Brazilian military—and nobody has even come close to replicating his spell. Our school's students may be talented, but do you think something like that would be possible for them?"

The journalists' faces twisted in displeasure. They understood that he was an expert and they were nothing more than amateurs. In fact, they had no idea how difficult Synchroliner Fusion was. With someone telling them there had only been one success case in the entire world, they couldn't obstinately insist it was possible for high school students, even at an experimental level.

But that had all been par for the course. What was unexpected for them, what made them unhappy, was his looking at the journalists *as though they were civilians.* It wasn't just Tsuzura doing it, either—it was the vice principal, the principal, the female teacher here, and the students. They felt that not a soul was affording them the respect *they deserved* as the *mouthpiece of society.*

"Today's nuclear fusion experiment was about whether it could be an energy source, an infrastructure for society. There are numerous issues that we still need to work out, but if a stellar reactor was implemented, humanity would be able to use far more abundant energy than what the sunlight cycle provides."

Tsuzura's eyes as he spoke were only on Kanda. The journalists realized, willingly or not, that they weren't even part of Tsuzura's consideration.

"How did you like it, Mr. Kanda? Our students have a willingness to make peaceful contributions to society, don't they?"

"Yes…they do. I think it's admirable that they're trying to contribute to our society's prosperity."

Overwhelmed by Tsuzura's unabashed coercion—what switch could have been flipped?—Kanda agreed reluctantly.

Tsuzura, with a somewhat shameless smile, bowed to Kanda. "I appreciate that, Mr. Kanda. I've taken the liberty of recording your words just now. I'd like to use them to encourage our students—would you mind that at all?"

"Well, I—"

"I wouldn't think there would be any problem."

"Ah, no. I would be more than happy to do it for the children's sake."

Kanda gave a perfunctory nod, his eyes averted, before leaving with a simple goodbye. Not leaving the schoolyard, but leaving First High. He couldn't tolerate any more of his statements, which were so far from his actual intent, being recorded, so he'd decided to call it quits for today.

Without a portable shrine on his shoulders, he couldn't remain in the festival—he had to leave the shrine-carrying procession. The journalists, too, without a choice, wrapped up their coverage and left First High behind.

Jennifer watched the Diet member and his rabble-rousing journalists leave, and as soon as they got out of sight, she turned to Tsuzura, who was next to her. "Tsuzura-sensei," she said, using *sensei* in Japanese instead of the loanword *mister* when referring to her fellow teacher—she was completely familiar with Japanese custom, and aside from her appearance, she was no different from a pure-blooded Japanese person. "Don't you think you went too far?" she asked.

Of course, if one were to call this kind of consideration also Japanese, it would definitely exhibit a prejudice against Americans.

"Well, this is embarrassing." Tsuzura really did seem embarrassed. "When they purposely twisted the students' disposition, I couldn't help feeling ticked off."

"Their disposition…?" It wasn't that she didn't understand the word. In truth, Jennifer knew Tsuzura from their Magic University days. Jennifer was significantly older than he, but at college they'd been in the same position—research colleagues. Friendly colleagues, if one had to say one way or another.

Jennifer was dubious about what Tsuzura had said because it wasn't like him. He passed as a weirdo at First High, but that was because of his *individualistic rationalism*, which discarded everything unneeded. Normally, he'd never have acknowledged the worth of something so based in emotion as "disposition." Normally, enthusiasm and purposefulness were things to be analyzed, not admired. Jennifer knew all that, which was why she'd let the question slip out.

And Tsuzura himself was aware of it. He was feeling bashful about it because he felt that talking about "disposition" didn't suit him.

"Well, you know… From a technical standpoint, the experiment leaves a lot to be desired. There's too much reliance on individual magic ability. It went well because of the group's members. There are a whole heap of issues we need to solve before this tech can ever come into common use."

Jennifer nodded at the explanation. That had been her opinion as well.

"But they're challenging the way society is by using magic and trying to change it. I think that mind-set is worth something, regardless of technological completeness. Their disposition is to try to change what they themselves mean to society, and I just thought that was really valuable."

Eventually unable to bear the embarrassment, Tsuzura looked away and added, "I know it's out of character, but still."

[14]

Thursday, April 26. Inside a cabinet, commuting to school, Tatsuya, who had been checking the news in his usual manner with his information terminal in his hand, suddenly looked mildly surprised.

"Brother, has something in the news caught your eye?"

His change in expression was subtle, like always, but Miyuki didn't miss this one, like always.

In the seat across from Miyuki, Minami also looked up. Her emotional expressiveness was restrained, but was by no means a constant poker face. The gaze she directed toward Tatsuya indicated that she felt an interest in the question Miyuki had asked him.

"It's the experiment I had you two help me with yesterday," answered Tatsuya in a volume such that everyone could hear him, even though Minami was sitting diagonally across from him. He shifted to face his sister. "Some of the articles are friendly, and others hostile, as we expected. But what I didn't expect…was this many friendly ones."

Miyuki encouraged him to continue, asking the question with her expression.

"Diet members know which way the wind blows, but I doubt journalists from big media outlets would put up the white flag at a gimmick like this. I expected more of them to grow stubborn and write more categorical articles in spite of reality. To tell the truth, I was going to use it as a foothold to make a counterattack and manipulate public opinion my own way."

After hearing Tatsuya's *confession*, Miyuki's eyes went wide. "This may be late in coming, but...you sure have a mean streak, Brother."

Miyuki wasn't seriously criticizing him, but all Tatsuya could do in response was give her a pained grin—though Minami, on the other hand, seemed genuinely appalled.

"Like I figured, there are some fairly hysterical articles, but...," Tatsuya went on, showing his portable information terminal to Miyuki. It showed a sensationalist title more suited to a tabloid site than a big news site. "I hadn't expected this," he finished, getting rid of the article and calling up a longer column on his terminal screen.

"'A challenge from the young people to the twenty-second century'? This newspaper is doing a recurring column on what we did yesterday?" asked Miyuki, tilting her head, perhaps feeling the same dubiousness as Tatsuya. Given the title of the column series, it was a critical piece that treated this revolutionary test by the young people in a favorable way. It was fundamentally at odds with the anti-magic activists' agitations.

"Yeah. Someone from this newspaper was there yesterday, so it's not strange the person wrote an article on it. But this paper had been distributing aggressively anti-magician articles until yesterday..."

"Then your stellar reactor must have quite impressed them, right?"

Contrary to Tatsuya, who looked like it was incomprehensible, Miyuki spoke as though that were the natural way of things.

"...If the journalist was one of the ones who liked going after new stories, it's possible they felt an individual sense of sympathy. It *is* a column, so I suppose there is a chance the entire editorial department is the curious sort."

Organizations were never monolithic. As they grew larger, their tendency to break apart grew stronger, which was something Tatsuya understood—maybe on an intuitive level. Sometimes one section would do its own thing outside the aims of the company. For the moment, Tatsuya took that as convincing enough.

In actuality, the situation wasn't that simple. The previous day's experiment had certainly been part of what suddenly caused a pro-magician-leaning tone to appear within big media outlets that had been completely anti-magic until today. Several more members of the media acknowledging the newsworthiness of high school students had frustrated a Diet member's plans, but those things, of course, weren't all there was to it.

Kanda's remarks, recorded by Tsuzura, had been delivered into the hands of the Diet member himself through connections from Tsuzura's Magic University days—along with a demand that, in a roundabout way, suggested he somewhat scale back his political activities on this front. That was one major reason the reports from his journalists had been limited in page space and their videos hadn't been run.

There was a fierce complaint from Principal Momoyama to the higher-ups in the opposition party, the Civil Rights party, about putting journalists on school property without prior discussion. With that, not only Kanda, but also the other members of the anti-magic camp, were forced to curtail their activities temporarily. From a certain perspective, the principal had very skillfully taken advantage of Tatsuya's plot.

And support fire had come blasting out of the industrial world, too.

"Hey, check that out, Tatsuya. They're doing this interview again."

The cafeteria during lunch. Leo was pointing at the video news pop-ups displayed on a wall-mounted screen. Tatsuya didn't even glance in the direction his index finger was pointed, continuing to eat his food in silence.

"It's rare for the Rosen family to appear on Japanese news, isn't it, Brother?"

However, while he might have gotten away with ignoring Leo, it was impossible for him to ignore Miyuki.

"Maybe there's been some sort of major change in their policies, including people with the Rosen name coming to Japan for new positions," he replied carefully, tellingly avoiding a chance glance at Erika or Mikihiko.

The large-format display screen was split into sixteen sections, and the interview with Ernst Rosen, Japanese branch president of Rosen Magicraft, was taking up four of them. Ernst Rosen was answering the newscaster's questions using fluent Japanese.

"——*We hadn't expected high school students to be able to use such advanced magical skills. The high skill standards of Japan have surprised me.*"

"Hey, that's a compliment."

"..."

Erika had been uncharacteristically maintaining silence for a while now. In her place—well, not really—Leo talked, sounding entertained, but Tatsuya turned a deaf ear again.

"*The First High students' successful experiment showed us the possibility that magic can become a technology that will bring further prosperity to human civilization.*"

"Wow," breathed Shizuku, straightforwardly impressed, no strings attached. "'Prosperity to human civilization,' huh?"

Tatsuya once again gave an inoffensive answer: "And we all worked very hard for it."

"Yeah. Miyuki and Honoka did great."

"I-I didn't really..."

As he watched Shizuku and Honoka start their routine, Tatsuya began to feel a question—what was Rosen after, exactly?—and something approaching surprise—they'd had the good sense to respect high school students' privacy.

The variety of unexpectedly friendly media responses to the fixed-reactor experiment had the First High students at an emotional peak. Some may not have been personally involved, but the fact that students at their school were being recognized by society, even if it was only on the surface, fulfilled their collective young desires for acknowledgement.

But there were, perhaps naturally, exceptions.

It was right after the final afternoon class, fifth period, had ended. As Takuma in Class 1-A was getting ready to head out for club activities, he was attacked again by unpleasant chatter for what seemed like the hundredth time that day. His female classmates were discussing the Rosen Japanese branch president's interview and the events of the previous day. Voices were extolling the girls in other classes who had been part of the experiment. Takuma abruptly stood up. He didn't bother trying to hide his irritation. The waves of peril coming off him shut the mouths of his chattering neighbors.

His attitude stood out among those of the others in the class. Nobody from Class A had been directly involved with the previous day's experiment. Kasumi and Minami were in Class C, and Izumi was in Class B. Class A hadn't even provided any of the support members handling the electronics. But most of the students—no, all the students except him—were as excited over the high praise coming from a world-famous corporation as though it had been directed at them.

Damn it, he thought to himself, but right now, he couldn't control his emotions very well. Praise for something the Saegusa family had done—that he believed they'd done, anyway—was unendurable for him. In the end, without a word to smooth it over, he left the classroom as though escaping.

The pent-up gloominess stuck with him during club activities, too. His spells were slipshod as a result of his lack of focus, and he failed several times at things he could usually do without difficulty, which built up his frustration even more. When it was time to leave, his ire had reached its peak.

For Takuma, today had been an utterly awful day.

While he was going home from school after getting his CAD from the office, he ran straight into Kasumi, her disciplinary committee armband on, in the front yard.

Now that club recruitment week was over, the disciplinary committee had gone back to its shift system. Patrols were generally a single-person affair, and that went for new freshmen, too. Kasumi was one of them. Considering the time, she must have been about to return to headquarters. So it wasn't the least bit strange when she gave him only a passing glance and tried to walk by him without saying anything.

It was probably all due to his persecution complex...

"That was a real nice job, Saegusa."

...him thinking she'd smirked down her nose at him.

"...What are you talking about?" asked Kasumi dubiously, stopping.

But ever since two evenings ago, when his father had given him the warning, the stress had been building up. To Takuma it looked like she was feigning ignorance.

Still under misapprehensions, Takuma vented his anger on her: "That little demonstration yesterday. Incredible—you even got Rosen's branch president to pay attention."

"Demonstration? Shippou, are you misunderstanding something?"

Kasumi was by no means a mild-mannered girl. She could put on friendliness, but for all intents and purposes, she was quick to get into a fight. She wasn't underhanded, but straightforward and blunt. Even now, she wasn't trying to hide her displeasure with the malice in Takuma's words.

"Don't play dumb with me. You knew a Diet member hostile toward magicians was coming yesterday, and that's why you put it together, isn't it? Very clever how you used Shiba to steal some prestige."

"Used him? That's a weird way to accuse someone."

Kasumi's objection turned slightly evasive—Takuma's remark

that they'd known of Kanda's visit beforehand was right on the mark. But he'd decided that all his deductions were actual proof.

"That was careless. He's kind of a big deal—not just here, but at all nine magic high schools. I have to give credit to the Saegusa for your shrewdness. Did you use your looks to coax him into it, just like your older sister? After all, if nothing else, you're both first-class attention whores."

"That's *bullshit!*"

Kasumi suddenly erupted, and her countenance was fierce enough that Takuma was momentarily speechless. But she was only beside herself for that instant.

"…Coaxing him? You have some pretty classless ideas, you know that? The Saegusa never even *consider* using their looks to gain an advantage. You know, you've got a pretty cute face—maybe you should give up on being a magician and start courting older women or something. Although, the only people actively looking for young swallows these days are probably creepy celebrities."

Takuma's face, this time, grew indignant.

Kasumi's raillery about birds lacked any deep meaning. Recently there had been an incident wherein a certain veteran actress, much talked about on yellow journalism sites, had been hiring boys as prostitutes, and that had left an impression, that was all. The old term *young swallows* referred to a man who was an older woman's lover and unequal in the relationship. She didn't know its actual meaning; she'd probably just picked it up from some gossip article.

But to Takuma, it sounded like an insinuation regarding his connection to Maki Sawamura.

"…Are you picking a fight with me, Saegusa?"

"You're the one who picked it first, Shippou. Besides, didn't I already say I'd beat you down so easy you'd never think of picking a fight again?"

They stared each other down. Their right hands were both on their left sleeves. The CADs they used were bracelet types. Both of them had already stepped over the line to make this a touch-and-go situation.

"You there! What are you doing?!"

"Both of you, put your hands down!"

But at the exact moment they were about to use them, voices from behind stopped them.

A male student's voice from behind Takuma.

A female student's voice from behind Kasumi.

Takuma rolled his left sleeve up with his right hand as he turned around, and Kasumi put her right hand down before turning around.

In Takuma's vision, a familiar male upperclassman with a severe look on his face had his right hand in his left breast pocket.

Takuma judged that he was trying to take his handgun-shaped CAD from his shoulder holster.

His counterattack was a reflexive one.

His left hand touched his CAD's switch.

The upperclassman still hadn't finished taking out his CAD.

I win, thought Takuma.

Then his body was rattled front-to-back, and he was concussed. Overcome with vertigo, he dropped to his knees.

Sensing the indications of magic activation behind her, Kasumi involuntarily turned around. She knew it was a bad move considering her position, but any activation of combat-use magic, even if it wasn't aimed at her, was something she couldn't ignore.

The two who had tried to use magic were Takuma Shippou, who had just been having a standoff with her, and her senior in the disciplinary committee, Morisaki—and just as Kasumi recognized that, the spell went off.

Morisaki's came first. Its impact was considerably weakened, blocked by Takuma's Information Boost, but his spell rattled the opponent's body forward and backward, which gave it more than enough effectiveness to cut off Takuma's attack.

"Drawless..." breathed Kasumi.

She'd been hit with no small shock. Takuma had clearly had the lead in readying CADs. Specialized types excelled over multipurpose types in the speed department, but even with that difference, Takuma should have been faster in that situation. That is, if Morisaki had been following the normal procedure: draw, then take aim.

But Morisaki had taken aim with only his senses and fired his spell while his CAD was still resting in its holster. It was a high-level technique called Drawless that was used with handgun-shaped CADs. Considering these CADs had assistance features that aimed in the direction they were pointed, it was difficult to fire one without drawing it. Morisaki, though, had done it without sacrificing the quick activation time that specialized CADs boasted.

Frankly, Kasumi hadn't thought Morisaki was that great. His magic program scope and event influence strength were both only average, and though his construction speed was high, it wasn't *that* high. She'd even had doubts as to why he'd been chosen as a disciplinary committee member with his level of skill, but now, she admitted honestly to herself that she hadn't been seeing the important part.

He was the same as always—she couldn't feel any more than average magic power from him. She was surprised. Upperclassmen could pull off stunts like this without having to rely on inborn magic power.

Looks like I'll have to keep on getting better, she thought, mentally making an enthusiastic fist.

"Kasumi."

But when her name was spoken by a relatively monotonous voice from behind, she popped up straight. "Kitayama...?"

As she turned around awkwardly, she saw Shizuku staring at her with a grimace on her face.

Escorted to the disciplinary committee headquarters by Morisaki and Shizuku, Kasumi and Takuma got a taste of what it probably felt like to rest on a bed of nails. The ones present right now were

Kanon, chairwoman of the disciplinary committee; the two who had brought them there (Shizuku wasn't on shift; she'd just happened to be passing by and gotten dragged into it); Hattori, chairman of the club committee; Tomitsuka, representing the executives; and Tatsuya, representing the student council for whatever reason.

"Kasumi, you're a disciplinary committee member. What were you doing? And you were on patrol, too..."

Kanon breathed a heavy sigh, and Kasumi looked away awkwardly.

"Shippou, I know you're aware that unpermitted magic usage is against school rules. Using it to pick a fight is a serious offense on its own, but to attack a committee member who came to stop you?"

Tomitsuka's laments caused Takuma to stiffen in place and lock his eyes dead ahead.

"In any case, I think learning the situation comes first," said Hattori.

Kanon nodded unhappily, looking down. "Seriously... Just when you think club recruitment week is over, we get even more trouble..." She impolitely scratched her head and set a sharp glare on Kasumi and Takuma. "I'll say this first. Kasumi, your offense stops at *attempted*. You won't be expelled, but you could be suspended. Shippou, you may not have been able to do anything, either, but you *were* starting to use your CAD, which means that in the worst case, you could be expelled."

Takuma took Kanon's declaration without moving a muscle. He was straining every part of his body not to start shaking.

"I want you to keep that in mind while you explain what on earth caused this."

Kanon's eyes went to Kasumi.

"Shippou insulted the Saegusa family."

Kanon's gaze shifted to Takuma.

"I was the target of an unforgivable insult from Saegusa."

Kasumi and Takuma knew better than to look at one another.

Kanon sighed. "Hattori, how do you think we should handle this?"

Hattori opened his closed eyes. "Shippou is part of the club committee. I'm not confident I can pass fair judgment."

"Yeah, but Kasumi is part of the disciplinary committee, too."

"Then we'll have a third party, one who isn't a member of either committee—the student council—decide."

As Kanon and Hattori looked at him, Tatsuya inwardly heaved a sigh. Things had turned out exactly as he'd expected them to. He'd only been sent here as student council representative because Azusa had sensed all the trouble and run away. Isori, too, had smiled and said that the student council president's proxy was the vice president, and then run away. There was a second vice president, but he couldn't exactly force this on his little sister, so Tatsuya had come ready to pull some chestnuts out of the fire. He'd been mentally prepared to deal with a troubling situation since the moment he'd entered the room.

"Can we not just have them fight in a match?"

Hattori's eyebrow twitched.

"Wait, you mean you're letting them off the hook?" asked Kanon dubiously.

Hattori didn't say anything, though. Tatsuya had an idea of what he was feeling right now, but that wasn't something worth talking about.

"If they can't solve their problems through talking, they can solve it through ability. The previous disciplinary committee chairwoman has said that's the recommended way at our school."

Tomitsuka was clearly surprised at Tatsuya's remark. But Kanon and Hattori's expressions implied they thought it was reasonable. Shizuku, for her part, was looking elsewhere sleepily, as though hoping this would be over soon.

"Unpermitted usage of magic is a serious offense, but I don't think we need to punish the ones who were stopped before they even did it. It happens a lot with freshmen anyway."

This time, Morisaki turned his face away, expression bitter. Fortunately, there was nobody here to drive *that* point home.

"If pride is on the line for both of them, I think letting their abilities do the talking so they can settle the score for good will keep this from dragging on forever."

"I think the vice president's opinion is fine. What about you, Hattori?" asked Kanon, without even pretending to think about his opinion.

"I have no objections. Shiba, could you do the paperwork?"

"Of course."

After agreeing to Hattori's request, Tatsuya headed directly for the stairs to get the approval paperwork from Azusa.

"Shiba?"

From behind him he heard Takuma's voice.

"Shippou, are you not happy with this?" rebuked Tomitsuka.

"No, sir! If you'll allow this match between me and Saegusa, I have a request."

Takuma was in no position to levy conditions. He would be aware of that himself.

"Go ahead."

Which was probably why Kanon told him to go on—driven by interest in what he might say.

"I'd like to fight not only against Kasumi Saegusa, but against Izumi Saegusa as well."

"Are you making fun of me, Shippou?!"

Leaving aside whether Kasumi's inquiry was polite given that she was surrounded by upperclassmen, it was still a reasonable one.

"Your reason?"

But Tatsuya's question to Takuma made her shut her mouth for now and listen.

"This is a match with our respective families' pride on the line. And everyone knows the Saegusa twins only show their true worth when they're together."

"In other words, it won't be a real victory unless you win against both of them at once?"

"That's right."

Tatsuya paused for a moment, then looked at Kasumi. "You heard him—is that agreeable to you, Kasumi?"

"I don't mind. I'll make him regret how egotistical he is."

"Then that's how we'll set it up," said Tatsuya, going up the stairs to the student council room.

When Tatsuya returned with written permission stamped with the student council president's final seal of sanction, Izumi was behind him, along with Miyuki and Honoka for some reason.

"Chairwoman, this just needs your seal of approval now."

"Uh, the seal? ...Where did I put that thing...?" said Kanon, flustered.

Behind her, Shizuku took a small, important-looking box out of a cabinet. Managing a smile that was clearly meant to hide her embarrassment, Kanon took the box and stamped the permission slip with the seal of approval.

Hattori cleared his throat loudly, as if to drive away the strange mood. "Where should we go for this?"

"Please use seminar room two."

The one who answered Hattori's question was Honoka. She'd come bearing the code to unlock seminar room two's doors, which everyone understood without being told.

"Will you be judging, Shiba?"

That question was from Tomitsuka. He'd been beside himself this whole time wondering why Miyuki was here.

"No, I will be an observer."

Miyuki smiled and refuted his assumption.

"In that case, Tatsuya?"

Shizuku's question had been directed at Tatsuya. But before he could answer, Kanon interrupted.

"That will be fine."

"I don't mind, either."

Hattori continued after Kanon. Neither of them seemed to have any plans to ask Tatsuya his opinion on the matter.

"...Then let's go. There's not much time left until closing."

Tatsuya had been the one to propose the duel. They wouldn't let him say no at this point. Suppressing a sigh, he urged everyone to get moving.

Moving to seminar room two were the combatants in this so-called "match"—Takuma, Kasumi, and Izumi; the judge, Tatsuya; the observer, Miyuki; the one with the door codes (to lock and unlock), Honoka; Tomitsuka from the club committee; and Shizuku from the disciplinary committee. There were eight in all. Considering the disciplinary committee's shift system, Morisaki should have been the one observing, but Shizuku had volunteered to stand in for him, so here she was.

Takuma felt like he'd been put in a difficult position with the members of this group. In his mind, Tatsuya and Miyuki were on the Saegusa side. With even the judge and the observer being enemies, he'd go into this match with a handicap—no, this was a fixed match.

On the other hand, Honoka and Shizuku were very much people he wanted to be allies with in order for the Shippou family to retake its *rightful position*. His belief was naive—that if he showed them his strength right now, he'd be able to talk them into it more easily. Still, he was a fifteen-year-old boy, so you couldn't blame him; his mentality matched his age. When you thought about it, Tatsuya and the others were the ones acting unlike their ages.

The situation had him at an absolute disadvantage—but the rewards he stood to reap for overcoming that and winning would be sweet.

By the time he finally confronted the Saegusa sisters, he didn't feel like he was in a difficult position anymore. It was all fighting spirit now.

Kasumi and Izumi couldn't be as aggressive as Takuma. Kasumi genuinely believed Takuma had randomly come along and forced this little relationship, while Izumi simply felt like she'd been wrapped up in something that was not her business. They didn't have any particular feelings toward the Shippou family. Him antagonizing them was just an annoyance. If he'd just settle down, he could get better grades on exams than they and get chosen as class representative for all they cared.

The two of them never had much interest in status or honor in the secular world. They liked being praised and loathed being insulted, but they never wanted to gain anything from others' esteem. In a sense, their lack of avarice came from their having been born with silver spoons in their mouths, but that hadn't been their choice.

Their desire was one and the same: They wanted to put this nuisance behind them, here and now. For that purpose, they'd thoroughly beat that nuisance down so that he'd never mess with them again. With that determination, they confronted Takuma.

Seminar room two was longer than seminar room three, where Tatsuya and Hattori had faced off a year ago, being designed for middle-range magic. The floor was split into blue on the near side and yellow on the far side, with a one-meter block on the front and back walls painted in red.

The blue area was Takuma's, and the yellow area was Kasumi and Izumi's.

Takuma had stayed in his school uniform, and was holding a large, thick hardcover at his left side.

Kasumi and Izumi had changed into training clothes that were easier to move in. The clothes were long-sleeved, ankle-length coveralls made of a thick fabric. If they'd been doing outdoor exercises in the artificial woods in the back of the school, they'd be wearing sleeveless outerwear that doubled as storage on top of that, but neither of them wore any now. The tight women's coveralls made their slender body lines stand out. The only one actively concerned about where to look, though, was Tomitsuka.

"This match will be conducted under no-contact rules," announced Tatsuya, standing on the border between blue and yellow. No-contact rules were applied to matches between people of different genders, as long as there was nothing crazy going on. (These rules were normally selected for matches between women as well.)

"I'm sure you all know this already, but I'll explain the rules just in case. You may not leave your colored area. Going into your opponent's area or into the red area constitutes a disqualification. Direct contact with the opponent's body is also forbidden. Touching their weapon will also disqualify you. However..."

Tatsuya spared a glance at Takuma.

"Weapons controlled remotely via magic are not against the rules."

He immediately returned his gaze to a position where he could see both parties equally.

"Lastly, any lethal attacks or attacks that can cause incurable wounds are forbidden. If I decide it's too dangerous, I will stop the match, so please keep that in mind."

For a moment, Takuma made a scornful expression that looked a lot like *Go ahead and try.* Tatsuya and Miyuki, as well as Honoka and Shizuku, all noticed it, but nobody criticized Takuma for the brazen attitude.

"Both of you, get set."

Kasumi and Izumi moved to the center of the blue area.

Takuma, without moving away from his spot close to the borderline, dropped the book he was carrying to the floor with a thud.

Tatsuya looked at all three of their faces in turn. They all nodded in the same way back to him.

After moving to the wall, Tatsuya held his right hand over his head, then quickly brought it down.

Psionic light sparkled, and magic fired.

Takuma and Kasumi were the ones exchanging magical fire, while Izumi deployed Area Interference and focused on defense.

One had to master both offense and defense by himself, and another could focus solely on offense.

The conditions were clearly advantageous for Kasumi.

"What do you think?" Shizuku asked Honoka softly.

"I guess they're about equal, for now..." Honoka whispered back, a little shaky.

Kasumi was mainly using movement-type magic, targeting Takuma directly or moving air masses to create gusts to hit him with. The method of fighting specifically for a ring-out. Takuma was protecting against it using Information Boost and a physical barrier.

Meanwhile Takuma, though he'd conducted direct attacks based on oscillation-type magic at first, had switched to creating pressurized air bullets and firing them as soon as he realized his way wasn't going to break through Izumi's Area Interference. Air Bullet was a popular spell, but its popularity only served to underscore its effectiveness. Izumi's Area Interference, however, was broader than he'd thought, and as soon as the bullet of air entered the territory she controlled, it dispersed. He was having trouble dealing any effective blows.

"Kasumi seems like she's trying to avoid hurting Shippou. That's why her attacks are so narrowly aimed."

"Yeah."

"Shippou...doesn't seem to know how to use Air Bullet yet."

"The same goes for Izumi, doesn't it?"

"Yep. If she can't place this entire room under her control like Miyuki, she won't be able to guard against Air Bullet with just Area Interference. Maybe they're both so talented that they never practiced refining how to use the spells."

"Well, they are freshmen."

"Mm-hmm, I suppose. We were kind of like that until the Nines, too, huh?"

Though not because he heard Honoka and Shizuku's conversation, Takuma felt strongly that he couldn't keep this up. He fought his impatience down, and while he wove his spells, he rallied his knowledge in search of a way to break through.

He didn't feel as though his magic power was less than theirs. He'd never lose, even two on one, and he was confident he'd win if he used his trump card. His trump card, though, carried a high risk of seriously injuring his opponents. He didn't think Tatsuya could stop his spell—he may be a year above him, but he *wasn't even part of the Twenty-Eight*—though he might disqualify Takuma for breaking the rules afterward.

That was Takuma's misgiving. However...

Damn!

Magic-manipulating combat actions performed while thinking. That likewise wouldn't get him far.

He overwrote the mass of air hurtling at him from behind with a Disperse spell. The firefight had given Takuma a near-perfect grasp on their difference in strength. Kasumi had the edge in scope, rapidity, and versatility of magic. Takuma had higher influence than she did, but Izumi and Takuma were nearly equals.

Takuma's Disperse—its power of influence won out, and the make of its magic program was simple and thus quick to activate—just barely disabled Kasumi's Wind Hammer. But upon being released from its compressed state, the air turned into a gale and shoved him forward. Wind Hammer's compression level was significantly lower than Air Bullet's. The released air didn't have the force to harm Takuma's physical body, but it was enough to cause him to lose his balance. He tilted forward, and his spell's aim angled down and away.

Of the factors that comprised Air Bullet, the bullet's size, the compression of the air, and the bullet's acceleration were constant values built into the activation sequence, while its firing direction and maximum range were variables input by the magician. There was no actual need to be looking in the direction you indicated, but it was easier to put your eyes that way, and that method was the most common one.

His bullet of air fired off downward. When the Area Interference net caught it, the bullet's compression released; it slammed into the floor quite a bit in front of where Izumi was standing, then slid the rest of the way to her feet.

With a short yelp, Izumi staggered. The unexpectedly strong wind current had blown past her feet and ruined her balance. When Takuma saw that, he caught on to his misunderstanding. What Area Interference had nullified was the air's compression and the acceleration being continuously granted to it—it hadn't been nullifying the kinetic energy that the air already possessed.

The air that was still up off the ground when the compression was released dispersed in all directions in the shape of a sphere. But the air that had expanded closer to the floor met with the floor's resistance, which limited the directions it could disperse in. Kinetic energy was added to the downward-facing flow's forward direction, turning into a strong airstream that had reached his opponent.

Essentially, I just have to fire it so that the attack doesn't get canceled out even if the spell does!

Takuma positioned seven air bullets in the space in front of him—six at the points of a regular hexagon and one in the middle. He fired the bullet at the center point, then the other six with almost no time between them.

The magic developed for the Shippou—at Lab Seven—was colony control. *Colony*, in this case, was not a group of biological organisms; it was an aggregate with no physical laws tying it together. It controlled several independent objects or phenomena individually as though they were a single creature. The technique of collecting hundreds of dry-ice bullets on a target rather than just raining them down was also an application of this colony control. Firing seven Air Bullet shots in tandem was a cakewalk for the heir to the Shippou name.

The first bullet's convergence broke against Izumi's Area Interference and dispersed. But the expansion of the six air masses that flew in a moment later surrounded it, blocking the air's dispersal, and pushed it forward since they were slightly behind it. As a result, the Air Bullet's density dropped, but it turned into a stone made of wind that attacked Izumi.

"Kyah?!"

Izumi's cry wasn't due to the stone hitting her. She cried out because she'd been suddenly pushed to the ground. Kasumi had jumped over to her; her speed was clearly reinforced by magic. She'd probably switched the movement spell she was about to aim at Takuma over to herself.

Movement spells that ignored the acceleration process placed a heavy burden on the body, and its being her own spell didn't change that. Plus, the one who had been pushed down would have taken equal damage. *Now's my chance*, thought Takuma.

He struck his hands together in front of his chest. The properties of sound in that area were reorganized. His clap's volume was amplified and its sound wave was narrowly confined before being fired toward Kasumi.

Even if the Area Interference disabled the spell, the volume would remain amplified. Even if the focused sound wave dispersed somewhat, it would strike the girl with the violence of sound equivalent to an acoustic grenade going off at point-blank range. It had enough punch to knock her out cold.

At least it *should* have.

But instead, Takuma's sound-wave assault was blocked by a vacuum gap Izumi had expanded.

The air was sucked into the vacuum gap. The gusts whipped up amid the shrill noise blew the sisters' hair around. Kasumi's hair was short, but Izumi's was somewhat long, and it turned into a very unsightly display, but a simple finger-comb through her hair was enough.

"Kasumi, are you all right?" asked her sister after sitting up. The other girl was still leaning over her.

"Thanks, Izumi. That was a close one," answered Kasumi, moving off.

Takuma's attacks continued. By alternating their activation of defensive spells, the twins were managing to hold out.

But there was no haste or panic on their faces.

"It looks like we were makin' light of this guy a little."

"Leaving aside your choice of words, it would appear so."

"Things are gonna get worse and worse."

"But we aren't about to lose, are we?"

"Course not. Izumi, let's do the thing."

"Yes, Kasumi. The same as we always do."

"I'll shoot."

"And I'll boost."

"Then here comes the countdown."

"Three!" "Two!" "One!"

"Cast!"

A moment after Kasumi gave the cry, the force of their magic sailing toward Takuma shot up several times over.

From behind him, from above him, from the sides—there came an event-influencing force like a whirlwind. This spell would be incomparably more powerful than anything thus far, and as soon as Takuma detected it coming, he switched his full-powered offense to a full-powered defense.

The spell he'd sensed was a combination of convergence and movement with gas as its target—gas flow–controlling magic. He didn't have time to read any further into it.

Expanding an omnidirectional airtight shield was almost entirely instinctual. The shield completed first for no other reason than that it had a simpler magic program structure than the spell Kasumi and Izumi had been about to activate.

A vicious wind blazed about within the room's narrow limits. No sooner had he felt a wind blowing from overhead to hold him down than he was smashed by gusts from both behind and the side. They threatened to blow him away along with the airtight shield he'd formed around him. Because its surface area was so far expanded, it was hit by more of the wind, receiving greater pressure. However, that didn't mean he could lower the degree of airtightness or shrink the shield. As the wind assailed him, his magician's senses had realized its composition was very heavily skewed toward nitrogen.

One spell to raise the nitrogen density in the air, and another to move the air where it collected. A compound convergence/movement spell: Nitrogen Storm. If he breathed in any of the air now that its oxygen concentration had been lowered so much, the hypoxia would knock him out immediately. If he shrank the shield so the airflow didn't carry him away, his body would quickly run out of oxygen.

He dug in, and at his feet, the pages of his book turned wildly. The book itself wasn't blown away because the magic wind was blowing around at knee height and above.

The large, thick hardcover he'd brought here... He dropped his gaze to its pages, each one imprinted with the same exact geometric pattern, and resolved to play his ace in the hole.

"Is that...Nitrogen Storm?"

"Yeah."

When Miyuki asked the question, her voice a mix of surprise and admiration, Tatsuya came back with a short affirmative.

"I suppose I should have known Saegusa's family would be able to master such advanced spells."

"They haven't mastered it, but still, it's really something."

In the sense that it was a spell that disabled an opponent by hypoxia, it fell into the same category as Mayumi's personal-combat trump card, Dry Meteor. She'd probably had something to do with Kasumi and Izumi pulling it out as a secret weapon. But in terms of spell difficulty, Nitrogen Storm was higher than Dry Meteor. It was hard to gather a large amount of carbon dioxide in one place for Dry

Meteor, given how little there was in the air, but the skilled control it took to maintain a certain gas makeup while directing its flow made Nitrogen Storm an incredibly difficult magic.

The twins' Nitrogen Storm, understandably, was conspicuous in its roughness of airflow control, which is why Tatsuya said they hadn't mastered it yet. But it was still definitely an advanced spell you'd almost never see on a high school level.

"So this is a multiplicative cast... The idea that the Saegusa twins only show their true worth when together isn't unfounded."

It was an advanced spell Kasumi and Izumi unleashed after having used relatively novice-level spells theretofore. It wasn't because Kasumi, in charge of offense, had held anything back on purpose; Nitrogen Storm was so difficult that Kasumi *by herself* couldn't activate it.

Kasumi and Izumi Saegusa were frequently referred to as the Saegusa twins, a normal name with a special meaning, because of a unique trait only they possessed. By *combining their strength*, they could use high-power, high-difficulty spells that would be impossible for them to use individually.

That may not have seemed very strange to someone who wasn't a magician, but this was an abnormal phenomenon. Certainly there were techniques whereby multiple magicians would perform a single ritual to execute wide-scale, high-level magic impossible to cast alone. With ancient magic in particular, while actual examples of its being used were few and far between, it wasn't unusual as a traditional method of casting. However, magic rituals of this variety always required a medium or process that could be shared with the five senses—something like an incantation, an altar, or a dance.

Multiple magicians merely activating the same spell at the same time wouldn't add their magic power together or amplify it in any way; only the spell from the magician with the strongest magic power would manifest its effects—the other magicians' magic power would actually just get in the way of the event alteration. Ritual magic performed by more than one person used complex or gigantic magic programs by splitting the work between the magicians involved so that they wouldn't stray from their particular section of the magic program. Chanting and symbols were guideposts that allocated each magician's magic power, or they served as circuits.

But Kasumi and Izumi amplified their magic power just by getting support from their CADs, in the same way one would activate normal magic. Plus, they didn't divide the magic program into parts—they combined their very magic power into one.

Kasumi aimed the magic program at the target and fired, while Izumi gave it event-influencing force. They didn't add their magic powers together but multiplied them to use the spell. They could do this because not only did they share the same genes physically, they were perfectly matched in mind, right down to the characteristics of their magic calculation regions. Takuma's analysis had decided Kasumi excelled in activation speed and magic program construction scope and Izumi in influence, but that had been a miscalculation. He'd thought that because that was how they'd been using their magic power. But their roles could have been switched, and they'd have been able to use the same spells in exactly the same way.

Not even genetic engineering could cause this—they were irregulars, and their irregularity was completely coincidental. And it was the secret to the Saegusa twins' power.

Takuma, who had been digging in and holding his breath, suddenly dropped to a knee, squatting to close the book whose wind-whipped pages seemed about ready to tear apart. A moment later, he opened its hard cover again. In that moment, all the pages turned into one big blizzard of paper and scattered.

The book he'd brought here was hardcover, not quite B5 size, and had 720 pages—it was thick and large. The pages were 182 millimeters horizontally by 256 millimeters vertically. All the pages had been shredded into pieces four millimeters square, leaving two millimeters still on the binding. The shredded pieces numbered 2,880 per two pages (or one sheet). With 720 pages and 360 sheets, the total number was 1,036,810.

Over a million tiny scraps of paper formed a tempest, going against the gales and pushing toward the twins. Obviously, these tiny scraps weren't just ripped pieces of paper. If someone had the kinetic vision to capture each individual piece as it danced and twirled in a complicated manner, they would notice that none of them bent or folded—and maybe that they'd turned into thin, square blades as though made of glass or some other hard material. As the million blades danced around, seemingly at random, they all moved to wrap themselves around the girls.

Kasumi and Izumi, as well as Tatsuya and Miyuki, were aware this paper storm was actually made of countless sharp blades. They knew the magic of the Shippou, too, and knew what this spell was.

Million Edge—one of the Shippou family's trump cards. Manipulating a million scraps of paper through colony control, turning them into bladed clouds to carve up an enemy.

The twins, while controlling Nitrogen Storm, activated a different spell. They took air that was filled with oxygen and rammed it into the paper blizzard from many directions, creating a scirocco hotter than the ignition point of paper through adiabatic compression, trying to burn the paper blades to cinders.

It was an arrangement of the Heat Storm spell. It was one difficulty rank higher than simply creating an adiabatically compressed air mass, and they activated it at the same time as Nitrogen Storm, but for now, it was well within the scope of the girls' abilities. Lab Three's research theme had been control of multiple spells of different types. The range of versatility of the magic they could activate and control at once, and the raising of that limit to its extreme, was the magician-strengthening program Lab Three had adopted. Lab Three was unusually open-minded among the magician development laboratories, and its fruits were used by Lab Ten as well. For Saegusa magicians, who had mastered the results of the multitype, multi-magic control also used in the Juumonji family's Phalanx and then transferred to Lab Seven, it was a skill that let them cast double or even triple, no matter how advanced the magic, without it even being difficult.

A suffocating storm swallowed up Takuma, and the air mass, over five hundred degrees centigrade, threatened to burn away all the paper scraps.

As the million blades were bathed in heat past their ignition point, they pressed farther toward Kasumi and Izumi, wanting blood, following Takuma's will as he was protected by the spell that had created them.

At this rate, Takuma would succumb to hypoxia, and Kasumi and Izumi would be riddled with countless wounds from the blades they couldn't reduce to ash. It was clear lasting effects would be a concern for both sides when this was over.

"That's enough!"

Tatsuya's right hand moved.

In his outstretched hand was a glittering silver CAD. A handgun-shaped specialized CAD called Silver Horn.

Nitrogen Storm.

Million Edge.

Heat Storm.

Three magic programs shattered, and a torrent of psions blew their shards apart.

Had Tatsuya's command to stop reached the three combatants' minds?

Amid the silence, with all the offensive spells blown away, Takuma, Kasumi, and Izumi all stood idly, dazed, unable to comprehend what had just happened. But not everyone was standing around wondering what had just gone on. The only ones stricken speechless were the three freshman combatants.

Tomitsuka's eyes were wide, too, but his expression didn't betray much shock. He was surprised, for sure, but it was more like he knew what had happened and thought it was incredible. The other three—Miyuki, Honoka, and Shizuku—merely looked mildly impressed.

Miyuki was actually the only one who *properly* understood what had happened, but the freshman trio couldn't even figure out the surface-level phenomenon: the fact that Tatsuya had used anti-magic to disable all their spells instantaneously.

"I declare both sides disqualified."

Tatsuya handed down his decision as the judge. Only then did the frozen freshmen reboot.

"What is that supposed to mean?!"

The first one to yell at Tatsuya was Kasumi.

"I said this before the match. Any lethal attacks or ones that could cause incurable wounds are forbidden, and that if I decided it was too dangerous, I would stop the match myself."

"Then what would the match's result be otherwise?" asked Izumi in a calmer tone than her older twin, but a firmer one than usual.

"Both sides are disqualified. In other words, both sides lost."

It wasn't a draw—it was a mutual loss. Tatsuya had purposely said it like that to imply that he wouldn't let them have a rematch, but he doubted whether Izumi or the others understood that.

"But if I may, Shiba, Nitrogen Storm is unlike Million Edge. It may possess a degree of lethality, but it wouldn't leave lingering aftereffects."

Izumi was essentially insisting that Shippou should have lost because he broke the rules. Takuma understood that right away, too. Almost without any time between them, he tried to voice an objection, but Tatsuya was quicker.

"Yes, Nitrogen Storm's power can be controlled to the point where it won't leave serious aftereffects on the opponent. But I don't think either of you had the time to think about that, Izumi."

Faced with Tatsuya's look of *Am I wrong?* the twins clammed up.

"That wasn't the case!"

In their place—well, not really—this time Takuma yelled at Tatsuya.

"It would have been finished before that happened!"

An amused—not the happy kind, but the interested kind—light went on in Tatsuya's eyes. "Are you trying to say you won?"

"Yes," declared Takuma proudly without flinching away from Tatsuya's cold stare. "Saegusa's Heat Storm wouldn't have been able to stop Million Edge. My attack would have reached Saegusa before Nitrogen Storm broke through my airtight shield!"

A sardonic hue found its way into the chill in Tatsuya's gaze. "In other words, you insist that if I hadn't stepped in, a million highly heated paper scraps would have completely ruined the soft skin of two freshman girls?"

He heard someone muffle a laugh. Actually, he heard at least two.

Blood rose to Takuma's face. It got red enough that everyone could see it clearly.

"In that case, Shippou, I declare that you lost by breaking the rules."

Before the excited Takuma could explode, Tatsuya made his assertion in a calm, even cruel, tone—that Takuma had lost. His voice was like cold steel, and it made Takuma hesitate to argue.

"I won't allow you to say you didn't know what would happen if they took the brunt of that spell." Takuma was on the verge of saying something, but Tatsuya had no intention of letting him make excuses. "Excessive attacks are only allowed in death matches. Not in a game with rules."

"But!"

Takuma raised his voice in opposition, more energetically than he needed to, as though clearing the pressure from Tatsuya that was entangling him. That one word alone made it clear that he was spent.

"Wouldn't that mean it was a foregone conclusion that if I used Million Edge, I would have lost?!"

"As long as you couldn't control its attack power, it would always be against the rules."

"But that's crazy!"

Tatsuya kept his cool as the freshman blew his top, and that only enraged Takuma more. His temper was so bad that it made not only Tomitsuka, his senior in the club committee, but also Kasumi, who had just been arguing with him, feel anxious.

"That would mean my trump card was restricted before the match even started! That's a hell of a handicap, don't you think?!"

"The conditions are the same for both of you. Highly lethal spells were equally forbidden for the Saegusa sisters."

For now, though, those two were the only ones concerned with where this argument was leading. The junior girls—Miyuki, Shizuku, and Honoka—simply watched Takuma with lukewarm eyes.

"That's cheap! They don't even *have* magic lethal enough to be restricted!"

"Nitrogen Storm is lethal enough in its own right. I didn't stop it at first because its power had been controlled to within the rules' limits."

Tatsuya's tone was clearly far from pleased. Takuma choked on his next words as cold stares descended upon him. Not only Tatsuya, either—he felt like the three upperclassman girls were sneering at him, too. Desperately, he searched for a thread to argue on.

"You, however, didn't have Million Edge's power under your control."

"That's a false accusation! I was in full control of the spell!"

His objection had no grounds whatsoever—it was reactive, emotional, and simplistic. Every junior in the room could clearly tell that Takuma's Million Edge hadn't been modified enough.

If Tatsuya hadn't just used his own judgment, but asked for everyone else's—Miyuki's, Honoka's, Shizuku's, and Tomitsuka's—Takuma probably would have had to back down. The members of

Tatsuya's in-group aside, if even Tomitsuka supported his judgment, it definitely would have been too hard for Takuma to force the issue on emotion.

"I was the judge of this match. I decide the outcome. I said that at the start."

But Tatsuya didn't do that. He was the one who made the judgment, a fundamental rule he didn't feel the need to bend.

"...Fine, I get it! Million Edge is the same as an overly aggressive attack! Why couldn't you have just said that at the start?! There were plenty of other ways I could have fought if I'd known it was against the rules!"

Takuma didn't realize that *his* remarks were the ones that sounded like childish excuses.

But everyone else did.

Tomitsuka's eyes as he looked at Takuma had gone from anxious to helpless.

Miyuki's had changed from lukewarm to sharp.

However, Tatsuya responded by pointing out Takuma's failings in his usual dispassionate manner. "Don't be a child, Shippou. You couldn't control its power because you lack experience. If you knew the conditions beforehand and still couldn't meet them, your level of skill is the only thing at fault."

"I don't want a Weed like you telling me that!"

The room fell deathly quiet. A tension, sharp enough to prick skin, filled the silence.

Takuma's face, dyed crimson, drained of blood and paled a little. He probably hadn't meant to take it that far. He seemed to realize he'd said something he couldn't take back in his rage.

Honoka and Shizuku paled, too, but for a different reason. They were afraid a blizzard was about to start raging right here in this room. Thankfully, however, Tatsuya spoke before that happened.

"So you're unhappy that it's coming from me?"

Takuma realized that his remark had been inappropriate on two different levels. The term *Weed* was not one he should have used in this situation at the very least, and Tatsuya was an exception who had risen in rank from Course 2 student to magical engineering student through his abilities. Takuma worked his mind, desperately trying to come up with a way to recover from this error. But he was cornered and his calm was gone; he was having a hard time thinking of anything that would help. Nevertheless, he couldn't keep his mouth closed.

"I… What I'm unhappy with is the biased judgement! It was only your subjective point of view that Saegusa could control Nitrogen Storm and I couldn't control Million Edge, isn't it? I was completely in control! Your decision is clearly biased toward Saegusa!"

"Shippou…you're being incoherent."

It wasn't Tatsuya who chided him, appalled, as he relied on emotional excuses like a child throwing a temper tantrum. Instead, it was Tomitsuka.

"You just said that if it had kept going, your spell would have done damage to the Saegusas that exceeded the limits of the match."

"That's because they used Heat Storm!"

Takuma's excuse wasn't wholly without logic. Unfortunately, though, it just sounded like he was passing the buck right now.

"Give it a rest, Shippou."

A lax voice interrupted Takuma and Tomitsuka. It had come from the mouth of Kasumi.

"If you really wanted to win that badly, then you can have it."

"Kasumi, are you okay with that?"

Amid the line of faces that looked shocked, though the intensity of the shock varied, the one who'd asked Kasumi that question was the one who probably knew her best: Izumi.

"Yeah. If you really think about it, we shouldn't have gotten that riled up. It was just an unofficial high school match, but we used a multiplicative cast, and then used it to multi-cast Nitrogen Storm and Heat Storm. That's going too far, no matter how you look at it. Shiba's right."

As her words implied, Kasumi looked as though she'd completely cooled off. Even her eyes when she looked at Takuma had waned from a look of hostility to one of disinterest.

"...If you say so, Kasumi."

Izumi accepted her sister's excuse pretty easily. She'd planned to be her twin's assistant for this in the first place. If Kasumi said it was fine with her, then there was nothing for Izumi to argue against.

Takuma was about to shout something, but used all his might to close his mouth. The angry words *That's bullshit* came very close to escaping his throat, but he realized saying them would be utterly unseemly. Thanks to the interval where everyone was too stunned to speak, he'd recovered enough of his ability to reason logically.

Kasumi walked over to Tatsuya, with Izumi following behind.

"Shiba, I'm sorry for the trouble."

Kasumi and Izumi bowed their heads to Tatsuya. Of course, Izumi's mind was 70 percent on Miyuki, which should perhaps be called amusing.

...Meanwhile, Takuma gritted his teeth and watched.

"But can I say one thing?" she asked.

Nevertheless, it wasn't like Kasumi to apologize and leave. At least, in this case, *not when it came to Tatsuya.*

"What?"

Tatsuya's expression had changed completely as well from when he'd been facing Takuma, and it now wore a slight pained grin.

"I—no, we didn't lose control of the spells. Stopping the match there was a mistaken decision on your part."

Kasumi jabbered at him quickly, her eyes strong, before leaving the seminar room without waiting for Tatsuya to answer.

"I, umm..."

Izumi, switching between Kasumi's back and Tatsuya's face over and over, seemed to be seriously disturbed, which was rare for her.

"Izumi?"

"Yes?!"

It couldn't have come as unexpected, but when Tatsuya said her name, Izumi's spine immediately straightened up. A moment later, she looked down, embarrassed she'd let herself get tongue-tied.

Without grinning at her, but without any harshness, either, Tatsuya, his face serene, continued. "Would you mind telling Kasumi that if she's unhappy with this, I would be happy to take her on anytime?"

Izumi's eyes widened—perhaps out of surprise. She immediately realized he'd spoken out of consideration for Kasumi, and it was seriously at odds with the image of him she had in her head.

"...I understand. Thank you very much," she answered, bowing deeply. After her bow, which was neither too long nor too short, she looked back up, then stopped in place for some reason.

"What is it?"

After Tatsuya prodded her, Izumi gave Tatsuya an honest smile for the first time.

"My opinion of you has *very slightly* gone up. I see you have *a bit* of what I would expect Big Sister's older brother to have."

Her sarcasm was so overloaded all the cargo could have fallen off it, but perhaps taken aback by the excessive bluntness, Tatsuya watched Izumi excuse herself and leave without saying a word.

In the seminar room after Kasumi and Izumi left, Takuma was still standing around in silence doing nothing. The juniors couldn't deny it seemed like he'd been left behind, but Takuma himself didn't think that way.

"Shiba."

He had wanted to speak with Tatsuya after the "nuisances"—at least in his mind—were gone. That was why he'd remained.

"Is there still something you want to say?"

Tatsuya's voice was still cold. There was nobody here to criticize that as childish behavior. As far as the conversations had gone in this room, at least, everyone had probably decided the blame lay with Takuma. In fact, even Takuma himself thought so now that he'd regained a degree of reason. But at the same time, he'd given up hope of apologizing, because it was too late at this point. He was stuck thinking that he needed to make up lost ground in a way other than by being courteous.

"I'm still not convinced."

"Of what?"

"That I lost by breaking the rules."

"Shippou!"

Sounding like he couldn't hold it in any longer, Tomitsuka raised his voice. But Takuma's gaze remained fixed on Tatsuya, and didn't move toward Tomitsuka.

"What is it you want?"

Tatsuya could have silenced Takuma's protests. From the outset, this match had been a relief measure for Takuma and Kasumi after they'd committed a serious infraction of school rules. In particular, it had been intended to rescue Takuma, who in the worst case would have been expelled. Whether it was partiality or outright cheating, Takuma wasn't in a position to quibble.

And yet Tatsuya was asking for his excuse. This wasn't him being kind; he just didn't want this trouble to drag on for a long time.

"Please, let me prove it to you."

"Prove what?"

"Prove that I was in control of Million Edge."

"How?"

"Please stay here with me—I'll use Million Edge and force you to surrender without harming you!"

Miyuki's slender eyebrows shot up at Takuma's words. But a white darkness had not covered the room.

Before her emotions could explode, the sound of a harsh blow and the sound of something hitting the floor went off one after another. The unexpected sight interrupted Miyuki's anger.

The one who had fallen to the floor was Takuma.

The one who had punched him down was Tomitsuka.

"...Tomitsuka?"

Takuma, his hands on the floor, looked up, his face looking like he didn't know what had just happened.

"Give it a rest, Shippou!" yelled Tomitsuka, growing red in the face. Expressions like *demonic* or *enraged* were altogether inapplicable—perhaps because he had unhandsome features to begin with—but it was clear that he was seriously angry.

"I've been listening to you as you do nothing but spout self-satisfied, incredibly rude things... Who the hell do you think you are?! Are you trying to say the Twenty-Eight are that far above everyone else?!"

"I...I didn't mean..." muttered Takuma from the floor, almost to himself. He had only sat up in place, doubtless because the shock had made him forget to actually stand all the way up.

Takuma truly hadn't noticed. He truly hadn't been aware. He was so insistent on the Ten Master Clans' position that he only ever looked up—he never bothered to look down. Actually, he might *face* downward, but he never *looked* that way. He didn't acknowledge the worth of the Shippou family because they couldn't become one of the Ten Master Clans. Unconsciously, he'd been looking down on magicians without the right to be in one of the Clans *the same way he looked down on his own father*.

"Shippou. If you want to prove your own strength, then you'll be with me! Or are you not satisfied with me? Not satisfied going up against the worthless Range Zero of the Tomitsuka of the Hundred?"

Overpowered by his friend's spirit, Takuma, still on his rear, backed away. Whether Tomitsuka pressed an attack or Takuma played the cornered rat finding courage in desperation, a precarious mood that foreshadowed a battle's start at any moment floated through the seminar room.

"Tomitsuka, please, calm down."

It was Miyuki's clear voice that cooled the flames about to ignite.

"As long as you don't have permission from the student council president and the disciplinary committee chairwoman, no matches will be allowed. And perhaps Shippou needs time to think anyway? He would also require time to prepare the Million Edge's activation medium."

"...You're right. I'm sorry."

Tomitsuka flushed at how even he'd been letting his temper get the better of him.

"Shippou, can you stand?"

In place of Tomitsuka, who retreated to the wall, Honoka went out in front of Takuma. She was truthfully indignant that Takuma had treated Tatsuya so rudely, but she was too nice a person at heart to leave an underclassman sitting on the floor.

"I'm fine!"

Takuma energetically got to his feet. His face was a little red because a girl he was trying to recruit for his own faction had seen him in such a sorry state—at least that was what he decided to think.

Tatsuya, who had been keeping quiet until now in the belief that interrupting would ruin the situation beyond repair, saw it was a good time and spoke.

"Shippou, I don't plan on fighting you. Tomitsuka, if you want to fight him, you should explain what's happening to Chairman Hattori."

"Er, I, yeah."

It was Tomitsuka who answered awkwardly. Takuma was staring wordlessly at Tatsuya.

"Honoka, would you mind closing up?"

"Of course, Tatsuya."

Tatsuya left the room briskly, as though saying he didn't want anything to do with any further quarrels.

Taking only Miyuki with him.

Unfortunately, however, Tatsuya wouldn't be escaping this incident that easily.

It happened about fifteen minutes after Honoka returned to the student council room after locking up, right as Tatsuya was getting up to go home for the day: The student council room doorbell rang.

"You can come in."

"Excuse me."

The one who entered through the door was the club committee chairman, Hattori.

Having a bad feeling about this—no, a firm belief about it—Tatsuya sat back in his chair.

Hattori walked over to Azusa, who had remotely unlocked the door in the first place, with a truly bitter, or maybe pained, look on his face.

It was a surprise to Tatsuya that Azusa, sitting at the desk, didn't seem frightened at all.

"Nakajou, this is really hard for me to say, and I'm ashamed to say it, but..."

"What's wrong, Hattori?"

Azusa probably couldn't do anything but answer like that.

"I'm sorry. I'd like permission for a match *again.*"

"Again?! Who could it be this time?"

One could call the fact that he didn't make excuses about this or that right now a virtue that reflected his serious nature.

One could also say he felt more responsibility for what had happened than Tatsuya, at least, who had predicted this turn of events and hadn't reported anything because he didn't want to get involved with it.

"Tomitsuka and Shippou."

"Shippou *again...?*"

Hattori and Azusa were of one mind, a fact the deep wrinkles in their furrowed brows attested to.

"...I foresaw he'd have some personality issues when he spurned the invitation to the student council. Maybe I should be scolding him for it and making him reflect on his behavior for this, too."

Miyuki and Honoka both nodded, but neither was visible to Hattori.

"But his talent is valuable. I think if he learned how to be a little humbler, he'd grow by leaps and bounds."

Miyuki and Honoka traded glances, using their eyes to say *What do you think?* and *Probably not*, but that conversation wasn't visible to Hattori, either.

"I decided a defeat would be better than a harsh reprimand to take him down a peg."

"Which is why the match... But is Tomitsuka all right with it? If that's the reason, wouldn't Sawaki be more certain to win—or you, for that matter?"

Now that Katsuto, Mayumi, and Mari had graduated, Hattori and Sawaki were currently considered the strongest at First High. ("Considered" because it was what the students thought; they hadn't had a tournament to prove it or anything.)

"I considered giving him the lesson myself, but Tomitsuka was very adamant. I've left Shippou's education to Tomitsuka until now, and he's not lacking in the strength department. That's why I'd like to trust him with this."

"Well, that's fine, then, right?" Isori, who had been listening quietly to Hattori's explanation thus far, gave Azusa a push. "Tomitsuka is strong. Like Hattori says, we won't have to worry about his skills."

The relationship between the Tomitsuka and Isori families was not a shallow one that was due only to each family's field of specialty. It wasn't strange that Kei Isori would know Hagane Tomitsuka's true strength.

"And Tomitsuka is serious, too. His disposition hasn't changed despite the way he was treated. I don't think letting him have a match against Shippou would turn out badly."

Azusa knew that, so she accepted Isori's advice without issue. "What day would they like, then? It's close to closing time, so without much time left, I can't permit it for today, but..."

Hattori already had an answer for Azusa's question: "Can it be the day after tomorrow?"

"Why not tomorrow?"

"I don't want to let him use the successive-fight excuse. I think we should leave a day in between for him to rest."

"The day after tomorrow is Saturday, so I'm not sure whether the seminar room will be free after school…" said Azusa, calling up the facility reservations herself. "Oh, seminar room three is usable after three. Is one hour okay?"

"Would you be able to make it two hours?"

"Well, it should be fine." Despite feeling dubious about Hattori's request, Azusa made the reservation for the seminar room. "I'll issue the permission slip."

"Sorry, and thanks for doing all this work," said Hattori, lowering his head in apology. His display provoked a little laugh from Azusa.

"…Did I say something weird?"

"Hattori, you're kind of starting to remind me of Juumonji."

Coming from her, that was beyond the shadow of a doubt a compliment. But Hattori, who considered himself clearly a different type from Katsuto, felt like she'd told him that he was trying to make up for his lack of ability by pretending to be someone else, leaving him in a fairly delicate mood.

Miyuki watched with concern from the living room as her brother relaxed on the sofa, having gotten changed in his room before her.

On the way from school to their house, Tatsuya had seemed deep in thought about something. Still, that was only how Miyuki felt, and no differences from his normal routines were apparent. When she spoke to him, she got actual responses. And he didn't remain passive in the conversation—he'd asked what Minami thought of school life, and gathered information about whether what had happened today was already a rumor among the freshmen.

But no matter how same-as-always he seemed, he was definitely worried about something, Miyuki was sure of it. It wasn't about whether she had excellent powers of insight or not; her gut just told her that her brother wasn't sure what to do.

Maybe it would be better to express it by saying their hearts were connected.

It was only recently that she'd become this strongly aware of it. Sometimes she wondered if it was some kind of telepathy. Whatever the real cause was, it was a joyful thing for her—simply being able to really feel like her heart was connected with his made her blissful.

She could notice her brother's worries like this. That, too, was a happy fact. Because of that, she grew unnecessarily curious as to what it was he was worried about. She couldn't find it within herself to look the other way when she knew he was worried.

"Brother?"

In the end, she decided to be straightforward and ask. Maybe their hearts were linked, but this was no telepathy—she couldn't read his mind. And even if it were a telepathic ability, looking into her brother's thoughts was something she would never, ever be rude enough to do. Even if there was something she could do for him, if she didn't know what that thing was, then she couldn't help him. (Incidentally, according to current, late-twenty-first-century research, telepathy could only read surface-level, verbalized thoughts.)

Receiving his permission, she sat down directly in front of him, and asked her question with (though she didn't realize it) a very serious expression.

"Brother, what are you worried about?"

Even if she intended to be straightforward, that may have been a little *too* direct. Tatsuya looked at his sister, seeming taken aback, but maybe that was why he didn't feel like evading the question.

"I'm a little concerned about Shippou."

"...Brother. If you ever consider his insolent attitude too much to tolerate, you need only tell me."

"No, no, Miyuki, don't be hasty." Seeing a dangerous light in her eyes that was one step from murderous, Tatsuya quickly waved his hands to the sides. "His attitude isn't what I'd call praiseworthy, but that wasn't exactly what I was concerned with. Besides, I don't have much room to talk about the attitude others take toward their elders to begin with."

"That is not true. You are an admirable person at all times."

He knew this argument was practically reflex for Miyuki, so Tatsuya decided not to comment on it. "What I'm concerned about is how Shippou can remain so aggressive. He turns down an invitation to the student council, jumps down the Saegusa family's throat, and doesn't care if he makes enemies out of upperclassmen."

"Perhaps he simply isn't thinking at all."

Tatsuya accidentally let a grin slip out at his sister's scathing opinion. "No, that's not how it looks to me. He has a very strong ambition to rise up in the world. When I watch him, I feel like maybe he's mad that he can't be in the Ten."

"...But if that was the case, I would think one would normally join the student council and try to build personal relationships."

"I think that would be normal, too."

Miyuki, suddenly surprised, put a hand to her mouth. "Then are you saying something abnormal is happening? Is that what you've been thinking about?"

"Well, yes, but..."

As Tatsuya was fumbling over his words, Minami entered the living room with an "Excuse me."

In her hands she held a tray with coffee cups on it.

Miyuki directed a resentful look at Minami, but Minami casually averted her eyes and pretended not to notice it.

"I've brought you some coffee."

"Right, thanks."

Tatsuya noticed the battle in their eyes, too, but he wasn't foolish enough to remark on it.

"Hey, Minami, I'd like your opinion, too. Would you take a seat?"

Tatsuya hadn't said this because he considered Minami's deductive prowess more helpful than Miyuki's.

Miyuki was too easily influenced by Tatsuya's thinking style. She had a tendency to look at everything from the same viewpoint as he. Tatsuya valued that as a way to complement his own analysis, but right now he decided he wanted ideas from a different viewpoint.

"Yes?" said Minami, not moving to sit down. She just stood next to the table, waiting. Glimpsing a firm sense of professionalism in that, Tatsuya stopped wasting time.

"What sort of impression does Takuma Shippou give you?"

"He's a fool who does not know his place."

There wasn't a moment's hesitation in Minami's answer.

Miyuki nodded deeply in the seat across from him. Seeing her out of the corner of his eye, Tatsuya regretted asking the question that way. He dismissed the pounding in his head as just his imagination. (And, in fact, it wasn't a physical occurrence.)

"...What is your reason for thinking that way?"

For now, Tatsuya decided to ask the reason why. Minami also answered that one without pretending to hesitate.

"He is like a wild dog. He snaps at everyone without thinking of interests or differences in strength. His indiscriminate offensive nature seems to indicate not that he believes he is the strongest, but that he believes he *must* be."

Takuma seemed to have considerably angered Minami as well, and before she knew it, her own thoughts were leaping off her tongue.

"That he needs to be the strongest..." Tatsuya didn't know how deeply Minami had thought about this, but her impressions felt oddly on the mark. "I wonder who could have riled him up like that."

That comment hadn't been directed at Miyuki, nor had it been directed at Minami. He was basically muttering to himself, trying to organize his own thoughts, but Miyuki didn't take it that way.

"Rile him up... Could this be how the Shippou family is raising him? Telling him that the Shippou's heir needs to be stronger than anyone else, perhaps?"

Miyuki's speculation was, if one had to judge, more appropriate for the Yotsuba family. But none of the three here realized that, because they were all up to their necks in this Yotsuba-esque principle already.

"No, I hear the Shippou family head, Takumi Shippou, is so discreet he's almost timid. He would exercise *some* caution in directing the family, regardless of what his true intentions are."

"Big Brother Tatsuya, it seems to me that this is not the result of someone riling him up but of someone inciting him or flattering him."

Miyuki was the one to respond to Minami. "You mean that someone is trying to take advantage of him rather than align their interests with his?"

"I hadn't thought that far...but I feel you are correct, Big Sister Miyuki."

As Minami nodded, Tatsuya mentally agreed with her. Yes—to put it in an ugly way, Takuma was *being made to dance like a puppet.* That was the expression that came to Tatsuya's mind when he watched the string of disturbances Takuma had caused.

"That's interesting. What could be their purpose...? Should I do a little digging?"

"Will you ask Sensei about it?" asked Miyuki, wondering if he'd inquire with Yakumo.

"Shall I connect you to Master Kuroba?" suggested Minami, wondering the same thing.

"No," said Tatsuya, disagreeing with them both. "This is all too vague to bother Master with, and I can't let myself ask for Aunt Maya's help. Still, by myself, this is..." He paused before shaking his head to clear his hesitation. "I feel like nothing good will happen if we leave him alone, but...there's no choice. I'll just have to watch him for a while."

A backward-looking conclusion, but he couldn't think of any other way to deal with it. If violent behavior was happening right in front of them, he could solve it through muscle by himself, but time and manpower were necessary for investigations. Maybe they weren't necessary with hacking skills like Sanada or Fujibayashi had, but with his current abilities, that was asking too much. He decided to be quiet about it and give up.

However, the god of trouble (or the devil?) seemed to want to sweat him to the last.

Just as Tatsuya had finished his coffee and was about to get up, the telephone rang. Seeing the call source, Tatsuya frowned in doubt. The one who had called was Kyouko Fujibayashi.

"Yes, this is Shiba."

Taking his response as a signal, the living-room display began to function as a videophone monitor.

"Good evening, Tatsuya. You weren't having dinner yet, were you? Can you spare a moment to talk?"

"I can, ma'am," answered Tatsuya, glancing to his side.

"Oh, they can hear this—both Miyuki and Minami."

The glance had indeed been a signal for them to excuse themselves, but Fujibayashi preempted him and stopped them. A thought crossed Tatsuya's mind—did she mean to get them involved? But more importantly, she spoke as though she knew all about Minami, which set Tatsuya heavily on guard.

"I actually wanted to talk about the disturbance the Shippou family's eldest son caused today."

"Could you wait a moment, ma'am?" interrupted Tatsuya. The topic she was trying to broach wasn't the kind he could just listen to without saying anything. "How do you know about that, ma'am? Unlike the Nine School Competition representative selections, that incident was off the books. You don't have an informant in our midst, do you?"

Fujibayashi looked like she was trying to stop herself from laughing. *"I'll have to give them a bonus. Not letting you notice that they've been watching you, of all people."*

"Watching me…?" asked Tatsuya, erasing his expression.

"Hmm… Well, not quite. They weren't watching you—they were watching anyone getting close to you. I instructed them not to pay direct attention to you or Miyuki, and it seems they've kept to that faithfully. Maybe that's why your senses didn't catch them."

"Why—it's because I'm a strategic-class magician, right?"

"Well, of course. The military can't exactly leave a strategic magician defenseless, can they?"

With a completely guilt-free smile, Fujibayashi revealed that she'd been eavesdropping and spying on them.

"I suppose you wouldn't answer me if I asked who it is."

"Obviously I can't tell you that."

Tatsuya sighed and gave up on the subject. Tatsuya and the Independent Magic Battalion had never been allies unconditionally. Besides, the logic of keeping a watchful eye on a strategic magician's movements, even coming from an ally, was logic he could understand.

"All right, ma'am… What did you want to discuss regarding Shippou?" asked Tatsuya, shelving the prior conversation for the moment and making an expression like nothing had happened.

Fujibayashi answered him with the same look she'd had when he picked up the phone. *"Just wondering if you wanted to know who's supporting him."*

It was as though she'd been eavesdropping on the very conversation Tatsuya and the others had just been having. "…Why would you think that?"

But Tatsuya knew he wasn't senile enough that someone could plant a bug in his own home, even Fujibayashi. And besides, if they *had* been listening to all their conversations at home, neither she nor her superiors would have done anything so careless as to let him know about it.

The Shippou family was one of the Eighteen Support Clans acting as assistants to the Ten Master Clans. Someone was exerting no small influence on its eldest son and heir. Doubtless that person's existence was a worrying element that a force like the Independent Magic Battalion, which saw magic as a crucial element of Japan's defense forces, couldn't ignore. Did it already have detailed intel?

The answer to Tatsuya's question was one of the two responses he'd expected.

"Because I was curious."

It would be dangerous to take that answer at face value. It wasn't fully a lie—but it couldn't have been fully the truth.

"I wanted to propose we work together on a little investigation."

But it was also true that her proposition was a life raft for Tatsuya. "What exactly should I do, then, ma'am?"

"I'll handle the home surveillance. I want you to come here when Shippou visits his supporter."

"That's something I would have liked to request myself, but...for what purpose?"

"We have the whole nonintervention thing when it comes to domestic incidents. Not our territory, and all that. But if it were you, you could just say you were worried about a younger student as their senior, right? Though I can't force a respectable *student to do anything dangerous, of course."*

The retort *But it's okay if it's me?!* didn't even come up in Tatsuya's mind. "Understood, ma'am. In that case, I accept."

"If he makes a move, I'll contact you. Miyuki, I'll be borrowing Tatsuya for a short while when that happens."

After hearing Miyuki comply with a taken-aback voice, Fujibayashi winked and hung up.

[15]

"I wonder who the traitor is…"

Gongjin Zhou's graceful eyes clouded as he gazed at the report automatically scrolling by. Wrinkles creased his brow. It was rare for him to show overt displeasure like this.

The date had just changed from April 26 to April 27 a short while earlier. He, however, didn't notice. That was how focused he was on the report in his hands.

The scrolling stopped, and Zhou looked up from the information terminal. After a brief sigh, he reached for the wineglass on the table. This was the third time he'd read over the report. He couldn't spot any mistakes in the text. He didn't seriously think there would be any, but in the end, he'd needed to borrow the power of alcohol, if only a small amount, to wipe away the sense of vain effort he felt after he finished reaffirming the unfortunate truth.

The report was a written investigation pertaining to the trend of public opinion. It was the result of detailed investigation on what non-magicians felt toward magicians, investigated through some illegal methods.

If this report had been on paper, it would have been quite thick, and it showed that ill feelings toward magicians had gone up since the end of the past year. The worsening just this month had been conspicuous. His media manipulation was certainly having results.

But they weren't all Zhou had been hoping for. It clearly hadn't reached the levels he'd calculated it would. Certainly there had been an unexpected factor, that play to the audience by those First High students. With only that irregularity, however, there was still an inexplicable dissociation between his projected values and the actual ones.

"Inexplicable, even considering Rosen's intervention... This must mean there is a media outlet that hasn't acted as I instructed."

He called something up on the screen—a views-per-day count on a video from a media outlet critical toward magicians. It was clear as day: a shortage compared to his plans. In other words, in the corporation that managed push-type video media, including television, someone had broken their promise.

"How foolish, to break a contract... I'm not interested in violence, but if I must."

All Zhou had done was shady business. Business that featured no contracts guaranteeing legality. That was why he needed to make sure the contracts were effective personally. Even if it had been a verbal agreement—no, *because* it had been a verbal agreement—he would use any means at his disposal. He would reward keeping agreements and punish breaching them.

"Come to think of it, it's already been a year since inviting Mr. Sun's nephew... That should be long enough to entrust a job to him."

Gongjin Zhou made his decision: He would borrow a *friend's* help and grant a penalty to the traitor.

Friday, April 27. Takuma stayed home from school.

He was this year's new student representative, and a celebrity among the freshmen. Many of his classmates knew about the disturbance he'd caused yesterday. And one day later, he was absent. All sorts of rumors were floating about the freshman floor.

——The Saegusa sisters had beaten him and he was asleep in bed.

——No, he was asleep in bed because an upperclassman had punished him.

——He wasn't injured, but he was holed up at home out of shock that he'd lost.

——He'd won the match, but he took responsibility for causing a disturbance and was voluntarily confining himself to his house.

——He had been ordered to confine himself at home, and from there he was plotting to overthrow an upperclassman.

Most of the rumors like these were based mainly on spite. But a few did among them did graze the truth.

"Big Brother Tatsuya, Takuma Shippou is absent today."

For those reasons, Tatsuya knew that fact before Minami faithfully reported it to him via text message, and he had a pretty solid guess as to why.

Takuma hadn't been ordered to confine himself at home. That wasn't a guess, but the truth. What was correct (or seemed correct) despite the rumors was the part where he was preparing for a match with an upperclassman.

Million Edge, which one could call the personal spell of the Shippou family, was a colony control spell one could activate without using a CAD. That was because it set the spell into preactivation standby mode in advance, then used the caster's psions as a key to trigger. It was a conditionally activated delayed spell. Leaving colony control's difficulty aside, the use of a delayed spell to omit manual CAD operation wasn't a rare one. In the United Kingdom, for example, the Goldie family's Magic Bullet Tathlum spell operated on the same principle.

Million Edge's unique trait lay in the technique that kept it in standby mode. You would use symbols to physically record a spell directly before its activation. At a glance, the technique appeared the same as for seal-type spells, but while those streamed psions through the symbols to create a magic program and alter events, Shippou's spell was only a conditionally activated delayed spell—you wouldn't need to build the magic program on the spot. When faced with an enemy, it wouldn't need time to set up.

In exchange, you had to record the magic's standby state beforehand. With seal-type spells, if you included the necessary information in the magic program's structure, even a machine could engrave the symbols. This was because it was fundamentally the same as saving an activation sequence to a CAD. But Shippou's spell actually used the same process as activating magic, so the caster had to record the spell.

Plus, the record itself could only be used once. Which made sense because it only released a spell that had been stopped right before activation; it was different in nature from the record of magic that could be used anytime that Tatsuya was searching for. In other words, Million Edge was a spell that took a lot of time to prepare beforehand.

Right now, Takuma was probably pouring his efforts into creating an activation medium for Million Edge for the upcoming match tomorrow. If he planned on winning it, it made sense that he'd need to take today off.

In any case, Minami had informed Tatsuya of Takuma's movements because Tatsuya had decided that investigating whoever his supporters were involved keeping track of him. Minami was worried that Takuma might contact the mastermind while they were still tied up at school, but Tatsuya believed that to be a groundless fear. Today was Friday. All teenagers, not just magic high school students, would be at school right now. Playing hooky might not earn someone a warning, but they would stand out. Takuma, who was at least trying to maintain this conspiracy, wouldn't want too many eyes on him. Tatsuya figured he'd only contact his backer after night fell. And anyway, Fujibayashi's team was observing him, apparently, so if anything happened, they'd contact Tatsuya.

Until night, Tatsuya decided to focus on his schoolwork like a normal student.

"Our disciplinary target is Yoshio Sawamura. President of the Culture Communication Network, otherwise known as CulNet."

As Gongjin Zhou spoke to the young man sitting across from him, Robert Sun, he placed a leather attaché case on the table.

Robert opened the case. Inside were an automatic pistol and a large knife, plastic explosives and a wireless detonator device, and a brass-colored ring.

"You'd like me to put an end to this man?" asked Robert in a surly manner.

Zhou shook his head, a regretful smile on his face. "Normally, yes, but unfortunately, Yoshio Sawamura is currently on a business trip to Paris," he said, handing Robert a large binder.

Robert flipped through the paper documents, which were unusual in this day and age. A young woman's photograph and detailed personal information were included.

"So his daughter instead?"

"It should be enough of a warning."

Robert clapped the binder closed and looked back at the attaché case. His eyes were drawn to the metal ring made of antinite.

"Does she have a magician guarding her?"

"He isn't a bodyguard, but recently, he has been around her frequently. He's still a child, but he does belong to the Eighteen Support Clans."

"I see." A savage grin came to Robert's lips. "A magician created by the Japanese military…"

Strictly speaking, Robert had the wrong idea. The Twenty-Eight—the Ten Master Clans plus the Eighteen Support Clans—were magicians who had been created by magician development laboratories, not by the military itself. But Zhou didn't intend to correct that minor misunderstanding. Magicians in Japan's military were targets of family revenge for Robert. He was enthusiastic now, and throwing cold water on that would be a foolish move.

"The schedule is written there. I could only prepare rings for two people, but I've several sets of guns and knives ready if you need."

"That's enough. I'll use them."

Robert Sun picked up the attaché case and binder and stood up, and Gongjin Zhou saw him off with a smile.

Tatsuya was reviewing his classwork after getting home when he looked up at the sound of the alarm at the edge of his desk. It was a signal from Fujibayashi. He hadn't asked her what methods she was using to do her observation, but the Independent Magic Battalion had little manpower, so she couldn't have been using numbers. She'd probably hacked into the roadside cameras' identification system to keep an eye on when Takuma went out. If she had, that would make him an accomplice to an invasion of privacy via unlawful usage of public systems, but he didn't feel at all guilty about it.

Putting morals to the side for the moment, or rather, never having thought about them to begin with, Tatsuya stood up from his chair—to meet up with Fujibayashi, of course. He told Miyuki and Minami to mind the house—in other words, to absolutely not come after him—and climbed onto his personal electric bike.

As they watched, Takuma disappeared out of a medium-rise building, part of a high-class apartment complex district. He didn't give any sign he detected followers. He did *seem* concerned about whether someone might be watching, but the way he was paying attention was amateurish and insufficient.

"It doesn't look like the Shippou family's head is putting his son through military training."

"To categorize it properly, ma'am, I believe that would be spy training. By the way, Lieutenant, why is Captain Sanada here as well?"

Tatsuya had parked his motorcycle at a station, and now he was observing from the back of a large sedan the apartment complex Takuma had entered. Next to him was Fujibayashi, a desktop-sized information terminal resting on her lap, and in the front seat was Sanada, operating a large tablet.

"Because if this kid has talent *and* a bone to pick with the Ten Master Clans, he'd be a perfect fit for our unit," answered Sanada, turning around in the front seat.

Tatsuya lifted his eyebrows slightly in surprise. "Do you plan on scouting him for the Independent Magic Battalion, sir?"

"Oh, would you not like that, Tatsuya? If you say you dislike Shippou, we'll have no choice but to give up."

Tatsuya scowled. "Why do you make it sound like I have any choice in the matter, ma'am?"

"Well, 'Specialist Ryuuya Ooguro' is our unit's greatest strength. We couldn't afford to put *him* in a bad mood."

This was a joke of Fujibayashi's, of course. But getting riled up about it now wouldn't lead anywhere good. That was what Tatsuya's gut instinct told him.

"...It's not exactly because I hate him, ma'am. I honestly don't care what he does as long as he doesn't meddle in my business."

"Well, they do say the opposite of love is apathy, right?" put in Fujibayashi. Tatsuya didn't deign to comment on that.

"...Then why *are* you helping with this investigation?"

With the baton passed from Fujibayashi to Sanada, the latter's question was a reasonable one, so Tatsuya couldn't keep his silence this time. "If guys like Blanche are backing him, then all making the Shippou settle down will do is make the next problem child appear."

Fujibayashi burst out laughing partway through Tatsuya's explanation. She was probably amused by his calling someone else a problem child. Not that Tatsuya especially cared.

"I see," Sanada said. "If it were just Shippou being rowdy, you could tolerate it, but if a second person, and then a third, and then a fourth show up, that would be an annoyance to you."

"An annoyance isn't all it would be, but...yes, sir." Tatsuya's answer was mixed with a sigh.

"Oh, looks like they're gonna start talking. Want to listen?" asked Fujibayashi, who had been having this conversation with an earbud in her opposite ear the whole time. Apparently she'd started hearing Takuma's conversation with the "mastermind" through the bug they'd planted on him.

"Yes, ma'am, if you don't mind."

Smirking at Tatsuya's response, Fujibayashi switched the sound output to the car speakers.

In general, Takuma didn't look very happy. At least that was the kind of boy he was when Maki Sawamura looked at him. Even when he was talking about how he'd gotten the top grades in the entrance exam and been chosen as the new student representative, he hadn't been visibly happy.

But today he was more disgruntled than usual. Maybe he thought he had the same face on as always, but it was clear as day to Maki.

She was an actress, a professional at faking facial expressions. On top of her naturally beautiful features, her acting skills allowed her to display whatever emotion she wanted on-screen—joy, anger, sadness, pleasure, tenderness, malice, love, or hatred—and they'd won her the number-one spot among young actresses. Her eyes could not be fooled.

"Takuma, I haven't had dinner yet today. It'll be light—do you mind?"

If she got right to the topic, she'd probably end up on the receiving end of his complaints and ire. Instead, with her meal excuse, she schemed to stall for time he could use to cool off.

"At this hour? Wouldn't that be bad for your figure?"

"That's why it'll be a light meal. It's mostly done already, so I'll bring it out."

Mentally giving a point to Takuma for not saying something rude like *You'll get fat*, Maki withdrew to the dining room.

What she brought out were thinly-sliced baguettes and hors d'oeuvres like cured ham, salmon, tomatoes, and avocadoes. They certainly appeared light, but that didn't necessarily reflect how many calories they contained.

Takuma had come after finishing dinner, but not caring about that, he reached for the hors d'oeuvres Maki had made. For about five minutes, Takuma's mouth was mainly used for eating and drinking. He didn't realize that the fruit juice he gulped to wash down the saltier hors d'oeuvres had a little alcohol mixed in. She'd used liqueur in the little bites as well, but he didn't notice that, either.

Timing it for when Takuma had cleaned up most of the "light meal" on the plates himself, Maki began to speak to him in the voice of an open-minded and accepting older sister. (Incidentally, this was when Fujibayashi switched the sound output.)

Takuma, who usually didn't like to show any weakness, was, *for some reason*, quite talkative tonight.

"...Oh, I see. That must have been mortifying for you."

Maki comforted the young man in a sweet voice that would have made any of her fans breathe a sigh. Right now, she was sitting next to him on a three-person sofa with her hand on his shoulder, peering into his face as she talked to him.

"I'm not mortified! It was never a fair fight to begin with! If we'd kept on going, I would have won!"

Takuma had been repeating that over and over for a while now, but Maki never let any distaste cross her face as she stuck with him. "Of course, Takuma. *In reality*, you would have won. You would have won the respect and the praise afforded to the victor. I think it only didn't happen because you were unlucky."

"You think so…?"

"Yes. People say luck is part of skill, but that isn't right. The *truly* skilled will always win *in the end* regardless of luck. But when you look at individual, smaller matches, luck sometimes affects the outcome. It's happened to me personally many times—where the stars didn't line up, and I didn't get a role I wanted."

With one hand on Takuma's shoulder, Maki put her other over the back of Takuma's hand.

A soft sensation stroked his skin, and a smell like honey stimulated his nose.

"So you'll be fine, Takuma. You just happened to have bad luck yesterday. A trivial match like that won't affect your future."

"I guess…"

They'd already gone through similar exchanges several times, but Takuma finally showed a different reaction. Internally relieved, Maki knew it would just take one more push.

"It's true. So cheer up."

Maki guided Takuma's hand onto her lap. Using seduction to achieve her ends went against her policy, but a timid Takuma was enough to pique her playful spirit.

Takuma's hand slid little by little from her knee toward her thigh, but it was Maki who was moving it that way. She was wearing a loose, open-front dress, the skirt long. But at the chest it was open wide, and its fabric was thin enough to see her skin through. Feeling Maki's skin through her skirt and with his will already slackened because of the alcohol's effects, Takuma's self-control began to wane.

Takuma brushed her hand aside and lifted his palm from her thigh.

A moment later, his hands were grabbing Maki's shoulders.

As the force pushed her down, she only made a token effort to resist.

"Oh, my. This has turned into something big."

Fujibayashi was clearly amused, but Tatsuya didn't give her a cold look. He didn't appear appalled or disdainful, either. His face was cool and calm and unconnected to such ideas as excitement or blushing.

"This may be convenient," he answered in an extremely dry tone as they listened to the steamy voices over the wiretap.

"Now, what might you be plotting?" asked Fujibayashi with interest, her expression still one of amusement.

"Recently the media have been buzzing with news of a female celebrity buying boys as prostitutes, ma'am," answered Tatsuya, his tone still businesslike.

"...A threat?" Cracks appeared in Fujibayashi's grin.

"It should be fine once in a while for *us* to be using the media."

"...I'm surprised you thought up something like that *so quickly*."

Sanada, who thought of all kinds of villainous plans when it came to technology, offered his opinion with a slight grimace. Although, judging by how he placed the emphasis on the words *so quickly*, he seemed to think that given more time he'd have thought of it, too.

"If this escalates into an actual crime, the damage the school receives will be too large and we might not be able to use this as a *negotiation* tool, so we should step in while we can write it off as only *attempted*."

Tatsuya, not budging from either Fujibayashi or Sanada's reaction, calmly proposed a plan.

While entangled with Takuma on the sofa, Maki had been coolly observing him—not that her own expressions of pleasure had been 100 percent an act, though. It may not have been as much as Takuma had drunk, but the alcohol she'd ingested was dulling the brakes on her reason. But even as her eyes looked enraptured, she watched through sober vision the boy's foolishness as he bent over her. She'd learned the trick to separating physical sensation from mental pleasure long ago.

So even if Takuma didn't realize it, Maki's clear mind realized something was wrong. The sliding door to the veranda was opening up with a soft noise. Without a doubt, and even though it had been locked. And regardless of the fact that crime-prevention mechanisms equipped with all the attack power the law would allow had been set up there.

The security alarm wasn't going off. The bodyguards didn't seem to notice, either.

"Someone! It's a thief!" shouted Maki as she pushed Takuma off her, intensely regretting her overreliance on the security system in not closing the shutters.

After rolling onto the floor, Takuma reacted to her shout.

Hastily, he stood up and turned to face where Maki was looking. But before he could make out the burglar, a mild shock ran across his features. By the time he realized something had been thrown at him, he was overtaken by an irresistible drowsiness and crumpled to the floor again.

"Takuma?!"

Because she immediately covered her mouth with her sleeve, the cry Maki gave turned into a muffled one. She had an idea as to the reason Takuma had passed out. She'd been shown the real thing alongside a prop once. What Takuma had taken in the face was a sponge ball loaded with an extremely fast-acting sleep drug. It wasn't the kind he'd wake up from in five or ten minutes, either.

Fighting her fear, Maki turned back toward the veranda. The sliding door and curtains were already closed. In front of them stood a figure all in black, including a black mask, with what looked like folded wings on his back—looking just like a mystery man from an old movie who was based on a bat. If he'd had wings on the sides of the mask, he'd have been perfect. The outfit was actually stealth gear using EM-absorbing fabrics, but there was no way for Maki to know that.

"My lady, are you all right?!"

Then, finally, her two bodyguards burst into the living room. Right as the wings on the mystery man's back fell to the floor. No sooner had they seen that than the two female bodyguards sprang toward the burglar.

Had he only brought one sleeping-drug ball? The thief in black didn't move from his spot and intercepted the women. Her bodyguards were holding indoor-combat-use clubs in each hand. These weren't simple sticks or police batons—their grips made of flexible material and their weight frontloaded on their tips wrapped in rubber, they were *weapons* that could also function as blackjacks.

A club swung down, and the mystery man calmly stopped it. Not with his arm, but with his palm, wrapped in a glove.

By taking a step forward and to the side, one bodyguard entered the blind spot provided by the other and placed herself in a position so that only one of her two clubs would reach. Because of this, there was now only one club he'd have to defend against. By stopping that one, he restricted the enemy's movements, and he launched a fist toward the bodyguard whose escape was now cut off.

The female bodyguard was easily sent flying.

The other bodyguard flinched as the combat force drew a straight line toward her.

The mystery man's movements showed no mercy.

Black fists shot out, one after another.

Maki's bodyguards were disabled, unable to even scratch him.

The mystery man walked in front of Maki, who had slumped on the sofa after her knees gave out, and spoke in a voice she remembered.

"Would you mind fixing your clothes?"

Maki then remembered she was in a half-naked state. Her dress was completely off, with only her sleeves left, and they didn't do much to hide her. Her underwear was still performing its duty, but traces of her *previous phase* were written in spots here and there on her exposed skin.

"Oh, but do you *want* me to put my clothes back on?"

Using all her strength to control her body and keep it from shaking madly, she started to use the coquettish acting directors had lambasted her endlessly for when she was still a new actress. If this mystery man was the boy she thought he was, then he'd fly right into her arms. She didn't know what he was after, but if they exchanged feelings, she was confident she could bring this in a direction that benefited her.

But her scheme stumbled on the first step. No, it didn't even have time to *take* that first step.

"Of course. Though if you insist, I do not mind."

Maki felt like someone had poured ice water over her head. A cold rage at her pride being wounded overrode her cowardice. With an irritated expression, she fixed herself up.

"...Is this fine with you? How long are you going to wear that *thing*, anyway? It doesn't look good on you, Tatsuya Shiba."

Her disdainful tone as she said "that thing" referred to the black mask Tatsuya, disguised as a bat-man, was wearing—which was actually a newly developed helmet of flexible material. Of course, what she'd *really* wanted to say was the name Tatsuya Shiba. In other words, it was to tell him she knew who he was. But even with his expression hidden behind the mask, Maki could tell plain as day that Tatsuya wasn't the least bit bothered—no, she was *made* to understand—

"Then let's move on to our negotiations."

—by the fact that Tatsuya ignored her provocation with extreme ease.

"Negotiations? What on earth are you after?"

Maki wasn't hung up on her own pride. She was well aware that she was the weaker party in this situation. She knew from the previous scene that violence wouldn't be a match for him. Her womanly weapons didn't seem to be much help, either. She realized her options at the moment were extremely limited.

"First, please listen to this."

That his choice of words was polite, like *normal*, bothered her. But that was utterly trivial up against the voices Tatsuya played from the terminal in his hand.

It was the voices of her and Takuma as they were entangled on the sofa.

"You were eavesdropping?! You creep!" Maki cried out despite herself, even though, considering the situation, such an insult wouldn't do her any favors. She thought *Damn it!* that very instant, but she couldn't suppress the ire in her mind.

"It would be a problem if this were to leak to the media."

But when Tatsuya stopped the playback and said that, Maki's mind passed through coldness and simply froze.

"There has been similar news recently… Even an idol past her prime can cause disturbances like that, so what about a beautiful actress who is, in fact, *in* her pri—"

"What do you want?!" shouted Maki hysterically, interrupting Tatsuya. She was angrier at herself for being so careless earlier than at the boy in front of her, who had come to her with a cowardly threat.

"I have two demands."

A calm voice, in contrast with Maki's, his uninterested baritone fostered anxiety in her.

"First, please cut off relations with Shippou. Oh, and I'm not referring to *those* relations, so please don't pretend you don't understand."

"Fine!" agreed Maki in a sulky voice, having been warned in advance when she had, in fact, been about to go on the evasive using such an interpretation.

"Second, please don't interfere with anyone high school–aged or below."

"…What do you mean by that?"

Maki wasn't playing dumb; she genuinely didn't understand what Tatsuya was after with that demand. She knew what the words meant, but not why he was demanding something like that from *her*.

"I don't know exactly what you're planning to do. It may actually be something that benefits magicians, but I don't have any interest in that. I'd just like you to stop disrupting things in my general vicinity."

"What…?" She looked back at the black-masked young man with a blank look.

"College students and older are adults themselves, so I don't intend to interfere with whatever you do with regards to them. As long as it doesn't disadvantage me. Will you accept these demands?"

"Y-yes… If that's all you want, then yes."

She felt taken aback. He'd pretended to break in and rob her just for that?

And that made it all the more uncanny. Unlawful entrance, acts of violence, and threats. If what he was doing came to light in a court of law, they'd definitely be considered serious crimes. And he had no hesitation in doing them anyway for something as trivial as this.

Realization dawned on her. *This boy doesn't fear the law, doesn't fear the state's authority…*

"Who *are* you…?" she asked with much trepidation. Reason was telling her it was better not to ask, but she couldn't help herself. This night was the first time someone with an unknown identity had ever caused her such unease.

"When I confirm your enactment of my demands, I will erase this voice data."

Her question didn't receive an answer.

"You have my thanks for making this negotiation worthwhile."

Putting the things that looked like folded wings onto his back again, he gave a contemptuously nonchalant remark and exited onto the veranda.

In haste, Maki followed after him.

But the boy garbed in black clothes had abruptly vanished from the veranda.

Tatsuya confirmed Maki peering *down* from the veranda from *above* before pulling his head back.

He was standing on the apartment complex's roof. His initial plan had been to use his foldable glider to descend to the ground, but he'd changed it after noticing a suspicious silhouette in the night sky.

The black shadow was a small aircraft. For a moment, he thought it was the stealth airship belonging to a certain department of the JDF's intelligence bureau that had been involved with the incident some months ago, but the vessel's shape immediately informed him that he was wrong. This was a commonplace type that media organizations and film companies used to record video from the sky. But it was painted all black, obviously for cloak-and-dagger uses. If a black video-shooting vessel was in the night sky, Tatsuya knew it could only be for sneak photography.

He called up Fujibayashi on his transmitter. "Lieutenant, do you have a read on the airship closing in on Maki Sawamura's apartment building?"

"Yes, I have it. I've had it since you went into the actress's room. I didn't think it would descend like this, though."

"Do you know who it belongs to, ma'am?"

"A TV station, based on its flight plan."

The corporation Fujibayashi named was a local cable channel in the south Kanto region that mainly covered celebrity gossip. Its affiliations made it a rival of the TV studio Maki's father had under his umbrella.

"Could they be going after a Maki Sawamura scandal?"

"I don't think the chances are zero."

Loathing had seeped into Fujibayashi's voice; probably an emotional reaction to the act of secret photography.

"Lieutenant, can you turn off the psion radars in this area? Five minutes would be enough."

"Are you going to stop them?"

"Yes, ma'am."

Meanwhile, Tatsuya had decided to interfere with their secret photography because he didn't want his negotiations with Maki to go to waste. If Takuma was caught on camera in Maki's room, then even if it wasn't in the middle of *certain acts*, that would be enough of a scandal.

"Do it in three minutes, Specialist," came the request from Sanada.

"Yes, sir."

Taking his favorite CAD, the Silver Horn Custom Trident, in his right hand, he looked up at the airship just as the gondola door opened and a rope ladder was lowered.

They won't stop at secret photography, they're even going to break and enter? thought Tatsuya to himself, ignoring his own acts moments earlier, before activating a jump spell toward the gondola entrance.

Tatsuya didn't understand the angry shouts directed at him as soon as he jumped into the aircraft. From their words he felt like it might have been a language from the East Asian mainland, but he had never learned either Pekingese or Cantonese.

But he knew right away the situation wasn't what he'd expected. Obviously, these men were no TV reporters. They had guns—pointed at him.

Of course, Tatsuya wasn't about to let them fire. He already had his Trident in standby mode in his right hand. He took zero extra time to switch his dismantling targets.

Five weapons were aimed at him.

Every one of them lost its form, and their pieces scattered about the gondola floor.

The reaction to his dismantling magic was a startlingly quick one.

The two on either end stuck their fists out toward Tatsuya. Brass-colored rings shone dully on their middle fingers. Psionic noise filled the gondola. Cast Jamming, propagated via antinite.

Two on the inside readied knives, then charged for him in the swaying gondola.

Tatsuya's finger moved twice on his CAD.

His information structure–dismantling spell wiped out the Cast Jamming noise structure, and all five of the villains were pierced through both thighs and crumpled to the floor.

But that wasn't the end of it. The man who had been standing in the middle—just before he fell, Tatsuya noticed him clenching his right hand.

Tatsuya dived out of the thrown-open gondola door into midair.

There was a flash and the sound of an explosion, and the aircraft went up in flames.

He knew, at least, that if he let it fall like that, there would be more to come. But he needed to prioritize something else right now. An airship falling on an apartment complex district would be a major tragedy.

Exposed to the blast winds, Tatsuya twisted his body around. He aimed his Trident CAD at the descending airship as its air bladder broke.

Falling while facing upward, he activated Mist Dispersion.

As he watched the airship wreckage vanish into dust, he called up an inertial control spell whose magic program was already recorded. A moment later, he felt a severe impact on his back.

Tatsuya had fallen onto the roof of a building outside Maki's apartment complex. For all the building's height and the short falling distance, the inertial control working though him was strong enough that it ended up being the glider on his back that cushioned his fall and managed to keep every bone in his body from breaking. Of course, if Regenerate hadn't been working, he probably wouldn't have ever walked again.

"Tatsuya, what happened?!"

Fujibayashi's voice, audible through the transmitter, sounded considerably panicked.

"Unknown. I believe the TV station would have the clues, ma'am. That aircraft appears to have been hijacked."

After adding, in a disconsolate voice, that maybe it hadn't been a hijack and maybe the TV station was in on it, Tatsuya picked himself up off the roof, from which the traces of his fall had been erased.

Robert Sun's failure in the Maki Sawamura raid operation became known very quickly to Gongjin Zhou. A subordinate who was standing by, the one he would have sent to the traitor with photographs of his daughter's murder had the operation succeeded, had informed him of it.

A falling, flaming airship vanished into thin air... The only person who could do that is...

Unfortunately, they hadn't been able to take any pictures. His subordinate's report was a noncommittal one as well, but Zhou correctly deduced who had interfered in the operation from the fact that the ship had disappeared in midair.

...Detestable. That man again?

Still, he only knew who the man was by his visage, the helmet covering his face, and his nicknames, Demon Right and Maheśvara. The invasion forces under Zhou's control during the Yokohama Incident had met a terrible end at the hands of this unidentified magician, too. One could even say that the huge blow they'd taken from Maheśvara had been a major factor in their invasion operation's failure.

The damage that the GAA forces had sustained during the Yokohama Incident in and of itself wasn't the least bit inconvenient for Zhou. He'd always hoped for the Japanese and GAA militaries to take each other down. Contrary to his plans, it had ended in one-sided victory for the Japanese, but in a way, a weakened GAA was exactly what he'd been after.

This time, though, he couldn't smile the matter away.

It looks like we'll need to seriously go after his identity.

At the same time, he felt the need to change the direction of the media manipulation he was in the middle of.

When all's said and done, Master's true wishes were to exact revenge against those who destroyed Dahan... My real target isn't an abstract notion of Japan's magicians as a group, but that one clan.

And Zhou knew someone influential with very special feelings toward that clan.

It won't be much—it certainly won't cause a family split—but there's no harm in giving it a try.

Zhou lowered his eyes to his glass of wine, which he hadn't drunk from yet, and began to assemble a plan in his mind.

[16]

Saturday, April 28, 3:00 PM.

Tomitsuka and Takuma appeared in seminar room three on time, as instructed.

Hattori would be the one judging this match. And for whatever unfortunate reason, or possibly it was just the natural course of things, Tatsuya was once again involved with a Takuma match as a witness.

Incidentally, as far as Tatsuya could tell, Takuma wasn't showing any aftereffects from the preceding night. Not only physically, but mentally as well. The actress had probably done a good job supporting him. But at the same time, that meant Tatsuya could assume she hadn't "broken up" with him. He figured that for a time, she would be watching and waiting.

An array of prominent guests were here as well, including Miyuki from the student council, Sawaki and Mikihiko from the disciplinary committee, and Kirihara from the club committee. Kirihara had permission to use his CAD, and not just for show.

Should they need it, he would be the peacemaker.

That, too, was because this match was being held under somewhat unusual rules. More accurately, exceptional rules had been added to it: There was no usage restriction on Million Edge. Nobody would stop it, regardless of how strong or weak it was. Only in the event that it was clear the opponent would sustain excessive injury would they stop the match. Thinking about it calmly, the risks for a rule like that were far too large. And it would be one-sidedly against the opponent. But the one who had suggested this rule was that very opponent: Tomitsuka.

More than likely, Tomitsuka had a secret plan to completely negate Million Edge. Takuma understood that, too, and he wasn't happy about it. He felt like he'd been told the Shippou family's trump card was little more than nothing. But this match had been put together because Takuma had argued against his being disqualified for using it. This was a rule he needed to welcome—not one to be unhappy with.

Tomitsuka and Takuma faced each other from a distance.

Today, Takuma was wearing outdoor training coveralls, too.

Meanwhile, Tomitsuka wore a magic martial arts uniform. It consisted of a long-sleeved, buttonless shirt with cushioning on the elbows and a loose, beltless pair of pants tight only near the ankles, with cushioning on the knees. On his feet were soft shoes for close combat. The wide rings on the eight fingers, excluding his thumbs, coming out of his fingerless gloves were input devices for his magic martial arts–specialized CAD. One ring corresponded to one button, and by moving his fingers or concentrating psions in them, he would relay his activation sequence choice to the actual CAD attached to the wrist of his glove. The rings had been covered with flexible resin-based cushioning, so he wouldn't be able to use them as weapons. That was official match style. In other words, Tomitsuka was completely in serious mode.

Hattori stood between the two and explained the rules. Still, there wasn't much to explain. It was mostly ceremonial.

Hattori stepped away from them, then raised his hand.

All at once, the tension grew. Everyone observing could feel the nonphysical waves—not psionic waves—clashing between Tomitsuka and Takuma.

Tomitsuka lowered his body slightly. Takuma put his right hand to his book, the activation medium, which he still held in his left hand.

Even those not participating couldn't move a muscle or make a peep. The room was deathly quiet, and they could even hear Hattori's intake of breath before he broke the silence.

"Begin!"

The first to move was Takuma.

Though it may be more accurate to say that Tomitsuka *didn't* move.

Takuma opened his book and grasped the first dozen or so pages in his right fingers. He ripped them out all at once—actually, they turned into a paper blizzard right when he put force into his hand.

Paper blades, each four millimeters square, numbering about eighty thousand in all. Instead of manifesting a million blades at once, Takuma seemed to have chosen the strategy of finely controlling a *small number* of them.

In response, Tomitsuka, without moving, just watched as the paper scraps flew toward him, separated into four clouds. He appeared to the others to be patiently saving his energy. And their judgment was correct.

White paper belts slithered through the air. They were like four snakes crawling through the clouds. Their fangs were aimed at the arms and thighs. Takuma first planned to deal damage to Tomitsuka's limbs to stop him from moving.

Right before the paper flows reached Tomitsuka, their lengths decreased, and their densities increased. Their march stopped—and a moment later, they suddenly accelerated. The swarms of paper blades circled about Tomitsuka's arms and legs, trying to tear his skin.

At the same time—

Tomitsuka released an explosive psionic light from his body. As the invisible light glittered, the paper blades reverted to mere scraps.

Eighty thousand pieces of paper lost their energy in midair, then turned into a paper blizzard that scattered and danced all over.

Sawaki, Kirihara, and Mikihiko each unintentionally raised a hand to their eyes. Tatsuya, Miyuki, and Hattori, too, squinted at the brightness.

They knew what this light was.

"Program Demolition…?"

A dazed murmur—it was Mikihiko's voice.

"Someone besides Tatsuya can use that at our school…? And he's in the same grade…?"

Program Demolition was an incredibly rare technique that almost nobody used. That was a fact and common knowledge, not just something Mikihiko had convinced himself of. And there were *two* people in his grade at his school who could use it. His shock was completely understandable.

"Maybe we should prefix that with *contact-type*."

This supplement came from Miyuki.

"That's right! I should have guessed, Shiba—you've got a good eye!" The one who agreed more eagerly than he needed to was Sawaki. "I gotta say, though, Tomitsuka's really into this."

As Tomitsuka's senior in the club, Sawaki already knew he could use what Miyuki called "contact-type Program Demolition." This technique, which could nullify magic that touched you, could be called Million Edge's natural enemy, since the latter changed simple paper scraps into flying blades via sustained, magic-induced event alteration.

Sawaki also knew Tomitsuka had suggested the special rule because he was confident in this technique. He'd been prepared for Tomitsuka to use it, but today, Tomitsuka was more *brilliant* than he'd anticipated. That was a happy thing for Sawaki—in many ways, Sawaki hadn't lost his boyish heart.

But unlike the upperclassman witnesses, Takuma didn't have time to be impressed. He knew full well what this exchange meant.

Million Edge wouldn't work on his opponent.

It had only taken one attack to inform him of that.

…No, it just means it won't work if I attack him head-on! I learned two days ago that magic is all about how you use it!

As Takuma told himself that and got himself pumped up, Tomitsuka watched patiently. He was full of options right now. Tomitsuka knew that if he wanted to, he could end the match right now. But that wouldn't mean anything. He knew just as well as Takuma that he couldn't let this match end so easily.

Finally, Takuma readied himself again. As he did, Tomitsuka increased his psionic activity. Takuma flipped through the book's pages—well, he pretended to do so as he went for the CAD on his wrist.

The spell he activated was Air Bullet. Seven compressed air masses shot toward Tomitsuka at a high speed.

Without watching the result, Takuma activated his next spell. Even he didn't think Air Bullets would be able to take Tomitsuka out. They weren't anything more than a distraction. Takuma tried to use a self-accelerating spell to go around Tomitsuka.

However, when Takuma reached that point, Tomitsuka was there waiting for him.

"Guh, gah!"

There were no rules against physical attacks. A combination body blow into a hook came. Unable to withstand it, Takuma fell to the floor. Only his stubbornness kept the activation medium book in his hand. Blowing away the mists threatening his consciousness with willpower, he searched for his opponent.

Tomitsuka looked at him without a follow-up. He always looked so friendly, even childlike, but now scorn was on his face, as though he were looking down at—down *on*—a filthy wild dog.

That was how it looked to Takuma. For a moment, the anger boiling within him overrode his fear. Kneeling on one knee, he opened the book in his left hand.

Twice the paper fragments of his initial eighty-thousand attack sailed toward Tomitsuka. This time, not split into four but combined as one. The more "colonies" were involved in colony control, the more its power waned. Takuma challenged Tomitsuka's Program Demolition head-on by combining the quartered magic power into one.

——But it was a feint. The real attack was the one he fired a few moments later.

The paper blizzard made of one hundred and sixty thousand pieces turned into scraps against the psionic light Tomitsuka released and scattered to the floor.

Then, as if piercing the white clouds, twenty thousand more blades, fired a few moments later, turned into a tornado and struck at Tomitsuka's feet!

Takuma knew he'd done it. All Program Demolition did was emit a large amount of psions. But Tomitsuka had to do more than that—he had to compress them tightly enough to blow away the magic program. He wouldn't be able to fire it again this quickly.

But Takuma's prediction was wrong. He only realized long after that it hadn't been a prediction at all, but a dream.

At the time, he didn't understand. Program Demolition and *contact-type* Program Demolition were similar but different techniques.

The moment the twenty thousand blades struck Tomitsuka's body, they turned into twenty thousand paper scraps.

This time, as Takuma stood there blankly, Tomitsuka delivered the finishing blow.

"That's enough. The winner is Tomitsuka."

Named the victor by Hattori, Tomitsuka gave a small bow.

Then he knelt next to his classmate, who was lying on the floor.

"Shippou, are you conscious?"

Takuma, moaning in pain as he was, was of course conscious. Tomitsuka had hit him so that he'd stay awake—this was what he'd wanted.

After coughing several times, eventually Takuma simply answered, "Yes."

"Then stand. Take a short rest near the wall."

"...All right."

Takuma, a sense of defeat pounded into him, followed Tomitsuka's instructions, not knowing why he was hearing them. He staggered over to the wall unsteadily, slowly, while holding his gut where he'd been hit, to the opposite side from where the observers were standing. Resting his back against the wall, he slid down it until he was sitting on the floor.

Once Tomitsuka saw that Takuma was watching him, he walked up in front of Tatsuya.

"...What is it?" asked Tatsuya eventually.

Tomitsuka, looking like he was having a hard time saying something, finally spoke. "Shiba, would you have a match with me?!"

The request, broached after some hesitation, was one that made Tatsuya tilt his head and wonder why.

With the suspicion-filled gaze on him, Tomitsuka averted his eyes uncomfortably. But immediately, he took a leap into that abyss—that was an exaggeration, but he *did* have enough determination to try bungee jumping, anyway—and looked back into Tatsuya's eyes.

"I want you to show your true strength to Shippou!"

His gaze burning brightly, Tomitsuka stared at Tatsuya. He probably envisioned a scenario in which Tatsuya accepted as a response to his own masculinity.

But Tatsuya's confusion only deepened. "I don't understand why...?"

As soon as he said that, Tomitsuka faltered so hard it was almost funny. "Uhh, right. I guess that was kind of sudden. What I mean is—"

"Could you show to Shippou what a match between two people who have true skill looks like?"

While Tomitsuka was busy being flustered, Hattori took up the explanation for him—and that alone was still incomprehensible to Tatsuya.

"If you want a match of true skill, wouldn't you and Sawaki be more suitable for it?"

"There's meaning in you showing your skill here, Shiba."

Hattori's explanation was nowhere near enough.

"Brother, it will be fine, won't it?"

But then support fire—and to Tomitsuka and Hattori, the strongest kind—came flying in.

"If they want you to set an example for an underclassman, I believe that's a role suited to a student council member."

The upperclassmen and classmates listening to her speak (except Tatsuya) for some reason all translated *student council member* to *brother*.

"In fact, I was just thinking that I'd quite like to see you display your strength as well, Brother."

Miyuki's motives were obviously different from Tomitsuka's. There was a metric ton of irritation behind her smile. And it had crossed the threshold of what he could safely ignore.

"…Well, if you say so."

Tatsuya changing his mind, or rather making a decision, should have been what Tomitsuka was after. But for some reason, Tomitsuka couldn't stop himself from feeling like something had just been spoiled for him.

And others, not just him, were feeling the same way.

Hattori had stretched out the reservation for this room because of this right from the start. All the seniors present already knew about the plan for this match. They'd gotten permission, too, so as soon as the battlefield was clear, they could start.

"Please, leave it to me."

The one who volunteered to clean up all the paper scraps strewn about the floor was Miyuki. She used her CAD, and without a moment's delay, an indoor airflow gently began to blow. It passed around the room's corners, whirling in a complicated fashion, and it barely took any time to gather the garbage in one place. Then Miyuki used the vacuum for the room's maintenance and sucked it all up.

She'd just performed a complex, elaborate spell as though it were nothing, a testament to her skill. The seniors looked at her with approval, Mikihiko and Tomitsuka gave sighs of admiration, and Takuma was shocked—leaving aside the process of hardening the paper scraps, the spell Miyuki had just used was technically superior to his Million Edge.

"Shiba, is that good?" Tomitsuka asked.

"Yeah, it shouldn't cause a problem."

Tatsuya handed his jacket to Miyuki. Now he just wore his school uniform.

"Do you want me to take my shoes off?" he asked.

"No, you can keep them on."

That implied he didn't care if Tatsuya used kicks with hard shoes.

Tatsuya and Tomitsuka faced off in the center.

Hattori would remain the judge. But this time, he skipped the rules explanation.

"Are you both ready? Then begin!"

Right as Hattori gave the signal, Tatsuya and Tomitsuka both pushed off the floor.

In complete contrast to the previous match, Tomitsuka charged aggressively straight for Tatsuya.

But Tatsuya's backing up was quicker.

In the blink of an eye, he jumped to the edge of the seminar room, then pointed his handgun-shaped specialized CAD at Tomitsuka.

Loaded into it was a dismantling spell: Mist Dispersion.

Despite the startled look Miyuki gave, Tatsuya pulled his CAD's trigger.

…And nothing happened.

Thought so.

Miyuki had a hand to her mouth, her face white, while Tatsuya looked as though he'd predicted this. When Tomitsuka came at him with a straight fist, pushed forward by a self-accelerating spell, Tatsuya jumped to the side to dodge it.

It hadn't been a failed show of strength—he'd predicted his Mist Dispersion would be neutralized.

Tatsuya's *vision* showed him an outline, covered in thick clouds and hard to make out—Tomitsuka's true form. It was Tomitsuka as seen from the information dimension.

The dense clouds were a psionic suit of armor, thickly covering his physical body and its information bodies.

Program Demolition was an anti-magic spell that used psionic pressure to separate a magic program from a target.

But Tomitsuka didn't fire a psionic bullet to blast away a magic program. With thick psionic armor to cover his "body," he was preventing any magic programs from getting inside.

If Program Demolition was a cannon, Tomitsuka's contact-type Program Demolition was a steel rampart. Plus, that rampart didn't possess such a structure as an information body. It was just a huge amount of psions wrapping around him chaotically. Piercing this wall and applying *direct* magic to him wouldn't be easy, even for Tatsuya.

If he attacked indirectly with an event caused by magic, the psionic armor wouldn't mean anything.

And as long as Tatsuya didn't use his retrofitted low-output virtual magic region, he was a flawed magician who could only use magic that directly affected a target.

After his fifth charge was dodged, Tomitsuka began to grow impatient.

He was called Range Zero—he didn't have any ranged magic tricks. But in exchange, he thought, he'd honed his close-combat magic skills to twice those of anyone else.

But his attacks were being handled with ease.

Not with magic, but by a combination of magic and martial arts.

I had guessed he'd be good, but not this good...

Frank admiration began to sprout at his opponent's skill level. At the same time, his fighting spirit began to boil.

But I won't lose. At this distance, I can't possibly lose!

Shippou disappeared from his mind. The goal of this match and his personal role in it also began to fade from his mind. His intentions were converging on one thing: victory.

"They're amazing! I knew about Tomitsuka's skill, but not that Shiba was this good."

"I'm surprised Tomitsuka can even match my man Shiba out there."

As he listened to his upperclassmen talking, Mikihiko was simply in awe. His opinion was the same as Kirihara's. He'd never thought they had a classmate who could rival Tatsuya in close combat ability. He felt like this was the first time he'd ever seen Tatsuya having a hard time.

Already, Tatsuya was getting to the point where he wouldn't be able to simply dodge the attacks. Soon he wouldn't be able to handle them without counterattacking. With his CAD in his right hand, he was handicapped. Because of the match rules, he couldn't strike with it. But without that, Tomitsuka's crazed offensive was driving him into a corner.

Suddenly curious, Mikihiko looked next to him.

Miyuki's expression was tense as she watched her brother, immersed.

Takuma, sitting on the floor with his back to the wall, was overwhelmed by the duel happening before his eyes.

At a glance, it just looked like they were brawling. Actually, kicking techniques were coming out sometimes, so it looked like a simple martial arts match. But each and every strike was woven with advanced magic. His shock was all the stronger because he'd been born with the ability to understand that.

Tomitsuka closed the distance too quickly to see. He was increasing his speed with a self-accelerating spell, but it wasn't a slipshod kind that implied speed was the only answer. He was controlling it, keeping it just barely within the mental zone where he could consciously keep up with it.

His footing faltered slightly. The floor was shaking with pinpoint precision each time his forward-charging foot hit the ground, rattling his senses. The vibrations were, of course, created by Tatsuya's magic. But even though he tried to send vibrations to where Tomitsuka stood, they were all being nullified by Program Demolition, which was constantly active (or at least appeared to be). Takuma had experienced that the hard way. But the *aftershocks* of the vibrations, created a moment later, were a purely physical phenomenon, and Program Demolition couldn't cancel them out. Had the ground been dirt or a sidewalk, the aftershocks probably would have been too small to perceive. But the seminar room's floor was made with suitable hardness and elasticity to both soften the impact of falling and to not interfere with movement over it. The magic-based interference had been in consideration of that.

It threw Tomitsuka's precise and accurate body-controlling calculations to the wind, causing him to pause to reoptimize his motions. Taking advantage of that slight window, Tatsuya pointed his CAD at Tomitsuka and pulled the trigger. And at *the exact same time, without any time for Takuma to perceive an activation sequence expanding,* an oscillation spell attacked Tomitsuka. It vibrated psions—it was both an oscillation-type spell and a typeless spell at the same time.

The spell didn't have enough strength to punch through Tomitsuka's defenses. Takuma guessed that was because the spell prioritized speed over power. He thought that the reason he couldn't actually perceive any of these activation sequences was that they'd been adjusted specifically for speed. Or maybe it was the CAD's specs that was responsible.

But even if it wasn't strong enough to knock Tomitsuka down, that didn't mean it had zero effect. Hit with an oscillating psion wave, the psionic field surrounding Tomitsuka also shook slightly. It became noise, a smoke curtain, and it dulled Tomitsuka's senses.

And the next attack was the real one. Palm strikes from Tatsuya's left hand fired out toward Tomitsuka. Takuma sensed that there was some kind of spell in his palm, too.

His attacks came one after another, none of them having the same pattern as any before, but Tomitsuka once again defended against them. With his Program Demolition–harboring right arm, he stopped the oscillation spell–harboring left palm. As an infinite variety of attacks pummeled him, Tomitsuka continued blocking them all with a single shield.

Tomitsuka's left hand struck out toward Tatsuya's stomach. The blow was slow, which actually made it harder to block; Tatsuya just barely let it slip by his right arm.

A spell triggered—Tomitsuka's acceleration magic, Exploder. As it was in the process of activating, Tatsuya's own Program Demolition destroyed it.

Tatsuya evaded the follow-up attack and took a leap to the side. On the sidelines, Takuma's eyes were glued to the action; he'd forgotten to breathe. He couldn't believe what he'd just *sensed*. And he felt fear, as well, from his own *magician's senses* being thrown so far out of whack.

Tomitsuka's acceleration spell—the one that had been canceled midactivation. Tatsuya had used that canceled event alteration as a springboard to activate his *own* self-acceleration spell.

Takuma wanted to shout, *You can do that?!*

If the shock to his mind had been *a little smaller*, he doubtless would have. He knew that if two event alterations were the same type, you could activate a second spell without getting in the way of the event-altering force of the first spell. And Exploder created an acceleration vector in a half sphere around its activation point, so acceleration to the side didn't break the basic premise of this spell.

But it didn't do anything—it just *didn't get in the way*. Taking advantage of someone else's spell and linking a new event alteration in the direction the natural law of resistance was weakened in? Takuma had never even thought of such a possibility.

What he was seeing before his eyes was still the same old magic he'd always used. Techniques belonging to the same system. But these spells were in a different dimension from his. Takuma's eyes were glued to the next-level skirmish unfolding in front of him.

I can't get any attacks to hit!
Tomitsuka was steadily losing his cool.·

They hadn't exactly been fighting for long. Not even ten minutes had gone by since the match started. But separate from his physical senses, his mind felt like it had been fighting for hours and hours.

He commanded the flow. Without a doubt, he had the advantage. He was confident of that. He had the initiative right now, and though he hadn't landed any clean hits, his blocked strikes were still racking up damage. He could feel it.

Still, Tatsuya wasn't the only one taking damage. Tomitsuka could feel it building up inside him, too, little by little. He'd blocked all his enemy's attacks. The damage he felt wasn't physical—it was, so to speak, illusory damage. But that illusion was still shaking his defenses a little at a time. The one constant built into the ever-changing attack patterns was an untyped oscillation spell. Those vibrations were rebounding off his wall, and at the moment they disappeared, the spell delivered a wave to the wall itself. He felt those waves rattling his psion particles, inflating his psionic field just like a solid undergoing thermal expansion, lowering its density all the while.

Tomitsuka couldn't fire his own psions far. The farthest he could expand them was so they tightly covered his body. This was the flaw that made him unable to use ranged magic very well. The magic scholar his parents had called had explained that his "core" was extremely rigid, strongly drawing the psions in, and thus psions that would normally have flowed out of him weren't parting from the source. What

Miyuki and Sawaki called contact-type Program Demolition was a product of what was, in a way, an accursed nature.

He'd already made his peace with this nature. He'd worked out how to use ranged magic *a little bit* as well, and had turned this characteristic into a weapon for close combat that other magicians didn't have. It was no more than a moderate defense against attacks that hit him with purely physical force like the shock waves Sawaki delivered by accelerating his fist—it was a club secret that the president of the magic martial arts club had given his own technique the embarrassing name "Mach Punch"—but he had absolute faith in it against spells of the sort where the magic program directly touched you.

Unfortunately, that psionic field that he shouldn't ever be able to expand was dispersing, little by little, under Tatsuya's attacks.

That fact gave Tomitsuka an indescribable shock. He wasn't just frightened, he wasn't just recoiling—he felt like he'd peered into the bottom of Pandora's box.

The never-expanding psion field kept expanding. Wasn't that just an impossible hope?

Tomitsuka desperately clamped down on his mind before that fact exhilarated him.

The person he was facing was not an opponent he could beat while thinking of *unnecessary* things.

Deciding it was time to settle the score, he decided to play his ace.

Psions flooded every part of Tomitsuka's body. Everyone who was watching could feel that, not just Tatsuya.

His body abruptly accelerated—and only Tatsuya and Sawaki realized it wasn't because of a self-acceleration spell.

The psionic particles enveloping his body like a formless cloud rapidly began to neaten. Under Tomitsuka's will, they were controlled into an orderly shape.

With more precision than before, Tomitsuka lashed out with a middle kick.

A heating magic program had been constructed in his foot. If Tatsuya took the kick, he'd take damage equal to that of a microwave oven showering him in electromagnetic waves. Using Program Demolition with his elbow as the affected point, he tried to block the heat magic—upgraded kick.

But just before Tomitsuka's right foot connected with his left elbow, it *unnaturally* came to a stop.

The heating spell had been nullified by the Program Demolition fired from Tatsuya's elbow. But Tomitsuka had worked that into his plans from the very start.

Still in his midkick pose, he sent out a right hook. No, not a hook— it wasn't a fist, but an open-handed strike. A slap, in other words. And there was no way he could have launched a powerful attack from a position where he couldn't put his weight into it.

And yet his open-handed strike was equipped with speed and power both. Tatsuya, who had lowered his waist to block the kick, was not in a position to evade the blow.

There was a dull *blump*.

"Brother!"

A silk-tearing cry rang out.

Tatsuya's body fell to the floor.

Tomitsuka, in a somehow doll-like pose with his right foot swung down, his right hand having followed through, and standing on only his left leg, blinked dubiously.

"...Didn't expect Tomitsuka to be so nasty. He went right after my man Shiba's eardrums."

Kirihara had seen that Tomitsuka's open-handed strike was delivered while his palm was cupped and the wind pressure was all focused on the point of impact.

"Whoa, he purposely got knocked back? I can't believe he withstood Tomitsuka's Self Marionette with that sort of movement. Shiba's good!"

While the two seniors were evaluating the exchange, Tatsuya

stood back up. As Sawaki had seen, he'd purposely rolled to create distance.

Tomitsuka's expression was suspicious because he'd felt a hard sensation, but he hadn't felt like he'd made an impact. If Tatsuya had firmed up his neck to keep his brain from shaking, he would have firmed up his waist and legs as well, which means Tomitsuka would have felt a strong impact. If Tatsuya hadn't fought against his blow and loosened up to be knocked back, the sensation that came back to Tomitsuka's palm would have been a soft one. That meant that Tatsuya had both tightened up *and* relaxed.

Leaving the surprise welling up in his mind for later, Tomitsuka activated Self Marionette again. It was a movement-type spell, a technique that moved his body using *only* the spell itself. He relaxed the muscles that would resist the magic as much as he could, then carefully put together a magic program that wouldn't exceed his joints' articulation.

It wasn't a spell with which he could move the way he wanted. Because of how modern magic worked, it only reproduced movements based on patterns. But as the previous attack had shown, he could deliver attacks that were impossible from an anatomical and dynamic standpoint.

He made his own body into a marionette, became a puppeteer to control himself, and struck out at Tatsuya with movements that defied all martial arts logic. Tatsuya was watching how the psions incident to his body were moving.

One magic program was covering his whole body. The technique was so complicated that even high-level magicians would have found it difficult to reproduce. The psions probably moved so they wouldn't get in the spell's way. The chaotic psions simply spinning around his body had organized, ordered themselves, and the information bodies were being reconstructed in such a way that they wouldn't allow any spells but Self Marionette near.

The orderless chaos transformed into an orderly cosmos.

Order was form, and form was structure.

Tatsuya's dismantling was the destruction of structure. It couldn't break the formless, but if something had form, even if it was only information, he could *dismantle* it.

The cloud of psions that hadn't had a form while covering Tomitsuka's body fell into a form in accordance with his spell.

Tatsuya understood this through Elemental Sight, his power to see the Idea's status—its form. And there, he *saw* the chance of a lifetime.

He injected psions into his CAD. He wasn't pretending to use it—he was going to use the dismantling magic stored within. The spell he chose was Program Dispersion.

The trigger was pulled.

Tatsuya's information structure–destroying spell blasted away Tomitsuka's *now-structured* armor.

An exposed combat puppet closed in on him.

A mass of psions condensed in Tatsuya's left hand.

Firmer, firmer—firm enough to pierce even Tomitsuka's armor if it came back up.

Not to hide his strength, but to grasp victory. He chose not his specialty magic, which *might* have been stopped by insufficient armor, but a magic bullet, which would *certainly* shoot through insufficient armor.

A high-pressure, high-hardness farstrike he'd learned to use against nonhuman foes—the AP Psionic Bullet (name courtesy of Yakumo)—fired from his hand and pierced the combat puppet that was Tomitsuka.

Taking the insubstantial gunshot, Tomitsuka careened backward on his own. This was a side effect of Self Marionette. That he'd been hit with a hard impact from the front had overwritten his magic program's variables. When the spell tried to execute with an inconsistent command, it threw a logic error and crashed.

Launched by his own spell, Tomitsuka fell to the floor, limbs sprawled, not moving. Because his muscles had been so relaxed, he didn't have any time to take the fall with a roll, which left him with a mild concussion.

"The winner is Shiba."

Hattori, having confirmed that, proclaimed Tatsuya the victor.

"Bro—"

About to say "Brother," Miyuki looked down. She'd probably forgotten herself and nearly dived into Tatsuya's arms before remembering her role and barely restraining herself.

When her face came back up, Tatsuya sent a smile her way.

She smiled back, and it was like a huge flower blossoming. Nodding to her, Tatsuya faced back the way he'd been turned.

He put his right-hand CAD back in its holster and walked over toward Tomitsuka, who was still on the floor.

"Tomitsuka, can you stand?" he asked, offering his right hand.

Tomitsuka remained on the floor as he grabbed it with his right hand.

"Thanks."

With Tatsuya's hand's help, Tomitsuka stood up. He was still a little unsteady, but the concussion didn't seem to have been very bad. He quickly got his feet back under him.

"Just like I thought—you're strong, Shiba," said Tomitsuka honestly, removing his helmet.

"Same goes to you. This one hurt." Tatsuya pointed to his reddened cheek and grinned.

A figure dashed by them.

"What—hey, Shippou!"

Without turning around, Takuma fled from seminar room three.

The empty space behind the robot club garage, nestled next to the outdoor training grounds, was used as a secret meeting place because people barely ever visited it.

But Takuma hadn't come here because he'd known that. He'd simply been running away from where others could see him, and that had led him here.

In front of a tree—not a particularly gigantic one with any special attributes, but a fairly large one—Takuma stood for a while, staring at nothing. But then, as though he couldn't hold in his nervous emotions any longer, he suddenly began to punch the tree with his right hand.

"Damn it, damn it, damn it!"

Over and over again, his fist met the bark.

"Give it a rest, Shippou. Look, you're bleeding."

Just as his swearing began to falter, a voice called out to him from behind.

Takuma whipped around. There, he spotted a miffed Kasumi.

"Saegusa, you—!"

As Takuma turned a sharp glare on her, Kasumi put up her hands and shook them. "Hey, don't misunderstand me. I wasn't following you or anything. It's a complete coincidence that I'm here."

After finishing, she walked up to Shippou with a frown. She took out a handkerchief, then folded it up into the shape of a bandage before taking the still-glaring Takuma's hand.

"What's that for?!"

"Great… The skin is peeling off, you know."

Scowling at the blood, Kasumi began to wrap her handkerchief around the confused boy's hand.

"Sorry, but I still don't have permission to use healing magic. You'd better get to the nurse's office."

Takuma didn't respond. He just stared at the handkerchief as the blood crept into it.

"Oh, you don't have to give that back."

"…"

Takuma still didn't move a muscle, so Kasumi sighed. "Looks like you lost pretty handily."

"…"

"Guess the upperclassmen wall is just too high."

"...How?"

Takuma's gaze was still lowered.

"Huh? How what?"

But now that Kasumi had finally gotten a reaction, she figured she'd respond accordingly.

"How the hell are they so strong?!"

A bitter cry. Probably the kind you'd use the expression *shouting himself hoarse* for, thought Kasumi—and she had a feeling she knew whom he meant by *they*.

"They're in high school, too, aren't they?! They're only one year above me! How are they *still* that freaking strong?!"

"Maybe there isn't a reason."

"What...?"

Houston, we have conversation, thought Kasumi, but she didn't say something that foolish, of course. "They're just strong because they are. I mean... If you really want a reason, they probably worked really hard to get that strong, right?"

"But I—"

"Yeah, I know you've been trying hard. I've been putting my best foot forward, too. But if they're stronger, doesn't that mean they've been trying even harder?"

"..."

"I'm not denying you have talent, here. Most of my strength comes from talent too anyway."

"..."

"But the strength you're so shocked at—maybe it came from something other than talent."

Takuma looked up and into Kasumi's eyes.

A single frustrated tear had fallen from his own.

"Anyway, I'm not really interested in this whole *being strong* thing. But if you want to get stronger, that's your problem—and I think your strength is something only *you* have."

Just like she said, she easily turned away from him and disappeared from Takuma's sight.

One more time, not with a fist but with a palm, he struck out at the tree trunk with his rage.

After parting with the club committee members, starting with Hattori, and returning to the student council room, Tatsuya sat at his desk and booted up his device's communication function. As his fingers darted over the keyboard with blinding speed, the message he was composing was for someone in the same room.

"Yes, Master?"

Active telepathy, its target restricted to only Tatsuya, came back in response.

"Have you doctored the data?"

His written communication, which he didn't want the other student council members to know about...

"As ordered, I recorded false data in real time."

...garnered the answer he was hoping for.

"Master, have I been of help to you?"

"Yeah, you did well," he replied to the evil spirit who had guarded his secret. "You can rest for today."

"Yes, Master. Entering suspend mode."

After ordering the doll to go to sleep, Tatsuya erased all records of his communication.

[Epilogue]

"That aircraft was stolen goods. The TV station is saying the request for a flight plan was done with stolen codes as well."

Tatsuya was taking a phone call from Fujibayashi in his room.

The conversation was about the aircraft he'd encountered the other night, and the results of the investigation into whether the people who had caused Tatsuya such pain with their suicide attack were terrorists, a mafia, or what.

"They seem to be the Chinese mafia, but unfortunately, we couldn't figure out any more than that."

But like Fujibayashi said, the investigation's results were unsatisfactory ones.

"The Chinese mafia—you learned where they came from, ma'am?"

"Yes, but not all of them. They had a bone to pick with you personally, too."

"…You don't mean No-Head Dragon?"

"Their remnants, anyway. We confirmed that Robert Sun, Richard Sun's nephew's cousin, led the heli-jack."

"His nephew's cousin, ma'am…?"

He was about to point out that that made him practically unrelated, but he swallowed it back down. He'd just remembered particular relatives of his own who were considered blood even at that distance.

"Well, he's practically unrelated. When No-Head Dragon collapsed, only a few close 'brothers' answered his call."

But that seemed to be something anyone would have thought. Still, now wasn't the time to be worried over something that trivial for too long.

"Of course, last night would have been impossible with that few men, so there must be a mastermind, or at least some kind of support..."

"Whom we haven't identified, ma'am?"

"Yes."

The situation was graver than Tatsuya had thought. That there had been a failed terrorist attack in the heart of Tokyo was bad enough—but whoever the mastermind was, even Fujibayashi's investigative skills couldn't root them out. Of course, at the moment, they had far too few clues, and he supposed he had to think about that as well. That, though, didn't change the fact that this opponent was not one to make light of.

What crossed Tatsuya's mind at this time was not *I hope this doesn't turn into a big mess,* but a more self-centered wish: *I hope Miyuki and I don't end up involved in this massive mess.*

A downtown at night. On a smaller road a short way from a main street, there was a shop.

Nakura checked the shop's name by its modest illumination.

This was definitely the place the *current* head, Kouichi Saegusa, had instructed him to come.

If you hadn't known there was a shop here, you'd have passed it by—the door was made from an inconspicuous alloy whose only merit was how sturdy it was. He opened it, then went up the stairs to the second floor. The surly man showed him to a private room, where the other party to the meeting had already arrived.

"I apologize—have I made you wait?"

"No, not at all. I myself only just arrived," said a handsome man brimming with charm and youth on an entirely different level from Nakura's as he stood from his chair.

"My name is Nakura."

"And mine is Zhou. Come, take a seat."

A young woman, pretty and charming—the exact opposite of the male employee who had shown him here—was waiting in the room, off to the side. At a glance from Zhou, the beautiful waitress led Nakura directly across from Zhou with practiced motions and pulled out the chair for him. After seeing Nakura sit down without hesitation, Zhou returned to his seat as well.

"Would you like something to drink?"

"I would perhaps like some *baijiu*."

Zhou's eyebrow twitched in surprise. As far as he knew, guests who actually requested alcohol after such pleasantries were rare.

"...In that case, though it may be commonplace, might I suggest the Maotai?"

"I'll leave it to you."

The wine came immediately after Zhou ordered it. Once the spirits were poured into their small glasses, Nakura and Zhou gauged each other's breathing and simultaneously downed the entire thing.

Placing his emptied glass in the middle of the table, Nakura peered into Zhou's eyes.

"Mr. Nakura."

The first one to speak was Zhou.

"My master wishes for an amicable relationship with your master, Mr. Nakura."

"My master desires to move forward with your proposal, *Zhou*."

Zhou gave a bewitching smile at Nakura's answer. "Well, well. I'm flattered to have earned your trust. Shall we move on to more concrete matters, then?"

"Our basic conditions haven't changed from what we previously informed you of."

"Yes, of course. I am aware. I would never do aught to bring disfavor to Master Saegusa, nor are my interests aligned with the GAA."

"And the media manipulation?"

"I'm well aware of that as well. I've already made arrangements to refrain from further campaigns targeting magicians *as a whole*."

"All right, then let's work out the details."

Zhou sent another signal to the female employee.

The beautiful waitress bowed deeply before exiting the room. The conversation inside would not be known to any but Nakura and Zhou.

Fin

AFTERWORD

First, I'd like to give a heartfelt thanks to everyone who purchased this book. I look forward to your continued support, whether this is your first one or otherwise.

Tatsuya, Miyuki, and their friends have advanced to their second year, and this episode was about their new underclassmen. Did it suit your fancy? This series will be going from the protagonist siblings' entrance into high school until their graduation, which means it can't be without year-advancement events, nor the renewal of human relationships that must come with them. As you can tell from reading this volume, characters won't disappear forever just because they've graduated, but I also have to put the new characters in the spotlight. Otherwise, there's not much point in introducing them.

What I need to think about in that regard is what personalities the new characters will have. I actually almost didn't struggle at all with character building for the new students. I already had rough ideas for all of them when I first began writing this story. Of course, there were several places that needed moderate revisions. The thing that changed most was probably Kento originally being a crossdressing boy. For understandable reasons, that was dropped when I was putting together the Double Seven arc's story line.

My headache is the new students who will appear *next* year. To be quite frank, their character profiles are blank slates... Well, thinking about episodes that will happen next year is unrealistic. But if this series safely makes it that far, you can feel free to laugh at the vestiges of the author's suffering.

Changing the topic, as you know, the Double Seven arc was serialized in *Dengeki Bunko Magazine*. My goal was to deliver brand-brand-new episodes to the fans as soon as possible...but it was a somewhat reckless experiment that I now regret.

I put my stories together without thinking about the factors that are going into it at the time, so I knew going in it would be pretty rough, but I hadn't thought it would be so full of holes... While writing, I was painfully aware that there was not nearly enough explanation about what was happening behind the scenes. I believe I was able to add in the bare minimum of supplements to this book edition—did it work out?

By the time this book is in stores, you will have all heard the big news. Actually, the Double Seven arc's serialization placed a heavy load on the entire staff, but I think I'll be putting them through even more in the future. I'm terribly sorry.

But all that's just what's happening backstage. The entire staff, including myself, intends to strive forward so that fans can enjoy *The Irregular at Magic High School* to an even greater extent, so I look forward to your support for this series in the future.

Tsutomu Sato

RIGHT AS SCHOOL BEGINS, WE'RE IMMEDIATELY THRUST INTO THE JUNIOR'S NINE SCHOOL COMPETITION ARC!

July 2096.

The biggest event of every magic high school student's summer, the National Magic High School Goodwill Competition Magic Tournament—nicknamed the Nine School Competition—is fast approaching once more.

First High's student council—headed by Azusa Nakajou as president and the Shiba siblings as co-vice presidents—is busy preparing for the games, but this year's Nine School Competition won't be anything the students expect!

With barely a month left before the competition begins, an unprecedented and far-reaching set of changes to various events and rules is announced, leaving every magic high school in a frantic rush to respond.

There's a new event in particular, the Steeplechase Cross Country, that's causing headaches not only for Tatsuya and his friends but for every other school's student council as well.

On one of the busy days when Tatsuya is developing strategies for the upcoming games, an anonymous message alerts him to another potential conspiracy targeting the latest Nine School Competition…

As the spectacle of the games occupies the stage, a secret battle begins to unfold in the shadows…

Tatsuya must to cut his way through Mount Fuji's man-made forests, which are enshrouded in darkness even during the day, for a chance to confront a plot rife with betrayal!!

The action-packed Volume 13 is set to be released in 2019!!

Now presenting your favorite magic school series in manga form!

See how the other half of the Shiba household lives! *The Honor Student at Magic High School,* 1–9 on sale now!

Art by Yu Mori | Original Story by Tsutomu Sato | Character Design by Kana Ishida

The
Irregular at
Magic High
School

Tsutomu Sato
Illustration Kana Ishida

Read the light novel that inspired the hit anime series!

Re:ZeRo
-Starting Life in Another World-

Also be sure to check out the manga series!
AVAILABLE NOW!

www.YenPress.com